“You are treading on dangerous ground, Miss Tremeer.”

His voice was silky, a warning.

“I am used to danger. You don’t scare me. Your Grace.”

And that was when the mood suddenly changed.

He was very close now, and something flared in his eyes, something hot and bright. Instinctively she felt herself respond. Her blood heated in her veins, and her breath caught in her throat. Her lips tingled as their eyes locked. He leaned in.

He was going to kiss her. It was a long time since a man had kissed her, and Gabriel looked as if he meant to kiss her very thoroughly indeed. She braced herself to refuse him, to slap his face if necessary, but as his warm breath brushed her lips, her eyelids fluttered and her heart knocked against her ribs, and she knew that she wasn’t going to do any of those things.

She was going to kiss him back.

Dreaming of a Duke Like You

SARA BENNETT

New York Boston

This book is a work of fiction. Names, characters, places, and incidents are the product of the author's imagination or are used fictitiously. Any resemblance to actual events, locales, or persons, living or dead, is coincidental.

Cover design by Daniela Medina
Cover art by Sophia Sidoti

Forever
Hachette Book Group
1290 Avenue of the Americas, New York, NY 10104
read-forever.com
twitter.com/readforeverpub

First Edition: October 2023

Forever is an imprint of Grand Central Publishing. The Forever name and logo are trademarks of Hachette Book Group, Inc.

The publisher is not responsible for websites (or their content) that are not owned by the publisher.

Forever books may be purchased in bulk for business, educational, or promotional use. For information, please contact your local bookseller or the Hachette Book Group Special Markets Department at special .markets@hbgusa.com.

ISBN: 9781538723814 (mass market), 9781538723821 (ebook)

Printed in the United States of America

OPM

10 9 8 7 6 5 4 3 2 1

This book is for my Sara Bennett readers, thank you!

Acknowledgments

A big thank-you to my agent Nancy Yost, and to my editor Madeleine Colavita. And as always much love and gratitude to my husband for suffering with me through yet another book.

Dreaming of a Duke Like You

Chapter One

November 1817, Cadieux's Gambling Club, London

Gabriel Cadieux rubbed his tired eyes and looked again at his ledger. He hunched his broad shoulders and settled his big body in his chair. He could have hired a bookkeeper to deal with such matters, but he preferred to keep a close watch on his monetary incomings and outgoings. That way no one could cheat him. The members of his staff were handpicked for their honesty and loyalty, but temptation was everywhere, and there were already too many people eager to relieve him of his hard-won blunt.

Five years ago at the tender age of twenty-two, Gabriel had won what was now Cadieux's Gambling Club from the original owner. The man's arrogance and his disbelief that someone so far beneath him could best him at cribbage had ultimately been his downfall. He had lost his club and, in trying to win it back, had increased the stakes and therefore lost a great deal of money besides. That night was the beginning of Gabriel's rise from nothing to something, and his chance to make a success of a life that until then had been lived on the edge of poverty and respectability.

Not that he was respectable now. To own a gambling hell was not exactly a respectable occupation. Some titled gentlemen did own them, and ladies too, but that was usually through necessity rather than choice. Gabriel did not fool himself into thinking he would ever be considered an upright citizen. He knew what he was and was perfectly content with it.

Now he ran his eye down the columns of figures, adding them up in his head, and was pleased to discover it had been a particularly lucrative night.

As usual his hard-earned profit gave him a feeling of immense satisfaction. That he, an unwanted bastard from a foundling home, should find himself in such a comfortable position. He had been lucky, certainly, and his head for figures had been enormously helpful when it came to gambling—especially in skill-based games such as cribbage. But he wasn't like most of the gentlemen who frequented his club, bored and desperate for entertainment. If losing everything on the turn of a card or the roll of the dice made them feel alive, then Gabriel was not going to dissuade them, even though he didn't understand that sort of mindset. He was pragmatic and hardheaded, and any risks he undertook were carefully thought out. He told himself he would never bet his home and fortune on the fall of a card. On the whole he was satisfied with his life as it was and had no intention of altering it.

That wasn't to say he could not be generous when it suited him, and sometimes when it didn't. He would do anything for his two best friends, and he had been known to toss a coin to the street beggars, especially if they were children.

He poured himself a glass of claret and leaned back, admiring the ruby red color against the lamplight. French, no doubt. Charles had a contact in the government who turned a blind eye to import and excise. Charles Wickley, his friend and partner in business, made himself very useful in various ways but particularly when it came to supplying the club with top quality spirits. Add to that the excellent chef he had employed to prepare two suppers nightly, and Gabriel was beginning to wonder how he had ever managed without him. Charles Wickley and Freddie Hart, both from the same foundling home as Gabriel, were his best friends then and today. Family was not always born of the same blood, or so he had discovered over the years.

Voices drifted up from the gambling rooms downstairs. Someone gave a drunken shout. It was late and although there would still be games being played—vingt-et-un, loo, or whist, among others—the final supper had been served. Soon his "guests" would be staggering off to their beds. The staff would then have the task of cleaning up and preparing the rooms for tomorrow night, when the whole thing would start again. In the early days, Gabriel had mingled a great deal more in those rooms. There were always men who had listened to the tales of Gabriel's exceptional skill, a skill that had raised him to his current place in the world, and were keen to topple him from his perch.

Occasionally Gabriel would play them, but the truth was he didn't enjoy the thought of losing. The club wasn't a recreation for him or a way of showing off. It was work. A means to an end. And these days he preferred to keep his distance from chancers with nothing to lose, such as the boy he had once been.

Cadieux's was his, and he wasn't about to risk it. He might have traveled a long way from his bleak childhood, indeed he was a fortunate man, but he would never forget where he came from, and he never wanted to go back.

He ran a hand over his face, feeling the rasp of his whiskers, and yawned. It was late, probably close to four in the morning. He tugged at his necktie, loosening it, and yawned again. He really should go to bed. His servant had lit the fire in the small chamber off his office, making everything comfortable. Gabriel paid for rooms elsewhere but most nights it was more convenient for him to sleep at the club.

A step sounded outside his door. He looked up.

Whoever was at the door tapped loudly.

No one bothered him unless it was important. A drunken player who had lost everything and wanted to blame the club rather than himself, or maybe it was Charles come upstairs for a late-night chat. It couldn't be Freddie. He was currently in the north of the country with his regiment, although he was due back any day.

Gabriel set down his glass. "Come in!"

The door opened and a woman stood there. She was wearing a hooded cloak over her gown, but the light on the landing was too dim to see more. She stepped inside his office and closed the door firmly, before turning to face him. She lifted her hood from her hair.

Gabriel hadn't asked for female company. His regular visit to the establishment he favored wasn't until tomorrow, and he was picky when it came to bed partners. Watching as she hesitated just inside the room, a mixture of shadow and light disguising her features, he could sense her unease. Her gaze flicked about her, lingering on the bookcase on the adjacent wall. He suspected he already knew why she was here. He drew breath and opened his mouth to speak, but she got in first.

"Mr. Cadieux?" She didn't sound like a native of this part of London, her voice far too refined, and now that she was closer, neither did she look like one. A lady. Not in the first flush of youth, not a debutante, but neither was she long in the tooth. Perhaps twenty-four or twenty-five, with dark hair glossy in the glow of the lamp and light eyes in a heart-shaped face. There were shadows under those eyes, and her wide mouth was drawn into a thin line, as if she was laboring under some difficulty.

"Madam," he began, attempting to bring their conversation to a close before it could begin. Once again she circumvented him.

"Sir," she said firmly. "I wish to speak to you about my brother, Sir William Tremeer. For his sins, he is a regular visitor to your gambling establishment. But you are probably aware of that." She waved a pale hand toward the ledgers on the desk before him. "I'm sure he features often in those pages."

She was correct. Sir William had been slouched over the hazard table earlier this evening, losing. His friend, an older boy, had smirked and egged him on to "throw the dice one more time" because his luck was bound to change. So not really a "friend" then, in Gabriel's opinion. Charles had noticed too and had warned Tremeer to go home. The boy was barely a man, innocent and foolish, the perfect victim to be fleeced by a more experienced gambler. Gabriel and Charles had discussed the matter, and both agreed this was not the sort of client they wanted in the club.

Cadieux's was known for honest dealing among its

clientele, and young, naïve, and with barely a penny to his name, the boy was running with a particularly reckless crowd. Some of the club's older players were shaking their heads and talking about going elsewhere. Gabriel could have banned him from Cadieux's, but that reckless crowd was made up of some of his most lucrative customers. The difference between them and William was they had the money to cover their debts, and he didn't. His losses to the house had been considerable and were still outstanding.

"Madam," he began again.

"Miss Vivienne Tremeer."

Gabriel sat back with a sigh. It wasn't often he had a lady in his office, and from the sound and look of her, she was the genuine article. "I don't mean to be rude," he began, when he meant just that.

"My brother has lost a great deal of money in your club, sir. Money he does not have. He tells me that you have not demanded payment so far. I'm not sure why you have been so lenient. Perhaps you think it a kindness. I hope so, because I have come to ask you whether you would consider forgiving his debt entirely."

Gabriel found himself staring into her eyes. They were light gray and surrounded by thick dark lashes. She was rather lovely, despite the strained look on her face. Gabriel knew little of ladies' fashion, but he thought her gray cloak covered a gown that was plainer than those usually worn by the gentry. Although perhaps she had dressed down to come to his club. That she was here at all was not unheard of, but it was unusual. The last lady who had come to beg him to "forgive" a debt had sobbed and wailed and flung herself all over him.

Vivienne Tremeer didn't look as if she was going to

do any of those things, and he found he liked her the better for it. Not that he was about to agree to her request.

"I'm afraid I cannot do that," he said at last. "It is not my habit to forgive debts. Paying a debt may be a matter of honor, but it is also a matter of business, and your brother knew this when he came to play at my tables. If he thinks he can send his sister to beg me to—"

She didn't let him finish. Her silk skirts whispered as she moved closer, coming to a stop directly opposite him. Gabriel knew a gentleman would rise to his feet, but he was no gentleman.

"He hasn't sent me to beg," she retorted, and he could see the tension in her slim body, as if she were strung so tightly that at any moment she might snap. "I came of my own accord. He cannot pay you."

Gabriel let his gaze slide over her. "I'm sure someone in his family will find the money," he said unsympathetically.

She laughed but there was no humor in it. "The bailiffs have taken most of our belongings, our house in Cornwall is falling down, and the only reason my aunt offered us shelter is because she has a horror of scandal. This may tip the balance in favor of the debtors' prison."

He said nothing, watching as she took a breath and appeared to gather the tatters of her self-control. There was something admirable in that, but he knew what was coming. He felt his stomach twist. Perhaps he could head her off before she spoke the words he dreaded.

"It's no use offering to share my bed, Miss Tremeer," he said gruffly, frowning darkly at her. "I do not accept physical favors in lieu of cold hard cash. I've never found it nearly as satisfactory."

Her gray eyes sparked and lit up like a bonfire. She

was furious, but she held it back, the rage bringing color to her cheeks and causing her hands to clench into fists as they rested on his desk.

"Not if you were the last man alive," she hissed.

He watched her turn, back straight, and walk away with long strides. The door slammed behind her.

Gabriel took a sip of his claret. He found he was smiling and wasn't sure why. Then, deliberately setting his glass aside, he put Vivienne Tremeer from his thoughts and went back to his ledgers.

Chapter Two

Vivienne had taken only two steps down the stairs and she was already regretting her wretched temper. Yes, the man was arrogant and rude, but she should not have let his words fire her up. She had come here for the sake of Will, and now her outburst had probably made matters worse. Cadieux might even demand the debt be repaid immediately, and then what would they do?

She settled her hood over her hair—at least it offered her some protection if she was to meet anyone she knew. Unlikely, but not impossible. A great many gentlemen seemed to frequent Cadieux's, and one of them might see her and tattle to her uncle. She was not so concerned the Viscount Monteith would care what she did, but he would be sure to speak of it to his wife, Vivienne's aunt, and she *would* care.

With a sigh she continued downward toward the shadows at the bottom of the staircase. She didn't see the man approaching her until he was nearly in front of her, and then they both gave a startled jump and came to a stop.

He was a skinny fellow, neatly and plainly dressed,

but with a fussy look to him. From an early age Vivienne had learned to sum up people upon first meeting; it was imperative when at any moment one might be confronted by a bailiff or one of her stepfather's unpleasant cronies. She thought this man had the look of a gentleman's steward or secretary.

"Ma'am," he murmured politely, cool eyes sliding over her with scorn. He was judging her morals and she realized he thought her on a visit to Cadieux's for the sorts of reasons Cadieux himself had spoken of. Vivienne lifted her chin and gave him her best baronet's daughter stare. To her satisfaction he dropped his gaze and bowed, before they proceeded to pass each other with difficulty on the narrow staircase.

He continued upward and she reached the lower corridor, pausing there a moment to take a deep breath and gather her thoughts. Will was waiting for her out in the coach. She dreaded telling him that her appeal to Cadieux's better feelings—he had none—had failed.

Cadieux's deep voice echoed in her head: *I've never found it nearly as satisfactory.* If she'd had a pistol, she might have shot him. She couldn't remember when a stranger had ruffled her feathers quite so thoroughly.

Above her she heard the visitor knock on the office door and open it. "Mr. Cadieux? I have some rather urgent news for you," he said, and then the door closed again, cutting off their conversation.

Vivienne hoped it was bad news. She was not normally a vindictive person, but life had worn her down, and recently she had begun to feel it more than usual. Her father the baronet had died when Will was still in his crib, and then her mother had remarried a scoundrel and a waster. Richard Sutherland had spent everything he could get his hands on, and would have sold Tremeer, their small estate in Cornwall, if it hadn't been left to Will. Vivienne had good reason to know just how devious Sutherland was, but she had still been dumbfounded when yesterday a letter arrived from old Mr. Davey, the lawyer who had handled her family's legal matters for decades. He had informed her that Richard Sutherland had been to see him, and Sutherland had drawn his attention to a clause in her father's will that he believed could be used to overturn it. The clause in question was copied in the old man's shaky hand.

> *Tremeer, house and lands, I leave to my only son William, to be held in trust until he turns twenty-one years if he be judged to be of sober character. If he be judged to be profligate, then he shall not inherit and I leave the dispensing of my estate to the discretion of my trustees.*

As Mr. Davey pointed out, the wording was open to interpretation. Did the baronet mean that Will must be of sober character on the day of his twenty-first birthday, still three years away, or must he be judged to be of sober character in the time before that birthday? It would be up to the trustees to show fiduciary responsibility, and act in the best interests of the estate. One of those trustees was Mr. Davey, and the other Sir Desmond Chamond, a neighbor of the Tremeers and also the district magistrate.

Does Mr. Sutherland have any proof that young Will is behaving in a manner that might be described as "profligate"? the old man inquired in his letter.

The letter had thrown Will into a terrible panic, and

he had admitted, when Vivienne had insisted, that he was in trouble. Deep trouble. The figure he mentioned took her breath away. A figure it would be impossible for them to repay in the next few days, weeks, or maybe ever. And yet they must try.

She had decided to see Cadieux at once—Vivienne judged herself to be the more likely to inspire Cadieux's sympathy—and perhaps the damage to Will's reputation could be repaired before Sutherland took advantage of it or the trustees became aware of it.

Really it was the worst news. Vivienne already blamed herself for their flight to London, although Will had insisted on coming with her. Their plan had been to stay with their father's sister, the Viscountess Monteith, until Will turned twenty-one, when he and Vivienne could safely return to Tremeer and take charge of the estate. With the power of his inheritance and the trustees behind him, Will would send Sutherland packing and hopefully begin to repair the damage their stepfather had caused.

But what if the estate was taken from Will and they were cast adrift? There would be no going home, ever, and they could not expect Aunt Jane to pay for their upkeep indefinitely. As it was, she begrudged every penny she spent on them. Vivienne had been grateful when she took them in, but she suspected her generosity was tempered by the knowledge that she would look bad in the eyes of her friends and peers if she did not. This way she could accept their congratulations on her Christian benevolence…and their sympathy for being lumbered with such disappointing relatives.

Vivienne had overheard Aunt Jane's tête-à-têtes with her friends enough times to know how she felt, but one conversation in particular stuck in her mind: *You are so* *good, Jane! I don't know how you can do it. I'm sure I couldn't take on that girl...*Of course the speaker had been quickly hushed when they saw her lingering in the doorway.

Because she was *that* girl. The scandalous one. The one whose reputation was ruined beyond repair and was therefore nothing but a burden on her kindhearted aunt. Never mind that the scandal had not been of Vivienne's making and certainly not her fault, unless showing kindness to one's neighbors could be said to be a fault. Another crime that she could lay at Richard Sutherland's door.

No, they could not stay with Aunt Jane any longer than necessary, and at the same time their aunt must not hear of Will's gambling debts. Their only hope was to return to Tremeer in three years' time, and now that hope was at risk.

The more Vivienne looked at their situation, the more the trap they were in seemed to narrow. Or perhaps it wasn't a trap, but a mine, like the ones her father had owned. As a girl at home in Cornwall, she had listened wide-eyed to stories of cave-ins and rising water levels, and men struggling to breathe as the earth pressed down around them. She felt a bit like that sometimes. Trapped and gasping for air and waiting for rescue, while horribly aware that no one would reach her in time.

She slipped through the door from the kitchen, ignoring the smirk from the server she'd bribed to let her up to Cadieux's office. In hindsight a waste of money, but she'd hoped that all the rumors were wrong and that the man had a heart instead of a lump of stone beneath his white linen shirt.

His necktie had been undone to show the strong column of his throat, and his shoulders broad and strong.

Oh yes, he was a handsome brute. Dark hair curling around his ears and tumbling over his brow, dark stubble on his jaw and cheeks drawing attention to his pink lips, and eyes black as the winter storms that came in from the sea at Tremeer. But as Vivienne well knew, sometimes the worst men were the most attractive.

The bookcase troubled her though. She had already decided Gabriel Cadieux was an uneducated, cruel fellow to whom nothing mattered but raking in as much profit as he possibly could. But would such a man own that quantity of books? So many that they were all but bursting from their shelves, and obviously well read. It didn't fit with her image of him. A vicious gambling house owner did not read romantic novels. More worrying than the anomaly of such a man enjoying fiction was one particular book on those shelves. A book Vivienne knew only too well. Seeing *The Wicked Prince and His Stolen Bride* had thrown her for a moment, until she reminded herself that by now there must be a great many persons in the country who had purchased, borrowed, or stolen a copy.

Outside she breathed in the chilly air. The coach was waiting around the corner and she quickened her steps. This was not a safe area for a lone woman to linger, and their coachman, Jem, had not wanted to remain here for longer than five minutes. He had raised his bushy brows at her while she had assured him that her visit was of the utmost importance.

She and Will had known Jem since they were small, and he had stayed on at Tremeer after their father died. He was always good for a visit to the stables and a ride on the back of one of the quieter horses. Of course most of the horses were gone now, sold off to pay Sutherland's debts, and eventually Jem had been let go. His final task had been to see Vivienne and Will safely to London eight months ago, to throw themselves upon the mercy of Aunt Jane. Worried about Jem and breaking the link with her past, Vivienne had given her aunt a heartfelt speech, listing Jem's long service and sterling qualities, and pleading with her to employ him. Perhaps the viscountess was feeling particularly charitable that day, or perhaps she saw Jem for the jewel he was, and she had agreed to take him on.

"There you be, maid." Jem called her by that affectionate Cornish word for girl, and it always warmed her heart. He was standing by the horses, his old tricorn hat pulled down around his ears. These days he might be more grizzled, but he was still fiercely loyal to the Tremeer siblings, and Vivienne was forever grateful for it.

"I reckon we have a gang over there working up the courage to rob us of our worldly wares." He nodded toward the corner where the shadows were deepest.

She doubted anyone would be brave enough to tackle Jem. He might be getting on, but he was big and bulky, and in his younger days he had excelled at bare-knuckle boxing.

"Thank you, Jem, we can go home now."

"All good?" He shot her a shrewd look.

"More or less as I expected," she said as he handed her up into the coach.

Will had been slumped wearily in the corner but as Jem closed the door, he struggled into a sitting position. There was a stain on his new waistcoat, but she tried not to let it make her cross. Her brother was five years her junior, and she had always seen it as her duty to look after him, until the scandal of eight months ago when he had come to her aid.

"Did he agree?" Will said anxiously, hope shining in his gray eyes so like hers. He was a slender boy of eighteen, handsome and good-natured, and it was only after they had come to London that he had changed. For the worse, unfortunately. It wasn't his fault, or not entirely. The charming but naïve young gentleman had been easy prey for sophisticated Londoners like Mr. Germaine.

"Vivienne?" Her brother spoke again, impatiently. "What did he say?"

"As we expected he said no. He's an unmannerly bully and—"

She'd hardly finished speaking when Will flung himself against her, breaking into noisy sobs, and she held him, stroking his dark hair as she murmured soothing words that meant nothing.

"I'm so sorry," he said, choking on his emotion. "I won't ever do it again, Viv. I won't, ever. If we can only extricate ourselves from this, then I will join a…a… monastery."

Vivienne bit her lip. "That is a good thought, but I doubt it will do. Although I suppose it might show you are of sober character."

Their grandfather Tremeer had been far from sober. A spendthrift and a gambler, he had left his son an estate weighed down with debt, and a lesson he had never forgotten. At least that was what Vivienne believed was behind the clause in her father's will. The baronet had been determined Tremeer would never again fall into unreliable hands, and because he had died before Will was old enough for his character to be judged, he had taken sensible precautions. Vivienne and Will had known nothing of that clause, and until he came to London Will had never gambled, so it would not have been an issue.

The city had changed matters, but if they could wipe the slate clean…

Vivienne took a breath. "I have my nest egg," she began, a suggestion she had made before. "Two hundred pounds might—"

And as before Will protested, shaking his head wildly. His eyes looked rather wild too. "No! Two hundred pounds won't be nearly enough. Besides, that money is yours and I refuse to take it. You might need it when I am in the Marshalsea," he added glumly.

"Then we will have to tell Aunt Jane."

"She will wipe her hands of us, send us back to Cornwall, and it is not safe for you with Sutherland in residence." His protests grew louder, and although Vivienne shushed him, she feared he was right. Aunt Jane would be furious with Will for risking his inheritance.

"She won't let Sutherland take the estate," she said, when he had calmed down. "She hates him, you know that."

"How do you know she won't keep it for herself? Aunt Jane might overturn the will and cut me out entirely."

Vivienne supposed there was always that possibility. Aunt Jane had grown up at Tremeer and still had an attachment to it, even if she abhorred her brother's family.

"Don't tell her yet," Will begged. "Perhaps Cadieux will change his mind?" His gloomy expression brightened. Her brother was about to have one of his flights of fancy—his moods recently had been careering wildly up and down—staggering home while dawn was breaking was taking its toll. "Perhaps after one glance he is now smitten with you, and will agree to anything you ask of him!"

Vivienne shook her head but couldn't help smiling at the thought of Gabriel Cadieux so agreeable. "I very much doubt he is smitten with me, Will. And even if such a thing as love at first sight were possible—which you know I gravely doubt—he is the sort of man whose heart will never rule his head."

"You believed in it once," Will said gently. "Before you-know-who."

"And that just shows you what a fool I was."

Will let her bitter statement pass, returning to the subject. "What if Cadieux's head tells him it is more practical to forgive my debt than to try to wring water from a stone?"

Vivienne doubted very much that was ever going to happen either. Cadieux looked as if he would have no trouble refusing a crippled child a bowl of porridge. But for Will's sake, and perhaps because she wished it were so, she agreed to wait a little longer.

Will gave her a sly glance. "There is always Annette. I'm sure she would loan us the money."

She quickly quashed that suggestion. "I am not asking our cousin to dip into her pin money for us, Will. Remember what happened when she paid for the hire of your horse when you wanted to go to that boxing match outside London? Aunt Jane will only find out, and poor Annette will have to forgo another one of her pleasures as a punishment."

"She doesn't do anything but read books," Will grumbled.

The memory of Cadieux's overburdened shelves sprang to mind, but she pushed it away again. "Nonsense. And even if she does read rather a lot, she doesn't deserve to have her pleasure taken away from her because of her kind nature. I won't do that to her. I know I was feeling less than charitable toward her last year, but that is all forgotten."

Will smirked. "I still can't believe you wrote that book. And that Annette had it published!"

"It wasn't meant to see the light of day," Vivienne said, but refused to be diverted. "Let us wait before we tell Aunt Jane. I have written back to Mr. Davey to instruct him to keep his ear to the ground when it comes to Sutherland and the will, and to send me word posthaste if he learns of anything more. Remember you do not reach your majority for three years, so perhaps he thinks he has plenty of time." Although knowing her stepfather, once he had a sniff of the money the estate would bring him, he would begin scheming.

As if reading her mind, Will said, "I don't know how he found out about my debt."

"He is a gambler himself, you know that. Some of his friends may have seen you at Cadieux's or word may have filtered back to Tremeer. But I think if he was certain about your situation, he would already have set about trying to overturn the will. We have to trust that Mr. Davey will be on the lookout and warn us in good time."

They fell into a dispirited silence.

Will leaned his head against her shoulder, and Vivienne rested her cheek on his soft hair. Their mother had rarely been available to spend time with her children. Once she remarried the awful Mr. Sutherland, she had been too busy with his constant demands and trying to keep everything they owned from being carried out to pay his debts. Vivienne had stepped into her mother's shoes when it came to her brother, although she hadn't realized how reckless he had become once they came to London. Mr. Germaine, whom Will now claimed to be his best friend, constantly led him astray. The man was wealthy enough, and so losing every night at the card tables didn't worry him, but he knew Will was poor and still allowed him to lose, in fact actively encouraged it! Vivienne just hoped her brother would see for himself how thoughtless his friend was, quite unlike a true friend, because the one time she had tried to open his eyes to Germaine's behavior, she and Will had their worst argument ever.

Germaine is my friend, my only friend, and if you knew how he had stood by me...how he rescued me from several unfortunate s-situations...Without him I would have been so much worse off. If you knew, Viv, you wouldn't be so hard on him.

Vivienne hadn't wanted to ask what those "unfortunate situations" were, but it wasn't difficult to guess what young gentlemen got up to in London.

Outside the coach window, the city had changed from the grubby streets around Cadieux's Gambling Club to the more salubrious avenues in the west of the city. Aunt Jane lived in Mayfair, in a square where only the most blue-blooded of aristocrats had their town houses. Old Georgian houses and old wealth. Not that the word *money* would ever be spoken aloud by her aunt and uncle. If one had wealth and breeding, then one spent one's days in leisure. Vivienne's hopes of finding employment for herself, and with it a mite of respect and independence, would be shot down without a second thought.

Her thoughts drifted back to Cadieux, seated behind his desk, his dark eyes watchful. What drove a man like that to become successful? Was he self-educated, as the books seemed to suggest? She realized she knew nothing about him other than the rumors Will had shared with her, and the conjuring of her own angry imagination. The outcome of their conversation might have been disheartening and disappointing, but it wasn't a moment she would soon forget. The man wasn't what she had been expecting. Heartless, yes, but also intriguing. Blunt and insulting, and yet charismatic. Indeed, she had not met anyone quite like him.

No, whatever happened, she would not soon forget Gabriel Cadieux.

Chapter Three

Grantham Estate, Sussex, England

The late November sky was gray, and rain had made everything soggy. A perfect day for a funeral. The little group by the Ashton mausoleum—a building as gray as the sky—were all dressed in black. Gabriel had expected to see more mourners, but of course the disgrace would have kept many of them away. He recognized the lawyer who had visited him, although he had forgotten the man's name. The fellow stood beside an elderly woman seated on a chair and wrapped in a heavy fur-lined cloak. Several servants huddled miserably nearby—no doubt the faithful few who remained with the Ashton family through thick and thin. Gabriel's gaze passed swiftly over them and stopped on the six daughters of Harry, the late duke, his father. The illegitimate daughters. Gabriel's half sisters.

They stood dutifully in a row, from oldest to youngest, heads bowed and hands clasped in a manner that seemed too good to be true.

Just then the eldest girl glanced up, and he had an impression of bright eyes and a sulky expression, before she lowered her face again. Gabriel bit back a smile. As he had suspected, their obedience was only skin deep.

"That's them then?" Charles murmured in his ear. "The six half sisters who go with the title?"

"They look harmless enough," Freddie said. His auburn hair and scarlet ensign's uniform seemed almost obscenely bright under the glowering skies and the mourners in black. "Pack them off to school is my advice, Gabe."

Freddie had just returned to London with his regiment, and when he heard Gabriel was to attend the late Duke of Grantham's funeral, he joined Charles and tagged along. For support, they declared, but Gabriel suspected it was more for entertainment. Not that he minded. He was extremely glad to have his two best friends at his side.

"Your advice isn't particularly useful," Gabriel responded.

Freddie wasn't to be repressed. "What about the mother? Shouldn't she be playing her part?"

"Lady Felicia," Gabriel said. "I don't know. Perhaps she is prostrate with grief."

Freddie snorted. "Prostrate with rage you mean. *You're* the bloody duke!"

Gabriel's mind was still reeling from the unexpected visit to his office by the Ashtons' lawyer. It was like a plot from one of the novels he devoured, but the dry little man who had come bearing the news did not look like he approved of fiction as a pastime.

"You are the legal heir to the dukedom of Grantham. Your mother, Eugénie Cadieux, the duke's mistress, was in fact his legal wife. She and Harry, your father, married

in secret. She was a penniless French émigré—very beautiful I believe." The man cleared his throat, having strayed from the point.

For a moment a face fought to clear itself from the shadows. A long-ago face. A beautiful woman with long dark hair who smiled down at him and whispered endearments. Gabriel forced himself to concentrate.

"The late duke's mother was unaware of the first marriage at the time of her son's marriage to Lady Felicia. Eugénie died when you were three years old, and you were placed in St. Ninian's Foundling Home for Boys. This was done at the request of the late duke's mother."

Gabriel gave the man a baleful look. "My grandmother sent me to a foundling home?"

He avoided Gabriel's eyes. "That is so. She believed the marriage with Lady Felicia to be the only legal union and therefore only she could produce a legal heir. It wasn't until Harry's death that the error was discovered."

"'Error'? He committed bigamy."

The lawyer ignored that. "The truth may never have been brought to light, but the priest who performed the marriage of your mother and father came forward and refused to be hushed. He insisted that he had been silent too long and the matter was on his conscience." Gabriel knew that the efforts to "hush" the man must have been robust, but evidently his conscience was even more robust.

"There are other children?" he asked with shocked curiosity.

"None who are legitimate. Your late father had six daughters with Lady Felicia, but they have now been declared bastards. You are the only legitimate heir to the dukedom and the Grantham estate."

A wave of dizzy nausea washed over him. He could

hear his heart beating fast. He watched, speechless, as the lawyer bowed obsequiously low before him and called him "Your Grace." Because it didn't seem real. Surely it was a dream.

But it hadn't been a dream.

"I'm not going to accept the title," he reminded his friend. "I'm saying no."

Charles raised an eyebrow, his fair hair tousled by the breeze. His handsome face appeared thoughtful as he recited facts that Gabriel already knew. "If you don't accept the title and all that goes with it, the daughters will receive nothing. Will be nothing."

Nothing. The word was stark, reminding him of his own past. Most men would probably jump at the chance of being a duke, but not Gabriel. His immediate response had been "No." As a self-made man, he didn't need a coronet to make himself feel worthy, and he was proud of his achievements. All he knew of dukes was that they were idle fellows who expected others to fetch and carry, a concept completely foreign to him. He had even more reason to refuse the offer now that he knew the truth of his beginnings and why he had been placed in a foundling home. Abandoned as a little boy when he could have grown up in a proper home. Why should he disrupt his life now to sort out the problems of those who had never given a damn about him?

But these girls standing before him, the privileged daughters of a duke, how would they survive if thrown upon the mercy of the parish? Unlike Gabriel, Charles, and Freddie, they had not learned to make their own way, and according to the lawyer, if Gabriel did not take up his unexpected windfall, then everything that belonged to the Dukedom of Grantham would return to the Crown.

It is what they deserve, that little boy's voice spoke angrily in his head. *For tossing you away when your mother died and trying to hide the truth.* His older and more pragmatic self knew why they had done it. Eugénie had been a poor, exiled foreigner, and Lady Felicia had the sort of aristocratic connections a family like the Ashtons craved. Eugénie was a mistake, Gabriel was a mistake, and so they had drawn a line through them.

But was any of that the six girls' fault?

He swallowed as his emotions seesawed. The sick feeling had returned to his stomach, with the addition of a hard kernel of worry and doubt. He was no loving brother, and the thought of taking on such a burden…his head ached.

Gabriel watched as the church minister finished droning on and the coffin was carried into the stone building where so many generations of Ashtons were contained. He shuddered, imagining being locked in there with sneering strangers, and decided he would rather be tossed into the Thames. The lawyer had insisted he come here today, despite Gabriel having no intention of agreeing to sip from this poisonous chalice when he was perfectly content with his life as it was. Perfectly content.

The lawyer might have said more, but if he did, Gabriel couldn't remember it. At the time, he had been busy trying to process the man's words, trying to come to grips with his stunning revelations, trying to believe this was not some feverish nightmare and orphan fantasy come true, all rolled into one. It was accurate that to be part of a family was the dream of every abandoned child, and those from St. Ninian's were no exception, but Gabriel and his friends had always been determined to make their own way in the world. They did not expect favors, or dreams to become reality; they were equal parts hard graft and single-minded ambition, with a dash of refusing to give up thrown in.

No, he told himself he didn't care that he had been given a family on a silver platter—a tarnished one probably—but all the same his new circumstances felt painfully real and raw.

He was a duke, part of the peerage, the nobility, and only the Prince Regent was higher in the land than he and his ducal peers. It was so far outside of his sphere—upbringing, education, aspiration—as to be ridiculous. Surely dukes were made from the moment they were born, molded into the required form, and not plucked from obscurity? Polite society would never open its arms to him in welcome. It would laugh at him for aping his betters. He would be an outsider in its ranks rather than inhabiting his current comfortable position as gambling hell proprietor.

But there was more to his decision than a fear of being mocked. Gabriel could shrug that off if necessary. The truth was Grantham was drowning in debt. Gabriel was an astute businessman, and he had contacts in that world, and it didn't take him long to discover the extent of his new family's financial ruin. His father had been the worst kind of duke, spending and spending and never putting anything back. If Gabriel agreed to become the next duke, he would have to turn the disaster around. It would be almost like starting all over again from the bottom. Did he want that? Was the title worth it?

The night the Ashtons' lawyer came to give him the news, Gabriel had drunk more claret than was his habit, and Charles had joined him. They'd thrashed out the pros and cons, asking questions they could not answer, and woken with aching heads and no solution to the problem other than Gabriel's stubborn determination not to agree to it.

"I'm happy as I am," he had told Charles. "I like beginning each morning knowing exactly what the day holds."

"Do you?" Charles had replied. "Sounds boring to me. Where's the challenge in that? Maybe you need a change, my friend."

A white flower had fallen from one of the wreaths that adorned the coffin as it was carried by the pallbearers into the maw of the family tomb. The delicate blossom had landed on the muddy ground in front of the youngest of the duke's daughters. Gabriel watched as the little girl stared down at it, then across to her oblivious siblings. Thinking herself unobserved, she stooped to pick it up, only to lose her balance and stumble. Her hands went to the muddy ground and she let out a distressed wail, before straightening up and holding out her hands in front of her as if not quite knowing what to do with them. Abruptly her little face crumpled.

Gabriel felt every sinew in his body tighten as the need to go to her rescue overcame all other concerns. The sensation was as unfamiliar as it was pressing, and he wasn't sure what to do with it.

At the same moment the stern-faced woman standing behind the girls—a governess or a nursemaid—moved swiftly to haul the child back in line. Her voice was a sibilant hiss, but the effect of her words was immediate obedience. The sister next in line took her sibling's grubby hand in hers, and after a few hiccuped sobs, peace was restored.

Gabriel started as Charles elbowed him in the side. "Poor little mite," he muttered. "First thing you should do is toss the governess out on her arse." Then, with a sly, knowing glance at his friend, continued, "*If* you take all of them on, of course."

Gabriel rubbed a hand over the bunched muscles of his jaw. "I'm not taking them on. I told you. I've refused."

"Standing firm, huh?"

Maybe the little girl had sensed their interest, because now her sad eyes turned on Gabriel. Suddenly all six of the sisters looked up, as if they were acting on some sort of unspoken directive, to stare at him. The eldest sullenly, the second eldest shyly, and all the way down the line to the smallest, whose woebegone face broke into a brilliant smile. It was as if the sun had come out on this wretched occasion, and despite himself, Gabriel felt his lips twitch.

"I can see how firm you're standing," Charles whispered beside him. "Not tempted at all."

This time Gabriel ignored him.

"Your Grace?" The lawyer had appeared and was bowing before him. "If you will come with me? The family wishes to meet you and discuss arrangements for the future."

He remembered the man's name. "Very well, Mr. Arnott, but I assure you I have not changed my mind."

"Of course not, Your Grace," he said soothingly. "You must do as you feel best. We are all in your hands."

Arnott set off toward the house, which was at some distance from the family cemetery. A jumble of chimneys and gables in stone the color of butter rose above grand old trees. The place looked old, and a bit of a mess, as various generations of Ashtons had added to it. This was Grantham, where his father, Harry, had lived and which now belonged to Gabriel.

If he wanted it.

Chapter Four

The Grantham estate was close to the Sussex coast in the south of England. The family name was Ashton, headed by the Duke of Grantham, and they considered themselves one of the leading families, having been here since Henry VIII ruled England. They had been active in the most important decisions throughout history, usually pulling strings from the sidelines. Scandals weren't unknown throughout those centuries, in fact Gabriel was sure there were plenty, but still he wondered if it would be his fate to go down in Ashton history as the *most* scandalous member of the family.

The grounds of the estate were vast, with swaths of green lawn and mature trees in every direction. The sea must be close though, because Gabriel could smell the salty air, so very different from the musty waters of the Thames. Just as this place was very different from the crowded, jumbled buildings of London, where he had grown up and now resided.

He thought he might have liked to wander about before he gave up his unwanted inheritance, but Arnott was setting a cracking pace. Charles and Freddie spoke in low voices, glancing anxiously at Gabriel every now and again, but he ignored them. The question he really wanted answered was one he couldn't answer, and neither could they.

Why him? Why had he been handed this terrible gift? Why not Charles, who would make an excellent duke, with his charming manners and friendly smile. No one would question why Charles should take on the reins of Grantham. Or even devil-may-care Freddie, who would certainly cut a dash as a duke. Gabriel knew he was not a social animal, he was solitary and intense and liked nothing better than to lose himself in the figures in his ledgers or the stories in his books.

They passed under a gatehouse, which Charles said reminded him of the Tower of London. "Are we going to have our heads chopped off?" he said with a grin. Freddie snorted as they walked across the graveled area that led to the front door. They were met by an ancient butler in blue and silver livery, who looked as if he had never smiled in his life.

"Welcome to Grantham, Your Grace. My name is Humber. The family awaits you in the state drawing room."

Gabriel, who would have preferred to turn and make haste back to London, nodded brusquely and followed Humber's dignified steps.

Freddie caught Gabriel's gaze and rolled his eyes with a smirk, while Charles had grown suddenly quiet, his usual good humor nowhere to be seen. Perhaps it was the atmosphere. The place was certainly grand, and it was difficult to pretend they were comfortable in such regal surroundings. The vestibule, with its marble columns, checkered floor, and hushed mood, made Gabriel want to whisper. He looked up at the glass dome high above, through which the gray sky threw its cool light upon them. The butler led the way up a curved staircase, and Gabriel noted the family portraits glaring down at them, before they reached a wide, carpeted corridor. A procession of doors with gold embellishments hinted at the opulence within, until at last Humber paused at a set of double doors and opened them wide. Before Gabriel could enter, the man spoke in a sonorous tone. "His Grace the sixth Duke of Grantham."

It did not help. Gabriel was already laboring under the burden of being in such an unfamiliar and taxing position, and he had to wonder why the servant had announced him in such a way when his old master was barely cold in his coffin. Charles muttered a curse, and Freddie stifled a laugh. Gabriel's gaze caught the butler's for a second. There was a glint of satisfaction in the man's eyes, as if he had fulfilled some long-held promise to himself, before he stepped aside and the drawing room came into full view.

Walls were papered in stylish silver and blue, reminiscent of the servants' livery, while lush landscapes hung at various intervals, and the portrait of an elegant dark-haired woman dressed in the fashion of the mid-eighteenth century stared back at him from above the mantel. The furnishings were upholstered in pale pinks and greens, sometimes striped, and a gold clock adorned with cupids sat on a side table, while beeswax candles helped alleviate the dullness of the day beyond heavily draped bay windows.

It was a room designed to exhibit the family's wealth and power, a tactic meant to intimidate, and Gabriel flushed as he realized he had been gawping about him like a chimney sweep let into the big house. Quickly he turned his attention to the gathered family members, grouped by the lit fireplace, and saw that they were equally as fascinated by him.

The old woman who had been at the graveside held center stage. She was obviously a person of importance, a close relative. Her posture was rigidly proud, the diamonds circling her throat incongruous against the mourning black of her clothing. Perhaps, like the room she commanded, they were meant to intimidate, and the dark eyes fixed on him were coldly authoritative. Gathered around her were the six daughters, the girls assuming the same obedient poses as before, their heads bowed. Until the oldest one shot him a heated and resentful glance from beneath her lashes. He caught a hastily repressed grin from the youngest girl, and then the oppressive silence was broken.

"Your Grace." Mr. Arnott was back by his side.

"Mr. Cadieux does not merit the courtesy of being 'Your Graced,' Arnott. He has not agreed to assume the title, nor the duties that go with it." Of course it was the old woman who spoke, her face a myriad of wrinkles, like a frozen puddle in winter when the ice has begun to crack.

"You're right, I haven't agreed," Gabriel said. "I—"

"You must. It is your duty," she interrupted.

"I beg your pardon, madam, but I have no duty to this family. I was abandoned at birth."

The six girls exchanged startled glances, as if they were not used to the old woman's pronouncements being met with dissent.

Something glinted in those dark eyes. Surprise? Disgust? Perhaps it was approval. He didn't have time to decide, because when she spoke again, her words pushed everything else from his head.

"I remember well. I was the person who persuaded my son to abandon you."

Beside him Charles stiffened, and, thinking he was going to launch himself at the creature, Gabriel put out an arm to stop him. He had forgotten Arnott still hovered at his side until the lawyer spoke again, this time his tone censorious.

"Mr. Cadieux, may I introduce your grandmother, Her Grace, Margaret, the Dowager Duchess of Grantham."

His grandmother? Of course it was, he realized. Who else could it be? He clearly remembered Arnott's words to him in his office when he first learned of his windfall. His father's mother had placed him in a foundling home to clear the way for her son to marry a better prospect and produce a better heir. This woman seated before him so callous and uncaring had done that to him.

An image came to him then. A child's memory, murky and dusty with time and distance. A woman with dark eyes like his own, and an icily posh voice. He had been called into the superintendent's office when he was ten years old. By then he had been a resident of St. Ninian's for almost seven years and knew nothing else. The woman had been seated by the window, and at first he hadn't seen her. He had answered the super's questions sulkily. Yes, he had been a good boy. Yes, he had minded his manners. Yes, he knew his alphabet and his tables. The questions answered satisfactorily, a silence fell, and that was when the woman spoke.

"The child seems bright enough, and he looks like Harry." She had said it with a hint of regret. "A pity he is a bastard."

"Your son has how many daughters now, Your Grace?" The superintendent sounded sympathetic, but knowing the man's sly tone, Gabriel was aware he was only pretending.

The woman's mouth turned down in disappointment. "Too many. We are praying that this time Lady Felicia will deliver him a son and heir."

"Who are you?" Gabriel interrupted. "Why are you here?"

"Boy, mind your manners!" the superintendent began with a growl, but the woman held up a hand to stop him.

She rose to her feet, and although he was already a tall boy, she was still taller. "I am nothing to you," she said frigidly, "and you are nothing to me. As for why I am here...I hardly know." She turned to the superintendent. "I have seen enough. I will not come again."

Gabriel stared back at his grandmother, reliving the memory. Why would the dowager visit him at the foundling home years after she had sent him there? He could ask her, but he wasn't sure the answer would help ease the sudden ache in his heart. His grandmother had abandoned him, tossed him aside as soon as his mother was gone, and the only reason she was speaking to him now was that she had been forced into a position that gave her no choice.

His silence had lasted too long.

"You have nothing to say?" the dowager said. "Did you think me dead?"

"No, madam." He spoke the truth through stiff lips, any need he might have felt to be polite gone. "I *hoped* you were dead."

The eldest of the girls gave a burst of shocked laughter, hurriedly covering her mouth and pretending to cough. She was ignored. The dowager did not so much as flinch. "Well, I am very much alive," she said forcefully, "and intend to remain so until the Ashtons take their place once more as one of the first families in the land."

He said nothing, and perhaps she took his silence as a judgment upon her actions, launching into an explanation of sorts. Gabriel did not think she felt any guilt though, and he would not have expected her to.

"At the time I sent you away, I thought you were of no consequence. Harry had married Lady Felicia and then proceeded to do his best to produce a son, unfortunately to no avail. We had all but given up thought of a male heir, and then Harry died and to my surprise I learned you were in fact the legal heir. And before you accuse me of child cruelty, I chose St. Ninian's for you because it had a fine reputation for educating boys and finding them worthy occupations."

She thought she had done well by him. Gabriel wondered if she had any understanding of how much he had lost by being abandoned. Yes, he had had an education and the chance of a worthy occupation, although he had never taken up the apprenticeship with the bookkeeper. Yes, he had left the foundling home with a burning desire to succeed. But what about love and care, kindness and tenderness? Surely even a bastard deserved an occasional hug and a soft word or two? Things he never had. Yes, he had his friends, but his mother was dead and his father unknown, and his grandmother had abandoned him.

"I assume she doesn't consider owning a gambling house a worthy occupation?" Freddie murmured beside him with a smirk.

The dowager hadn't finished. "You do not have to like me, Cadieux, just as I do not have to like you. We are here to do our duty, and yours is to step up and become head of this family."

"And if I have no desire to do so?" His voice sounded harsh and dry.

Her gaze held the disdain that was becoming familiar to him, and her eyes were as dark as his. Gabriel had always assumed his eyes came from his French mother, but he saw now they were his grandmother's eyes. The realization was not one that pleased him.

"You have a gambling hell, I believe?" she asked, her mouth curled in derision. "You won it in a game of chance. Oh yes, I know all about that. And yet you knew you would win because you are a man who weighs up the odds in any given situation. Looks at all possible sides to an argument." Her cold smile told him his expression had betrayed his surprise that she had bothered to learn his character. "There is no risk here either. All you have to do is agree and sign some papers that Arnott will place before you, and you will become the Duke of Grantham, with a fine estate and a London town house. A few other bits and pieces, land and houses and so on," she said with a careless wave of her hand, as if she were speaking of buttons and beads. "All yours. I would call that an easy day's work for a man like you."

No, she did not know him as well as she thought, if she believed that greed was what would sway him. Gabriel did not want any of the items she had listed, even if they were unencumbered by debt; she would not win him over that way.

"Without your consent, everything will be lost to the Crown," she went on evenly, still attempting to persuade him, but he could see from the way her fingers plucked restlessly at the lace on her gown that it was now an effort for her to remain calm. She must be furious. All her plans gone awry. "Everything will go into the coffers of the Prince Regent to spend on that ridiculous pavilion in Brighton."

Charles huffed a laugh. "Surely that's treason," he said. "Isn't it, Freddie?"

Freddie straightened his cuffs. "A form of it, no doubt."

Regally, the dowager ignored them. "Well?" she demanded of Gabriel. "I must have your answer."

"I have no wish to step into the shoes of the man who gave me up because his mother told him to." Gabriel heard the bitter twist to his voice. He told himself he shouldn't care what she had done, but he found he did. He did!

"Is it an apology you wish for?" Her brows rose in genuine surprise. "Are your feelings hurt, Cadieux? If I say I am sorry, will that convince you to agree?"

Gabriel didn't know what he wished for. Not an apology, no, he didn't want that from her, because it would mean nothing. Suddenly it was all too much. This room, these people, the weight of the great house and its past pressing down upon his shoulders, until he felt as if he were going to sink into the richly colored Turkish carpet at his feet.

"I'm hungry."

The tense standoff was broken. The smallest daughter turned to her siblings and wailed dramatically, "I'm starved!"

"Hush," one of the others said.

"You have to be patient, Edwina," said another.

But the child would be neither hushed nor patient. "Why are we here?" she demanded. "I want to go to the nursery and play with my dolls."

"The child misses her father." The dowager was still watching him, and Gabriel strove to make his face a mask. "Without his protection she has nothing. I believe the workhouse has been mentioned, although I don't think it will come to that. I have a cousin in Bristol who might take her in. He is of course a vicious brute, but that shouldn't worry you, Gabriel."

Until now he had been "Cadieux," and hearing his given name in her mouth was a shock. He knew that the girls would be destitute without him, and the image that formed in his mind now was very real. And his grandmother, curse her, had finally homed in on his weakness, and before he could steer her away, she carried on, digging deeper.

"You have not been introduced to your sisters, have you?" She pointed them out as she spoke. "Olivia is twenty years old. She was meant to make her debut last year, but due to Harry's illness, it was put off. We had expected her to make a brilliant match, but that will not happen now. She has a tendency to sulks and fits of temper, and who will put up with those character faults without the dukedom of Grantham to sweeten them?"

Olivia shot her grandmother a look of loathing before lowering her blue eyes.

"This is Justina, she is eighteen. I think she would make a good governess. She is quiet and biddable and always has her head in a book."

Justina shifted uncomfortably.

"Roberta is sixteen, and she is a great rider, always getting into mischief. I think she would make a perfect stable hand."

Roberta gave a pleased laugh but quickly covered her mouth. Freddie snorted in response, and the two of them exchanged an amused glance.

"Antonia is twelve, and it is far too soon yet for her to have developed any particular traits. She may be vivacious, or she may be dreadfully dull. Georgia is eight and I rarely notice her. And then there is Edwina, who is four years old."

"Five," Edwina corrected her. "And I'm hungry."

"Do be quiet," hissed Olivia. "Do you think he cares if you are hungry? He doesn't care about any of us, you silly child. He doesn't want to be here. Why would he want to take us all on? *I* wouldn't! The only reason he came was to laugh in our faces."

Edwina stared up at Gabriel, and her lip wobbled. Unlike her dark-haired sisters, her hair was light brown and a mass of unruly curls, although her eyes were the same shade of blue as her siblings'. "He does c-care," she retorted. "I know he does. Do you care?"

Gabriel had no answer. If he said yes, then his grandmother would pounce on it, and if he said no, Edwina would probably burst into sobs. Thankfully Charles broke the silence. "Why do all of your granddaughters have the feminine version of masculine names?" he asked curiously.

The dowager turned her gimlet stare on him. "We have not been introduced, young man."

Gabriel met his friend's startled gaze. "This is Mr. Charles Wickley, Your Grace. And this is Ensign Freddie Hart."

"Only my friends call me Freddie. My full name is Alfred Hart, ma'am," Freddie informed her, with his irrepressible grin.

"I see." She sniffed. "To answer your question, Mr. Wickley, my granddaughters have the feminine version of masculine names because Harry and Felicia chose their names before the happy event. I believe they hoped, foolishly as it turned out, that this would promote an heir. Once it was discovered the children were female, they kept the names, more than likely because Lady Felicia could not be bothered to change them."

Obviously she did not think much of her daughter-in-law. Gabriel opened his mouth to ask where Lady Felicia was at the moment, but did not get the chance.

Suddenly the dowager clapped her hands, startling everyone. "Girls! Make your curtsies please, and then you may be excused."

All six rose obediently, curtsied, and filed from the room. The door closed behind them, leaving only Gabriel and his friends with the dowager and Arnott.

"Now you know what is at stake," his grandmother said. "You can step up and save your sisters from the penury that awaits them, take your proper place in society, or you can skulk away into the shadows of your vile club. Your mother was a beauty, I grant you, though a poor creature, but you have Ashton blood in you, Gabriel. I will expect you to rise to it."

She reached for an ebony cane, and a moment later the door closed for a second time.

"Bloody hell," Freddie muttered. "I never thought I'd say this, but it makes me glad I don't have a family."

Mr. Arnott made one of his sudden appearances, followed by another bow. "I will call upon you in two days' time," he said. "I must have an answer then, Your Grace…sir."

Gabriel's gaze slid past him, to the portrait of the elegant woman above the mantel. He realized now that it was his grandmother as a young woman. She was not beautiful, her face strong rather than pretty, and she was not smiling. She looked formidable, and that at least had not changed.

"Two days," he repeated, "and my answer will be the same."

Arnott cleared his throat. "I feel I should clarify the dowager's words. Yes, there is the estate and the house in London, as well as various other entitlements, but it would be wrong to believe there is a fortune involved."

Gabriel gave him his attention, appreciating the man's honesty. "You mean there isn't?" he asked, as if he didn't already know.

Arnott shook his head regretfully. "Far from it, I'm afraid. Your father and his father before him spent most of what remained in the estate coffers."

"Thank you." The lawyer could have kept that from him, and Gabriel was grateful that he hadn't.

"Does your grandmother know how much you make from the club?" Charles said as the three men left the room. "Perhaps she's after *your* fortune, Gabe."

Outside it had begun to drizzle, the trees wet and dripping, and the ground marshy underfoot. Gabriel told himself he couldn't wait to get back to the warmth of his club, the familiar surroundings he valued and where he felt safe. He strode swiftly to the coach, his companions hurrying by his side. He noticed the two of them exchange a glance, but they didn't speak, and he was glad of that. He had nothing more to say to anyone.

Just as the coachman opened the door for them and lowered the steps, there was a cry from the house. He turned back in time to see Edwina's face at an open window in one of the upper stories, waving her hand to him. A moment later she was hauled back into what was probably the nursery, and the window slammed shut.

Gabriel's mouth twitched.

"Are you going to do it?" Charles was watching him

curiously, a hint of concern in his blue eyes. The dampness in the air was making his fair hair curl. "I know I said it would be a challenge, but I wasn't aware just how much of a challenge."

"Of course he's not," Freddie scoffed. He threw himself down on the leather seat and stretched out his polished black boots. "Save those poor girls from the horrors of poverty? I think it would do them good to experience life as it really is."

"The workhouse," Charles said thoughtfully. "They won't last long, at least there is that."

"They'd probably murder the youngest one after one day," declared Freddie.

"What was her name?" Charles said.

"Edwina," Gabriel answered, and then swore when he saw the laughter in his friends' eyes.

"Of course, she may be sent off to the brutish relative in Bristol. But I'm sure that will be equally good for her."

Gabriel tuned out their teasing. He didn't want to do it. He felt that sick, twisted feeling in his stomach at the thought of doing it. Bitterness filled him at the memory of his grandmother who, with one word to the superintendent, could have turned a life that was harsh and miserable into something so much better. But she hadn't. And now she was asking him to do his duty as if it were the easiest thing in the world.

"Gabriel?"

Charles and Freddie were watching him curiously.

"You don't have to do it, you know," Charles said softly. "No one will think any worse of you if you say no."

But that wasn't true, was it? There were six reasons for him to say yes, and six persons who would think worse of him if he didn't.

He was not a coward, but he rarely took risks. The dowager was right when she said he liked to weigh up both sides of an argument before he made his decision. He was trying to do that now, but he kept seeing Edwina's face, and hearing his grandmother's precise voice as she listed the awful possibilities ahead of them, followed by Olivia's passionate cry—*He doesn't care!*—and Gabriel very much feared his decision had already been made.

Chapter Five

Christmas Eve, 1817, London

It was still early in the morning, and Vivienne had hoped Will would be in the breakfast room. A letter had come from Cornwall yesterday, and she had read it with relief, but when she went to find her brother, he had been out somewhere. Old Mr. Davey had written to inform her that he and the other trustee of the Tremeer estate, Sir Desmond Chamond, had met with Sutherland, and come to the decision that there were no grounds for the baronet's will to be overturned.

> *Young men are inclined to sow their oats, but there is no cause for alarm. Sir William has not yet attained his majority, and once he does, we have every expectation of him becoming a sensible and honest gentleman, just like his father.*

The letter had an almost jovial tone, and did much to calm Vivienne's fears. For the past month she had been on tenterhooks, wondering what was happening in Cornwall and expecting any moment to hear from Cadieux. But in fact she had heard nothing from the gambling hell owner, although for reasons she'd prefer not to delve into, the memory of her visit to him kept playing on her mind.

She was not an expert when it came to gambling matters, but the fact that they had not heard from Cadieux was a good thing, surely? Had he mislaid the paperwork? No, more likely he was charging them interest. She shuddered at the thought. The horrible truth was she would have to ask Aunt Jane to help.

Aunt Jane did not like her niece and nephew, and Vivienne was not quite sure why, although she suspected it had something to do with Helena, Vivienne's mother. The viscountess had never forgiven Helena for marrying Sutherland after the baronet died. It had been a love match, on Helena's side at least. Sutherland was a handsome man, and could be charming, keeping the truth about his character hidden until after the wedding. Aunt Jane blamed her sister-in-law for the impoverishment of the Tremeer estate and the diminishing of the Tremeer family's standing in the local community. The viscountess believed that Mrs. Sutherland could have put a stop to her husband's excesses, although Vivienne doubted that was even possible. Her mother became chattel upon marriage, and all that was hers became Sutherland's. What would Aunt Jane think when she learned of Will's thoughtless behavior? Like mother like son?

And then there was the matter of Vivienne spending a night with Benjamin Jones, alone without a chaperone, which had subsequently ruined her reputation. It was a mistake, and one that Sutherland had quickly turned to his own advantage. Vivienne's father had settled a sum of money upon her for when she married, and Sutherland knew it. Ever on the lookout for easy pickings, he had sought to take advantage of Vivienne's situation and force her into marriage with Benjamin. In desperation Vivienne and Will had set out for London and thrown themselves upon Aunt Jane's mercy. Vivienne could not fault her aunt's response once she had learned the truth—she had been furious. Benjamin had been bundled out of the country as quickly as possible, and Aunt Jane had done her best to hush things up. But it was too late, and the scandal had leaked anyway.

In hindsight, Vivienne and Will were fortunate that their aunt had offered them a roof over their heads instead of washing her hands of them altogether. "At least in London I can keep an eye on you both!" she had declared. And they *were* grateful, despite being aware that her kindness had more to do with her belief that their mother was a bad influence, and their stepfather a worse one, than any real family feeling.

Returning to Cornwall was not something Vivienne wanted to think about. Bad enough to have to live in Tremeer with its falling-down roofs and overgrown grounds, and not be able to do anything about it. But Vivienne had no desire to spend her time avoiding Sutherland's lecherous friends and his schemes to marry her off.

Life with Aunt Jane may be far from perfect—Vivienne was treated as an extra pair of hands when the servants needed help, or an untrustworthy and unwelcome relative who had disgraced herself once and needed watching so she didn't do it again. At least she was more certain now that if they held fast for the next three years, Will would inherit Tremeer and they could return in circumstances very different from the ones in which they had left.

Will wasn't in the breakfast room, but it wasn't empty. Annette, normally not an early riser, was already seated in a chair by the window, a teacup at her side, staring out at the garden. There was enough sunlight to turn her fair hair into a halo and set aglow the lacy white collar that framed her pretty face with its normally unruffled expression.

Only her expression wasn't unruffled today. There was a frown wrinkling her brow, and her mouth was turned down.

Apart from Will, Annette was Vivienne's favorite relative, although her gentle nature made her popular with everyone. Even Aunt Jane's frosty smiles were less frosty when she looked upon her only child, while Vivienne couldn't remember when she'd last had even a hint of a smile from that direction. Will said that Annette was in favor because she was smart enough to agree to all of her mother's plans, even when secretly she disagreed, while Vivienne tended to say what she thought. Vivienne thought that Will was probably right, but not because of any scheming on Annette's part. Her cousin hated fuss, and agreeing with Aunt Jane was always the safer option.

Vivienne wondered if that was the reason Annette was allowing herself to be pushed into the path of a man who was completely wrong for her, simply in order to please the viscountess. Marriages in the circle the Monteiths moved in were rarely more than business arrangements hashed out between families, with daughters married off without much regard to their own wishes. Almack's was rightly known as the marriage mart. Mr. Sutherland, deep in his cups, had once told Vivienne that girls were for bedding and breeding, and no use for anything else. Did Annette really want to find herself in the company of such poor creatures?

"Good morning." Annette had heard the clink of the silver coffeepot as Vivienne poured herself a cup. As she added cream, she thought that her cousin's smile was as sweet as ever but there were definite dark shadows under her eyes.

"You're up with the lark," Vivienne teased, sitting down opposite her. "Is there a reason?"

"The sun is shining and the rain has stopped."

"Do you have an engagement to be somewhere? A visit to an old school friend and her family?"

"That's next week." Annette glanced away. "Today Ivo and one of his sisters are paying us a visit. Didn't Mama tell you?"

Of course she didn't. She would not want her scandalous niece contaminating the room. Ivo, the Duke of Northam, had called yesterday, and taken Annette riding in the park, while his sisters often took Annette shopping. It wasn't difficult to see that Aunt Jane was keen to form a match between the duke and her daughter, and if Annette could bring Northam up to scratch, then she would make everyone happy. Well, everyone apart from herself.

"Ah. And you rose early to try on all of your gowns," Vivienne teased gently.

"There's nothing wrong in looking one's best," Annette said seriously.

"Did you want me to stay with you?" Vivienne asked carefully.

Annette chewed on her lip. "Mama will probably not

like it. She has got it into her head that Ivo disapproves of you. I can assure you, he doesn't."

No, it was the duke's mother who disapproved of her. She and Aunt Jane had been at school together and were still bosom bows, and so Annette had grown up with Ivo and his sisters. For years the two older women had been determined to join their families in marriage, and now that Annette was of age, the pressure was mounting.

"Ivo is good company," Annette said, as if she suspected Vivienne thought otherwise.

"I don't know him as well as you do, but I have always found him cordial," Vivienne agreed. "You don't think he can be a little…wild? There was that curricle race through Hyde Park last month that caused such a fuss. And what about the boxing match he took part in? Don't you find yourself wondering what he will do next?"

Annette's expression grew serious. "Perhaps he is a little spoiled. His mother and sisters worship him, and they want to see him settled. Mama believes I can act as a steadying influence."

"Are you saying that you will marry him to please his family and yours?" Vivienne was smiling but her question was sincere.

"Of course! I would hardly marry someone my family did not approve of."

"There is that I suppose." Vivienne hesitated before adding, "But it does sound rather lukewarm. Don't you want a love match? I thought that was what you had always promised yourself, Annette."

Her cousin stared back at her with a frown. "He and I will deal very well together. And our families will be so happy. I do want to make them happy."

"But he has not proposed yet?"

That Ivo hadn't asked Annette to marry him despite all of the encouragement he was receiving was a matter of some disappointment to Aunt Jane and Ivo's mother.

"He will." Annette drew a deep breath. "And once we are wed, I'm sure he will change. This is nothing more than high spirits."

Vivienne was not confident about that—Ivo was twenty-seven, and if he was going to give up his reckless behavior, then he should have done so by now. Before she could voice more of her concerns, her cousin hurried on.

"Last night I reread *The Wicked Prince and His Stolen Bride* and I realized how very like Ivo the prince is. Not that Ivo would steal me away anywhere and—and ravish me, his mother would disapprove of that. But in looks he is a match for the prince."

Vivienne was startled into silence. The book—and it had never been intended to be a book—had begun life as letters to her cousin. A saga that Vivienne had created out of thin air when Annette told her she was miserable and lonely and wished Vivienne could come to stay. Knowing how much Annette enjoyed reading romances, Vivienne had made one up. It was the most preposterous story but a great deal of fun, and Annette had loved it. Loved it so much that she had mentioned it to Ivo's cousin, Harold, who was a partner in a publishing company. Harold had demanded to see it, loved it too, and the two of them had arranged to have the stories published in book form. Vivienne had known nothing of it until a charmingly bound book arrived, written by "A Lady," and she had acknowledged the story as her own.

It had been a shock, and although Annette had promised to tell no one—Aunt Jane would be furious if she knew—Vivienne was always worried she would forget and let the secret out. And that would be all the more shocking because Annette had made her own extensive improvements to *The Wicked Prince and His Stolen Bride*, which to Vivienne's mind made it a far better book.

"I don't believe I was thinking of anyone in particular," Vivienne said now. "I just wanted to make you smile."

"Will you write another? You should. You have a gift."

Although the money from the sales—which had been surprisingly lucrative—had been most welcome, Vivienne was ambivalent about repeating the experience. "You wrote just as much of it as I. What about that section in the middle where the prince's family tries to save the bride? I wish you would take some of my earnings."

"Certainly not!" A flush rose in her pale cheeks. "I told you Harold did enjoy reading it, and he has asked me several times whether 'the authoress' will be writing another. I even have a number of exciting ideas for a sequel." Her pleasure in the idea faded quickly, and Vivienne knew she was thinking of her mother and the disgrace that would ensue if the truth ever came out.

"Oh!" Annette had thought of something else. "Did you hear the latest on-dit?"

"Which one?" Vivienne asked dryly. "The wife of the marquis who threw her bonnet over the windmill and ran off with the coachman? Or the Prince Regent's latest extravagance?"

"No, much more interesting! Do you remember that the Duke of Grantham died recently? He had been ill and there were all those daughters and no male heir. You must remember! Well, a new duke has been found, and he is the owner of a gambling club. It is quite the scandal. Can you imagine? He has never been in society before and will not know how to behave. I wonder how he will be received by the ton." Annette shifted in her chair, a wriggle of excitement. She did enjoy a good gossip. "How awkward for the family. I'm sure some people will cut him for his humble origins, although he is said to be quite rich, so perhaps he will not care. I think I will feel sorry for the poor man."

Vivienne stared back at her while she rambled on. There was only one gambling club owner she knew of, but it could not be him. Could it? Was that why the man with his urgent news was knocking on Cadieux's door the night she left?

"What is this gambling club owner's name?" she asked as casually as she could manage.

"Gabriel Cadieux. His mother was French. Jenny was full of the news." Jenny, Annette's maid, was always eager to pass on the latest gossip to her mistress. "The Frenchwoman was the late duke's mistress, or so everyone thought, but it turned out the pair were married. It could have been hushed up, but some person who was present has come forward and put the cat among the pigeons. Now all of the daughters are disinherited and the gambling club owner is the new duke. Can you imagine what the Dowager Duchess of Grantham must be feeling? She does not go about in society much these days, she is very old, but she was always so haughty. So proud. I don't mean to be unkind, but I remember she cut Mama once because of..."

Her voice trailed off as she remembered what it was Aunt Jane had been cut for. Vivienne also remembered the reason—it was because of Benjamin and her.

Annette's cheeks flushed with embarrassment as she rushed on, trying to cover her faux pas. "They will have to bring the poor man up to scratch if the dowager is to be satisfied. I don't envy him one little bit."

Gabriel Cadieux with his dark eyes and tumbling dark locks, a duke? It beggared belief.

"The family has kept the whole thing hushed up until now, because they weren't certain that Mr. Cadieux would agree. He wasn't keen to be the next duke, can you imagine? But now he has agreed and the story is everywhere. Why do you think he would say no to such an elevation?"

She let Annette run on, concocting scenarios that neither of them could answer. Vivienne made sounds of interest when required, but she was no longer listening. Once her amazement had passed, she found herself wondering whether this piece of news explained why Cadieux had been too busy to demand payment of Will's debt. Once her cousin began musing on her old school friend and whether she had changed a great deal from the girl she had known, Vivienne made her excuses and went to find her brother.

He was still in bed, the curtains drawn, and the atmosphere in his chamber stale and unpleasant. Vivienne threw open the sash window and let the fresh air in before she turned back to the bed.

"Will? Wake up, Will!"

With a groan he rolled over and blinked up at her. His eyes looked red and swollen, while his skin had a greenish pallor. She could smell the brandy coming off him in waves.

"Oh, Will," she sighed.

"What?" he muttered, covering his face with his hands. "God, I feel awful. Close the window, would you."

"No, you will expire if you lie in here any longer. Where were you last night?"

Will swallowed, and dropped his hands, but avoided

her gaze. "Germaine asked me to go with him to White's. I'd never been there and he signed me in."

"White's?" Vivienne raised an eyebrow. "Don't you need rather a lot of blunt to be a member?"

Will shot her a sideways look. "It's enough that I'm a baronet. Besides, I'm sure Father was a member."

"More likely Grandfather. That's probably where he gambled away his fortune."

Will's mouth turned sulky.

Vivienne wasn't about to be diverted. "What did you do there?"

"We had supper. It was awfully good, Viv. Some sort of Frenchified chicken. And afterward we chatted with a few of Germaine's friends."

"Did you play?"

"Only a few hands."

Vivienne groaned. "Will! How could you?"

"I know, I know." His words fell over each other in his haste to excuse himself. "I'm sorry, Viv. I didn't stay long, made up some excuse, and Germaine covered my losses. He said it was the least he could do, after the trouble at Cadieux's. He's very good like that. I know you don't like him, but he has been a good friend to me. He said he would take me shooting at his family's country house and…"

He rattled on. Vivienne wanted to shake him. Shake him until he stopped behaving so stupidly and finally realized how much he was risking. Which reminded her…

"I have two pieces of news," she said, slipping the letter from Mr. Davey from her pocket and spreading out the single sheet.

Will eyed it balefully. "What is it?"

"Read it."

Will covered his face with his hands again. "Must I? My head aches so."

"I think you will want to hear this." When he made no move to take it, Vivienne proceeded to read him the letter. By the time she had finished, Will was staring at her through his spread fingers.

"Does that mean I will inherit after all?"

"Yes. But, Will, you must take care. Sutherland will be watching."

"I am taking care. I am being very good no matter what you seem to think."

"There is still the matter of your debt to Gabriel Cadieux."

"Can't you let me enjoy the good news before you remind me of the bad?"

"I'm not sure if it is bad." She grinned at him. "Cadieux is now a duke."

"He's a what?"

Vivienne began to explain, and his eyes grew wider and wider as the tale went on. It did sound incredible, but Annette believed it was true because Jenny had told her, and Jenny was never wrong when it came to town gossip because all of her relatives were in service. They were like a spy network, with ears in every grand house, or most of them.

"He'll sell the club, surely?" Will said, interrupting her wandering thoughts. His face had regained some of its color and he had sat up, resting back against the headboard. "Why would he keep it? If he's a duke, he will have so many better things to do. He'll sell the club and I will be free."

"Then your debt will be sold with it." Vivienne hated to quash his excitement, but they needed to be practical.

Will deflated. "I don't think he will sell my debt, it's worse than that. Cadieux is the sort of man who will hold on to it and force me to repay it, even if he doesn't need the money. He probably thinks he is doing me good. He certainly won't forget. Word is he never does. The last time he spoke to me…well, I wish now I had listened to him."

Vivienne looked at him in surprise. "What do you mean? When did he speak to you, Will?"

Will shrugged and then winced. He began to massage his temples as if that might help. "He came downstairs to the cardroom and spoke to me and Germaine. Me, mainly. We had been playing deep and it was late. I wanted to stop but I was so far in debt and I kept hoping I could win back a little of what I had lost. Luck can change, Viv. If you can get onto a run of good luck, then you can turn yourself around. Germaine says—"

Vivienne had heard enough of Germaine's pronouncements. "And did you? Win some back?"

He shot her an uncomfortable look, his mouth turning sulky. "No."

"What did Cadieux say to you?"

Will seemed to have no trouble remembering the conversation. "He asked me if I knew what I was doing, and shouldn't I be home with my wet nurse. Everyone in the room laughed. Germaine knocked over his drink he was so amused."

"He embarrassed you." It was never a good thing to embarrass Will; he had had enough of that from Sutherland. And he would be especially touchy about it in front of his friend Germaine.

"Yes, he did." Sitting up in his nightshirt, Will was gangly and thin, and without the bored man-about-town expression he had taken to affecting, he looked very young. "Until then I had been thinking I would leave. I did not like how Germaine was being so reckless, betting on everything, throwing good money after bad, and I was thinking up an excuse to leave. But then Cadieux said *that*, and I decided I wasn't going anywhere. I thought I'd show him. So I lost more and more money. Charles Wickley, who helps Cadieux run the hell, said I was a fool and because I was so young and f-feckless, I was giving their club a bad name."

"No wonder Mr. Cadieux doesn't want to forgive your debt," she said. "Oh, Will, why didn't you listen to him?"

"It wasn't my fault," Will retorted, but he refused to meet her eyes. Then he slipped back down beneath the covers and pulled them over his head so that his voice was muffled. "Yes, it is my fault. They were right. I'm so sorry, Vivienne. What are we going to do?"

"Pray he's too busy being a duke to remember us?" Vivienne suggested. "I can't imagine it will be easy for him. They can dress him up, but scratch the surface and he will still be the same heartless gambler. His grandmother, the dowager, is known to be a bit of a dragon. She cut Aunt Jane once, did you know?"

"Did she?" Will sounded delighted. "What for?"

But Vivienne diverted him with "Perhaps she wasn't holding her teacup in the correct manner."

Will chuckled.

"Anyway, while he's playing at being a duke, it will give us time to find the money to repay him." She pulled down the covers. "Will? Do you think Germaine would lend you some of it?"

Will grimaced. "I think he would if he could, but it is rather a lot and he says he's used up most of his allowance already. If his father cuts up rough, he'll have to return to the country to rusticate."

Vivienne wished he would; at least with Germaine out of the way, she might be able to talk some sense into her brother. But then again there were plenty of others like Germaine out there, and Will was more than likely to find them.

"I have my nest egg. I know it's not enough but perhaps—"

"No, it isn't."

"And you haven't been back to Cadieux's?"

"They won't let me in. I did consider trying to win some back, but I was refused entry." He sounded upset, but all the same Vivienne was tempted to give him a lecture. Another one. His next words changed her mind.

"When is Northam coming today?" he asked. "He's bringing his sister, isn't he? The younger one? She always cheers me up."

That hurt. Vivienne supposed it was true that she wasn't very jolly these days, and they always seemed to be at odds, but that was hardly her fault. If Will wanted her to cheer him up, then he shouldn't cause her so much worry. All the same, perhaps this was not the right time to remind him of his mistakes.

"I think they are..." she began, before she saw that his eyes had closed and he either had fallen back to sleep or was feigning it. He looked innocent and rather sweet, reminding her of the brother she loved. With a sigh Vivienne left him to his dreams.

Gabriel Cadieux a duke! The idea was tantalizing, something to while away the time as she went about her day. From gambling hell owner to duke—it sounded like the premise of one of Annette's romance novels. Perhaps

Vivienne could fashion something out of it? *The Wicked Duke*? If she did write a book about Gabriel Cadieux, she would make him generous and kind, and he would instantly forgive Will's debt. Fiction indeed! No, it was more likely that he would be the villain, a coldhearted cad. Yes, that would be far more satisfying.

Chapter Six

March 1818

"Vivienne! Wake up! Please, wake up…"

Vivienne blinked, struggling to shake off the fog of sleep. She had been having a rather nice dream and wanted to continue with it, but it was already slipping out of her grasp. Someone was leaning over her, speaking in a harsh whisper, and whoever it was sounded frantic.

"Viv, I need to tell you something important."

"Will? What on earth—"

"He's in London! He was there tonight and…and he said he'd tell Davey…"

Her brother was making no sense. Abruptly she sat up just as he leaned in, and they bumped heads. With a whimper she fell back onto her pillow again while Will groaned and clutched at his forehead. "Ouch," he muttered.

Thankfully the throbbing in her head was brief and Vivienne opened her eyes again. Her gaze narrowed as she took in Will's disheveled appearance in the light from a candle he must have brought with him. "What on earth are you doing here?" she demanded. "Have you been out on the town again?"

"Yes," Will said, still rubbing his head. And then hastily, "No!" as Vivienne opened her mouth to tell him what she thought of that. "I meant to say I was out but I wasn't gaming. I swear I wasn't. Germaine asked me to sit with him—he says I give him luck—and that's all I did. I sat beside him. I've been so good since Christmastide, but we've heard nothing from Mr. Davey, so I thought it would be all right."

Vivienne considered his wide-eyed stare. "You have been good, Will. And we haven't heard from Mr. Cadieux either. The Duke of Grantham I mean. It's almost too good to be true."

She had come to the hopeful conclusion that the duke had forgotten all about them. He must be very busy with his new life, learning to be a peer of the realm. Vivienne expected any moment for him to be unveiled, like a work of art, for the ton to admire. Or deride. There was certainly a great deal of interest in him.

"That's what I thought." Her brother's comment brought her back from her wandering thoughts. He flopped onto the bed beside her. "That's why I went with Germaine." He shot her a sideways glance and chewed on his lip.

"Is that what you woke me up to tell me?" she asked uneasily, knowing there was more.

"No." He turned his head and she saw how pale he was, even in the candlelight, his gray eyes like saucers. "I saw Sutherland," he blurted out. "That's what I came to tell you."

"You what?" Vivienne started up again, as if she

needed to be on her feet to hear what she already knew was bad news. Will caught her hand and stopped her, holding it painfully tightly.

"I saw Sutherland. I was sitting beside Germaine while he played, and I dozed off, and the next thing I knew Sutherland was there. Looming over me."

"H-he's here? In London?" Vivienne tried to grasp that awful thought. It was a year since they had left Tremeer to take refuge with their aunt, and she had not missed her stepfather one bit. Now Sutherland was here in London, no doubt getting up to all sorts of mischief. Another thought came to her. "Is Mother here too?"

"No, she's still at Tremeer. I asked him that too, and he said he couldn't enjoy himself if she was looking over his shoulder." He swallowed as if his mouth was suddenly dry. "I thought he was a bad dream at first—hoped! But he was real. He kept calling me 'dear boy,' you know how he does, in that fake jovial voice, while all the time I could see in his eyes how much he hates me."

"Envies you," Vivienne corrected him. "He envies you, Will."

She knew that was true. Sutherland came of good family but had been cast out in his youth because of his bad behavior, and had had to scheme and connive his way into a respectable enough position to lure their mother into marriage. He could have made a fist of their union, could have been a loving husband and a kindly stepfather, but all too soon his true nature had come to the fore. He envied Will because he saw him as the boy Sutherland could have been if his life had turned out differently. But there wasn't time to go into all of that when Will was staring at her, words trembling on his lips.

"Never mind," Vivienne said quickly. "Tell me what he said to you."

"He said he had heard I was gambling away my inheritance and he'd come to see for himself whether it was true."

"He said that in front of everyone?" Vivienne gasped.

"No, he took me into a private room. I didn't want to go, Viv. I was damned...dashed scared, but he sort of tugged me along. Once the door was shut, he started on about the gambling. He called me 'profligate'! I tried to tell him about the letter we'd had from the trustees but he scoffed at that, said Davey was our creature through and through, but Sir Desmond was now his bosom bow."

"He's wangled his way into Sir Desmond's good graces," Vivienne murmured. "That's not good news." As one of the trustees of their father's will, Sir Desmond was in a powerful position.

"That's what I think. Ingratiated himself with Sir Desmond in that sickening way he has when he wants something. He told me that Sir Desmond believes there is a good chance of overturning the will. That it isn't fair a loving stepfather should be cut out of the estate."

"Isn't fair!" Vivienne felt equal parts fury and fear bubble up inside her. "Hateful man," she gasped.

"He was gloating, Viv, as if he'd already won. He said that he'd heard a rumor that I owed a great deal of money for a gambling debt he knows I cannot pay, and he was going to prove it."

"A rumor? He must have a spy at Cadieux's." Unless the duke himself had been Sutherland's source of information? Vivienne found she did not believe that though. She might not know the duke well, but somehow idle gossip about his patrons' affairs did not fit with the man. "What else did he say?"

Will groaned and covered his face with his hands, his voice muffled. "That once Davey heard about my gambling debt, he would turn against us because he would see I wasn't fit to inherit Tremeer."

Vivienne could well believe that Davey would see the blemish on Will's character as damning evidence against his suitability to inherit. Loyal as the old man had always been, he was also a stickler for "doing the right thing."

"What can we do?" Will had dropped his hands and was watching her with a bleak expression on his face. "How can we stop Sutherland? If he overturns the will and takes Tremeer, then…" His shoulders slumped. "There will be nothing left to go home to."

There was only one thing they could do. "We need to pay the debt," Vivienne said, "so that Sutherland has nothing to use against you. Even if he finds out more about it, you will have paid it and can show Mr. Davey and Sir Desmond a clean slate."

"Pay the debt," her brother repeated dully.

"I will have to talk to the duke." She squeezed his shoulder. "Go to bed, Will. We can talk again tomorrow. And don't worry, I won't let that man steal your inheritance."

Will hesitated. "You know, while I was sitting beside Germaine, I was thinking about us. Living here on Aunt Jane's charity. It's worse for you, Viv. I've seen how she treats you, like one of her servants, and I know I haven't been much help. I've caused you so much more trouble. I told myself that when we return to Tremeer I would make it up to you. I'll be the best brother in the world because you deserve all the good things. And now I don't even know if we'll have a home to go back to."

Tears filled his eyes and she reached to give him a hug. "Oh, Will," she whispered, her arms tightening. "Don't despair. It will be all right. I'll speak to the duke, and Sutherland will go away. I promise."

It was silly. Vivienne knew she should not promise something she did not know whether she could make happen. After a moment Will sniffed and sat up, wiping his eyes with the heels of his hands. Outside a blackbird began to sing, heralding the dawn.

"Go to bed," she said again. "Get some sleep."

Will nodded and left her alone, the door closing quietly behind him. Vivienne lay, her thoughts churning, listening as the household came to life about her. *I'll talk to the duke*, she repeated to herself. *And this time I'll make him listen.*

Chapter Seven

Gabriel tugged at his cuffs. The tailcoat was more than snug, it was tight, and fit him like a second skin. But then it was meant to. His cream knee breeches and the midnight blue tailcoat were the traditional wear for attending a ball, according to his new valet. The man was eyeing his form now with a satisfied expression, and Gabriel tried to ignore his own discomfort, and his growing desire to tear everything off and replace it with his familiar shabby jacket and buckskins. He felt like he couldn't breathe, and opened his mouth to voice his protest, only to catch the man's smile.

"You will get used to the fit," Francis said. "And more importantly, you look very well. Sophisticated and fashionable without veering into dandy territory, Your Grace."

Gabriel wondered whether he would ever get used to being called that. "If you say so," he grumbled.

Francis smiled again and then bit his lip, as if he wasn't sure smiling was acceptable in a valet.

The young man had been Gabriel's choice, and against the wishes of his grandmother. She had sent along an older, much more experienced applicant to instruct Gabriel on how to conduct himself in society. Five minutes in the company of the superior valet and Gabriel had taken against him. He felt as if he were being judged or, worse, sneered at. Then Francis had appeared to be interviewed for the post on the off chance that he might be hired, having lately left his employ when his master retired from London to reside permanently in his country house. Francis was on the short side and compact, with brown hair and bright blue eyes that seemed to sparkle at a challenge. He was also enthusiastic, and a breath of fresh air despite his lack of experience. Gabriel had chosen Francis over protests from the dowager and the senior valet, and Francis hadn't let him down. Best of all, he made Gabriel feel as if they were on this journey together.

Over the past months, he had patiently led Gabriel through confusing choices of apparel for the day, the night, for riding in Hyde Park, for the theater, for making morning calls, for visiting gentlemen's clubs... in fact for every conceivable occasion. He had listened to his master's complaints and then gently explained why Gabriel was wrong, before he continued to steer him in the right direction like a determined little tugboat. Gabriel would have been amused, if he hadn't been so unsettled by the whole experience.

As well as learning how to dress and conduct himself in polite company, Gabriel had spent time in Sussex with the Grantham steward, going over estate books and learning just how far into debt his father, Harry, had driven them. He had never known his father, and while he appeared to have been an affable sort of gentleman, he was also irresponsible and weak. Gabriel had seen plenty of similar men in his club, and he tried not to despise him. Until he noticed how Harry had dipped into his inheritance whenever he wanted new horses or a curricle, or anything new, really. There had been fully staffed residences leased for his mistresses—yes, Eugénie wasn't the only one—and although Gabriel told himself to be pragmatic…it wasn't easy.

All of that aside, he had enjoyed dealing with the estate matters far more than the other parts of this duke business. He even noted several pages where the steward had made mistakes, whether inadvertently or on purpose, and sums of money were missing. Gabriel made the decision to look for someone more competent or more honest, or both. The dowager wouldn't like it. Their steward had been with the family for many years, and she seemed to value what she considered his loyalty. Gabriel thought it was more likely the man was supplementing his income with Grantham profits, and his grandmother would just have to learn that when it came to money, the new duke had his own ideas and meant to implement them.

"You need not stay long at the ball, you know," Francis said mildly as he collected the crumpled cravats discarded by Gabriel in his attempts to tie a decent knot.

"Don't I?" Gabriel heard the hopefulness in his voice.

"No. You just need to show your face, make a few bows so that people see you and know you are perfectly comfortable with the change in your circumstances."

"And am I? Perfectly comfortable?" Gabriel mocked.

"Oh yes, sir. Very comfortable indeed. Born to the role, in fact."

Gabriel couldn't help but smile at his valet's gentle teasing. Francis had that effect on him. "I never know what to say," he admitted as the man gave his coat a final brush down. The dowager's advice on conversing in a manner befitting a duke had been blunt and unhelpful.

Persons beneath your rank should be grateful you bestir yourself to speak to them at all, but if you find yourself in an awkward silence that you feel you must fill, then mention the weather.

As he rode in the ducal coach to the Farnsworths' ball, Gabriel found himself questioning why he had agreed to this if he disliked it so much. Why had he pushed aside his doubts and fears, and said yes to something he didn't enjoy? Had he really been persuaded by his grandmother's insistence that he "do his duty" when she had abandoned him as a child, clearly unconcerned whether he lived or died? There was still the mystery of why she had visited St. Ninian's when he was older, but he had not asked her. Their relationship did not allow for tête-à-têtes or reminiscences—it mostly consisted of her speaking and him listening. No, his grandmother hadn't swayed him, it was the sight of his half sisters, silent as they watched him, knowing that it was he, a stranger, who held their futures, their very lives, in the palm of his hand. And he'd discovered he couldn't abandon them.

Gabriel had thought his life had been hectic before, but being a duke seemed to fill up even more of the minutes in his day. Olivia, the eldest, was to make her debut as soon as a suitable mourning period had been observed. According to the dowager, that would give Gabriel enough time to learn how to conduct himself in the world he now inhabited. But Olivia's coming-out wasn't the only thing that needed careful thought and planning. At some point the girls would have to marry. Suitable spouses would need to be found, and not just for his sisters. The dowager had told him in no uncertain terms that he must find himself a wife.

"It will have to be someone who can stomach your appalling past and is willing to turn a blind eye to it, but the title will sweeten that pill. The Ashtons are an old and highly regarded family, and there will be plenty of young ladies who would consider themselves fortunate to walk down the aisle with you."

Gabriel narrowed his eyes at her. "You want me to marry someone who only wants a title?"

"Of course. Did you think she would fall in love with you? Love is for the lower classes, and you have risen above that, Gabriel. Remember, everything you do now reflects upon the family. Under no circumstances must you bring more scandal upon us. Your wife will be as pure as the driven snow."

How could he forget when she was always reminding him? It seemed that everything he did right now was for the sole benefit of his family. Gabriel had launched himself into his new life without any real thought for what lay ahead. Oh, he knew what he needed to do for his sisters and the estate, but what about himself? What would his life be like in five years' time, or more?

At the moment the future seemed cloudy, but as someone who liked to plan ahead, Gabriel was keen to push aside those clouds and take a good hard look at the possibilities. Would he be married to his grandmother's choice of wife with children of his own? Settled into a life that might seem less foreign to him by then? Or would he still be a bachelor, focused on running the family finances and acting on his sisters' behalf.

That last thought rather lowered his spirits. Recently he had discovered it was a lonely business being a duke.

Of course he had his friends, but although they supported him as much as they could, they found his new life rather bewildering. The idea of someone who truly understood his current situation was beginning to appeal more and more, although the face of that person was just as cloudy as his future.

Gabriel realized his hands inside his gloves were sweating, and wiped them surreptitiously. He was a study in understated elegance this evening, tasteful without being ostentatious. He had no reason to be nervous. None at all.

"You are not an exquisite," his valet had reminded him. "We do not want you to ape the excesses of that crowd, Your Grace."

Gabriel simply wanted to avoid any errors, and looking the part of the Duke of Grantham seemed a good start.

Charles and Freddie were going to be here to give him encouragement—he had been pleasantly surprised, not to say relieved, when his grandmother agreed to vouch for them—and he looked about as he was ceremoniously announced at the door. Only cold stares greeted him, with some curious glances from behind painted fans and lifted hands. Mocking whispers and cruel comments no doubt. Gabriel told himself that none of that mattered. He had had worse. He had survived worse, and he would do so again.

His hosts the Farnsworths said all the right things, the polite words falling from their lips, while their eyes remained avid with curiosity. Although his grandmother no longer ventured into society unless absolutely necessary, Gabriel was aware that it was through her influence he had gained an invitation tonight. Not that the gossip surrounding his ascension to the dukedom didn't play a part. Everyone wanted to take their first look at the new, improved version of Gabriel Cadieux.

"Tonight may be disagreeable," Francis had warned him, "but once it is over, then nothing, be it a ball or a soiree or a whatever, will ever be quite as disagreeable again."

Gabriel tried to take comfort from that as the Farnsworths busily introduced him to their other guests. He spent some time answering polite questions—"Try to use more than one word, Your Grace"—or making reference to the unseasonably warm evening. And all the while his shoulders felt as if they were set in stone, and his jaw ached from clenching his teeth into false smiles.

He was simply not comfortable in society, and he knew that had nothing to do with the newness of it. He much preferred the noisy, shabby confines of his club, and his cluttered office and the ledgers that spoke of his rising bank balance, because every penny he made took him further away from his past. He felt safe at Cadieux's, it was his world and he reigned supreme, while here he was a novice. He was very much out of his depth, and despite all the preparations, he felt as if he were drowning.

And then he saw her.

Gabriel would have recognized her anywhere, which should have struck him as strange, but he didn't have time to ponder it. Miss Vivienne Tremeer in a pale blue gown with a cream underskirt, her heavy dark hair pinned up and entwined with blue ribbons. She was with a group of people, looking very much at ease with her surroundings. And so she would. She must be a lady who had been brought up to negotiate the pitfalls of the polite world she inhabited, unlike Gabriel. As he watched her smile and converse, he found he envied her. *She* was not drowning.

He did not approach her. The memory of their meeting at his club would make matters awkward between them, and at the moment he was feeling awkward enough. Gabriel turned away and had taken a number of steps when a familiar, sneering voice spoke behind him.

"Cadieux. Oh, apologies, *Your Grace*."

Gabriel turned to face a man with a harsh, lined face and hard eyes. Sir Hubert Longley was one of Gabriel's most enthusiastic gambling club competitors, but the ill feeling between them stemmed from more than his jealousy over Gabriel's profitable hell. Sir Hubert had once owned the club that was now Gabriel's, and although he had two more, he had neither forgotten nor forgiven the way Gabriel had won it off him.

"Longley," he murmured, with a polite bow.

Sir Hubert returned the civility. "I'm surprised to see you here," he drawled. "I thought the Farnworths would have taken more care when they drew up their guest list."

Gabriel met those vicious eyes and forced another fake smile. "Well, you're here," he said.

"Gabriel was invited because he is a novelty, while you are tediously obsolete." A familiar voice spoke from the side.

Charles. Relieved, Gabriel looked around. Freddie was here too, and they were both glaring at Sir Hubert as if they could turn him into a toad by simply wishing.

Gabriel's tense muscles finally relaxed. His mouth twitched into a genuine smile at the expression on Sir Hubert's face as the man struggled to think of some clever rejoinder. The orchestra started up with a jaunty tune, and he remembered that this was a ball and in the normal way of things, he should be asking a woman to dance.

He felt cold and hot at the same time. Gabriel had never in his life danced. He could not dance. And even if he were foolish enough to ask one of the ladies, he was certain they would refuse him. His plan tonight had been to discuss the weather and chat with his friends, and then leave.

His gaze strayed over Charles's shoulder, searching for the door, and there she was again.

Vivienne Tremeer was standing to one side, once more appearing at ease. Her dark hair shone, the heavy coils twisted through with the pale ribbon that matched her plain but elegant gown. As if his glance had drawn her attention, she turned her head and their eyes met. Her face lost its calmness. He saw recognition.

Not if you were the last man.

Several other emotions flitted over that lovely face in quick succession, and he remembered she had a temper. She set down the champagne glass she was holding and took a step toward him.

For the sake of Olivia, tonight needed to be a trouble-free affair. He had been particularly cautioned by his grandmother that he should avoid anyone who might cause him to do or say things that were unwise.

Pretend not to care, Gabriel. If you do it often enough you won't have to pretend, was the dowager's advice. *You are the Duke of Grantham, and everyone else in the room is below you.*

He glanced about furtively. People weren't looking, not yet, but they would if Vivienne Tremeer began demanding he forgive her brother's debt—something he had not had time to consider during his transition to the dukedom. Not that that was the entire truth. He could have insisted on repayment, but every time he thought of it, every time he reached for his pen to sign the letter of demand, he remembered her standing so bravely before his desk, and his hand stilled. And now his forbearance was to be rewarded by a scene.

As Vivienne Tremeer headed determinedly in his direction, Gabriel started forward in a single-minded effort to divert her before this escalated into disaster.

Chapter Eight

Viscountess Monteith had swept Annette away through the crush to greet the Duke of Northam's mother and his sisters, but Vivienne was content to remain where she was, alone with her grim thoughts. Here by the draped doors open to the terrace, she could at least breathe in some fresh air. Despite Aunt Jane's resistance, Annette had pleaded that Vivienne be allowed to accompany them to the Farnsworths' ball, and for once Vivienne was happy to add her pleas to her cousin's. She had even indulged Annette by allowing her to choose her costume and oversee the arranging of her hair. But pleasure wasn't the real reason Vivienne was here.

Will's run-in with Sutherland last night had made clear to her just how very precarious their position was. When her brother had arrived home early this morning, shaking and distraught, Vivienne knew she needed to act. She could have bearded the dragon in its den, otherwise known as Cadieux's Gambling Club, but she did not think he would be receptive to her there, even if he happened to be in his poky office. Here, in the full glare of society…? Well, that was another matter.

When she had heard of Mrs. Farnsworth's boasts that the Duke of Grantham was to make his first social appearance at her ball, it had seemed the perfect place for her to confront him. The duke could hardly refuse to speak to her before the Farnworths' guests. To do so would depict him in a bad light, and that must be something he was keen to avoid.

Last November Vivienne had thought that the duke forgiving Will's debt was a real possibility. Now she wondered if she had been indulging in the sort of fantasy that had led her to write *The Wicked Prince and His Stolen Bride*. A hardheaded, coldhearted man like Cadieux was as likely to forgo what was owed him as to fly to the moon. So during the sleepless hours after Will returned home, she had worked out a new plan. It wasn't much but it was all she had.

At the same time, she admitted she was curious to see the duke in his new setting. Had the unshaven and handsomely disheveled man she remembered from the upstairs room in the smoky gambling hell been transformed into a Beau Brummel? It seemed unlikely. That man, his dark eyes reflecting the lamplight as he watched her intently from behind his desk, did not belong at a ball. She could not imagine it. He would be so far out of his depth that she wouldn't blame him if he took the coward's way out and didn't turn up.

The sound of raised voices caught her attention. A group of gentlemen stood nearby, and she recognized one of them as the unpleasant Sir Hubert Longley—he was someone she avoided whenever possible—but the others were strangers to her. A handsome, fair-haired man with a charming smile, and a red-haired soldier who clapped another man on the shoulder with hearty exuberance. The recipient of the friendly blow was a stranger too, tall and very elegant, clean shaven, and with his dark hair swept back apart from one lock that lay upon his brow.

Her gaze sharpened. It couldn't be. And yet it was. It was *him*. Gabriel Cadieux, the gambling hell owner with the heart of ice, and the new Duke of Grantham. And he was looking back at her.

Did she read unease in those black eyes? It was as she had suspected, he did not want her to cause a scene, and Vivienne was more than ever prepared to make one. This was her chance to force him to listen to her. Her last chance because Sutherland was closing in.

She set down her champagne and took a deep breath, but before she had taken more than a few steps toward him, he was striding purposefully toward her. Her heart gave a stutter. Apprehension, she told herself, because he didn't look happy to see her, those eyes without warmth beneath his frowning brows, and his mouth drawn into a tight line. He was determined to stop her, and she was equally determined not to let him.

"Your Grace…" she began at the same time as he said, "Miss Tremeer."

As she came up from her hasty curtsy, he took hold of her arm and leaned down from his greater height to speak close to her ear. His citrus-scented pomade filled her senses, and the flutter grew to a palpitation.

"Let us get some air."

She would have protested, but to her amazement he was already bundling her out through the open doors and onto the balustraded terrace.

Vivienne pulled out of his grip immediately, backing away. "What do you think you're doing?"

His outward transformation into the Duke of Grantham hadn't changed his overbearing attitude, and his voice was as gruff as she remembered from the night at the gambling club. "You were going to make a commotion. Don't deny it, I could see it in your eyes."

"Why should I deny it?"

"So you *were* going to cause a scene?" He frowned at her and crossed his arms. He had just treated her in a manner that stung, as if she was something to be dealt with. A problem to be removed. A threat he had to neutralize. And for some reason the fact that he looked like the perfect duke while he did it made her even angrier, but that anger was coupled with a dose of reckless bravery. Because what had she to lose?

Vivienne's words tumbled out. "Of course I was going to make a scene! I still might. I wanted to embarrass you into agreeing to my request. This is your first social engagement as Duke of Grantham, and I'm sure you'd do anything to prevent the gossips from labeling it a disaster."

At first he looked surprised by her frankness, and then wary.

She drew a breath before he could answer. "Speaking of gossip…surely even you must realize that a tête-à-tête, alone, with an unmarried woman who is not related to you, is a social faux pas. Your Grace."

His expression hardened, probably because of the animosity in *Your Grace*. "Should I have let you try to blackmail me, then? I assure you I would have refused. I don't care if everyone at this ball whispers behind my back. Let them laugh at the boy from the orphanage in his grand clothing aping his betters."

That was plain speaking indeed! This seemed to be the night for it, and Vivienne was oddly pleased that he thought her a female capable of hearing the unvarnished truth. "I didn't know you were in an orphanage" was all she could think of to say in return.

But she could see that Cadieux was already regretting his hasty honesty. He ran a nervous hand over his face and seemed about to tug at his beautifully knotted cravat. He stopped himself in time, and smoothed down the lapel of his tailcoat instead. Grudgingly she had to admit that whoever had prepared him for this evening had done a sterling job. Although he obviously wasn't enjoying it. She could tell that behind the polished outer shell, the man was miserable.

Somehow knowing that made her feel a little more at ease with him, as if he had suddenly become more approachable.

"Can we speak about my brother now, Your Grace?" she asked him calmly. "If you are to further damage my reputation, I would like some compensation."

His awkwardness left him and he was steely-eyed again. "We have spoken about your brother and I have refused your request. The matter is at an end."

"It may be at an end for you," she said, trying not to grit her teeth. "No doubt you have a great deal to be getting on with, but my brother's debt is very much in the forefront of my thoughts."

"And yet it has taken you this long to return to it."

"I was waiting for you to send the bailiffs in," she snapped. "Why have *you* waited so long?"

Something shifted in his eyes, as if the subject wasn't one he wanted to discuss. Before he could answer, she hurried on.

"I do not know the Ashton family intimately, although your grandmother did cut my aunt once." His eyes gleamed as if that amused him, but she ignored it and carried on. "I do not know your financial circumstances, but I suspect you do not need my brother to repay his debt to enable you to put food on your table. You must be a very busy man with so many duke-type things to be getting on with."

"*Duke-type things*?" he spluttered.

"I had hoped your good fortune might incline you to be more generous to Will. Come, what does his little debt matter to you now? It would not even pay for the polish for your boots," she bluffed.

That sparkle in his eyes again, a gleam of amusement, before he snuffed it out. "My good fortune? Is that what you call it?"

"Well, isn't it? You have a title and all the trappings that go with it. You even look the part." She waved a hand over him, taking in his elegance.

He reached for his cravat but again stopped himself before he ruined it. Was he uneasy? Had she actually pierced some tiny soft place in his stony heart? "You make me sound as if I were actively pursuing the title. I did not ask to be a duke, and I would have avoided it if possible. I had no choice."

"No choice?" she said with disdain. "I wish someone would offer me a dukedom. I'm sure I'd find a way to make use of it. You have everything and I…my brother has nothing. Do you really expect me to sympathize with you? Your Grace?"

His eyes flared as she tacked on the title. She had made him angry, but Vivienne didn't care. He had everything and he *should* be happy. Wasn't that how it worked in novels? The poor but deserving hero was discovered to be a rich, titled gentleman—not that Cadieux was deserving—and lived happily ever after.

All that was needed now was for him to marry the perfect lady and fill his enormous house with lots of little dark-haired, dark-eyed children.

There was an ache in her chest, and it was so sudden and so surprising that she simply stared at him.

"What is it?" He took a step closer, his hand held out as if to take her arm. If he touched her…the thought of it made her feel ridiculously breathless, and she shook her head quickly. He dropped his hand back to his side.

"What nonsense," she murmured to herself. A burst of laughter came from inside the room as she tried to gather her scattered thoughts. "Will told me that you tried to stop him from playing so deep," she said. "I wanted to thank you for that, at least, although I believe it was more to do with the reputation of your club than my brother's welfare."

The infuriating man shrugged. "I don't enjoy watching innocents being fleeced by sharps. But you should thank my friend Charles, he noticed your brother's predicament first."

"I shall, when I discover who Charles is."

That twitch of his mouth again. She was glad he found her so amusing.

"My stepfather is in London. Richard Sutherland. Has he been to your club?"

He frowned. "Not to my knowledge. Why, is he going to run up a large debt too?"

"Probably. He is trying to find out about Will, and I would be—" She straightened. "I would be grateful if you did not give him any information about my brother's visits to Cadieux's."

He seemed to be considering this and then nodded once. "I do not gossip about my patrons and nor do those who work for me. Your brother's secrets are safe."

She felt slightly dizzy with relief, but she shouldn't have been surprised. Gabriel was nothing if not straightforward. However, she wasn't done yet. Vivienne glanced about her. She really shouldn't be out here, her aunt might notice, and Annette certainly would. But she needed to say the words she had come to say.

She moved a little closer, and his eyes narrowed suspiciously.

"Your Grace. I have a proposal I hope you will accept…or at least consider."

His eyes narrowed even more, and she wondered uneasily if he thought she was going to offer herself to him. That was what he had been expecting at their last meeting. He could not know that Vivienne was the last woman in the world to make such a bargain.

"What proposal?" he asked brusquely.

"I will pay you two hundred pounds toward my brother's debt, all the money I have in the world," she added with a trace of bitterness. "You can look upon it as a down payment, a…a promise. It may take some time for us to pay off the remainder of the debt, in fact it will take a very long time, but I can assure you, we *will* pay it off."

He stared at her blankly for a moment, and then he gave a bark of laughter. He shook his head and laughed again.

Vivienne knew she should be angry, but it was difficult to feel anger when you were filled with despair. Not that she wanted him to see how deep the pain went. "I presume that is a no," she said with stiff pride.

He cleared his throat, shook his head again, and seemed to sober. "Do you know how much your brother owes me?" He had leaned down slightly, his eyes intent on hers, and stated the figure in pounds, shillings, and pence.

Vivienne stared back at him. The sum was slightly

higher than Will had told her. He may not have realized, but it was more likely he was in denial. Her two hundred pounds really was like a drop in the ocean. Vivienne felt anger raise its head, mostly at Will but also at Gabriel, and with it came the sensation that she might burst into tears. Despite her determination not to show emotion, he must have seen, because he stilled, watching her carefully.

"My offer stands." Her voice was dull in contrast to the bright sparks of pain inside her head. "My brother will come into his inheritance in three years, when he turns twenty-one, and we will then be in a position to repay you. Presently we are paupers living on our aunt's charity."

"Three years?" he burst out. "A gambling debt must be paid promptly, Miss Tremeer. Maybe if your brother had learned to be responsible for his own behavior, he would not have found himself in this position. I see a great many gentlemen more interested in amusing themselves than thinking of what comes after. Their fortunes run through their fingers like water because they have not had to earn them. Your brother is young and has a chance to learn from his mistake. He should not be relying on his sister begging—"

"Begging!" It was too much. His words hurt and all the more because she knew some of what he had said was true, or at least the truth as he saw it. But not everything was black and white, there was often a great deal of gray, and the story of Will and Vivienne was not, as he seemed to think, a simple tale of two selfish, bored siblings in London. Will had only come to the capital for her sake, to keep her company when she was forced to leave their home. He might have behaved in a reprehensible manner since, but he was still her caring brother, and she knew he would protect her to the end. Vivienne longed to explain that to the duke, to compel him to understand, but these were secrets she did not share with anyone but those closest to her.

"Isn't that what you're doing?" he added cuttingly. "Hoping I will feel sorry for you and let you off the hook?"

"I admit I thought that back in November, but now I know better. I can see you have not the ability to feel sorry. You are made of stone."

"Italian marble. I am a duke, after all."

His droll comment was like a flint on dry tinder. How could he joke when their future was in his hands? Her temper boiled over. "You great pompous, conceited, selfish oaf. You...you..." She spluttered to find more insulting words.

He laughed, that bark of amusement forced from him.

"I hate you," she responded irrationally. She was breathing hard.

"You are treading on dangerous ground, Miss Tremeer." His voice was silky, a warning.

"I am used to danger. You don't scare me. Your Grace."

And that was when the mood suddenly changed.

He was very close now, and something flared in his eyes, something hot and bright. Instinctively she felt herself respond. Her blood heated in her veins, and her breath caught in her throat. Her lips tingled as their eyes locked. He leaned in.

He was going to kiss her. It had been a long time since a man had kissed her, and Gabriel looked as if he meant to kiss her very thoroughly indeed. She braced herself to refuse him, to slap his face if necessary, but as his warm breath brushed her lips, her eyelids fluttered and her heart knocked against her ribs, and she knew that she wasn't going to do any of those things.

She was going to kiss him back.

Chapter Nine

A throat was cleared. Loud enough to startle Vivienne. Guiltily she and the duke jumped apart, shocked to find they were no longer alone, and both swung their heads in the direction of the sound.

It was as if she had forgotten all about the ball, so caught up was she in the moment. A glance at Gabriel's startled expression made her suspect he felt the same. A chill ran through her as the possible consequences of her irresponsible actions crowded in on her, and her heart began a sickening knock for an entirely different reason. Another second and they would have been mouth to mouth, locked in an embrace. And if Aunt Jane found out, she would be incandescent with fury. She would be furious anyway, if she learned Vivienne was out here alone with Gabriel. The least she could expect were harsh words and recriminations, reminders of that other time with Benjamin, only this time she would deserve them.

Her head cleared and she took stock. The throat clearer was the handsome fair-haired gentleman she had seen with Gabriel earlier. Dressed plainly, apart from his shockingly bright blue-and-gold-embroidered waistcoat, he appeared to be a bird of paradise hiding under dull plumage. He gave her a curious look before he turned to her companion.

"Gabriel, if you don't come in now, your absence will be noticed," he warned. "Freddie has done all he can to hog the limelight, but people are starting to wonder."

The newly minted duke groaned and rubbed a hand over his face, plucking at his cravat as if he wished he could tug it loose and toss it away. Suddenly he seemed so supremely uncomfortable, and the surprising thing was Vivienne understood how he felt. She had often been the outsider, even in her own family.

"What is he doing?" Gabriel demanded of his friend.

"A rendition of some army ditty. I'm hoping most of the guests won't recognize it, but a few might. I won't sully your ears with it." He glanced meaningfully at Vivienne.

Gabriel laughed, and it was genuine. "I was hoping to get through this evening without causing any ripples, but it looks like that's not going to happen. I'd better go in and make excuses for him." His gaze slid to Vivienne, the laughter dying from those black eyes. There was still a trace of heat but that was rapidly fading too. "My regrets, Miss Tremeer, I must leave you. I am needed."

She remained on the balcony staring after him, only belatedly aware that the other man had also stayed. He was observing her with interest, and she returned the favor. He wasn't as tall as his friend, and there was a sparkle in his blue eyes and a charm in his expression that was quite the opposite of the intense seriousness of the duke. Although Gabriel had smiled at her, and he had even laughed, so he wasn't always solemn.

"Gabriel neglected to introduce us." The man gave a

polite bow. "I am Charles Wickley, his friend and business partner."

"Vivienne Tremeer." She curtsied reluctantly, but his name had sparked a memory from her recent conversation. "I should thank you, I believe. You warned my brother about falling even deeper into debt. Sir Will Tremeer," she added when he gave her a quizzical smile.

She could see he knew the name and was already putting the pieces of the puzzle together. "And you are here to plead his case to Gabe…the duke?"

"Try to, yes." She bit her lip. There was no harm in asking, her pride was already in tatters. "I don't suppose…"

Charles held up his hands as if in surrender. "I'm afraid I never interfere in Gabriel's business. I assist him in the running of the club, but it belongs to him. He makes the decisions."

Vivienne didn't know if that was true, but she didn't blame him for steering clear of any controversy. Besides, she had run out of arguments. The open doors leading into the ballroom beckoned to her, reminding her that she was tempting fate by delaying. "I should go back," she said. "My aunt will be wondering where I am."

"Of course. It was a pleasure to meet you, Miss Tremeer."

He might be charming, but she wasn't sure she trusted him. Charles Wickley hid a lot behind his smile. The duke wasn't afraid to say what he felt, even if it wasn't what she wanted to hear, and she rather thought she preferred him because of it.

Vivienne nodded coolly and slipped back into the ballroom. On the other side of the room, where the orchestra was set up, there was some sort of commotion taking place. The music had come to a stop, and she could see the duke's tall form beside the red-haired soldier as he tried to extricate them from whatever the trouble was. There would be gossip. Those who believed Gabriel Cadieux the gambling hell owner had no business being here in the first place would use this to justify their opinion. They would mutter about the lower orders knowing their place, despite his being the legal son of a duke, and form ranks against him.

She wondered if he would care. The first time she had met him, he had seemed very comfortable in his own skin. Not the sort to let others' opinions of him govern his actions. And yet just a moment ago he had been determined to stop Vivienne from causing a scene. She wondered what it was that was making a man who had lived most of his life outside of society start to follow the rules. There was a reason, and although she shouldn't be intrigued by it, she found she was.

"Vivienne!" a voice hissed, and her attention swiftly returned to her own predicament.

Annette stood in front of her, one of the Farnsworth girls in tow. The girl began to chatter away as usual, and Vivienne answered with her usual politeness, but Annette wasn't listening; she was staring at Vivienne.

"Vivienne, Mama is coming. Here." Annette took her arm in a firm grip.

"Where were you, Vivienne?" Aunt Jane was already sailing toward her, and she didn't look pleased. "We are leaving. You are lucky you were not left behind."

"Vivienne was overheated," Annette said quickly. "She felt faint and she was taking some air, Mama."

"Was she indeed?" Aunt Jane didn't look entirely convinced, but just then one of her friends came up to speak to her, and she turned away to reply. Miss

Farnsworth had found someone else to talk at, and the two cousins were as alone as it was possible to be in the middle of a ball.

"Where were you?" Annette half whispered, giving her arm a little shake. "Mama was starting to say you couldn't be trusted and she would send you home to Cornwall."

"Aunt Jane has been saying that ever since I arrived." Vivienne bit her lip, knowing she sounded ungrateful. "I'm sorry. I was just…I was…" *About to kiss a man I have only met twice.*

"Who is that gentleman?" Annette was looking beyond her, wide-eyed. Charles had also returned to the ballroom, and gave them a quick smile as he walked past, in the direction of his friends.

"Mr. Charles Wickley. He is a…eh, an acquaintance of the Duke of Grantham."

Annette's blue eyes widened even more. "Have you met the duke, Vivienne?"

"Yes."

Annette seemed to expect more, but Vivienne didn't know what else to say. Disappointment was heavy in her heart, but at least she had won a promise from Gabriel not to tell Sutherland about Will. Suddenly she wanted desperately to leave this evening behind her.

"He's very…" her cousin began thoughtfully.

"Overbearing? Yes, very. And also rude."

Annette gave a surprised laugh. "I was going to say he's very handsome."

"Handsome is as handsome does," Vivienne quoted stupidly.

That piqued Annette's curiosity, and she was obviously about to ask more questions, so it was just as well Aunt Jane returned.

"Come, Annette…Vivienne!" Her frowning gaze swept from one to the other, as if she suspected mischief. Silently they fell in with her as they began to make their way out of the crowded ballroom. "I had the misfortune to be introduced to the new Duke of Grantham," she informed them coldly.

Vivienne felt Annette's glance on her. "Why was it a misfortune, Mama?" her cousin said, while Vivienne added, "I'm sure most of the people here tonight would envy you, Aunt Jane."

"Would they indeed? Well, I do not think I should be envied. I may not be intimately acquainted with Her Grace the dowager duchess, but I cannot agree with her decision. No good will come from raising a lowborn gambling club owner to such a high position."

"Do you think he had a choice?" Vivienne said, remembering her conversation with the man in question.

"A choice?" her aunt spluttered. "A creature like that would jump at the chance! I agree that he spoke politely enough and bowed correctly. Someone has been at work there. But beneath it I could see the coarseness. I have heard that the daughters were like wild animals before the dowager tamed them. How can they enter society when they have no idea how to behave or what is expected of them? At least you are well versed in etiquette and decorum, even if you sometimes ignore the rules," she added, with a dark look at Vivienne. "No, the dowager will rue the day, you mark my words." She gave her warning with such relish that Vivienne was reminded the viscountess and the dowager were not friends.

She bit her tongue to stop any of the arguments she might have put forth. For instance, was it so wrong to want to improve one's position in life, even if it meant stepping out of one's allotted rung on the ladder of society? Aunt Jane had never been in a desperate situation, a situation similar to the one Vivienne was in now. A sleepless night and sheer worry had begun to overwhelm her—she had that trapped feeling again. If fate offered a secure way out, she suspected she would take it.

But then, she reminded herself, Gabriel did not need her to fight in his corner. He was not a pauper or in reduced straits. He had his own source of income, his own life. And yet he had made the decision to be a duke, although he obviously wasn't completely happy about his change in circumstances. She remembered the bitterness in his voice and wondered again why he had agreed to step into such a complex arena.

No, she would not feel sorry for him. Outside on the terrace she might have said some things she should not have, but her temper had seemed to attract him rather than repel him. She remembered the heat in his eyes, and the certainty that he was about to kiss the life out of her. Was it wrong of her to wish he had? She rubbed her arms as her skin prickled with goose bumps.

"Do make haste, Vivienne." Aunt Jane's impatient tones broke through her thoughts. "Or are you still feeling faint?" Her glance was skeptical, and Vivienne reminded herself what was at stake.

"No, Aunt Jane, I am quite well now."

Her aunt had already turned away. Suddenly Vivienne was tired, so tired. Living up to her aunt's expectations and constantly failing was exhausting. Trying to help Will and preserve the Tremeer estate was almost beyond her. She wasn't happy with her lot, in fact she was miserable, and although they might be on different sides in this battle, perhaps she and the duke had that in common.

Chapter Ten

"Come on, Ensign Hart, it's time to go."

Freddie looked up at Gabriel with a lazy lopsided grin. He suspected his friend had been half-sprung before he arrived at the ball, and the Farnsworths' expensive champagne had pushed him into bosky territory. Charles had mentioned that Freddie was drinking heavily since his return from his regiment's time in the north, and there must be a reason for it. Gabriel knew he should have noticed that without being told. He had been neglecting his part in their friendship because of the dukedom, and while it was true he had a great deal on his mind, Freddie had been his friend for twenty-four years.

"Are you sure?" Freddie blinked slowly. "I thought everyone was enjoying my singing."

"You're lucky you weren't thrown out on your ear," Gabriel retorted. It had come close, but he had given an apology to the Farnsworths before Charles had arrived and proceeded to charm them all. His friend had also told several untruths about Freddie being a war hero and one of Wellington's favorites. Gabriel hoped the dowager didn't hear about that and demand an explanation, though he was sure there were plenty of helpful and malicious busybodies here tonight who would love to share the news. He was just glad his first social engagement as a duke was over and he was leaving. And it could have been worse. He could have been discovered on the terrace with Vivienne Tremeer calling him names while he loomed over her. He could have been found kissing her breathless.

She made him reckless. She heated his blood. He wasn't sure why, but she unsettled him, delving into places in his mind and heart he rarely allowed others to go. It was as if they, strangers as they almost were, had some sort of emotional connection. He had wanted to explain to her why he had taken on the dukedom, for God's sake, and why it was in her brother's interest for him not to forgive the debt. She must have thought him insane.

He had obviously pushed her beyond ladylike behavior, and he'd enjoyed it. Stripping away her carefully chosen words until she was spluttering insults. Seeing her gray eyes flare and her cheeks flush pink as her temper ignited. She was a passionate woman. He would have kissed those lush lips, and he thought she wouldn't have pushed him away. Whatever was between them, whether it was dislike or attraction, or both…it was dangerous, and he needed to be careful.

A hand touched his arm and made him jump. Charles was watching him with a curious look, and Gabriel told himself it was ridiculous to think his friend could read his mind.

"They are sending for the coach," Charles said with a quizzical smile. "We can wait outside."

"Good." He said it with relief. "Let's get out of here."

"What was that about?" Charles lowered his voice as

they made their way to the door. "You and Miss Tremeer? It looked as if you were about to—"

"Nothing. It was all about nothing." He cast around for a change of subject. "Did you and Freddie come in a hackney?"

"Yes, we made our own way here. Once the ball was over, we thought we could spend the rest of the night doing whatever you want. Put all of this behind you."

Gabriel felt his shoulders relax as they descended the stairs to the street. "Thank you. I'm grateful." His friends knew him well enough to understand he'd want to lose himself, forget that he was a duke, and shrug off his new, heavy responsibilities. They could visit familiar haunts, where they would be left alone, and no one cared who they were or what they did as long as they could pay. Drinking dens, whorehouses, and clubs where men fought with their fists for the sheer joy of it. The sort of rough-and-ready places Gabriel had always felt comfortable in. Or at least he had, until now. *Now*, everything he did seemed to be viewed through the lens of what it meant to the dowager and his sisters.

"I need a woman." Freddie's announcement interrupted his turbulent thoughts as they stood outside the Farnsworths' town house, awaiting their coach.

"Why stop at one?" Charles replied cautiously. He exchanged a glance with Gabriel. "What's the matter, Alfred? You have seemed out of sorts ever since you got back from the north."

"Why should anything be the matter?" Their friend muttered the question to his boots.

Charles sighed. "Freddie Hart! You have always worn your heart on your sleeve. It's in your name. Now tell us what is the matter so we can cheer you up."

Freddie blinked owlishly at him. "Hart on my sleeve? Are you serious?"

"Never mind that," Gabriel said. "Charles is just playing. Tell us what happened when you were up in the north?"

Freddie seemed to deflate. "There was a girl," he said dully. "Pretty girl, but clever too. I thought…well. Her father turned up and decided I wasn't good enough for her. He'd made some inquiries and found out about St. Ninian's and my lack of family or prospects."

"Lack of prospects?" Gabriel said irritably. "You have risen through the ranks at lightning speed. What on earth is wrong with your prospects?"

Freddie shrugged. "Not good enough for him, evidently. If it was you"—with a sideways glance at Gabriel—"well, that would be different. A duke. What father would turn down a duke for his daughter?"

Gabriel gave him a hard stare. "Is my being a duke going to be a problem for you? Because if it means you won't be my friend anymore, I would as soon walk away from Grantham and all of this nonsense."

Freddie's hazel eyes widened comically. "You'd walk away?"

"Of course. We've been friends for twenty-four years, and that means more to me than any of these ridiculous trappings." He waved a hand around him at the other groups of well-dressed guests waiting for their vehicles.

He meant it. He would walk away, although he hoped Freddie would not make him. He had given his word to the Ashtons, and whatever else he may have done in his life, he had never broken his word. "Being a duke is bloody hard work," he went on. "I'm not finding much to enjoy about it."

That wasn't strictly true. He was very much in his

element when it came to the financial side of the dukedom, and he felt as if he could contribute far more by dragging the estate out of the red than he could by attending balls and making polite chitchat.

Arnott had sat him down for hours to discuss how funds needed to be found for his six half sisters, and an amount set aside for each of them for when they married. Funds that weren't available because his father used the estate as his personal piggy bank. Something needed to be done to turn matters around, Arnott had said. Someone competent had to take charge. And, with a spark of excitement, Gabriel knew he was that person.

Gabriel understood things like economy and profit. He recognized his aptitude when it came to business, and he would be far better engaged in returning the dukedom to a reasonable state of order than wasting his time trying to convince the ton to accept him. His grandmother had even threatened him with Almack's, but he was convinced he would be refused entry. He had heard the patronesses were most particular when it came to attending their deadly dull events.

"What if I stay in Sussex and run the estate?" he had said to the dowager hopefully. "Then I won't embarrass myself or anyone else."

But no, that wasn't good enough. "The head of the family must be seen," she had informed him icily. "I don't care what you do when you are out of the public gaze, but while you are in it, remember who you represent."

The Ashton family name meant nothing to him, and he hated the thought that everyone was watching him, just waiting for him to trip up. He told himself that in five years' time he would laugh at the memory of his first social outing, but it didn't help much right now.

"Sorry." Freddie's sheepish voice brought him out of his thoughts. "I didn't mean to take out my foul mood on you, Gabe. I'll always be your friend, you know that, no matter how high you fly."

Gabriel snorted a laugh. "And I you, Freddie."

"What are you going to do about the Tremeers?" Charles had been watching his two friends with a warm smile, but now he was returning to the scene he had witnessed on the terrace.

Gabriel managed not to groan aloud. He should have known Charles wouldn't let it go.

"Where on earth did you get that waistcoat?" he tried, but Charles wouldn't be distracted.

"The Tremeers," he repeated sternly. "I expected you to have demanded payment long before now. What's stopping you?"

A good question and one he found difficult to answer. Gabriel knew he was dithering over Will Tremeer's debt, and it had something to do with the boy's sister. Was he growing a conscience? Had becoming a duke and taking on the care of his six sisters made him soft? If that was the case, then it was damned inconvenient.

"I've seen plenty of boys like Will Tremeer," he said irritably. "We both have. You know that wiping his slate clean isn't the answer. The boy's weak and his sister's indulgence won't help him stand on his own two feet. Besides, I've worked too hard to lightly hand any of my blunt over."

"She won't give up, you know," Charles said with a grimace. "She's a lioness and she'll fight until she wears you down. Looked like you were about to give her what she wanted on the terrace, or was I mistaken? She's probably desperate, Gabe. If you'd been seen in a compromising position, she could have used it to force your hand."

"She could try," Gabriel said, but found to his dismay that he was actually looking forward to further encounters with Vivienne Tremeer. It had been years since anyone had challenged him so fearlessly, and that moment together on the terrace had made him feel achingly alive. Charles may believe she was trying to trap him into ungentlemanly behavior, but he hadn't been there. Gabriel knew artifice when he saw it, and Vivienne hadn't been pretending. The way her eyes darkened and her lips parted, promising so much passion and pleasure…he almost groaned aloud at the memory.

"So that's the way the wind blows, eh? The delectable Vivienne. You have fine taste, Cadieux."

Surprised, Gabriel turned to face the new speaker. Sir Hubert Longley smirked up at him, the degenerate lines on his face deeply etched in the lamplight and giving him a grotesque look.

"I beg your pardon?" he said in a voice that sounded unnervingly like his grandmother's.

Sir Hubert ignored him and carried on. "Have you offered to make her your ladybird? She would jump at an association with you now that you are a duke. The Tremeers are penniless, you know. The boy is a gambler too, or so I hear. Owes you quite a large sum of money, isn't that so?"

"Where did you hear that?" Gabriel snapped. He had told Vivienne he did not gossip about his patrons and that was true.

"I keep my ear to the ground." The smirk turned into a sneer. "You'll need a mistress if you want to be a proper duke, and I'm sure the lovely Vivienne will be more than willing to please."

The man's tone was offensive, and Gabriel was

suddenly filled with a white-hot anger. But it was more than Longley's words, because even as he objected to the thought of insulting Vivienne in such a way, a provocative image flashed into his head. Vivienne lying upon the opulent bed he now slept in, her hair tumbling about her, her gray eyes slumberous as she smiled up at him.

God! I really am losing my mind.

Without him being aware of it, Gabriel had fisted his hands into Sir Hubert's jacket and now he tightened his grip. Sir Hubert went up onto his toes—he was a great deal shorter than Gabriel—and his face began to turn an alarming puce color.

"You insult the lady," he said through gritted teeth. "Do not let me hear you do so again."

"You are very proper for a bastard who made his fortune by stealing my club!" Longley snarled, not to be stopped.

Gabriel stared at him in amazement. "I won your club fair and square, and you know it, Longley. You are a fool and a bloody poor player. No wonder your other clubs are on the slide. You see, I keep my ear to the ground too. Would you like me to take them over for you?"

Sir Hubert looked as if he'd like to call Gabriel out for that, but he was at heart a coward. "Get your hands off me," he growled instead.

Gabriel let him go with a shove, and the man stumbled back a few steps before he righted himself. "You are high in the instep for a street urchin," he sneered. "Vivienne Tremeer is too good for an uncouth brute like you. If anyone is going to sample that sweetmeat, then it will be me."

"You!" Gabriel burst out, the words coming from some emotion inside that he barely understood. "Do you think a woman like that would look twice at you?"

"Are you jealous?" Longley scoffed. "She's not yours to decide what she does or does not do."

"She is mine." Rage made him breathless, and he dropped his voice. "As any woman you threatened with your foul intentions would be mine to protect."

Before Longley could respond, Charles was crowding him and then gave him another shove. "Go home and sleep it off, Longley, before I plant you a facer."

"You'll be sorry," Sir Hubert said furiously as he stomped away. "I'll make you sorry, Cadieux."

"Are you all right?" Freddie looked surprised by the sudden escalation into violence. "Why did you let him get under your skin? You know what he's like, Gabe. He lives to rile you up. Ignore him."

"Yes, I should have. God, this night just gets worse and worse." Gabriel ran a shaky hand over his jaw and, hearing the rumble of a coach, turned to see if it was his.

And found himself face-to-face with the very woman he and Longley had just been squabbling over.

Vivienne stood at a short distance from him, her cloak wrapped around her against the chill, her face leached of color and her eyes full of emotion. She had overheard at least some of the conversation, that much was obvious. Gabriel stared back at her, at a loss of what to say or whether to say anything at all, but before he could decide whether an apology was appropriate, she had turned away and hurried toward the coach that had just drawn up.

She wasn't alone, but in the company of a fair-haired young woman, and an older woman he vaguely remembered from the ball. The senior of the trio was giving him a disparaging stare, but he had had plenty of them tonight. A footman drew down the steps of the coach—it had an insignia on the side—and they entered the vehicle.

For someone who said she had no fortune, the coach looked fine enough, but Gabriel knew he could not judge by appearances. He remembered Vivienne had told him she and her brother were dependent on the good graces of an aunt. It was true she had painted a rather wretched picture of her state of affairs, which made sense when he remembered Longley's words. But as to whether she would sell herself to the highest bidder to escape her situation…? Gabriel was well aware there were some women who did, but he could not believe that someone as proud as Vivienne Tremeer would be among them.

Was he wrong though? He frowned after their coach as it trundled off, replaying their conversation from the terrace. There had been nothing that hinted she was willing to enter into such a transaction, or at least he thought not, but he was inexperienced when it came to the nuances of polite conversation. If he demanded immediate repayment of her brother's debt, would she really put herself up to the highest bidder? And would her brother allow it? But then he had already seen Will Tremeer swayed by his own desires and by personalities stronger than his own. Who was to say the boy was not callous enough to encourage his sister if it meant they could both live more comfortably until he came into his inheritance.

The questions left him feeling sick and unsteady on his feet. Doubt filled him. Was he doing the right thing standing firm on the Tremeer debt? What if his intractability led to Vivienne sharing a bed with a creature like Longley? His first impression of her may have been that she was no bit of muslin, far too proud, and well aware of her own worth, but he didn't really know her. He could be wrong.

"Gabe?" Freddie was eyeing him oddly. "What is it? You're not about to cast up your accounts, are you?"

"No. I just…Sorry."

"Don't take any notice of that fathead. He's jealous of you, always was."

"Come on!" Charles interrupted them, linking their arms with his and tugging them toward the ducal coach, which had finally arrived. "Let's drink and be merry, my friends."

"Oh God, yes," Freddie muttered in a heartfelt voice. "Let's do that."

Gabriel put on a smile and told himself to forget his problems, at least for now. Tomorrow the gossip about the ball and his lack of polish would do the rounds, he was certain of that, but he couldn't do anything about it now. And if it reached the ears of his grandmother…well, he would remind her that he was a gaming hell owner first and a duke second.

But even as he tried to forget, listening to his friends chatter and laugh, he couldn't stop his mind from returning to Vivienne and Longley. The expression on her face when he refused her offer, that mixture of resignation and desperation. He reminded himself that Vivienne's decision hadn't really anything to do with him. He was running a business, a profitable one, and there was a reason he was so good at it. And yet…if it had been Olivia in a similar situation? Or Edwina? Would he turn away?

Gabriel knew in his heart that he wouldn't.

Chapter Eleven

Vivienne stared blindly through the coach window at the passing nightscape. The weather had turned and it had begun to rain, a misty mizzle that suited her mood exactly. Aunt Jane had asked her to draw the curtain, but she had pretended not to hear. In this confined space she felt as if she couldn't breathe. She could hear her aunt rattling on about Ivo and Annette, but she wasn't listening. She was remembering the scene she had witnessed outside the Farnsworths'.

Gabriel Cadieux and Sir Hubert Longley almost coming to blows.

Over her.

"Are you sure he fully appreciates your feelings, Annette?" the viscountess said, giving her daughter a dubious glance. "I don't understand why he hasn't proposed to you yet. He has had ample opportunity and still he delays."

Annette was quiet, barely responding to her mother. Perhaps she too was wondering why Ivo was procrastinating. The joining of the two families in marriage was important to the Monteiths and the Northams, and

Annette must feel as if she was failing them both. Vivienne knew the viscountess loved her daughter, but these questions were causing her to look rather anxious, and Vivienne wished she would stop.

"He did dance with you four times. Such marked attention cannot help but be remarked upon," the viscountess went on thoughtfully. "What do you think, Vivienne? He is smitten, there's no other word for it, and yet he waits."

Vivienne was tempted to tell Aunt Jane to stop interfering and leave Annette and Ivo alone to sort out their future together—how could Annette even want to marry a man like Ivo, so completely different from her ideal husband?—but that would never do. Vivienne and Will's residency at the Monteith house was tenuous at best, and it would not take much for them to be sent off back to Cornwall. Especially if Annette was to marry the duke. Her aunt would not want anything to tarnish that triumph, and if it meant ridding herself of her scandalous niece and nephew, then she would happily take the opportunity.

"Do close the curtain, Vivienne! Whatever are you staring at?"

Vivienne closed the curtain but there was a small gap to one side, and she continued to gaze through it. Her thoughts were crowding in on her, each one struggling for supremacy, and she fought to keep a wave of panic at bay. Her offer to Gabriel had been turned down, and she couldn't blame him. Why would he accept her pitiful nest egg? No wonder he had laughed! An awful sense of helplessness threatened to overwhelm her, and she shivered.

Her thoughts turned to Longley, and now a spark of anger warmed her. His sister was married to a marquis, and only his important relatives prevented him from being shunned by decent society. Even then his reputation was too much for some to swallow, and there were places he was not invited to. She had always loathed the man. He had a way of cutting out the vulnerable from the strong, and using their weakness for his own benefit. He was known to be a predator of young women. Vivienne had learned from their first meeting that he was aware of the reason she was in London. Only last week he had tried to engage her in intimate conversation, offering to help her out of her awkward situation. She had turned his words aside with a polite smile, pretended not to understand him, and then pretended to remember an important engagement elsewhere. But growing up with Richard Sutherland had taught her a thing or two, and she knew what Longley was about all right. He was offering to buy her, to pay off Will's debts in return for her company in his bed. Vivienne knew some women would be inclined, or forced, or fooled into taking such an irrevocable step, but she was not one of them.

Was that why Gabriel had looked so furious? Longley must have made some lewd insinuation about her. She hadn't heard their entire conversation, but she had heard enough of it to know Longley had been baiting Gabriel.

That Gabriel had seemed to defend her had felt precious. She was attracted to him, there she had admitted it, and to see him behaving in such a way had lifted her heart. Until…

She is mine.

Shocking as those words would be to any woman, they were worse for Vivienne. She had been the subject of manipulation once before, and it had destroyed her reputation and driven her from her home. She would not allow it to happen again.

Vivienne shuddered as the coach rumbled on. They had both been suffering from a fleeting madness on the terrace, a lapse of judgment in the heat of the moment. But maybe it wasn't that at all, at least on his part. Could Gabriel have already been considering using Will's debt to persuade her to take a carte blanche? It seemed ridiculous. She did not know him well, but what she did know made her think he would find such a thing abhorrent. And yet, remembering the way he had grabbed hold of Longley, as if…as if he was warning him off. What she had thought of as a man protecting her reputation could just as easily have been two men fighting over ownership of her.

Then the new Duke of Grantham had said, his gruff voice full of anger and resolve, *She is mine.*

She leaned her heated cheek against the window and closed her eyes with a shudder. Because even if the idea of bartering Will's debt for his sister's compliance in the bedroom had not already occurred to the duke, then Longley had made certain of it.

The house was very quiet. Vivienne's uncle, Fortescue, Viscount Monteith, was no doubt in hiding in his study, smoking cigars and drinking brandy and admiring the paintings of his horses that hung on his walls. He bred race horses at his property in Devon and had won several prestigious events, and he usually came to London only to cast his eye over the livestock for sale at Tattersall's. Vivienne was certain he cared more for his horses than his family. Not that Aunt Jane seemed to mind. It had not been a love match, according to Helena, Vivienne's mother. The viscount required a wife to run his household and give him a child—he didn't seem to care that he had only the one and she was a girl—while in return Aunt Jane had money to spend and an entrée into the best society. Not such a bad bargain, and Vivienne had seen what turmoil a love match could cause—she had only to look at her mother and Mr. Sutherland.

And yet who could resist the allure of a man who would love you just for you? Vivienne wasn't immune, despite her experience with Benjamin and Sutherland. She dreamed of marriage and children and happy ever after, but such dreams were not practical. In three years, when she returned to Tremeer, then perhaps…But when they went home, Will would lean on her all the more, at least until he was settled into his role as baronet.

They were climbing the stairs on their way to bed when Aunt Jane was called away by a servant bearing news of some domestic crisis. While she was distracted, Annette grasped Vivienne's hand in a tight grip. "Come to my bedchamber," she whispered. "We can share Jenny instead of you waiting."

Jenny was Annette's personal maid, but Vivienne shared her. Aunt Jane did not think it worth employing another maid for her niece, although she could easily have afforded one. Just another reminder that she did not consider Vivienne a permanent resident of her home.

Tonight Annette's eyes looked a little wild, almost desperate, and Vivienne didn't hesitate. She allowed herself to be tugged into her cousin's room. Jenny was already there waiting, and began to unbutton and unhook the two women. Annette's fair hair had been pinned into a becoming style, and now as she sat at her dressing table, it had to be unpinned and brushed out and braided before bed.

"You looked beautiful tonight," Vivienne said, meeting her cousin's cornflower blue eyes in the looking glass. "If Northam isn't smitten with you, then there's something wrong with him."

Annette's gaze slid away. She fiddled with a bottle of the strawberry water her mother had insisted she use to fade the freckles that appeared on her face every summer. "He was most agreeable. Almost like a…a brother."

"Oh, Annette—"

Jenny had finished with Annette and was turning to Vivienne, but Annette spoke up, aware of the maid's listening ears and penchant for gossip. "We will manage, thank you, Jenny. Take yourself off to bed."

The maid was quick to obey, she looked asleep on her feet, and a moment later the two cousins were alone.

Annette's shoulders slumped. "I know, thinking of Ivo as my brother is not what I should be doing, but I'm sure he considers me another sister. How can I marry him, Vivienne? It would be just awful for both of us."

Vivienne tried to think of something helpful to say, but Annette was already speaking again, eager to share her woes.

"He is always charming and kind, but we are completely wrong for each other. He was telling me about some silly carryings-on, and I admit it made me laugh, but at the same time I thought, 'If he were my husband, I would find him very tiresome.'"

Vivienne hesitated but it had to be said. "You have to tell Aunt Jane. You cannot enter into a marriage you dread just to please her."

Annette stared at her and then shook her head. "She has such high hopes. It would break her heart, and not just her, but it would disappoint Ivo's family too. They talk about us as if we are already married!"

The silence was heavy. Annette looked up, and there were tears in her eyes. "What am I going to do?" she said on a sob, and the next moment she was in Vivienne's arms.

Vivienne let her weep for a time, holding her soothingly. Eventually Annette took a shaky breath. "You are very good," she said in a husky voice. "The best of cousins. I don't know how you put up with me when you have so many problems of your own. And mine are so, well, silly."

"They are not silly at all," Vivienne reminded her.

"A happy marriage does not always start out as a love match." Annette spoke the words girls of her class learned from the cradle. "One has to put aside one's expectations in such circumstances."

How desperately sad is that, Vivienne wanted to say, but instead she gave a diplomatic murmur of assent.

Annette sat up and mopped at her eyes. With her hair down and her face washed clean, she looked more like a child than a woman of one and twenty. "I wish Mama did not keep on and on about it. I want to enjoy the Season and instead I am in a state of constant worry."

Annette was the sweetest girl, but unlike Vivienne, her character was not strong. She could be easily worn down by the viscountess chipping away at her confidence, or her desire to please everyone apart from herself.

"Surely Ivo is aware of the situation? His mother is probably giving him broad hints. And anyone can see his sisters long for you to be part of their family."

Annette thought a moment. "You would think he would be aware. I wonder sometimes…" She bit her lip. "I should not say this, it feels disloyal, but I wonder if he prefers to let matters unfold rather than taking an active role."

"What if you spoke to him, explained your feelings…?"

Annette pulled a face. "That is not the way things are done."

Vivienne wondered why not. If Annette and Ivo were as close as her cousin believed, then could they not discuss the future? Was Annette afraid to push him? She suspected that Annette, like Ivo, was happy to leave the situation alone and hope it sorted itself out. The Duke of Northam was a pleasant and polite man, but Vivienne had never noticed any great passion in him, apart from his reckless leanings. Any great depth of anything, really. He was one of those people who were happy to drift through life in the shallows, without causing any ripples.

"I wish you would write another book. With a happy ending. Perhaps it would come true then! Will you write another one, do you think? Harold was asking me last week when he was visiting Ivo's sisters."

Annette flushed, her gaze sliding away, and if Vivienne had not been so distracted, she might have wondered whether it was the thought of Harold that brought the color to her cousin's cheeks.

"Annette—"

"Oh, he doesn't know you are the author. I promised not to say."

Vastly relieved, Vivienne took a moment to respond. "I wrote *The Wicked Prince and His Stolen Bride* to entertain you, that was what was so enjoyable about it. And I used every wild and desperate machination I could think of in that book. I doubt I have any left." That was true enough, but there were moments when Vivienne had considered dreaming up another book, perhaps when they finally returned to Tremeer.

Thankfully Annette left it there, though the subject she turned to next was just as uncomfortable. "Do you wish you had married Benjamin?"

Vivienne was surprised, but after Annette's confessions about Ivo, perhaps this was a night for confidences.

"No. We barely knew each other. Granted," she went on cynically, "he seemed to warm to the idea of marriage once it was put to him by my stepfather." Sutherland had wanted to gain control of Vivienne's marriage settlement. "Nothing happened, although no one believes me, your mother among them. But I am grateful to her for taking me in a year ago when I landed on her doorstep."

"I believe you. But I don't understand why…" Annette gave her a curious glance. "You spent the whole night with him, Vivienne! Couldn't you have insisted he take you home?"

"In hindsight I should have *walked* home," Vivienne said heatedly. "I was visiting the Jones family—one of Benjamin's sisters was ill and I brought a basket." As the daughter of the big house, Vivienne had considered it her place to support the Tremeer tenants in times of need. The basket was a kindness and had been full of delicious foods like cold pasties and saffron buns. "Benjamin's mother kept me there far too long, and when I went to leave, I discovered my horse was lame. I could have walked home, but it was late and had begun to rain. Benjamin offered to drive me home in the farm cart. Halfway home one of the wheel spokes snapped, and we tumbled into a ditch. Neither of us were hurt, but by now it was even later and wetter, and…there was an inn nearby. It seemed only sensible to go there and get dry and have something warm to eat. The parlor was empty, and my chair in front of the fire was very comfortable and I fell asleep. Benjamin should have woken me, but he said he didn't like to presume. When morning came and I realized…I panicked and hurried outside, and found the vicar riding by on his pony."

Annette sighed. "Most unfortunate."

"As for marrying him after that…no. We would have been miserable, or at least I would have been. Benjamin was very pretty, and I admit I enjoyed looking at him, but he wasn't much good for anything else. Certainly not practical in any way. I would have had to be wife and mother to him."

Annette was holding back laughter. "I'm sorry, it isn't funny, but the way you said it. Is he still in the army?"

"Yes. Doing very well. He always could ease his way out of a difficult situation. You know your parents bought him a commission after the scandal? To get rid of him I suppose, but my mother tells me his family believe it has been the making of him." Vivienne sighed and tried to shake off her disappointment.

Annette reached out to clasp her hand. "He's done better than you from the business. Is that what you're thinking?"

It was. She had suffered far more from that comedy of errors than Benjamin, but the more she saw of the world and its unfairness, the more she thought that was the natural way between men and women.

"Let's not talk about the past." She spoke resolutely. "Shall you help me with my hair?"

Annette stood up, giving Vivienne the chair, and proceeded to remove the pins and ribbons from her hair. The sensation was soothing and Vivienne closed her eyes, enjoying the attention. Not that Jenny wasn't proficient, but she was always in such a hurry, and Vivienne was not very important. Just another job to be done quickly so she could get back to those who really mattered.

"I thought Will might be at the Farnsworths' tonight." Annette's voice brought her back.

"So did I."

"I don't want to alarm you, but Mama thinks he is getting in with bad company."

Vivienne *knew* he was getting into bad company, but she would not tell Annette about that. Her cousin would try to help. Best to keep her out of their mess as much as possible.

"When he takes over Tremeer, you will be able to help him," Annette said confidently. "You are so good at taking charge. And you always know just what to say and do, Vivienne."

"Yes, I suppose so."

"A pity you cannot help the Duke of Grantham," Annette went on blithely. "I think he will need all the help he can get. Imagine being thrust into such a position, and with six sisters! Mama says they haven't a clue how to behave in polite society. You could teach them."

"Me?" Vivienne gasped when she had recovered from her startlement.

"Yes, why not? You may not go about in society very often, but you are very adept when you do. For instance, tonight you knew just what to say to that silly Miss Farnsworth, and the other evening, when Longley tried to monopolize you, you acted as if you hadn't a clue as to his meaning. You were so very polite that he could not accuse you of insult."

"I did not realize you had heard that," Vivienne said quietly.

"Well, I did. You were the perfect lady. Even Mama says that Aunt Helena has taught you admirably, and you know what she thinks of your mother."

"My mother always hoped I would marry well. Before Benjamin. Now she simply wants me to marry *someone*. An unmarried daughter of four and twenty years is unacceptable to her."

"You have plenty of time," Annette said calmly.

Vivienne tried to imagine herself in the role of Gabriel's tutor and giggled. Annette caught her gaze in the mirror and smiled, before finishing brushing out her hair. It had been a very long time since anyone had shown her such care. She closed her eyes again. Vivienne tried not to feel sorry for herself too often—that moment in the coach had been a rare occasion—but Annette was right when she said it was always Vivienne who sorted out everyone else's problems. It was always she who shouldered their burdens and tried to make things right. Vivienne always put others first.

She longed, just once, for someone to put *her* first.

Chapter Twelve

Ashton House, Mayfair

Gabriel had arrived home not long after midnight, cutting short his night on the town with Charles and Freddie. His encounter with Vivienne Tremeer at the Farnsworths' ball had left him feeling unsettled. One thing was clear, she needed his help, and he had considered and dismissed a number of ideas to do just that. None of them were quite right. Forgiving her brother's debt went against his business principles, and taking her paltry two hundred pounds in partial payment made him feel uncomfortable. But he kept thinking of that foul creature Longley, and the urge to do *something* only grew stronger.

Eventually he rose and rang for his valet. His latest outfit was first rate, according to Francis, and he did look very well. Almost like a stranger. The barber had arrived this morning, and Gabriel now sported the smoothest shave he had ever had. For a man who had never cared for appearances apart from making sure his face was washed, matters had certainly taken a drastic turn. He found himself swaggering slightly as he descended the stairs.

"Your Grace."

Humber, the butler, waited at the bottom of the stairs. Gabriel's grandmother and half sisters had arrived last week and were now ensconced in the Ashton town house. He had been dining with them most evenings, making awkward and reluctant conversation. Gabriel broke out in a cold sweat at the very thought of more moments like that.

Humber's monotonous tones continued. "Her Grace, the dowager duchess, wishes to speak to you when it is convenient. In the blue sitting room."

"What if it isn't convenient?" Gabriel said.

The man smiled faintly, as if the idea of refusing such a request was just too ridiculous to be serious.

Yes, it was as he had thought. His grandmother wanted to speak to him *now*, whether it was convenient or not. As he made his way to the blue sitting room, which overlooked the rose garden and generally received the morning sun, Gabriel reminded himself that he should not feel intimidated by the old woman. He was a duke and head of the family, and as such he should show the dowager the respect that her position deserved, but as a person...well, she warranted nothing from him.

Gabriel had familiarized himself with the town house since he had taken up residence. The housekeeper had given him a tour, along with a dissertation on the history of the family and the importance of some of the furnishings and ornaments—*This tapestry was given to the family by Queen Anne...The ormolu clock was a gift from the king of France...One of King Charles's mistresses was an Ashton, and this is her portrait...*

And so it went on. Gabriel didn't know whether to be impressed or made uneasy by his grand relatives. When he was a child at St. Ninian's, he would have been happy with one or two simple folk. A grandmother who smiled when she saw him, fed him when he was hungry, and gave him a warm hug. A father who looked at him with pride no matter what he did. The Ashtons were not proud of him, he was certain of that. For his grandmother and sisters, he was a means to an end, and it seemed to him that he was working extremely hard to reach that end.

He missed his gambling club. He missed the sense of familiarity being there gave him, and knowing he could confidently deal with every problem that came up. It was a safe harbor, but his ascension to the dukedom had taken him out of that harbor into a rough and unfamiliar ocean, where at every turn he might make a misstep and sink the boat.

The butler opened the door with a flourish. "His Grace the sixth Duke of Grantham, Your Grace." Why did the man persist on announcing him with his full title? At first he had thought that this was simply protocol, until he noticed that no one else did it.

The dowager had looked up at his entry with an icy stare, and Gabriel stepped into the room. The door closed behind him, cutting off his escape.

"Don't concern yourself with Humber," she said, reading his mind as she always did. "He started at Grantham as an underfootman, in the early days of my marriage. He is loyal to a fault, but he has his quirks."

Gabriel wondered what any of that meant—was Humber special to her for some reason? He considered asking her, before changing his mind. Whatever secrets his grandmother had, she could keep them, he told himself as he moved into the room. The sun made patterns on the floor, and the windows were slightly open, bringing in the scent of the early roses. As usual his grandmother was dressed in sober black, as befitted a mother whose only son had died.

When he had taken his place as the head of the family, Gabriel and his valet had discussed his own attire but decided that because of the "awkwardness" between father and son, it did not seem necessary to wear a black jacket or a crepe armband. Indeed, Gabriel had felt it would be dishonest for him to do so.

His grandmother spoke, and eerily, once again their thoughts were aligned. "I have decided that six months will be quite long enough for Olivia to forgo social engagements. She will make her debut on the ninth of May, which gives us seven weeks to prepare. I know it will be rather a rush, but we can delay no longer. By then everyone who is anyone will be in town. Until she is properly out, she cannot attend public engagements and feel comfortable in society. Everything in her future hinges on her launch here at Ashton House."

She made Olivia sound like a ship about to sail. "I bow to your deeper knowledge in these matters," Gabriel murmured.

The dowager gave him an irritated look. "Sit down, Gabriel, you are making my neck ache."

Gabriel sat. Today he was wearing fawn pantaloons and a dark blue jacket—he favored the color—and his Hessian boots. He had never before been as fashionably turned out as he was these days, and he was even beginning to take an interest in what others were wearing. Was that a good thing? He wasn't sure. The other day Francis had tentatively laid out some inexpressibles for his perusal beside his usual pantaloons, but they were scandalously tight, and although they seemed all the go among the fashionable crowd, Gabriel wasn't sure he was quite ready for them.

"Your sisters—" his grandmother began.

"Half sisters." His correction was automatic, but he wasn't sure he still made the distinction. They were all in the same lifeboat after all.

Her eyes narrowed. "Your *half* sisters have not received the sort of education and training I would have wished them to have. 'That woman' was not interested in preparing them for entry into the world of their birth. She rarely left her bedchamber, and now she rarely leaves her bed. The girls are scarcely able to converse, and as for dancing or playing an instrument!"

Gabriel assumed "that woman" was Lady Felicia, his father's wife, whose marriage had been declared illegal. Given the circumstances, he wasn't sure he blamed her for not leaving her bed, and he suspected that having six children, each one a disappointment, might play upon one's nerves too. Especially when they had ultimately been declared illegitimate.

"Why didn't you see to their education?" he said, and earned himself another icy glare.

"I did not realize how serious matters were until Harry died. I have visited Grantham rarely since his marriage…well, his supposed marriage. 'That woman' and I never got on. But then Harry died and I was needed." She leaned forward and her teacup rattled, and it was the first real sign of emotion Gabriel had seen in her. "The girls were like wild animals, romping about the garden or frequenting the stables with all manner of unsuitable persons. The little ones had not had their hair brushed for a week, and their clothing was stained. It was quite outrageous. I was appalled, and I soon brought them into line, but not without a great deal of sulking and protesting on their part. I was obliged to employ a governess known for her rigorousness. Pascoe has worked wonders on them, but there are still times when they betray their lack of decorum."

"I can imagine," Gabriel said dryly, remembering his sisters at the funeral, their heads downcast, their hands folded, and yet rebellion seething in their breasts.

"The girls will require dancing lessons, indeed lessons in all manner of things to make them fit to take their place in polite society." She eyed him up and down in a disparaging way. "I think you should join them. No one will think it odd if you wish to spend time with your new family."

"Dancing lessons?" Gabriel asked in shock. "I hardly think…"

"Come, we both know you have no accomplishments, Gabriel. Apart from winning at cards." There was a glitter in her eyes but whether of amusement or disapproval, he was unsure. "I have arranged for a dancing instructor to call promptly at two this afternoon. I will expect you to be present."

Gabriel stared back at her, a myriad of thoughts racing through his head, mostly denial. He was surprised when his grandmother looked away first, taking a sip of her tea, although he suspected it was cold by now. He wanted to refuse. He wanted to refuse to have anything to do with dancing lessons or anything else. Surely he had already played his part? What more did he need to do?

Plenty more. Too late now to wish for a different outcome. He had agreed to do this, he had put himself upon this path, and he could only go forward. This mess wasn't his sisters' fault, just as it wasn't his. His father, Harry, had created this tangle of family relationships, and Gabriel knew he had the capacity to make things better, financially at least. For a start he could see the estate out of dun territory—he had already begun that process—and that would set his sisters up for the future. He could help them in practical ways—he was good at that—but as for dancing lessons and conversation…God help him.

"I was planning to visit my club this afternoon," he said stiffly. "I haven't been for a week, and there are matters that need my attention."

She waved a dismissive hand. "You should sell it. You have no need for it. I believe Sir Hubert Longley would be happy to—"

"No." His reply dropped like a stone into the quiet of the room. He was not giving anything to Longley, not after last night at the Farnsworths' ball.

He glanced at his grandmother. Had she heard about his altercation with Longley? Was that why she had called him in here, to dress him down like the three-year-old she had abandoned? He'd rather go head to head with Vivienne Tremeer again than be scolded by his grandmother. *Much rather*, he decided with a smile.

The dowager was watching him curiously. "You are not at all like Harry," she said abruptly. "He was the sweetest boy imaginable."

"And look where that landed you."

She looked away, her mouth turned down, but he thought it was with pain rather than censure. Harry had been her son, her only son, and no matter what he had done, she must miss him.

"We were speaking of the dancing lesson," she said, and her dark eyes so like his dared him to refuse.

"Very well," Gabriel sighed, the hint of grief softening his stance.

She gave a brief nod, as if she had expected his obedience all along, but he thought there was a touch of relief too. The tension about her neck and shoulders seemed to suggest she wasn't as confident of his compliance as she pretended to be.

"At two then," she said, as if he could forget. "Ring for a servant on your way out. I have invitations to write."

He was dismissed. Gabriel stood up and left the room. His appetite for breakfast had waned, but all the same he should eat. If he was engaged this afternoon, then he would need to visit the club this morning and see what Charles had to tell him. His friend had taken over most of the running of the place now, but Gabriel remained the owner, and the major decisions were still his. He hesitated and then decided that before he left he would at least pour himself a cup of coffee and butter some toast.

He hoped to have the place to himself, and strode through the door of the breakfast room before he saw that it wasn't empty.

The six girls were there.

Gabriel stopped, wondering if he could back out again without being noticed. Unfortunately they had all looked up at his entrance, and before he could decide whether it was better to face it out or turn tail, a cheerful voice rang out.

"There you are!"

Edwina hopped off her chair and skipped over, taking his hand in hers. Her fingers were warm and slightly sticky. "I know I shouldn't be here," she said confidentially, "but breakfast in the nursery is awful. And I wanted to be down here. With you."

Gabriel wasn't sure whether to be flattered or frightened. "That's nice," he said with an awkward smile. "Good morning, eh, everyone."

Olivia shot him one of her sullen looks. Justina smiled and wished him a shy good morning, and there were murmurs from the others. Gabriel allowed himself to be led to the table by Edwina, who made sure to sit beside him. Georgia, the next youngest sister, gave him a doubtful look, as if he might do something disgraceful at any moment. He poured himself a cup of coffee, his appetite having completely gone. He had things to do at his club, and he was tempted to retire there indefinitely. Until recently he had slept in the rooms above the gambling area, but his grandmother had persuaded him to move into the ducal residence.

Edwina chattered away, telling him about her plans for the day, and the other girls put in a word or two, sounding either timid or grudging. At the same time they eyed him curiously, as if he were a foreign body in their midst—which he supposed he was—while he responded self-consciously. It occurred to him that none of them, including himself, seemed to know how to converse in that easy manner he had observed among the guests at last night's ball. If they had difficulty here in their own home, how on earth would they fare in society?

When he rose to his feet, wishing them a good day, Edwina followed him. Once the door was closed behind them, he heard a burst of sound from the girls left inside, as if his presence had restrained them in some way and now they could let themselves go.

He took a breath. "I really must—"

"Olivia is cross." Edwina interrupted before he could make his excuses.

"I can see that," he said cautiously. "Do you know why?"

"She hates being the eldest. She is afraid she will become like Mama and have to marry a man who doesn't love her and have a baby every year. She was hoping when Father died that she could make her own life, do the things she wanted to do, but then we found out we had no money. And that Mama wasn't really Father's wife. She has fallen into a melancholy, did you know that?"

"I suspected."

Edwina nodded her head sadly, curls bouncing, but she couldn't stay sad for long. Her sunny smile broke out. "And now you are here! I'm so glad you're here. You can mend everything for us. You can, can't you? Justina says you are awfully clever."

That explained Olivia's sulks anyway. Maybe he should tell her that he was just as miserable? And it was nice of Justina to say he was clever, but he had the impression she was rather a nice girl and would say that even if she didn't believe it was true.

"Before Grandmother came to stay, we had a wonderful time. Did you know, we went out every day? Roberta made up some wonderful games for us to play, about pirates and highwaymen. She says a girl can be a highwayman too. Or a pirate. Olivia said they were silly, but I think she enjoyed them just as much as the rest of us. And then when it was hot, we swam in the pond at the bottom of the garden. That was when Grandmother found us. She was very angry."

"I suppose she was worried you might drown."

"Oh no, the pond isn't deep. I think it was because

we had no clothes on. But it would be silly to swim in our clothes, wouldn't it?"

Gabriel didn't know what to say. He could imagine the dowager's face when she saw them. He wasn't surprised she had taken strong action to right matters.

"Now we have Pascoe," Edwina said dully. "She's our governess and she's horrible. She won't let us do anything. She says discipline is the most important thing, but where's the fun in that? I wish we could go back to before, but Olivia says we are doomed to be ladies."

Olivia appeared to have a turn for the dramatic. All the same, Gabriel understood her sense of loss, and sympathized too. For a time they must have felt like normal young ladies…well, the sort that ran wild like children in the London slums. But it could never have lasted. They were duke's daughters, and they had a role to inhabit, just as he did.

"Will you dance with me this afternoon?" Edwina interrupted his thoughts.

He blinked. "Of course," he said, trying to sound enthusiastic.

It must have convinced Edwina, because she smiled happily and skipped away down the corridor. He suspected she was going to bother his grandmother. He hoped so.

Chapter Thirteen

As Gabriel entered Cadieux's, he was reminded again just how much he had missed his club. Even the smell of it—last night's supper and alcohol and the sweat of men. Well, not so much the smell, so perhaps these days he was more fastidious. All the same he found himself smiling as he strode through the familiar gaming rooms and climbed the stairs, impatient to set foot in his office.

The door was open, and Charles looked up. He was bleary-eyed, his fair hair an untidy mop, as if he'd been running his fingers through it. "What are you doing here?" he said. "I thought you'd be busy in Mayfair being the duke."

Gabriel approached the desk. It didn't have its usually tidy appearance either, papers scattered about and an ink blot on one of them. His fingers itched to straighten things, create order, but as Charles was eyeing him rather belligerently, he resisted the urge and instead sat down in the chair opposite.

"I needed a breather from being the duke," he answered, with a shrug. "And I wanted to catch up on what's been happening here. And to see you, of course."

Charles observed him for a moment, as if weighing up the validity of his words. He shrugged. "You just missed Freddie. He said he'd call back for lunch, so if you're still here..." He raised an eyebrow as he waited for Gabriel's response.

"I will be. I have no plans until two o'clock." Why had he said that? Now Charles would ask what he was doing at two, and he really didn't want to talk about bloody dancing lessons. But Charles didn't ask. He reached into the pile of papers on the desk and pulled out a sheet of figures that looked familiar.

"Perhaps it's time we dealt with this."

Gabriel took the paper from his hand and peered at it with a frown. As he thought, it was a list of the debts Will Tremeer had run up at Cadieux's.

"Damn the woman," he muttered.

Charles sat up straighter and looked more interested. "I assume that the woman in question is Miss Tremeer? She's the reason you are so loath to demand repayment?"

Gabriel met his friend's quizzical blue eyes. "Yes. I thought..." He ran a hand over his jaw and just stopped himself from disarranging his cravat. "After Longley's foul remarks last night, I began to wonder whether demanding repayment might push her into doing something she didn't want to."

"You mean accept a disreputable offer from Longley?"

"Yes. Him or someone else."

"Has she asked you to forgive the debt?"

"Yes. At least she had a proposal whereby she paid me a small sum and I would wait until her brother inherited to receive the rest."

Charles chuckled. "So you said no and then tried to kiss her?"

Gabriel shook his head. "Actually, I think the kissing part was mutual."

Charles lifted his eyebrows. "Was it indeed?" There was a pause while he tapped his fingers against the cover of a ledger. "You should speak to her, Gabe. About Longley and what she plans to do. She probably needs a friend."

Charles was far more knowledgeable when it came to how women thought. He seemed to find navigating the twisting paths of their minds a great deal easier than Gabriel, who had always steered clear of entanglements. He preferred to satisfy his bodily needs without involving his emotions. Not that he was cruel, he was never that, but neither did he open his heart. He knew it was because his childhood had led him to associate love with betrayal. He didn't want to risk being hurt again, so he kept himself closed off. Charles and Freddie were different, and he would trust them with his life, but he had kept a distance between himself and the rest of the world.

Ironic that he now found himself responsible for the entire Ashton family and the cumbersome machine that went with it—servants and tenants, the Sussex estate and the London town house, a hunting box somewhere or other, as well as the several business ventures his father had entered into that were now languishing.

He decided it was time to change the subject.

"Has the club been busy?"

Charles gave him a look that was a cross between amusement and irritation, but decided to let it go. He nodded. "Very. I think your new status has brought in a lot more customers, all wanting to see where you sprang from. I even had a few of the bright-eyed sort asking if you were available for a game or two. I told them no."

Gabriel grunted. "I'm sure my grandmother would be

pleased to hear about that. The Duke of Grantham playing hazard in a common gaming club, even if it does belong to me. She wants me to sell, Charles."

It was Charles's turn to frown. "And will you?"

"No. The club is the only thing these days that is completely mine."

"What, that monstrous house in Sussex isn't yours?" Charles mocked.

"It doesn't feel like mine," he admitted. "Grantham belongs to the family, and I am expected to look after it and leave it in a better condition than I found it. Which won't be difficult. My father spent every penny he could on pleasing himself with never a thought for the future. Because of him the estate is encumbered with serious debt, the tenants' houses are falling down, and his daughters are penniless."

"You'll turn things around." Charles spoke confidently. "You're exactly the right person for the job. You'll do them proud, Gabe."

Gabriel gave him a quick look and found his friend smiling. Charles knew him so well; he could see Gabriel's self-doubt as if it were written on his face. "I'm not sure they'll feel like that. I'm an interloper, an undeserving beneficiary of my father's stupidity when he married my mother. I will never be seen otherwise, and to be honest, Charles, I'm not sure I care."

"I think you do care, or you would if you were honest with yourself," Charles said, but then held up a hand when Gabriel opened his mouth to argue the point further. "Let's not talk about it. You're here to see what's been happening with the club, so let's do that. In fact I could use your help with a few matters. Here, take a look at this."

As Gabriel leaned forward to read whatever it was

Charles pointed to, he felt a huge wave of relief. This is what he wanted, this was why he was here. The club was his own place, and he could forget about everything that awaited him back at the town house. Despite his fashionable clothes and new title, he could be himself.

The dancing lesson was to be held in the drawing room. Furniture had been pushed against the walls, clearing a large space, and by the time Gabriel arrived from his lunch with Charles and Freddie, the dancing instructor was there. Mr. Marks was a tall young man with a scraggly beard, and an older lady who looked very like him sat at the pianoforte, ready to play.

After all the teasing he had been subjected to by his friends once he had confessed the nature of his two o'clock appointment, Gabriel was prepared to relax and accept the situation. How bad could it be? Awkward, yes, but he had dealt with worse. For instance, Charles and Freddie had reminded him of the time he had to break up a brawl at the club when a patron was assaulted by his furious wife and accused of spending his winnings on another woman. Or when a teacher at St. Ninian's had threatened to throw Freddie from the window and they had to wrestle him to safety.

Surely an hour or two in the company of his sisters and a caper merchant would be mild by comparison?

"Now, if Your Grace will stand here, each of the ladies can take turns partnering you. In the meantime, the spare ladies will have to dance with each other."

"We should have found more gentlemen," Roberta complained. "Why didn't we?"

"Who were you thinking of?" Olivia said sarcastically. "Humber?"

Roberta poked out her tongue, and Edwina shrieked with laughter. For a moment the room descended into chaos. Luckily their grandmother had been called away on some errand or other, and Pascoe was elsewhere, so they were alone.

"You can dance with me," Justina said. Gabriel had noticed before that she was ever the diplomat when it came to smoothing over any issues with her more difficult sisters. "Then when the duke is free, you can dance with him. We all can."

"You can call me Gabriel," he said.

They exchanged glances, and then Edwina was standing in front of him, giggling. "My turn, Gabriel," she said, lifting her hands to take his. "You should ask me if I wish to dance first though, isn't that right, Mr. Marks?"

The instructor assured her it was. He prattled on about dance cards and the importance of carrying one, but Gabriel wasn't listening. He was concentrating on his steps and failing miserably.

When he had twirled Edwina clumsily around the room several times, and she refused to give up her spot, Justina tried to persuade her sister it was time for someone else to take a turn. There was a tussle as Edwina fought for her place, and more unruly shrieking as someone pulled someone's hair.

"Ladies, ladies!" Mr. Marks shouted. "This is no way to behave!"

To Gabriel's dismay no one took any notice of him, and in the end Olivia wrestled her youngest sister away, causing a deal of squawking and complaining, and took her place a little breathlessly. In contrast to Justina's kind smile, Olivia's glance was scornful as they counted their steps.

"I thought you'd know how to dance," she complained.

"No," he replied, feeling exposed and flustered. "There has been no call for it up until now."

"Well, what *can* you do?" she demanded, her eyes fixed on his face interrogatively.

His cravat seemed suddenly very tight, but he resisted tugging at it. "I'm not sure I should—"

"Grandmama is not here to scold," she retorted. "And our governess is unwell. How sad." There were some unkind giggles over this and conspiratorial glances.

"She ate too much plum crumble," Edwina spoke up. "She's greedy."

"Hush, Edwina," Justina murmured. "That isn't kind."

"But it's true," Edwina protested. "You can't scold me for telling the truth."

As the lesson threatened to descend once more into anarchy, Mr. Marks called for their attention. "Concentrate on your steps, ladies, please! Now, again, one, two, three!"

For a time there was silence as they did as they were told, but the peace could not last.

"We know you own a gambling club. *A hell.*" Olivia spoke the words with relish.

"I bet you can box too!" Roberta said eagerly, her eyes shining as she spun past with one of the younger girls.

Once more Mr. Marks tried to regain their attention, the pianist starting up with a flourish, but the girls took no notice.

"I do own a gambling club," he said. "And I have been known to box, although my fighting skills were honed on the street rather than a club for gentlemen."

They stopped and stared at him in amazement while Mr. Marks twittered angrily.

"Have you actually punched anyone?" Roberta, the bloodthirsty sister, asked him in an excited whisper.

"Yes. Usually when there's trouble at the club I have men who sort it out, but there are times when I have to help them."

"So you're not really a gentleman at all." Olivia spoke dismissively, but some of the sulkiness had gone from her pretty face. There was even a gleam of interest in her blue eyes.

Gabriel decided to be truthful. "I'm doing my best to be one. I need help though, and that's why I'm here."

"We can help you!" Edwina piped up.

"Eh, thank you, Edwina."

"My debut is soon," Olivia said, her flippant voice at odds with the tight grip of her fingers in his.

"And are you looking forward to it?" Gabriel asked curiously.

Her gaze met his, briefly, before she looked down at her slippers.

"Head up!" Marks ordered.

She jerked her head up with a grimace and then sighed. "No," she admitted. "I am not looking forward to it. I feel out of my depth," she added, surprising Gabriel with her sudden candor. "And Pascoe is quite useless. All she does is shout and then punish us if we get something wrong. I need someone to help me through the endless protocols that Grandmama has listed. Talk to this person, say this, do this, make certain I am amusing but not too amusing, don't giggle, hold my fan just so…It's exhausting."

"I agree with you there," Gabriel murmured as they made another turn about the room. "Bloody exhausting."

Olivia spluttered a laugh, her eyes wide. She was an attractive girl when she wasn't scowling, big blue eyes and dark hair and pale, flawless skin. A little shorter than Justina and Roberta, she wasn't quite as slender but had a pleasing plumpness. No doubt the gentlemen of the ton would flock to her like bees to honey, and perhaps he would have to use his boxing skills on them.

They danced on as Mr. Marks corrected a step here or a step there. Gabriel partnered each of the sisters, and although they were far from being the polite young ladies their grandmother expected them to be, he found it wasn't such a chore after all. In fact he was enjoying himself, especially as he grew more confident in his movements, and there were laughter and smiles all around. Until the dowager returned and fixed her stern gaze upon them.

By then the lesson was almost done, and it only remained for him to bow, and his sisters to curtsy, as if they really were in a ballroom. As he went to move away, Olivia, who had been his partner once again, leaned in closer.

"We can help you to practice being a gentleman," she whispered, for his ears alone, "if you help us be ladies. We can help each other. Don't you think?"

Just for a moment she looked very young and a little frightened, and he noticed the dark shadows under her eyes. It was as if she had opened a door to him, just a little, and he needed to say the right thing to step through. But he hesitated too long, uncertain what he should say, and the moment was lost. She had already resumed her familiar sullen expression, casting her eyes up.

"Please yourself," she said airily.

The dowager clapped her hands. "Girls! Please thank Mr. Marks."

They behaved very prettily now that they were being watched, and Gabriel felt his lips twitch into a smile. The dancing lesson had been a revelation to him, and he felt as if he knew his sisters quite a bit better than before. He also recognized their shortcomings—the Farnsworths' ball had opened his eyes to that. There were still frustrations, particularly with Olivia, but Gabriel knew now that her behavior was a mask she used to hide her real feelings. They were alike in that, and he felt a connection with her.

There was no such problem with Edwina. She was perfectly open and when she was present, the atmosphere around them felt a lot more relaxed. It was as if she was acting as a bridge between her sisters and Gabriel, and he was glad of it.

"The lesson went well?" The girls had left the room and he was alone with his grandmother. She was watching him, probably reading his thoughts. She had an uncomfortable talent for that.

"I think so." They needed a hundred more lessons at least, but he didn't say that aloud because it would not help. The dowager would only set Pascoe onto them and make matters worse.

"I have to return to Grantham. 'That woman' is letting things go to rack and ruin. She has sent the housekeeper away. Again. Someone has to take charge of the household." She looked as if she was fully prepared to be that person.

"How long…?"

"I don't know. Some weeks I should think. The girls will remain here. They have a lot more to learn but Pascoe will deal with that."

"Are you sure Pascoe is the right person to guide them?" Did his grandmother know how much the girls loathed the woman? Surely there was someone better to help them? The question sparked an idea and he almost didn't hear his grandmother's response.

"Most certainly. They need to be ready for Olivia's coming-out. So do you. She will partner with you for her first dance." She must have seen the apprehensive expression on his face before he could hide it, because she added, "You will do your sister proud, Gabriel."

The praise was unexpected, an echo of what Charles had said to him earlier, and her words caused a warm spark to flare in his chest. But that idea was bubbling away in his head and he didn't have time to consider the dowager's rare praise. Snippets of the girls misbehaving, and the useless Pascoe, and last night at the ball where Vivienne Tremeer showed him just how a lady should conduct herself. Well, perhaps not out on the terrace—his mouth twitched. But the idea was sound. He turned it about, looked at it from several ways, and he could find nothing wrong with it.

Gabriel ran a hand over his jaw, feeling the bristles. He would need another shave before he saw Vivienne and laid out his plan to her, and the sooner he did that the better. The only question then was...would she agree to it?

Chapter Fourteen

The letter had come just as Vivienne was thinking about bed.

The Viscount and Viscountess Monteith, with Lady Annette, were dining with Ivo and his family. Annette had cast a longing look at Vivienne as they moved toward the door.

"Come, Annette, we'll be late. Vivienne can keep herself busy helping Jenny with the mending." Aunt Jane showed her teeth at her niece in what was meant to be a smile.

I'm not a servant. Vivienne closed her lips on the protest that sprang to them. She was here because of her aunt's charity and she knew it, and what good would protesting do anyway? Now that the duke had refused her offer, she and Will had no option but to ask their aunt for the money to repay the debts. They had finally reached rock bottom.

Will had gone to a boxing match and was still not home. Tomorrow they would both approach Aunt Jane.

Vivienne knew she could not let it drag on any longer. The dread of the confrontation, of Aunt Jane in a rage, was weighing her down. The viscountess tended to rehash all of Vivienne's past wrongs when she was angry, making her feel even lower than she already did. No doubt it would be extremely unpleasant.

Would her aunt send Vivienne home as well as Will? Or should she go anyway, despite what awaited her in Tremeer? It would be neither pleasant nor safe to live in a house with Sutherland. Indeed, there were few things she could think of that were worse. Her stepfather and his machinations to see her married had been the reason she fled. Her mother would be glad of her company though. In no time she would be listening to Helena's complaints about her husband, not that they weren't justified, but there was nothing Vivienne could do about the state of their marriage. She remembered her last meal at Tremeer, before she set off for London. The beef had been so tough she could hardly eat it. Everything in the kitchen was prepared with an eye to cost, and Vivienne doubted that had changed. She supposed there would be more empty spaces on the walls where paintings used to hang, and there would be bare corners in the rooms where the better furniture once sat.

Last night at the Farnsworths' ball had faded enough that she could tell herself she must have been imagining the new Duke of Grantham's interest in her. Yes, she was attracted to him, but she had been burned before by a man. It was a reminder of the danger of impetuous behavior. Sir Hubert Longley was being his usual unpleasant self, and Gabriel had taken exception, and anything else was down to her imagination. If she ever saw him again, Vivienne would simply pretend it had never happened. And yet she would miss their clashes, the spark in his inky dark eyes when he looked at her, and the sense that there was more, much more, to learn about him.

No, Vivienne did not want to go home, not yet, but she may have no choice.

Jenny was tired and not her usual chatty self. They worked in silence until at last Vivienne finished sewing on a torn flounce and set her work aside with a yawn. "That's enough for one night," she declared.

Gratefully Jenny agreed and hurried off to bed. Vivienne was on the stairs on her way to her own bedchamber when one of the servants informed her that a letter addressed to her had just arrived.

It seemed a strange time for a letter, but she took it with a puzzled thank-you. The writing was unfamiliar, so not one of her mother's missives, the lines crossed so many times to save on postage that it was barely legible. She made her way sedately to her bedchamber, and once the door was closed, she ripped the letter open.

> *The Duke of Grantham requests Miss Tremeer's presence at Cadieux's Gambling Club as soon as possible.*

All sorts of wild thoughts careered through her head, but before she could begin to make sense of them, she saw the addendum at the bottom in Will's handwriting.

> *Please come, Vivienne! Tell Jem to bring you. I need you. Will.*

For a heartbeat she stood frozen, clutching the letter and staring down at it as if it could speak. But there was no time to dillydally. Will would not have asked her to come if it wasn't urgent, and she could not pretend that Gabriel had forged his hand in some insane plot to get her to his club. It was most definitely Will's writing.

Her mind turned immediately to more practical matters.

Had Jem driven the coach to the Northams' tonight? If it was inclement, he often sent the undercoachman, claiming his bones were too old to go out in the cold, but tonight it was reasonably fine. All the same, before she found a hackney, she would look for her old friend.

Hastily she dressed in outdoor clothes designed not to attract attention—a plum-colored gown with a plain collar, and her second-best cloak, dark gray and voluminous. Everyone was abed apart from Aunt Jane's maid and Uncle Fortescue's valet, but they would be waiting in their respective rooms to be summoned once their master and mistress returned home. Jenny would be waiting too, for Annette, but from the look of her earlier, she was probably dozing.

It took only a few moments for Vivienne to steal out the back door and make her way through the gate that led into the mews. It was late, the only illumination the stars, but she knew her way. Sometimes when she was particularly lonely she would visit Jem, pretending to be there to feed the horses apples but really just to listen to him talk in the familiar dialect of home.

She slipped into the stables, breathing in the scent of the horses and hay. Muted light trickled down through the uneven boards that made up the floor of the space above, where Jem lived. Her luck was in, and, relieved, she climbed the narrow unadorned stairs. Soon she was face-to-face with Jem.

"Miss Vivienne!" He looked shocked to see her. "What's happened? Is it your brother?"

"Yes. I need you to take me to him, Jem. He's at Cadieux's, the gambling club. You remember?"

"I remember." He didn't look happy.

"I think he's in trouble, Jem. I have to go."

He grumbled but he was already moving to find his boots and his coat. The fireplace was sending warmth into the small space, and a candle sat on the table by his chair, along with a metal cup. Other than the basics, there wasn't much in his room, and it occurred to her that although he had made himself comfortable here in London, it wasn't home. Was he lonely? There had been a woman once he had courted, but he had left her behind at Tremeer, and although Vivienne felt guilty about that, at the same time she was glad he was here with her and Will.

Once dressed, Jem pinched out the candle and led the way back downstairs.

"The coach isn't here," he said, "so we'll have to take one of the horses, and you can ride pillion with me, maid. Just have to hope they don't notice it missing and wonder where I am."

"I'll take the blame," Vivienne said. "Don't worry. And anyway…" She bit her lip, and then the words spilled out. "Will and I will more than likely be returning home soon. It doesn't matter if Aunt Jane punishes me for this as well. I'll make sure you aren't blamed, Jem."

He stared at her, his craggy face slack with surprise. "What do you mean you're going home? That's no place for you. 'T ain't safe."

"It can't be helped," she said, and reached to take his calloused hand. "Thank you, Jem, you know how much you mean to us. I'll miss you."

He said nothing, but she saw the emotion in his eyes. She was glad when he turned away to saddle the horse because otherwise they would both be in tears.

Cadieux's was abuzz with activity. Loud voices came from the gaming rooms as players shouted and laughed in that stupid drunken way she recognized when men were in their cups. Sutherland and his cronies sounded the same. Last time she had been here, it was early morning and things had been quietening down. Now, at midnight, the hell was at its zenith.

She slipped through the room, cloak covering her from head to toe, and took a relieved breath when no one stopped her to ask what she thought she was doing. Soon she was climbing the staircase to Gabriel's office.

The door opened to her knock, and Charles Wickley stood there. "Miss Tremeer," he said. His blue eyes were bright with amusement, as if he found the whole situation a joke, and stung, she lifted her chin and gave him her daughter-of-a-baronet stare.

"Let me in," she said.

He grinned and obediently stepped back, and Vivienne looked past him into the room. It was much as she remembered it, perhaps less tidy, but her gaze had already found her brother. He was slumped in a chair by the fireplace, while the duke loomed over him.

"Will?" she cried, and hurried protectively toward him.

At the sound of her voice, her brother gave a start and looked up, his face drawn and pale, and seeming much older than his eighteen years. When she reached him, he gave a gasp that she knew was the precursor to a sob, and

Vivienne knelt and flung her arms around him, at the same time glaring up at Gabriel.

The duke was watching her, and she was momentarily distracted by the expression on his face. Wariness certainly, but also something that was almost like longing. She didn't believe it had anything to do with her, but more likely from seeing the affection shown between herself and her brother. This was a man who had been brought up in an orphanage, she reminded herself, just as he wiped his face clean of anything at all.

"What is happening?" she demanded. Will was trying to burrow into her shoulder. "What are you doing here?"

He mumbled against her. "I'm sorry, Viv. Germaine said he saw Sutherland here, and I wanted to—to..." He groaned. "I thought if I could stop him from finding out about my debt and telling Mr. Davey, then..."

His voice trailed off, and she pushed him back so that she could see him properly. "Did you find him? Sutherland?" Her voice wavered.

He shook his head miserably. "I didn't intend to stay, but Germaine wanted to. Remember I told you he thinks I am his good luck charm. And I was drowning my sorrows."

"Drowning them rather a lot I think." She tried to make her voice stern. "Whatever were you thinking, Will?"

He looked up at her, his eyes bright with tears. "I was thinking that it isn't your job to dig me out of this hole. That's all down to me."

He looked so disconsolate. All of the anger and bluster had drained out of him. "I've been a fool. I just...when we arrived here, I felt so free, as if I could do anything and it wouldn't matter, and instead I turned into a man like Sutherland."

"You're not like him, Will, but you're young and I think you were enjoying being free a little too much. You lost sight of what is important."

"I don't want to go back to Cornwall," he said desperately, giving her a wild look. "Especially if I lose Tremeer. Living under Sutherland in what should have been my home? I think I'd die."

Her heart ached for him and, briefly, she was tempted to relent, but Vivienne hardened her resolve. It was long past time to stand firm, for Will's sake if not her own, and if her change of mind had something to do with the warning about her brother that Gabriel had expressed last night, then she refused to acknowledge it.

"It wouldn't be forever," she said, trying to sound more confident than she felt. "And Aunt Jane won't let Tremeer leave the family. If you can show her you have changed, you can still come into your inheritance in three years. Perhaps…"

Will cocked a skeptical eyebrow.

"Don't make any decisions. I want to put a proposal to you both," Gabriel interrupted, and they looked up at him.

Vivienne's eyes widened incredulously. Was this when the duke asked her to be his mistress? Was he truly not the man she had thought him?

"Miss Tremeer."

The sound of her name in his mouth scattered her thoughts and brought her head up. Gabriel was holding out his hand, waiting for her to give him hers so that he could help her to her feet. With a reluctant glance at Will, she slid her gloved fingers into Gabriel's, aware of their warm strength as he gripped her firmly. She expected him to let her go once she was upright, but he didn't, instead leading her away from Will to stand before the crowded bookshelves she remembered from last time. She tried not to let her eye seek out *The Wicked Prince and His Stolen Bride*.

"Before you say anything," she began, "I overheard you and Sir Hubert Longley, last night at the ball. If you are about to offer me an indecent proposal, then save your breath."

He stilled, his expression a mix of emotions. Anger, concern, and perhaps hurt. "You think I asked you here so that I could coerce you into immorality?" He sounded wounded, and she knew she was correct about the emotion she had seen his eyes. He *was* hurt.

"You never intended to do such a thing, did you?" She peered up at him, trying to read his expression.

There was that twist to his lips, and her gaze slid over them and the dark stubble on his jaw. He looked like the man she had met here back in November, Cadieux the gambling hell owner. At the time she had thought him a handsome brute, but he was far more complex than that. Aware that he was still holding her hand in his, she pulled away as if bitten. His dark eyes mocked her.

"You may be a tempting armful, Miss Tremeer, but I do not take advantage of ladies in distress." Now he sounded irritated.

"Tempting armful?" she repeated in a snappy tone. "You are not convincing me, Your Grace."

He ignored her. "Let me remind you of our history, Miss Tremeer. You came here and begged me to forgive your brother's debt—"

"Matters were desperate. I felt I had no option."

"Yes." He stared at her in silence for a moment, and

she felt on edge. If he wasn't going to use Will's debt to lever her into his bed, then what was he thinking?

"What if I have found another way to clear the debt? A way that will be mutually beneficial to both of us."

Vivienne shot her brother an uneasy glance, but he had his head in his arms. "What about Will?"

"I'll come to your brother in a moment. I have a proposal to put to him too, but I'd prefer him sober." He nodded to the coffeepot and cup that sat on the hearth by her brother's chair.

"How can we clear Will's debt?" she asked through lips that were suddenly dry. She ran the tip of her tongue over them and felt his attention.

He bent his head so that they were very close, and his warm breath, brandy scented, brushed her cheek. And there was that dip and dive in her stomach, the quickening of her pulse. She tried to ignore the effect his closeness was having upon her, but it was there, just as it had been on the other occasions they were together. "Explain to me first," he spoke gruffly. "I want to understand why you believed me such a monster."

Vivienne swallowed. "I overheard you and Longley. My experience of him…of men like him led me to assume…" She waved a hand. "My stepfather and his crowd would not have hesitated to take advantage of a desperate woman."

He observed her in frowning silence. Did he want more? What more could she say without delving into matters that were far too intimate? Vivienne shifted uneasily. "I suppose I imagined a…a pied-à-terre where you would require I repay you penny by penny in bed." She said the shocking words lightly, as if they meant nothing, but he wasn't fooled.

"I apologize. That was never my intention." He spoke with quiet sincerity. "Those who know me are aware I am not that sort of man." He tugged at his cravat, but it wasn't his usually perfectly tied one, so it didn't matter. In fact she saw now that he was wearing buckskins and a loose jacket over a soft, well-washed shirt. Not his fashionable gear at all. It was as if he had left the duke at the door.

He had never wanted to hurt her. Although she couldn't entirely blame herself for believing the worst, it was time for her to apologize. "No, it is I who am sorry. It is just that…Sir Hubert has spoken previously to me about the matter of—of debt, so I am aware of his intentions toward me. Seeing him there with you, I thought…wrongly, I know now, but at the time…"

His mouth tightened and his eyes blazed. Was he still insulted, or was he angry on her behalf? She had not the time to decide before he quenched the emotion.

"I may be a hard man, but I am not a cad," he said bluntly.

She liked that about him, his bluntness. It was something she should have remembered before she flew into a panic. If Gabriel had wanted her to be his mistress, he would have asked her straight out instead of leaving her to second-guess him.

"Last night you offered to pay me two hundred pounds"—over near the hearth Will groaned—"and the remainder of the debt in three years when your brother inherits. Do you still stand by that?" He stretched out his hand to her. "Are we in agreement?"

"Yes."

"Then let us shake on it."

Once again she placed her hand in that big, warm grip. It unnerved her, the feeling of his palm against hers, the squeeze of his fingers. "Thank you." Her voice sounded shaky. "I hardly know what to say. This means a great deal to me…to us both."

He nodded, still watching her.

She found she didn't want to let go, but that was ridiculous. She removed her hand and felt the loss. The ticking clock on the mantel caught her attention, and gratefully she looked away from Gabriel to its face. It was late and she had already been here too long, with Jem waiting. She and Will needed to get back to Mayfair. She had much to think of, and to be grateful for. She and Will would not have to ask Aunt Jane for anything. They could remain in London, and if Sutherland tried to overturn the will, he would not be able to prove anything. They were safe, but it had yet to sink in properly.

"We have trespassed on your time for long enough," she began politely.

He cocked his head to the side, considering her. "Because a single lady should not be in a place such as this? It is against society's rules. That is correct, is it not?"

Surprised and a little uneasy, she nodded. "Very much against the rules. But as you are aware, Your Grace, I am in a position where the rules must be put aside, for now at least."

"But you are mindful of them. You are a well-brought-up young lady, versed in ladylike accomplishments?"

Where on earth was this conversation going? "Even my aunt acknowledges that I can be the model of respectability…although if she could see me here now…"

"Yes, I thought so." He looked relieved. He seemed to prepare himself. "I have a further proposal to put to you, Miss Tremeer. More of a request. Will you hear me out?"

Surprised, she studied him. He was his usual intense self, but there was a flicker of something in his eyes she could not identify. "You can ask me, but that doesn't mean I will agree," she said.

He smiled politely. "Here is the deal. I will wipe out the entirety of the debt, and I will forgo the two hundred pounds, but I wish for something in return. Not"—with a sharp look when she opened her mouth to respond—"for any physical favors. I can buy them elsewhere."

Well, that was rude, but it certainly put her in her place. Vivienne swallowed her protest, and then realized what he had said. "All of the debt?" she repeated. "That is…this is most generous, Your Grace. But…"

He didn't let her finish, moving to the desk where Charles was standing. The two men had a brief, murmured conversation, and then Gabriel picked up an envelope. "Everything is in here," he said. He held it out to her.

She wanted to burst into laughter, or tears. Should she believe him? Was he really setting her free from the worry and strife of this past year? She took one step and then another, and her hand was trembling badly as she took hold of the envelope.

When he did not let go, her startled gaze flew to his. He looked apprehensive enough to cause her heart to give an anxious thump.

"This is not easy for me." He grimaced, glanced at her through his lashes as if he was…embarrassed? Ashamed? She gave a jerky nod to show she understood, when she didn't understand at all. He let the envelope go and gave his cravat another tug.

What on earth was the matter with the man? A moment ago he was in complete charge of the situation, and now he was floundering, seemingly out of his depth.

Was his request not a matter of business? Because it seemed to Vivienne that when it came to business, Gabriel was perfectly relaxed, knowing what he wanted and how to get it, but when it came to the social side of his new life, and the expectations placed upon him, he struggled.

"What is it?" she prompted. "What is your request? I think you must know it would have to be terrible indeed for me not to agree to it." She gave a nervous laugh.

Charles interrupted. "Perhaps before you launch into this matter, Miss Tremeer would like a cup of coffee, or a glass of wine, Gabe? I'm sure I could do with a brandy."

Gabriel wasn't to be diverted. "Perhaps we will take a brandy together when Miss Tremeer agrees."

She looked from one to the other, her mind feeling sluggish. It had been a long night and there was much to be grateful for, but now she was beginning to wonder if she had celebrated too soon. She tried to temper her sense of caution. Gabriel had shown himself to be anything but a cad, and whatever it was he was about to ask her…well, she trusted him.

"Tell me what you want," she said, and saw the relief flare in his face.

Chapter Fifteen

He met her clear gray eyes and was startled to find them full of trust. In *him*. After her confession that she had thought him capable of using his position to force her into his bed, her belief made him almost cheerful.

He didn't consider himself a good man, not entirely, and there had been a moment, when Longley made those foul suggestions to him, that he had imagined what it would be like to have Vivienne Tremeer in his bed. He hadn't followed through with it, he would never have done that, but the thought had been there…So although he wasn't certain he deserved to be looked at as she was looking at him now, he felt as if he had just played a game of hazard and won.

When Gabriel didn't answer, Charles cleared his throat. They had discussed earlier what was about to be said, and he seemed to find it amusing that Gabriel was so tongue-tied around Vivienne Tremeer.

Gabriel ignored him. "Last night at the Farnsworths' ball," he began.

Vivienne sighed. "I hoped we could forget about the Farnsworths' ball."

Gabriel ignored that too. "I saw you there. I watched you before we spoke on the terrace. I remember thinking you looked so comfortable when I was so uncomfortable. You knew what to say and what to do, Miss Tremeer, as only someone who has been born to that world can. I envied you."

Her gaze sharpened. "I am used to it," she said. "I have grown up in 'that world' as you put it. Not London so much as the smaller polite circles in Cornwall, but they are in essence the same. And you did not seem *un*comfortable, Your Grace. Well, perhaps a little." Her smile wrapped around him, and he actually felt its warmth.

"I'm not thinking of myself." He plowed on. He really didn't need her smiles, the curve of those lush pink lips, or he would lose his thread completely.

"Then who are you thinking of?"

"My sisters." Memories of the dancing lesson filled his head, and his sisters' misbehavior, but also Olivia's worried expression and Edwina's wise little face. After Olivia's request for help, after seeing his grandmother's reliance on the hated Pascoe, Gabriel had made the decision to help his sisters navigate the rocks and shoals of polite society. And he had immediately thought of this woman. It had felt like a revelation to him. Yes, she was the very one! And with her debt to him, she would hardly say no.

"Your sisters?" she prompted.

"They have not had the advantage of learning those rules you speak of. They have been neglected and ignored, and now they've been thrown into a situation where they are expected to behave like the daughters…or the sisters, of a duke."

He sounded impassioned, and her eyes widened in

surprise and perhaps alarm. Gabriel resisted the urge to pull off his neckcloth and throw it in the corner in frustration. Why was it so surprising to her that he should feel the need to help them? Perhaps it was time to be utterly and completely honest.

"They need help, Miss Tremeer. *We* need help. Olivia has her debut soon, and she is feeling overwhelmed. We all are. My grandmother is expecting a great deal from all of us, but particularly Olivia, and at the moment she is a hoyden."

Vivienne almost smiled as she considered his words. "You need someone to teach her the ropes—the, eh, rules. Is that what you're saying?"

"Yes," he said, relieved. "And I thought you could be that person."

She stared back at him for so long his hopes began to fade. Was she choosing a polite, ladylike way to refuse him? Would she rather be in debt to him than take this way out? He had set his heart on her helping them, and if she refused him…He wasn't even entirely sure why her acceptance meant so much to him, only that she had seemed the perfect solution to his problems. And there was the debt. His hard business head had reminded him they could make a deal and, as she was beholden to him, he could ensure she did not speak of her part in it.

"Your Grace…"

"For God's sake call me Gabriel! Or Cadieux." Now he sounded impatient as well as frustrated. Keeping him dangling was worse than an outright refusal.

"By rights you should be Grantham now," she reminded him with a teasing note in her voice.

"Grantham then!" he said gruffly. "But please not Your Grace. It makes me feel like a fraud."

She opened her mouth as if to address that, and then decided to let it go. She gave a brief nod and to his relief returned to the subject. "Not that I don't want to be debt-free, but isn't there someone else you could ask? A relative, a friend? Someone more suitable?"

He wanted to grind his teeth. "Aren't you suitable? You seem utterly suited to me."

Vivienne shot him a look from beneath her dark lashes and chewed on her lip. This reticence seemed very unlike her. The Vivienne he knew had always been quick to say what she thought without fear or favor, even if she was wrong.

Longley's sneering voice crept into his head. There had been a scandal, something that the vile man seemed to believe brought Vivienne into his reach. And Vivienne herself had mentioned that her situation with her aunt was tenuous because of that scandal. Did that mean she really was unsuitable for the role he had hoped to persuade her to play?

He leaned closer, dropping his voice so that Charles couldn't hear. "Tell me what's wrong. I'm tired of this dillydallying. If there is a reason you think you cannot agree to what I ask, then tell me so directly, and we will deal with it."

She made a sound that was half laugh and half sigh. "You are very forthright, Your…Grantham. Very well, I will tell you why I am reluctant to agree, and then you can decide whether or not you can 'deal' with it."

He waited, watching her face and the emotions flitting over it. He did not touch her but he wanted to. Run his finger over the smooth skin of her cheek, brush his thumb over her soft lips, breathe in the warm floral scent of her hair. Something about her drew him. Since their first meeting, he had found himself thinking about her far more often than seemed sensible. But this was not the time to let his thoughts drift from the point. Again he reminded himself that there was a reason she had believed the worst of him, and he had a hollow feeling that he was about to hear it.

"I told you that my brother and I came to London to find shelter with my aunt. My stepfather is an unpleasant man, an inveterate gambler and liar, and he has wasted my father's fortune and would have sold off his estate too if it wasn't left to Will."

"There are many men like that in the world," Gabriel said, trying to hide his impatience. "My father for instance. Go on, tell me."

She half smiled. "You are very high-handed," she murmured, but proceeded to do as he asked. Her voice was steady, but he could tell it was an effort to dredge up her past to him, who was near enough to a stranger. "There was a scandal involving me and a young man from the village. The son of a farmer."

Gabriel tried not to be disappointed. Who was he to judge her after the life he had led? She would not be the first to be taken in by a smooth tongue and a handsome face. All the same, the thought of her and another man… He had to work hard to mask his emotions. He must have succeeded well enough because after a brief examination of his face, she continued.

"I will not tell you my whole sorry tale, but I made a mistake and my stepfather sought to take advantage of it by forcing me into marriage. I have a…a dowry, and he thought to take that from me as soon as the ceremony took place. My brother and I fled to London, to my aunt. She took us in and hoped to avert the scandal, but unfortunately word had already spread. Perhaps she thought that people would forget, but it has been over a year now and it is still not long enough. A reputation once lost is lost forever, or…something like that."

Now she met his gaze directly, and he saw the depth of her pain. "So you can see, Grantham, that although I would very much like to help you and your sisters, and clear our debt completely, I am not the right person. You are already dealing with a scandal of your own, and associating with a woman with a blemished reputation would only make things worse."

His first thought when she finished was to ask her the name of the creature—because that was how he thought of this boy. Had she been in love, or had he gulled her into thinking he loved her? Perhaps he pressed her, wearing her down, until she agreed to ruin herself for him. For that was what she meant, wasn't it? This boy had ruined her, and despite the efforts of her aunt, the scandal had not gone away.

No wonder she had not trusted him.

The telling of her tale had been difficult for her, and she had lost some of her color. "You are brave," he said. "Thank you for explaining to me. I'd like to ask you more, but that would be ungentlemanly of me, and I am doing my best to at least pretend to be a gentleman."

"Thank you," she murmured, relieved.

"Miss Tremeer, as unfortunate as your circumstances are, I can't help but think they make you even more qualified to help my sisters. Who better than you to understand the pitfalls Olivia faces? Gossip, rumor, walking a line that would allow her to please her grandmother and pass muster with the gatekeepers of society. These are all tasks you have mastered."

Surprise sparked in her eyes, mixed with hope.

Encouraged, he went on, musing to himself as much as Vivienne. "Pascoe, my sisters' governess, is not the person to help boost their confidence. She is a bully and is more likely to make matters worse. I saw the way she dealt with Edwina at my father's funeral."

Vivienne eyed his darkening expression with approval.

"My grandmother places too much trust in Pascoe. She is old, and her skills lie more in arranging social events and seeing that those people who matter are present. I am sure she cares for her granddaughters, loves them even, but her capacity to deal with six young ladies is limited. She can smooth their way into society, but they need to be ready to take that first step without stumbling."

He met Vivienne's gaze again. She seemed perfect for the task. An accomplished lady, whose care for her brother showed warmth and generosity. Olivia needed someone to befriend her, someone nearer her own age, someone she would listen to, and the other girls needed a role model, someone who could encourage them to behave less like wild animals. Gabriel was aware that in that situation he was hopelessly out of his depth, and besides, there was too much family nonsense simmering between them. Yes, Vivienne was perfect, and he had neither the time nor the inclination to find another woman when the one before him now was eminently suited to the job. Even her "tarnished reputation" was a bonus in his eyes when it came to guiding Olivia through those hazardous shallows and into safe waters.

"We can make it work," he said abruptly, his mind made up. "Agree to my request, and I will see that our agreement is kept private. My grandmother will be leaving for Sussex soon and will be away from some weeks. Once she is gone, I will have free rein at Ashton House."

Vivienne looked surprised, and a flush stained her cheeks. "I still don't—"

"Yes or no, Vivienne." He cut through her protests, impatient now to get on with things.

She still seemed inclined to protest—a foolishly heroic gesture that would gain her nothing—but as she searched his gaze, something in her changed. Her chin lifted with a determined air, and she stared back at him with resolve. Ah, that was better.

"Yes," she said. "Then it is yes."

He felt relief so profound he wanted to shout. Instead he gave her a curt nod. *Thank God.* Now he could set matters in train for Olivia and the others.

Behind him Charles cleared his throat. "Haven't you forgotten something?" Charles appeared to have been unapologetically eavesdropping. There was a smirk on his lips.

Gabriel stared at him. "Forgotten what?"

"The boy," his friend reminded him, with a nod toward Will, still slumped, dozing, in his chair by the fireplace. "We need to discuss him."

Vivienne's eyes had been darting between them, a wrinkle in her normally smooth brow. "I thought you said if I agreed, you would forgive Will's debt?"

She sounded anxious, and Gabriel gave his friend a warning glare. He didn't want her backing out now.

Suddenly, Will, who was awake after all, lifted his head blearily. "If you change your mind, I'll have to ask my aunt for help to pay off the debt, and she'll send me back to Cornwall." He swallowed. "For the best perhaps. I'll be out of your hair then, Viv."

"Will," she began to protest, but Gabriel interrupted.

"Listen to what we have to say before you start feeling sorry for yourself."

The two Tremeer siblings gave him their attention, neither of them looking particularly pleased. Charles chuckled. "I suggest you hear him out," he said. "He may be bossy but he has a good heart."

Gabriel shot Charles an irritated look. "You're not helping," he said. Then, before anyone else could interrupt: "Because I am currently busy being *a duke*, Charles is left to run the club on his own. He needs help, someone he can train up, someone who knows enough about the place and what we do here to enable them to be a help and not a hinderance. We think that person might be Sir William."

Abruptly Will straightened, almost falling out of his chair. "Help run Cadieux's?" he squeaked. "Me? I thought you said I was detrimental to the reputation of your club!"

Charles shrugged and Gabriel sighed. "Yes, at the time you were, but you're young. You're still able to learn," Gabriel said. "Could you turn into one of those thoughtless young gentlemen whose only pleasure is losing money on the fall of the card? That's a possibility, but we're giving you the chance to stand on the other side of the table and see what we see. And there would be no gambling allowed on your part, that needs to be understood. It will open your eyes to what some of your peers are up to. We'll expect you to learn and work hard, and if your being here doesn't suit either of us, then we'll soon tell you."

"I've observed you play," Charles added. "You know the games, even if you lose more often than you win. You have a knack for remembering the rules, and you have a head for numbers. In that way you remind me of the duke here. I think you could be perfect for my apprentice, if you are willing to do as Gabe says."

Will turned to his sister. "I…Viv, what do you think? Aunt Jane will have kittens if she finds out."

Vivienne tried not to laugh. "Probably." Then her amusement left her. "I wonder, though, whether the trustees will decide this is a sign of profligacy. Could Sutherland use it to overturn the will?"

"As your brother's employer I will answer any questions the trustees may have," Gabriel said quickly. "I am offering him a responsible position, and although this is a gambling house, there will be no gambling on his part."

"If Cadieux's is good enough for a duke, it should be good enough for anyone," Charles said with a wink. "Besides, our reputation as respectable employers is known to everyone."

Vivienne thought a moment before turning back to her brother. "What do you want to do, Will?"

His eyes shone. "I want to say yes," he declared. "It would be something to do, wouldn't it? And a way of repaying my debts too. I know the duke has set them aside and I am grateful, really, but I'm beginning to think I won't feel comfortable if I don't repay them properly." He shrugged his shoulders as if his skin prickled at the thought.

Charles chuckled. "Well said," he declared.

Will flushed and shifted uncomfortably, not seeming to know how to respond to the compliment.

Gabriel had had enough discussion. "Then that settles that. What of you, Miss Tremeer? You haven't changed your mind? Your brother employed here won't put your own position in jeopardy?"

He could see her mind working. "No more than usual," she said with a wry smile. "But remember, you have been warned, Grantham. If I bring trouble down upon your head, then it will be your own fault."

He had been warned, and he had taken account of her reputation. On balance the risk was worth it. With Vivienne on his side, some of the burden of being a duke and brother of six sisters would be lifted from him. The truth was her agreeing to help him made him feel lighter already.

"My grandmother will return for Olivia's debut on the ninth of May. That gives us seven weeks. How much time will you need, do you think?" he asked in a practical voice.

"To turn them into exemplary young ladies?" She was laughing at him, he could see it in her eyes, although her expression was sober. "I don't think we have enough time for perfection. But I expect I will be able to help them at least pretend to be well-brought-up young ladies, and negotiate the worst traps before Olivia enters the ton."

"Then we have a deal." And this time when she smiled, Gabriel smiled back.

Chapter Sixteen

Are you really sure this is what you want, Will?"

Vivienne tried to read her brother's expression. She could see uncertainty and doubt, but at the same time there was a glow in his eyes, as if he could visualize a future that hadn't been available to him before. Boredom and apathy had led him into his current trouble, and now he would have something to do. But a gambling house! Vivienne shuddered at the thought of her aunt finding out—and the trustees of the will, would they really accept Gabriel's assurances? Surely there could be no objection? She rather thought that if there was then Gabriel would "deal with it."

"I'd like to try," Will said with sudden decision. He glanced rather shyly at Charles and Gabriel, and his voice faltered. He looked very young. "That is, if you really mean it."

"Then stay a moment while we discuss your duties," Charles told him kindly, a warmth in his blue eyes that Vivienne thought boded well. "You might even make a start tonight, if your sister is agreeable."

"Germaine wanted me to meet him at White's," Will

remembered with a frown. He found three pairs of eyes fixed on him and shuffled uneasily. "That is...I don't have to."

"You definitely don't have to," Gabriel said firmly. "He may be your friend, but he is exactly the wrong sort of friend for you. Wealthy and careless with his money, reliant upon his father to bail him out of trouble. He will stroll through life without really achieving anything, while you have the chance to strike out on your own."

Will began to protest.

Vivienne stepped in. "I know you care for him, Will, but it will not hurt to distance yourself." She watched as her brother struggled with his decision, hoping he made the right one.

"I want to stay here tonight," he said at last. "Please, Viv," he added, as if worried she might refuse and drag him from the premises and fling him into Germaine's arms.

"Of course you can." She squeezed his shoulder. "I'm proud of you," she added, close to his ear.

He gave her a grin she had almost forgotten. It was the grin he used to give her before they came to London, and she missed that closeness between them. Since they came to Aunt Jane's, she had become the person in charge of him rather than his sister. Now her heart felt lighter, as if, thanks to Gabriel, that millstone had been lifted from her.

With another squeeze of his shoulder, she turned to the door. Behind her, Gabriel and Charles spoke in soft voices, but as she stepped out onto the landing, she heard Gabriel's footfalls behind her.

She must get used to calling him Grantham, especially if she was going to be seeing more of him. But she knew that in her secret heart he would always be Gabriel.

"I'll walk you to your coach," he said as she started down the stairs.

Vivienne almost stopped. When she had asked Jem to bring her to Cadieux's, she hadn't imagined riding pillion behind her groom might come back to bite her. "No need. I'm sure you are busy," she said, hoping he wouldn't follow her any farther. The noise from the gaming rooms was muted, broken by the occasional shout of anger, or triumph.

"This is not a safe area for a lady" was his gruff response. "I will see you to your coach."

He wasn't going to let her go. He was too stubborn, and he cared about her safety. The thought was warming, as if he had put his arms around her, but she'd prefer he didn't discover her unconventional behavior. When they reached the bottom of the stairs, Vivienne took a breath and turned to face him.

"What is it?" he said, searching her expression. "Vivienne?"

Did he know he had called her by her name? She wondered if it was as natural to him as it was for her to call him Gabriel, before she pushed aside the distraction and told him the truth.

"I didn't come by coach. My uncle and aunt are out, and I could not wait until they returned. Your message sounded urgent."

His brows came down in a frown over his dark eyes. "Then how did you get here?" He paused. "A hackney?"

He didn't sound happy at the idea. Would he revise his opinion of her as a person suitable to teach his sisters the rules of polite society? She reminded herself that a man like Gabriel Cadieux could hardly be shocked by such a little thing. Could he? Well, she would have something to say to him if he were! All the same, it was best to tell him the truth—there had been enough misunderstandings between them.

"Not exactly, Grantham."

He wasn't budging, dark eyes still fixed on her face, waiting for her explanation. Even though he looked more approachable in his old clothes—not the fashionable duke—her heart still gave a nervous little drum tattoo under his scrutiny.

"Jem, our groom, brought me." He opened his mouth to speak, but she hurried on. "I've known him since I was a child at Tremeer, he was our groom there too. And I trust him. He is one of the few people in this world I do trust."

His frown didn't go away, but she told herself she wasn't going to make excuses for conduct that was really none of his business. She turned and walked toward the back of the club, into the kitchen, and refused to feel relieved when he followed.

Several servants noticed him and quickly began to chop things or wash plates.

"Next time let me know you are coming, and I will send my coach," he said from behind her.

"Really? The ducal coach?" Vivienne glanced over her shoulder and tried not to smile. "Would that be wise, Grantham? If you want to keep this a secret, then you will have to restrain your gentlemanly urges."

"I am perfectly able to restrain myself," he said, but she heard the amusement in his voice. Perhaps it would be all right after all and he wouldn't change his mind. Because if he did that, they would be right back where they started.

"You said the dowager duchess will be out of town?"

"Yes, so you have no need to worry about meeting up with her. The girls will be staying with me in London. I only have to find a way to deal with Pascoe, and the coast will be clear."

"The governess?" She thought they sounded like conspirators—Napoleonic spies—and hid another smile.

"Yes. The bully. My sisters hate her."

"Oh. Sounds like a governess I had when I was in Cornwall. Before my mother dismissed her."

"Why did she dismiss her?"

"It was either that or pay her, and we had no money."

As soon as she said it, she felt her cheeks burn. She should be long past feeling ashamed when it came to life at Tremeer, but telling Gabriel felt different. What must he think of such a ramshackle admission?

Jem was waiting outside. Slouched against the wall, he looked half-asleep, but as soon as he heard them approach, he straightened up. His gaze went to Gabriel, and a scowl deepened the lines on his craggy face as he stepped into the light spilling from the door. Vivienne already knew what was coming.

"Who be this then, Miss Vivienne?" Jem demanded, his voice suddenly far more Cornish than usual. It was the voice he used whenever he sprang to her defense. She might be grown up now, but to Jem she would always be a child.

"Jem," she said firmly, trying to convey with her eyes and expression that he should not say anything insulting. "This is the Duke of Grantham."

"Oh, is it!" Jem declared with a sneer. "Methinks this duke has been Gabriel Cadieux up until now, and the owner of this hell."

Vivienne wished he would be quiet. She knew it was

worry for her that was making him so mouthy, but she would rather not insult the man who had just asked for her help and was willing to take Will on.

But Gabriel didn't seem bothered. "I am," he agreed. "And I would rather be the owner of this hell and nothing more, but it seems I have no choice but to be a duke. Don't let that concern you though, Jem. Treat me as you would if I was still Cadieux."

"Aye, I will," Jem said belligerently, leaning forward so that his face was in Gabriel's. The two men were of a similar height, but Jem was thicker in the shoulders and body.

"Jem, that's enough," Vivienne said sharply. "We should go now."

That was when Gabriel saw the horse. He looked up and down the street, and then back to the lone animal, and comprehension filled his face. "No," he said, sounding as stubborn as Jem was belligerent. "You will wait until I arrange a hackney, Miss Tremeer."

"Certainly not," she said, with a flush in her cheeks. "I have ridden pillion behind Jem since I was old enough to ride at all. We will be perfectly safe, and it is best if we don't wait. My uncle and aunt might be home now. We can avoid them discovering we were out."

"Aye," Jem agreed, with feeling.

When Gabriel said no more, merely tightening his lips, Jem made his hands into a step for Vivienne. He threw her up onto the saddle with more enthusiasm than usual, and then swung himself up in front of her. The jolt of landing caused her hair to tumble down and over her eyes, and hastily she tucked it back, before straightening her skirts to a more respectable length. She faced Gabriel, expecting him to be glowering up at her.

He wasn't. Instead there was a curve to his mouth and a gleam in his dark eyes, as if he found her very amusing.

Vivienne looked away. She knew her cheeks were already flushed, but the look in his eyes made them feel even hotter. She must appear a proper romp. Once again she wondered if he would change his mind about introducing her to his sisters.

But it seemed not.

"I will arrange a meeting between you and my sisters soon," he said. "You won't change your mind, will you? I know you have agreed, but they can be rather overwhelming. There are six of them." He said it as if he were introducing her to a pack of hounds from hell.

"Are you trying to frighten me?" she said, and it was only then that she heard the teasing note in her voice. Oh God, was she flirting with him now? Her cheeks grew even hotter. "We shall deal very well," she hastened to add in a cool, polite voice.

His smile grew bigger. "I know you will." A slight bow of his head. "Goodbye, Miss Tremeer."

"Goodbye, Gabriel."

His dark eyes lit up.

It was only when Jem huffed as they turned away that she realized she had called him Gabriel instead of Grantham.

"I hope you know what you're doing, maid," the groom muttered. "Playing with fire you are, with that one."

"Why do you say that?" she asked, more curious than annoyed. "Does he have a reputation with the ladies?"

It hadn't occurred to her before, but it was quite likely Gabriel was just as much of a womanizer as Sutherland and his cronies. Though she didn't think so. There was a core of decency running through him, and his care for his sisters…well, she wouldn't admit it aloud, but seeing it, hearing it, made her almost…envious. No one in her life had ever looked after her quite like that.

"No reputation that I know of," Jem answered, glancing at her over his shoulder. His gaze slid by her, taking in the grimy houses and narrow alleys. They were passing through the shadowy parts of London, and although the streets were quiet, they were never deserted. "Not that he's a eunuch, maid, but I've heard o' nothing dastardly attached to his name."

"Did you check up on him, Jem?"

He grunted.

Well, of course he had. Vivienne smiled. There was someone who was looking out for her after all.

"What is it about then? You and Cadieux?" he growled.

Vivienne didn't hesitate in telling him about the deal she had made. If she was going to be making clandestine visits to Gabriel's house, then Jem would have to know about it so that he could help her. When she had finished, he shook his head but didn't scold her as she'd half expected.

They were riding through the better streets now, and nearly home. When Jem drew to a halt in the mews, they noticed that the coach had returned. Vivienne wasn't really worried that anyone would hear her creeping into the house. After their evening of being wined and dined, her aunt and uncle would be dead to the world and snoring.

Jem stood at the open door with her but stopped her as she was about to slip inside and make her way to bed.

"You and the duke, eh?" he said, and there was a twinkle in his eyes. "Who'd have thought?"

"It isn't like that. If I help him out, we can be rid of Will's debt. We will finally be free of it." She paused, it occurring to her that if they really were free of that constant worry, then she would be at rather a loose end. And then she reminded herself that she had six reasons to keep busy in the coming weeks. "We're just…well, I suppose in a way we're friends in adversity. We can't be more. You know that, Jem."

The groom's face sobered. "Don't let Sutherland find out. He'd be here in a flash, trying to twist money out of him."

Vivienne shuddered. "I wouldn't let him within a hundred miles of Gabriel."

Jem looked surprised at her vehemence, and then he nodded. "Good night, Miss Vivienne."

"Good night, Jem. And thank you."

When she reached her bedchamber, there was a note slipped under the door. Annette must have thought her sleeping, at least she hoped so. She picked it up, reading it by the candlelight.

"Oh!" Vivienne gave a relieved laugh, and then covered her mouth in case anyone heard. It seemed that luck was very much on her side. Ivo had invited Annette and her family to his country house for a fortnight. There were to be picnics and parties and other arrangements to entertain the large number of guests.

We are all invited, Annette wrote. *Please do say you'll come!*

No doubt the Monteiths would be hoping for a proposal while they were there. Vivienne would make excuses, assuming her aunt would want her to come, which was doubtful, leaving her free to visit Gabriel and his sisters and teach them how to make their way through the traps and snares of society. Being a lady, she knew, meant being aware of what might trip one up and avoiding it. She was going to enjoy herself, because she had a feeling the next few weeks were going to be very enjoyable indeed.

Chapter Seventeen

Gabriel stood while Francis eased him into his jacket, the tight fit making it impossible to dress on one's own. His valet circled him and gave a satisfied nod. "You look very well, Your Grace. And the inexpressibles? Are you satisfied with them?"

Gabriel had sworn never to wear the damn things, they were so tight and left little to the imagination, but Francis had convinced him to try them at least.

"You have the perfect figure for them," he'd insisted. "And with no need for padding."

"Padding?" Gabriel had arched his brow.

"Some gentlemen require it." Francis had a twinkle in his eye.

"Satisfied? They do look rather, eh, impressive," Gabriel admitted, and wondered whether he was becoming vain. But he reminded himself he had a position to uphold, a role to play, and if wearing the damned inexpressibles was part of it, then he would do as he must. At the same time he was rather pleased with the man reflected back at him from the looking glass. He certainly looked like a fashionable duke about town. He found himself wondering if Vivienne Tremeer would think so when she arrived this morning. Once the dowager duchess removed to Sussex, Gabriel had sent a message to Vivienne asking if she was available to begin fulfilling her part of their bargain. She had responded with the news that her aunt was away for a fortnight, and she would be more than happy to spend that time with the girls.

There had been a frisson of excitement running through him ever since he had received her news, as if he'd been living through a long, cold winter and his days were about to become brighter.

"And Madame Annabelle, the modiste?" his valet said, giving a final brush to the shoulders of Gabriel's jacket. "Is she satisfactory?"

Francis had recommended Madame Annabelle when one morning at breakfast Olivia had announced she had nothing to wear, before giving Gabriel's fashionable outfit an envious look.

"You are always so well turned out," she'd added wistfully.

Gabriel had felt a flush of pleasure that she should think so, but it hadn't lasted long. Not when all of his sisters were staring at him. His inexperienced gaze had slid over them, and for the first time he realized that they looked quite…dowdy. Yes, they were neat and clean when he knew that had not always been the case, but he could also see that the hem on Edwina's dress was too high, which obviously meant she had grown several inches since her dress was made. Olivia had a threadbare patch on her shoulder, and Roberta had a tear in the ankle of her stocking that she kept picking at and making worse.

"Doesn't Pascoe—" he had begun, but was drowned out when the girls responded with shouts of derision.

"As long as we sit up straight and attend to our lessons, Pascoe doesn't care if we are woefully out of date!" Olivia declared.

"Your grandmother..."

Again he had been howled down. "She wears black. And she hasn't changed her style since last century." Roberta this time, while even peacemaking Justina shook her head in dismay.

"Your mother?" he tried. "Isn't it a mother's job to see her daughters dressed properly?" He wasn't sure why he said it, when obviously Lady Felicia had long ago given up her motherly duties.

"She refuses to leave her bed. Still!" had said Olivia.

"I'll see what I can do," Gabriel had replied, but none of them had appeared to think much of that answer. Gabriel had left the room lacking even more confidence in his abilities than before when it came to his sisters. *This* was why he needed Vivienne's help. Something needed to be done, and he wasn't the man to do it. He knew nothing of ladies' fashion, he was only just beginning to understand gentlemen's. As he had climbed the stairs, it occurred to him that if anyone could help, then it was his valet.

As he'd hoped, Francis had considered his request and then put forward the name of a dressmaker he was acquainted with. "She is just starting out, so she will have room on her books, but I assure you she is excellent. And young. Your sisters will feel more comfortable with her than they would with some of the older, more established modistes."

Every day Gabriel thanked God that he had made the decision to hire Francis rather than the man who had been his grandmother's suggestion. Even when Gabriel was aware that Francis was stealthily smoothing over his rough edges, he was happy not to put up too much of a fight. For instance, who would have thought when this started that he'd be wearing these damned inexpressibles?

Gabriel brought his mind back to the present and became aware he hadn't answered Francis's question about the dressmaker.

"I have made an appointment with Madame Annabelle, thank you, Francis. Miss Tremeer will accompany my sisters."

When he had given his sisters the news, Edwina had suggested Gabriel come with them. Trying not to shudder, he'd made some excuse, but from the glances the girls had exchanged, he didn't think he'd been believed.

"Who will go with us then?" Olivia had said. "Pascoe?"

Howls of dismay.

"No, not Pascoe. Didn't I tell you? Pascoe is setting off to visit her family in Scotland tomorrow."

After dropping several broad hints, which she ignored, and in fact caused her to redouble her efforts to make his sisters' lives miserable, Gabriel had been reduced to paying the governess a bonus. She was to remain in Scotland indefinitely. Pascoe's smirk seemed to suggest that had been her plan all along.

"Scotland? Then…?" They looked at each other, wide-eyed.

"I have arranged for Miss Tremeer to accompany you," Gabriel had said in a voice that brooked no argument, or so he hoped. All the same he was mentally crossing his fingers. "She is a young lady who is familiar with the rules of society and has agreed to, eh, help you. She will be arriving tomorrow and staying for the day, and each day after that, until…" Until his grandmother returned, but he couldn't say that. "Until she is happy that you can at least play the part of young ladies."

More glances had been exchanged between the sisters. "Will Miss Tremeer be like Pascoe?" Edwina's voice wobbled.

"Most definitely not," Gabriel reassured her. "She will visit during the day and return home at night. Like a…a friend or a guest."

This time they had seemed intrigued rather than dismayed, but before they could ask any more questions, Gabriel had left the room.

"Very good, Your Grace," Francis replied now, but he was smiling. "I am always glad to be of help." Gabriel avoided his gaze, wondering if his face betrayed him. It was ridiculous to be so affected by the thought of seeing more of Vivienne when their arrangement was purely business.

Unfortunately, a moment later he was informed that his steward had chosen this day to come up from Grantham to enable Gabriel to catch up on estate matters. He thought about sending the man away again, but it would only put off the inevitable. Grudgingly he headed down to his office, condemning himself to working, while promising himself that after this morning, his time would be his own.

The man's bookkeeping hadn't improved, in fact it was worse. And he seemed to think himself above Gabriel, treating his questions with contempt, until Gabriel had finally had enough and shown him the door. Although he wasn't looking forward to what his grandmother would say when she heard, he refused to see the estate diddled or mismanaged, or himself insulted, because of some ridiculous sense of outdated loyalty to family retainers.

Once he'd dealt with the steward, he had no more

urgent appointments or engagements for the next two weeks, and he knew the club was in safe hands with Charles. Yes, he would have to start the tedious task of looking for another steward, or even consider taking on the role himself, but for now Gabriel was free. And he was going to fulfill his wish of spending more time with her. *Them*, he reminded himself.

As he descended the stairs, the afternoon stretched out pleasantly before him. His sisters and Vivienne awaited him, and he couldn't pretend there wasn't a definite spring in his step. At the bottom of the stairs, he turned and headed toward the door to the garden, telling himself his sense of urgency was simply because he was looking forward to seeing what progress she had made with his sisters. Nothing more than that.

As soon as he appeared, Edwina came barreling toward him as if he was her favorite person in all of the world. He caught her and lifted her high into the air, her little booted feet kicking, and she gave one of her loud shrieks. Her face was alight with joy, and the same emotion filled him to bursting. It was because of Edwina, and seeing her misery the day of his father's funeral, that he had taken on the others. Not that he would ever tell them that.

As he lowered her carefully back onto the lawn, he caught sight of Vivienne.

She was smiling at the scene before her, face flushed, her eyes bright, and once more that feeling washed over him. Joy, but now with a dash of anticipation and a sprinkle of longing. Their eyes held and he wanted to say how much he appreciated her being here, that he wished he could spend more time with her, that her being here made him happy.

But he had waited too long and she turned away, tucking a loose strand of hair behind her ear, her green muslin skirt belling out around her ankles. It was plain, apart from the pink bow tied under her bosom, and the matching pink ribbon on her long tight sleeves.

She was beautiful and elegant, but Gabriel felt doubt crowd in. He couldn't tell her how he was feeling. He wasn't even sure exactly what he *was* feeling.

Vivienne was pointing toward the riot of flowers in the perennial border while she spoke to the older girls. Gabriel could see there was a table and chairs set up nearby. As he made his way over to them, he heard Roberta say rebelliously, "I think that is the worst idea."

As always Justina was quick to step in and smooth matters over. "Hush, Robbie! Just because you would rather be riding a horse. Miss Tremeer, I would very much like to learn how to paint with watercolors," she added stoutly.

Roberta gave a rude snort, but Vivienne just smiled at the girls. "It was but a suggestion," she said, "because young ladies must have accomplishments. It is de rigueur. You will be quizzed about yours by the old biddies, you can be sure." And then, giving Gabriel an uncomfortable glance, said, "Excuse me, I mean the senior ladies of the ton. They place great stock on one's accomplishments, and although I wish it were otherwise, you must meet their expectations."

"Vivienne wants us to learn to draw and paint," Olivia shared with Gabriel. "But of course Roberta doesn't want to."

"Is there some other accomplishment Roberta can master?" he said.

Roberta seemed to consider his question seriously

before answering, "I'll wager I could win the next curricle race to Brighton."

Vivienne bit her lip but Gabriel could see by the glow in her gray eyes that she was enjoying the exchange. "I'm sorry," she said. "I don't think the patronesses at Almack's will be impressed by that, Roberta."

"If I were a man, I would be able to do as I pleased," Roberta muttered. "It isn't fair."

But Olivia, full of her own concerns, spoke over her. "Almack's?" she wailed. "Grandmama insists I should be seen there and I dread it."

Vivienne touched her arm. "You needn't. It is an honor to be allowed entry, although I have heard the suppers are rather unappealing."

The girls stared at her curiously. "You've 'heard'?" Olivia repeated. "Don't you know?"

"Well, no." Vivienne flushed. "Despite my aunt's best efforts, I have never danced at Almack's."

"Never?" Even Justina was amazed by this. "But you are lovely and—and so refined, Miss Tremeer!"

Vivienne didn't seem to know whether to be amused or flattered that they thought so highly of her. She colored and shot a glance at Gabriel.

"But why have you not been there?" Edwina demanded in her usual direct manner.

Vivienne sent him a silent plea for help, and Gabriel stepped in. "I am sure I will not be allowed in there either," he said stoutly.

"I'm sure you will," Olivia retorted with a sullen curl to her lip. "Roberta is right. Gentlemen are given a great deal more leeway than ladies. I think that is so unfair. Don't you agree, Miss Tremeer?"

He suspected Vivienne probably did think it unfair

but was trying to be the sort of person he wanted her to be while she guided his sisters along the prickly paths of London society.

"Miss Tremeer says she is not a proper person." Edwina spoke airily. She had been bent over a flower observing a bee and now she glanced up, her curly mop of hair waving all about her round face, and smiled. "But I think she is the most perfect person I know."

Vivienne caught her breath. Gabriel opened his mouth to say the words on the tip of his tongue before he stopped himself. *So do I.*

"Proper doesn't mean she isn't nice," Roberta said impatiently. "It means she isn't respectable."

That caused an uncomfortable silence. Vivienne was even more flushed than before, and after one worried glance at Gabriel, she again focused her gaze on the girls rather than him. Her voice was firm.

"Nevertheless, I am the daughter of a baronet and that makes me qualified to tell you, Roberta, that it is unacceptable for a single lady to drive a curricle on her own, or take part in a wager. Or indeed to gallop through Hyde Park!"

Roberta laughed, as Gabriel suspected Vivienne had meant her to.

"What else, what else do you know!" Edwina cried.

"Oh, let me see…When Olivia attends her coming-out ball, she will not be able to stand up for more than two dances with the same partner. Unless it is her brother."

"Then I will dance every dance with you, Gabriel," Olivia announced.

"I know that a lady cannot call upon those above her in rank unless they have called first and left her a card," Vivienne went on. "That a lady should never drive down a London street where a gentleman's club is situated. And that she should ignore servants at mealtimes."

The girls stared at her in amazement. "There, Justina," Olivia said, "I told you not to thank the servant who served us at dinner. No wonder she gave you that look."

"Does Grandmama know you're not a proper person?" Georgia said, evidently stuck on that one point. "I don't think she'd want us to spend time in your company if she knew that."

They began to argue among themselves. Gabriel knew they were on shaky ground here, but he refused to have any aspersions cast at Vivienne.

"Imagine your grandmother's expression when she returns to London and sees your ladylike demeanor. Let's keep this a secret until then so that we can surprise her."

The girls exchanged glances, and he was glad they understood his meaning without him having to spell it out. He thought he'd made himself clear on the matter a week ago, but perhaps it was useful to repeat the need for secrecy.

"I won't breathe a word," Edwina promised.

Gabriel wondered whether him telling them not to be honest with their grandmother was a responsible thing to do. But to hell with it. They were enjoying Vivienne's company, and she was doing a great deal of good.

"Pascoe tried to teach us table manners," Olivia shared. "She struck our fingers with a cane if we picked up the wrong utensil."

He froze in horror. "Good God, I should have sent her to gaol rather than Scotland!"

There was startled laughter at that, before Vivienne shooed them once more in the direction of the paints. "Now, ladies, I want you to attempt a garden scene. It need not be a masterpiece, but you should try your best. Then, when you are asked, you can say quite truthfully that you paint 'a little.'"

Roberta muttered rebelliously, but all six of them flopped down at the table and proceeded to paint. Gabriel's mouth twitched as he observed them. They looked as if they were being sent to the guillotine. Vivienne's maid joined them, watching as if she had never seen the like. The girl looked as if she was too frightened to meet his eyes let alone speak, but he supposed her being there fulfilled the necessary proprieties.

"Who on earth is that?" he asked, with a nod in the girl's direction.

"Her name is Wen, and she's Jem's niece—you remember Jem the groom? He sent for her when I told him of our plans, and he has sworn her to silence. She is so excited to be here in London that she will never tell anyone, you can be sure."

His gaze slid over Vivienne's softly rounded cheek, the curve of her lips, lifted into a smile as she watched his sisters arguing over what color a particular spring flower was. She glanced at him to share the moment, and then her lashes swept down as she became aware of his stare.

If he didn't speak soon, she would leave him and join the girls, and he didn't want that.

"I hope this isn't—" he began at the same time as Vivienne said, "Your sisters are not at all as I expected."

"In what way?" he answered, surprised.

"They are very natural," she said.

"Could that be because they have not had the correct upbringing for this world we've all been thrown into?" He hesitated and then rushed on, "Are you sorry you agreed to take them on?"

"Oh no! I am enjoying their company very much. I hope you don't mind…I am rather frank with them."

"I want you to be frank, Miss Tremeer. I want us to be frank with each other. I have always preferred plain speaking, as you know."

She gave him a serious look. "Yes, I do know. And I am happy to visit if you are happy to have me. I have nothing much to keep me occupied at home, nothing that I enjoy anyway," she added with a wrinkle of her brow.

Gabriel considered what he could say about that, but he decided he didn't want to rehash old ground. He wanted to savor this moment together.

Perhaps Vivienne had come to the same decision, because when she next spoke, it was in a pleasant, conversational tone. It reminded him how good she was at this social chitchat. "Olivia tells me that she has never learned any of the accomplishments a lady should learn, and I wondered why. You said their upbringing was unconventional?"

"Their mother, Lady Felicia, didn't pay attention to them. The family wanted a male heir—that explains their names, if they haven't told you already—and each time a girl was born, their parents lost interest, hoping that they would have a boy next time. When Harry, my father, was ill, Lady Felicia ignored them completely and they were left to run wild on the estate until Harry died and my grandmother arrived to take them in hand."

"Oh. I think they enjoyed running wild." She bit her lip. "I can't blame them, really. But I'm trying to show them that not everything about their position in society is tedious. And they are genuinely trying hard to reform themselves. It just isn't the same, is it, as being free to be yourself?"

Gabriel thought a moment and then said glumly, "No, it isn't."

"You speak from the heart." Her smile was back, teasing him.

"I do."

"And yet you have learned to fit your own role so well." She gestured to his elegant clothing, her eyes seeming to linger on the shape of his legs in the tight pantaloons, before dropping to the mirrorlike shine of his boots. "You *look* like a duke."

He grinned. "Outwardly anyway. Underneath this fine outfit I am as wild and untamed as my sisters."

That seemed to unsettle her, and her eyes flew to his before she looked away and fiddled with her collar. He watched her, wondering what she was thinking, before she seemed to regain her equilibrium. "That's as may be, but you are a good brother. They are lucky to have you."

Why was she avoiding his gaze? Was it the thought of him being wild and untamed? The idea brought him a step closer. "At first they resented me, but I think we have come to an understanding. At least I hope so." He had had enough of the subject, so when she opened her mouth to continue it, he headed her off. "Will is doing well at the club. Charles says he is a quick learner. He seems to have the knack of smoothing over those trickier moments when gamers' tempers grow heated."

Vivienne's face shone with pleasure. "He is enjoying himself, and it is doing him so much good to have a reason to get up in the mornings. Until he came to London, he wasn't used to idle time, and I don't think it's good for him."

"I don't think it's good for anyone, but I see it all the time. A recipe for disaster."

"Yes." She looked at him knowingly. "I can't imagine you were ever a young gentleman with nothing to do."

He felt as if she could see right through him, and it was uncomfortable. He hid so much of himself from others that for her to understand him so easily made him feel as if he were stripped bare of all his fine clothes and stood before her just as he was. It…unnerved him.

"I was never a gentleman," he admitted.

"No?" Her eyes widened before her lashes swept down to hide whatever it was she felt. But there had certainly been something in those gray eyes, because he found he had forgotten whatever he was going to say next. His breath quickened and his heart beat faster as if he were coming down with a sickness.

She swallowed, and maybe his ailment was infectious, because she seemed to have trouble catching her breath too. He could see the pulse fluttering in the hollow of her throat, and before he considered the consequences, brushed his fingers lightly over the place. She gasped at his touch but did not move away. The warmth of her body, the now familiar floral scent of her hair, enticed him to take more liberties.

Gabriel leaned down to whisper in her ear. "We are like two peas in a pod, are we not, Miss Tremeer? Both of us playing our parts and hiding our true selves from the world. But I see you and I think you see me."

She turned to face him. "You do?" Her voice had a husky quality to it that made him bolder.

The idea came to him that he could easily kiss her. She was so close and her lips deliciously half-open, as if waiting for the press of his. What would she taste like? Sweet, he thought, and welcoming. Her breath gave a hitch as though she wanted that kiss too, and at the same time he gave a name to the symptoms they were both suffering. Desire. He desired Vivienne in a way he could not remember ever wanting anyone before, and she was responding.

He might even have done so, he was already moving to capture her lips, when there was a shout from Edwina as his youngest sister demanded attention. Gabriel came back to himself just in time.

And just as well, he told himself, as Vivienne looked away, flushed and flustered. Kissing a young woman in his garden was not acceptable behavior, but to do so in front of his sisters would show a lack of courtesy that was completely deplorable.

Chapter Eighteen

Vivienne moved away to a safe distance, but her skin prickled as if his presence behind her were another physical touch. She had been trying to maintain a calm and polite veneer, but Gabriel had burrowed his way beneath her public mask and threatened to overturn her.

Outwardly this wasn't the down-to-earth man who had spoken with her at the gaming club, putting his deal to her, winning her over with his intensity and his honesty. This was the Duke of Grantham, dressed in his fashionable clothes, dazzling in the spring sunlight as he flirted with her, as she tried to keep her eyes from his broad shoulders in that stylish jacket and his strong legs in those tight pantaloons. And he *was* flirting.

What on earth was wrong with her?

It wasn't as if she hadn't seen a good-looking man before. And yet something about Gabriel tipped her off balance, made her forget her usual caution, and despite knowing it was never going to go anywhere, that anything between the two of them was impossible even if he were interested, she couldn't help this foolish lift in her chest.

Was he attracted to her too? Did he feel this frisson between them whenever their eyes met? Did he dream about her as she dreamed about him? Because if he did then she was in a great deal of trouble.

Vivienne squirmed inside to admit it, but since they had come to their agreement, she had dreamed of him every night. And they were not the sort of dreams she could discuss with her mother or Annette. Naked dreams, mouth-to-mouth dreams, skin-to-skin dreams, leaving her heated and achy. The way in which he had stared at her lips just now, the barely there touch of his fingers, had reminded her of those dreams. Just like when they had argued on the terrace at the ball, she wanted him to kiss her, she wanted to kiss him, but this time it was Edwina who had interrupted them and not Charles.

She took a breath and told herself to forget about all of that. She was here to pay off Will's debt by helping Gabriel's sisters, offering them advice and support for their entry into society. Particularly Olivia. She had taken to the eldest girl immediately, understanding what lay behind her rebellious gaze and the watchfulness that hid a multitude of confidence and self-esteem issues. Olivia didn't want to be a duke's daughter, she didn't want all eyes upon her, she wanted to be able to do and say as she pleased. Unfortunately that would never happen, not now. The girl could not go back to those carefree days, so it was up to Vivienne to give her the assurance to take on her new role and step into her place in the ton.

As for Gabriel caring for his sisters…perhaps it had surprised her in the beginning. She knew he wanted to help them secure their futures, but at the same time she had expected some carelessness on his part, some hint of selfishness, because that was the way men were, wasn't it? Only he wasn't like that, and he impressed her over and over again. For a man who had been abandoned by his family and left in an orphanage and then had to make his own way in the world, Gabriel had taken on the responsibility of being a duke with flair and fortitude.

And he had so much faith in Vivienne. She felt humbled. He believed in her, and his belief made her all the more determined to excel at the role he had asked of her. And that certainly didn't include her making eyes at him and dreaming of him naked. She needed to put up a barrier between them to protect herself.

"Miss Tremeer?"

She jumped guiltily. After a moment of struggle to compose herself, she turned with a polite smile, hoping he hadn't noticed her skittishness.

Gabriel's dark eyes narrowed. He had noticed, and the corners of his generous mouth tugged up. That mouth… Vivienne swallowed and halted her thoughts before they could stray deeper into dangerous territory.

"You don't mind going with the girls to Madame Annabelle's next week?" he said.

She waved a hand as if she hadn't a care in the world. "Of course not. I look forward to it."

"We are taking up a great deal of your time, Vivienne," he said quietly, his voice soft and gravelly.

She felt it low in her belly, like an ache. This was wrong, so wrong, and once again she attempted to barricade her unruly emotions. "I haven't much to do," she assured him. "The servants run the house, and all they require is for me to appear for meals and to deal with any disputes that arise. My cousin has already sent me one letter, begging me to change my mind and set out for Ivo's country house posthaste."

Gabriel looked unsettled. "And will you?"

"No. My aunt wouldn't welcome me even if Annette would."

He breathed a sigh of relief. "Is it wrong of me to say I am glad you are staying?"

She laughed. "Not at all. I am glad too."

Once again she couldn't seem to look away, but neither could he. If they had been alone, she was not sure she would have been able to trust herself, but once again, it was Edwina who broke the moment, complaining about the lack of green paint. An argument broke out between the other girls as to who had used it all.

Gabriel shook his head in despair and strode forward, Vivienne trailing behind him. "I think there has been enough painting for today," he said, trying to sound stern but failing miserably.

"Can we practice our dancing?" Edwina wailed. "I want to dance."

"Mrs. Marks isn't here to play the piano," Gabriel responded.

"Miss Tremeer can play, can't you, Miss Tremeer?" Six pairs of eyes were fixed on her with a mixture of pleading and hope. Olivia's gaze slid from her brother to Vivienne with a shrewd look that made Vivienne all the more aware of the need to hide her attraction when it came to Gabriel.

"Miss Tremeer does not want to play," he said. Then, raising his eyebrow: "Perhaps that is not one of her many accomplishments."

"I can play," she said. "If you don't mind a few fumbles. I am afraid I have not kept up my practice."

"Very well," Gabriel bowed. "I will leave you to it."

But he was laughing when he said it, and sure enough

he was howled down. With the younger girls clinging to his hands, refusing to let him go, they made their way into the house.

He was so comfortable, as if he had found a place within this strange new world he had had to learn to inhabit, and Vivienne found that very attractive.

"We will take turns," Edwina said importantly when they reached the drawing room. "I will go first."

Roberta snorted but Justina sorted them into pairs with her usual gentle, practical manner. Vivienne made herself ready at the piano and began to play.

It turned out to be one of the most enjoyable afternoons she had ever experienced. Watching Gabriel dance with his sisters, listening to their bickering and laughter, even more aware of how much they had come to care for each other. The only thing she wished for was to have taken a turn about the room with him herself.

I must be sensible, I really must.

Eventually it was time to go home, with promises to return the following day and teach the girls how to curtsy.

"I know how to curtsy!" Edwina insisted, and gave a creditable performance.

"But there are different curtsies for different occasions," Vivienne said. "The more important the person, the deeper the curtsy. And there are different forms of address too. You must learn them all."

Olivia shuddered.

Gabriel took Vivienne's hand in farewell. "Thank you." It sounded heartfelt.

She tried not to glance back as she and Wen made their way to the front door. Jem was waiting outside.

"You're getting in deep, maid," he muttered, helping her and a silent Wen up. "This can't end well."

"I don't care," Vivienne said blithely. "I am enjoying myself. I am happy, Jem. For the first time in, oh, forever!"

He gave her a long, unsmiling look. "I reckon you are," he sighed. "And that's what worries me the most."

Chapter Nineteen

Over the following days, Gabriel felt his life change. Vivienne being there, taking on some of the burden of his sisters, lightened him but also filled him with a sort of elation that was new to him. The girls were happier too, and he had heard only good things from them whenever he asked about Vivienne. "She knows exactly what to say on every occasion! Even at a doll's tea party!" Edwina had given Vivienne her seal of approval. The others had giggled at that, but Gabriel did not laugh, his face serious as he said, "There is no one better than Miss Tremeer to guide your steps." That had caused another round of giggles, or in Olivia's case, a roll of her eyes. "You *would* think that," she'd said.

Something about his reply had amused them in a way that Gabriel completely failed to understand. Best, he had decided, not to try.

He tried to be present at most of Vivienne's "lessons," telling himself that he was also learning, but it wasn't always that. Well, if he was truthful to himself, it never was. She brought a new dimension to his life, a missing piece, and he suspected it was the same for his sisters.

They were getting to know each other better, and all because of Vivienne.

For instance, there was yesterday's luncheon, where she had given them a lesson in table manners. At times it had been frustrating and hilarious, but it had also been sweet and poignant as they shared their stories.

"I'm too hungry," Edwina had wailed. "How can I eat 'politely' when I'm so hungry?"

Gabriel had opened his mouth, then closed it again when Vivienne spoke.

"If you are invited to a luncheon at someone else's house, then I suggest you have something to eat before you go, because in my experience the meal will be delayed for some reason or other, or it will not be to your taste. So fill up first, and then you can pick at your food like a bird."

"Or go straight to the pudding," said Antonia, who did not say a great deal, but when she did, it was received with instant agreement.

"You'll get fat if all you eat is pudding." Georgia could be relied upon to put a damper on things, and as usual the others howled her down.

By now Gabriel was used to the squabbles at mealtimes, and once he might have been worried Vivienne would decide it was a lost cause and walk out. He knew her better now, and once again her patience impressed him.

"Well, that is why young ladies need to be busy," she said, raising her voice. "Dancing and walking, riding, and various other forms of sport."

"What sort of sport?"

"I believe archery is very popular."

"You mean with a bow and arrows?" Roberta's eyes gleamed. "We used to have archery contests at Grantham."

"Now"—Vivienne smiled at her charges—"let us have some polite conversation."

Wails greeted this, which made her bite her lip on a laugh. Her eyes met Gabriel's across the table and he shrugged his shoulders, mouthing the word *hopeless*. She shook her head, still smiling. She was wearing a simple blue gown today, her hair in a coiled arrangement on her crown, with a few dark curls framing her face. He found himself wondering what she would look like with her hair loose about her bare shoulders and how it would feel sliding through his fingers. Would it make a cave about them on his bed as she knelt over him as he kissed her? Worshipped the curves he had imagined beneath her clothing so many times? The image was so vivid he wasn't aware how long he had been staring until Vivienne turned away, color staining her cheeks.

"Come now," she said, regaining her composure, "you cannot sit in silence while you eat. Conversation is important, and once you learn the trick of it, it is not at all difficult."

"But grandmother scolds us when we talk at the table." Edwina again, indignant.

"You won't always be under your grandmother's eye," Vivienne reminded them. "Before too long you will be responsible for making your own way in the world, and it will be easier if you follow the rules."

Roberta spoke up. "Not if they try to make us eat something we don't want to."

"'Specially pig's cheek," Edwina added, screwing up her face at the very thought.

Vivienne sighed. "You are lucky you have a choice. I have had to eat things I'd rather not, and I'm sure your brother is the same." She gave Gabriel a look, widening her eyes, and he took the hint, launching into a tale of mealtimes at St. Ninian's.

"The broth was so thin I would have fought every boy there for a slice of pig's cheek."

Olivia reciprocated when he finished. "After our father died and our mother went to bed and stayed there, most of the servants left. We had to cook our own food. Luckily Justina remembered some recipes."

"Very simple ones," Justina said with a blush.

"Roberta made up horrible names for them." Georgia was disapproving.

"Blood and guts!" That was Edwina, of course.

"Toad's brains." Antonia's blue eyes sparkled.

"It sounds as if you had a great deal of fun despite the deplorable circumstances," Vivienne said gently. "You are very brave and resourceful girls. I don't think you will have any trouble at all when it comes to behaving like the sisters of a duke, not if you put your minds to it. It may not be as much fun but…you are lucky, you know. Your brother is working very hard to see that you have as many choices as possible in the future and you won't be forced into a thorny situation. You have so much to look forward to."

Gabriel was touched, and his sisters seemed sobered. Perhaps it was Vivienne's tone as much as her words, as if she wanted them to make the most of their good fortune because her life was not so fortunate. Concerned, he tried to meet her eyes, but she looked away and began explaining the importance of using a soupspoon correctly.

He thought of that moment now as he headed toward the racket coming from the drawing room. Mrs. Marks was pounding on the piano accompanied by the less-than-delicate thump of his sisters' feet on the floor.

Gabriel knew that Vivienne's current state of affairs was not ideal, although he hoped that by removing her brother's debt from her shoulders it might be improved. But the truth was he had forgotten the real reason she was here. He just knew that every day he had something to look forward to. The idea of a future without her in it was so dismal that he didn't want to think about it. Instead he wanted to enjoy these rare moments and hope that, somehow, he could have more of them. He had even begun, cautiously, to imagine his life with Vivienne permanently in it, tiptoeing around the idea as if wanting too much all at once would ruin his chances of it happening.

A shriek that surely belonged to Edwina brought him back from his musings, and as he opened the door, he could hear Mr. Marks desperately clapping his hands for silence. The scene before him was one he had witnessed before, the girls standing red-faced and rebellious, while the dancing master spluttered about what was proper conduct for ladies. He searched for and found Vivienne, seeing that she had noticed his entry. She looked relieved to see him.

"You make dancing boring," Edwina muttered.

Mr. Marks heard her, his mouth dropping open with shock. "Boring? Dance is an art!"

Roberta sniggered. "What? Like a painting? We've already tried painting, and that was boring too."

"Enough!" Gabriel strode into the room, making the girls jump. "How will any of you attend a ball if you can't dance?"

"We don't want to attend balls," Olivia said, and it sounded as if she spoke from the heart.

Gabriel decided to ignore her, and the others. Vivienne was watching him with interest now, and he held out his hand. "Miss Tremeer and I will show you how it's done," he said. When she placed her hand in his without hesitation, he drew her closer, smiling down at her.

"Are you sure about this?" she whispered, leaning in close and bringing with her that light floral scent that was hers alone. "We won't just make matters worse?"

"Can we make it worse?" he whispered back.

She smiled and again he found himself lost in her eyes. The gleam of amusement made them glow, coupled with the delightful curve of her lips, as if she was perfectly happy to be here in his arms. Perfectly willing to go along with his suggestion. Because, he reminded himself, she trusted him, and that was something he had never expected to find so very attractive. He had always avoided deep emotion when it came to women, aware that his father—and he hadn't learned the truth back then—had "loved" his mother only to abandon his son when she died. Last year, when Gabriel discovered Harry was his father, it had seemed more important than ever to avoid situations that put his heart at risk. Love was like a trap that one fell into, causing pain to those who loved as well as everyone around them.

And yet his resolve appeared to be weakening the longer he spent in Vivienne's company. Gabriel wasn't sure that was a good thing, but he didn't seem able to help himself.

The pianist resumed, and they took up their positions and began to move. Vivienne was a good dancer, able to make allowances for his fumbles, and they soon found their rhythm. Gabriel forgot about their audience, or why they were doing this, focusing on the woman in his arms. Her dark curls were dancing, her face warmly flushed and her eyes sparkling. He turned her around the room faster and faster, only vaguely aware of the girls squealing and enthusiastically clapping their hands. Vivienne looked like a young girl herself, all her care fallen away, as happy as he felt. And all he wanted to do was to keep dancing with her.

Eventually she cried out breathlessly for him to stop. "You're making me giddy!"

He slowed, and when he came to a halt, she stumbled against him, so he held her safely in the circle of his arms until her balance returned. It felt good, it felt right, her soft curves fitting to his harder shape as if they were meant to be together. Her forehead rested against his cravat as she clung to his shoulders, and he felt her warm breath through the cloth, against his skin. It seemed to him then that she was as reluctant to let him go as he was her, but eventually she made to move back.

"All right?" he asked, bending to peer into her face. Some more curls had tumbled down, hiding her expression, and he tucked them back.

She cleared her throat and nodded as she looked up, but he thought she looked a little paler than before and cursed himself for his rough treatment of her.

"My apologies..." he began, but she stopped him by pressing a hand against his chest.

"No, it wasn't the dance. I was just..." She stopped and tried a smile, a smaller one than before. "I am well." She glanced at their audience, as if only just remembering them, and leaned in close to him again. "I think you have proved your point," she murmured.

Gabriel turned to his sisters; they looked more excited by the demonstration than he'd expected. "There, you see," he said, rather breathless himself, "dancing is not boring."

Mr. Marks seemed even more impressed. "His Grace is a remarkably robust dancer." He cleared his throat. "Now, ladies, once again, take your partners."

Before Gabriel could think to escape, he was overwhelmed by his sisters demanding he be their partner. He couldn't help but laugh as he tried to fend them off. When he met Vivienne's gaze over their heads, he saw her face was alight with amusement and something softer he couldn't place.

"Save me, Miss Tremeer," he begged.

"Sir, I fear you have worn me out," she retorted, placing a hand against her brow and assuming a delicate pose.

It was only when the dancing lesson finished that Gabriel realized Vivienne was no longer in the room.

Chapter Twenty

The library offered Vivienne sanctuary from the noise and rambunctiousness of the Ashton sisters. She also needed some time to calm herself after the dance—or was it a romp?—with Gabriel. This man was so different from the one she had first met that night at Cadieux's, full of fun and laughter, his smile bright enough to light up a room. And it was as if his touch had made a permanent impression upon her so that she felt it still.

Up until now Vivienne had not had much joy in her life. When was the last time she had done something for the sheer pleasure of it? She smiled at the memory of Gabriel's laughing face as he spun her around and around. She knew she wasn't mistaken in thinking he had enjoyed himself too, the heavy weight of his responsibilities cast aside, if only for a few moments. Vivienne liked to see him happy, she liked it a great deal. It made her wonder what sort of man he would be if he were able to set aside his cares more often. Or share them.

Although Vivienne was a practical woman—she knew dreams very rarely came true—she let herself consider the idea of herself and Gabriel. Together. Was such a thing even possible? He with so much obligation and only just learning the ropes of being a duke, and she with her scandalous past and doubtful future. Although none of that had seemed important over these past days, when every moment had felt special, reality would come crashing down soon enough. And she wished, she yearned, to stave it off a little longer…

The door opened and a deep voice, full of satisfaction and perhaps a little relief, said, "There you are."

"I was taking a moment." She looked up with an instinctive smile as he strolled over to the chaise lounge.

Gabriel ran a hand through his hair, messing it up even more. He wasn't as well turned out as usual, his cravat rumpled and his jacket askew. "I'm not surprised. This is all rather exhausting, is it not?" He paused in the act of sitting down, as if it had occurred to him he was behaving impolitely. His direct gaze focused on her. "May I?"

"Please." Vivienne made room. He was a large man, and he took up more space than her. She folded her hands in her lap, aware she should point out that they were alone together without proper chaperonage. And she would have done so if she were doing her job properly, but right now driving him away was the last thing she wanted to do.

"I haven't had time to read any of these books," Gabriel said abruptly, frowning at the shelves that surrounded them. "I'm not sure they're my cup of tea."

"They do look rather grim," Vivienne agreed. "Do you…do you read a great deal?" He did, she already knew, watching him curiously as he answered.

"One of my teachers at the foundling home discovered I had a liking for reading. Romances, mainly." The corner of his mouth kicked up as he grinned. "He tried me with the classics, but I prefer my reading to be lighter. Takes my mind off things."

Vivienne nodded. "My cousin Annette is a great reader." She wondered if she should mention *The Wicked Prince and His Stolen Bride* but decided against it. He would be able to tell she was keeping secrets; he seemed adept at reading her.

"Reading is a habit now, and I cannot break it. Don't want to," he admitted. "I have all the latest novels sent to me. As ridiculous as some of them are, they take me out of myself for an hour or two. Charles laughs but then he's not like me. I spend a lot of time in my head, and I need a distraction."

"You have a great deal on your shoulders," Vivienne agreed. "And reading can be the ideal distraction."

"Lately I have wondered whether my current life might make a good story. Or perhaps it's too unbelievable for even the most voracious readers."

"But such a tale would appeal to everyone, surely? The hero rises from nothing only to discover he is a duke. Despite the odds, he sets out to rescue his family. All it needs is a happily ever after."

When he was silent, she wondered if she had said too much, but when he glanced sideways at her, she could see he was moved rather than irritated. "Are you certain I am the hero in this story, and not the villain?"

"Oh, the hero, definitely. If you were the villain, you would have refused to help, or set out to revenge yourself upon the family that abandoned you."

He raised his eyebrows. "You are good at this." Then, his smile almost tentative, he asked, "And the happily ever after? How does the hero achieve that?"

She pretended to ponder his question, but his attention

was making her reckless, her barricades perilously close to crumbling. It was almost as if they were discussing more than books, as if their surface conversation was actually about something far deeper.

"It depends, I suppose. Does he choose an aristocratic wife who will look good on his arm, someone his peers will envy him?"

"A wife with a spotless reputation and a blue-blooded family, who will marry him for his title, even if she despises him as a man?" He spoke the words as if they were bitter in his mouth. "Does he have another choice?"

Her heart was beating rather frantically now, as if she were about to tumble into that dark, intense gaze fixed upon her so unwaveringly. She ignored the warning, seemed incapable of protecting herself. "Of course. That wife is probably the one most people would advise him to choose."

"And if the idea of such perfection does not appeal to him?" he persisted with a twist to his lips.

Vivienne pretended to consider his question. "I suppose he could choose another, someone who does not see him as a title, but as a man. Who will stand at his side during challenging times." Vivienne knew it was incredibly reckless to say such a thing. Did he know she was talking about someone like herself? He would laugh at her, or pity her, and certainly think her a naïve fool. Vivienne wanted to flee the room, but if she did that, he would know for certain she was talking of herself. All she could hear was the sound of his breathing; she dared not meet his eyes.

His hand hovered a moment before landing on the chaise lounge, between them. His fingers twitched as if he would have liked to grasp hers, and then stilled. "Which wife would *you* recommend our fictional hero marry?"

"If his place in the ton, in society, matters to him, if he wishes to gain the acceptance of his peers, then he must choose the first wife. He would be foolish not to."

He nodded slowly, considering her answer. There was something else on his mind, she could tell, and she knew if she waited, he would tell her. He stared at the empty hearth in a grim fashion and admitted, "I am out of my depth, Vivienne. With my sisters, with my place in society…with everything. My grandmother only tolerates me because of my money and my ability to make more, while despising me for everything else."

She placed her hand over his. Without a glove, his skin was warm, so warm, and when he turned his hand over, his strong fingers wrapped around hers as if he never wanted to let her go. Her breath hitched.

"Gabriel, you do so much more for your sisters than pay for their food and their keep. You show them your own efforts to master this new life, no matter how difficult that can sometimes be. When you enter a room, their faces light up." He opened his mouth to argue with her, but she stopped him with, "Yes, even Olivia's. They trust you, and they know you have their best interests at heart. Yes, they are noisy and silly, but they won't always be like that. They might argue with you about their future, but they know that soon—very soon—they will have to accept who and what they are. You are leading them by example, and they love you for it."

His dark gaze had been fastened on hers, but now it slid slowly over her face, as if cataloging every inch, before landing on her lips. He leaned in even closer and this time there was no one here to stop them. She met him halfway. A tentative brush of warm lips on warm lips sent a warm tide surging through her. A feeling that had been unfamiliar to her before she met Gabriel. A mixture of desire and need and longing, and hope. Foolish, foolish hope.

"Vivienne," he sighed, and kissed her again, the soft brush of his lips firmer now but still chaste. He wasn't about to ravish her, which should have given her comfort. Instead she wanted more. She was greedy and she wanted everything.

"I wish," she said softly as they separated. *I wish you could choose me. I wish this were forever.*

He leaned in for another kiss, desire making them clumsy as his nose bumped hers. He angled his face and found her mouth, and there was nothing gentle about this kiss. Vivienne heard herself make a sound at the same time as he groaned. He cupped her jaw with his hand and deepened the contact, his tongue sliding between her lips and seeking hers.

Bliss. Every part of her being focused on the heat of his mouth and his body, pressing to hers now while she strained to get closer still. Their earlier dance had taught her just how she felt in his arms, and she wanted more. Her hand imitated his, reaching to stroke his jaw, feeling the rasp of his whiskers, before sliding around to his nape and running her fingers through the short, crisp length of his dark hair.

This, she thought. *This is what I want.*

Then the door opened. Abruptly, with no warning, and several pairs of feet pounded into the room. One moment they had been lost in the wonder of an intimacy so much more than physical, and the next they sprang apart. Gabriel stumbled to his feet and pretended to be examining the bookshelves while Vivienne patted at her hair. There was a giggle from one of the intruders, and then Olivia said, her voice full of amusement, "Here you both are! We were wondering about the next lesson. I think you said you wanted to see how well we were doing with our curtsying, Miss Tremeer."

"Yes, I…I did." She felt shaken, shocked at her own lack of restraint and the risk she was taking. As she led the way to the door, she did not look at Gabriel, suddenly afraid of what she might see.

"Are you coming, Gabriel?" Olivia turned to him, eyebrows raised in a teasing fashion as if she was enjoying her brother's discomfort.

"I have some letters to answer," he said in a gruff voice.

Vivienne turned to look at him despite herself and saw that he was straightening his cuffs with sharp, jerky movements.

"If you will excuse me, Miss Tremeer." His gaze met hers briefly, but she could not read him. She wondered then if he was regretting what had happened between them. Well, of course he was.

The door was almost closed when naughty Edwina piped up. "Or we could learn *kissing* instead, Miss Tremeer."

Neither Gabriel nor Vivienne answered her.

Chapter Twenty-One

Gabriel made his way to his study and closed the door. He needed time alone, to think, to remind himself of his priorities. Because they were becoming hopelessly entangled with the sort of dreams he wasn't sure he should be contemplating.

But what had he expected? He had asked Vivienne here, knowing he was partial to her, and now he was holding her while they danced and sharing smiles with her during her lessons with his sisters, and feeling…feeling happier than he had in years. There had been something missing in his life for a long time, and it was only now that he understood what it was. *Vivienne Tremeer.* The kiss they had shared, although to call it a mere kiss was to vastly understate it, was so far beyond his previous experience he felt as if he had reached the stars.

Had he really believed himself hardheaded enough to control any unfortunate impulses? He had thought himself a pragmatic businessman with a firm plan for his future. Well, she had shattered those illusions. When he had held her tight against him and plundered her warm mouth, he'd known that he didn't just want to hold on to her for a few weeks. He wanted so much longer than that. He wanted a lifetime.

Gabriel put his hands over his face and groaned.

There had been women in his life before. Not ladies, nothing of that kind. His weekly visits to the bawdy establishment he favored had been all about scratching an itch. Since the night Arnott came to see him, he hadn't been back, and he could pretend that was why he was hot with desire for Vivienne. But he'd be lying to himself, because this was much more than a physical urge.

The women he had slept with…well, he had never really tried to get to know them. He certainly hadn't been interested in building something more with them. Now he was a duke, and he was aware that men in his position usually kept a mistress. His father had had three that Gabriel knew of—the estate books had named them, a column for each, with the amounts spent on their upkeep neatly tallied. His mother was there, under Eugénie Cadieux.

Seeing her name like that, next to the page with the estate breeding stock, had chilled him to the bone. He had felt shaky for days afterward and had decided that he absolutely did not want a mistress. And he knew that even if he asked Vivienne to be his turtledove, she would refuse.

So where did that leave them?

His gaze dropped to the desk as he sat down, and that was when he saw a letter waiting for him. Had the dowager read his mind somehow, even from as far away as Sussex? Because he recognized her hand, and reluctantly broke the seal and spread out the thick sheet of spidery writing.

At first he was simply relieved there was no mention

of the steward he had dismissed, because she would eventually hear of the matter. He knew he would have to justify his decision, which was tiresome when he was not used to his rulings being questioned. But as he read on and the true nature of the letter sank in, his chest filled with a hard ball of anger and anxiety.

Gabriel, I have arranged for you to meet the Earl of March's eldest daughter. You will find Lady Edeline both beautiful and accomplished, and indeed the perfect wife for a duke of Grantham. She will also be the perfect foil for the Ashton emeralds, which I intend to bequeath to you. March knows about our family scandal and is prepared to overlook it since I have assured him you are nothing like your father.

The earl and his daughter will be guests at Olivia's coming-out ball, where I will introduce you. I expect you to dance with her and behave in a manner befitting your position as the head of the Ashton family.

She signed her name with a flourish.

And then, beneath that, in a scrawl even more spidery than the rest of the letter.

I am aware that this will not please you, Gabriel. Please don't ignore my instructions and fall into a sulk, like Olivia. You need a wife, and I am doing my best to find you an appropriate one. Lady Edeline will do very well, being sweet natured and biddable as well as beautiful. I want a great-grandchild before I die.

Gabriel crumpled the paper in his fist and threw it toward the fireplace, cursing as it struck the screen and rolled across the hearth.

In the library, when Vivienne had told him what sort of wife he needed if he were to succeed, she might as well have called that faceless woman Lady Edeline.

A woman with perfect breeding and blue blood who would look well in the Ashton emeralds, which somehow his grandmother had managed to keep from slipping through Harry's careless fingers. He knew that marriages like this were commonplace in the circles he now inhabited, but the idea of it…He couldn't do it.

He wouldn't do it.

Would he?

With another groan he flung his head back and stared at the ornate ceiling.

It was Olivia's ball and he was attending, so he had no choice but to meet the woman. His grandmother knew that. His sister was working hard to make herself a success, so how could he refuse to play his part? Well, he would meet Lady Edeline, but he would not marry her. For all he knew she was dreading this whole business just as much as he.

His grandmother reminded him of a spider in the middle of a web, spinning away. He should have known that despite her being in Sussex she would still be plotting and planning for the further aggrandizement of the Ashton family. But Gabriel wasn't sure he could make himself unhappy for the sake of that family. Marry a woman he didn't know and couldn't love just so that the Ashtons could carry on?

That thought brought him up short.

How did he know he couldn't love her? Perhaps she really would be the perfect wife for him. But the fact was he *did* know. Even if she were the perfect wife for the Duke of Grantham, she was not the perfect wife for Gabriel Cadieux.

Because he already knew the woman who was perfect for him. Vivienne Tremeer with her tarnished reputation and ramshackle family. He could not have set his sights on anyone less suitable.

He stayed at his desk as Vivienne left, his sisters' voices calling their goodbyes to her, until silence fell once more. Normally he would be there to call out his own farewells, but not tonight. He felt as if the happiness that had enveloped him over the past days, culminating in today's passionate kiss, was vanishing before his eyes. Only the stark reality of his future remained.

He thought about escaping to the club, where he could relax in familiar surroundings with his friends, but his mind was too full of questions and doubts. He stayed home, and his sisters joined him for dinner. Thank goodness no one mentioned him kissing Vivienne, or perhaps his stony face did not invite teasing. He did his best to take part in their conversations, but he kept circling back to Vivienne and his grandmother's letter. His sisters exchanged glances and raised their eyebrows when they thought he didn't notice, but he kept his own counsel.

Afterward, Edwina persuaded him to read her a bedtime story, and then he went back to his study and sulked, just as his grandmother had said he would. He also drank far too much brandy. By the time he went to bed, his head was spinning, depression had settled over him in a black fog, and he had achieved nothing.

Apart from the physical attraction between them, Vivienne was someone he could talk to in an open and honest fashion. He could discuss the girls with her, and she understood the difficult situation they were in. Why was she forbidden to him? Did he care that he would bring more scandal to the family by marrying an unsuitable woman? No, he didn't, but he knew it would affect his sisters, and hadn't all he had done so far been for them? Could he really risk losing the whole game with one reckless throw of the dice?

Over and over he reminded himself of what was at stake until he felt as if he were surrounded by dark clouds, and yet some foolish glimmer of hope continued to shine though. Refused to be quenched. It burned on. Absurd it might be, but he wanted her, he wanted her so much that his heart ached.

Gabriel must have slept, but at some point he woke suddenly, feeling disoriented. And cold. He shivered. For a moment he was an abandoned, sniveling boy having wandered from his bed, and found himself lost in the great halls of St. Ninian's.

But he wasn't a small boy, he was a grown man, and he was standing in his breeches and shirt on the landing.

He had been sleepwalking.

Thank God he hadn't bothered to undress. He looked around in confusion. The lamp that was always left lit on the table at the head of the stairs barely pierced the shadows, and the unfeeling eyes of his ancestors glared down at him from the portraits on the wall. One of them in particular had a nasty sneer, and in his confused state it seemed to be directed at him.

He jumped as someone spoke his name, and at the same time he felt a familiar hand in his, the small fingers warm and sticky. He looked down, and Edwina peered up at him, her big blue eyes full of concern.

"I couldn't sleep, and Justina said if I ever couldn't sleep, I could come to her room," she half whispered. "And then on the way there I saw *you*. You were walking about, Gabriel, but you were asleep. With your eyes open."

He hadn't walked in his sleep for years. When he was a child it had happened often, and either Charles or Freddie had kept an eye on him, sneaking him back to his bed before anyone noticed. There were times when he evaded them though, which had resulted in consequences. After he left St. Ninian's, there had been moments when he would wake to find himself in some area of the empty club instead of his bed, but over time, as his life had become more settled, that had stopped. Because he knew from experience that he walked when his mind was disordered. It was as if that inner turmoil sent him up from his bed to walk the dark halls, just as he had as a child.

And now he was walking again.

The burden of a new family and an encumbered estate was bad enough, but he had not walked because of that. It was the letter from his grandmother that had tipped the balance—the thought of marrying a woman he did not love and spending the rest of his life with her. The idea was so cold, and Gabriel was far from being a cold man.

Edwina gave his hand a little squeeze, bringing him back to the silent house. "Are you unwell, Gabriel? Should I get Justina?"

With an effort he pulled himself out of his head.

"No." He cleared his throat and made his voice firm. "No, I was just…You're right, I was walking in my sleep." He bent down closer to her, placing his hands on her narrow shoulders. "Sometimes I do that. Best not to tell anyone, Edwina. I wouldn't want them to think they have to tie me to my bed at night."

She gasped and shook her head wildly.

It relieved him to see how horrified she was. At St. Ninian's they had done that, when the walking was at its worst. The memory of his wrists and ankles being fastened, of being held prisoner, could still make him squirm. He didn't really think anyone would do that to him now, but all the same he didn't want to be judged. He imagined if his grandmother found out, if the ton found out, they would think even less of him than they already did for what even he considered a weakness.

"I won't say a word," Edwina promised. "Now come with me, Gabriel. I will take you back to your room so that you're safe."

Her kindness made him feel curiously shaky. "Thank you," he said softly. "And I'll be sure to lock the door this time."

She nodded as if she thought that was a good idea, and they made their way back along the corridor to the ducal bedchamber. She smiled and squeezed his hand again and left him there.

Gabriel didn't expect to sleep now. How could he, when he was worried about walking, and what it meant? How could he be the man he was expected to be when he couldn't even control his own impulses?

He needed to talk to Charles and Freddie—perhaps they would have some ideas. He closed his eyes, comforting himself with that thought, but it was Vivienne who came to him as he drifted off at last. Vivienne's clear gray eyes gazing into his, and her teasing smile. Vivienne, whose mere presence seemed to have the ability to lift his spirits, to make everything better, and yet he was not allowed to have her. Despite everything he now had, he could not have her.

It seemed to him that the world was a very unfair place.

Chapter Twenty-Two

Madame Annabelle's little establishment was close to Covent Garden, and not the better part, although it was certainly not in the worst. Gabriel had arranged for Vivienne to accompany his sisters, but before the day of their visit, she had made some inquiries of her own.

Madame Annabelle did not inhabit the same sphere as the mantua-makers to the higher echelons of the ton, but there were good reports from those who had availed themselves of her service. And because she was new, her list of clients was not long, and with six girls to dress, Madame Annabelle would be eager to please the Ashton family. Vivienne imagined that if Annabelle played her cards right, Grantham and his sisters would keep her in work for many years to come.

She would have shared her information with Gabriel, but he had been missing more often than not since their kiss in the library. Vivienne wished she knew what he was thinking, but she could guess. He was distancing himself from an unsuitable distraction. Their bargain had only ever been about the repayment of Will's debt by her helping his sisters to be ready for their new lives.

The physical attraction between them had always been there, but neither she nor Gabriel had intended it to go that far.

Now it was over before it had ever really begun and, painful as it was, Vivienne was determined to finish her part of their bargain.

Madame Annabelle's premises were a little cramped, but madame's assistants were friendly and attentive. The younger girls were soon dealt with; they needed only a couple of outfits each that might be worn in company, as they were hardly likely to show their faces often in society. The older three needed more care, particularly Olivia. Most importantly, she needed a dress to wear for her coming-out. Vivienne knew the girl was expected to make a splash on the night of the ball, but that was just the beginning. If she was a hit, then she would be invited to many more events. But even if she wasn't a hit, her social standing would mean she must attend soirees and picnics and rides in the park, just to name a few of the likely occasions.

Olivia carried much of the burden of her family's hopes, and Gabriel's attempts to help his sister must make her feel she had to succeed, if only to please him. And of course she knew if she was a success, people would begin to, if not forget, then tend to ignore the scandal that had enveloped the family after Harry's death.

It was a lot to expect from Olivia, who until recently had lived a life without rules and restrictions, or the expectations of others. Now that Vivienne had come to know her, she thought Olivia was inclined to melancholy and low moods. It made sense. But this should be an exciting time in the girl's life, and Vivienne was determined to persuade her to enjoy it.

Once five of the girls were dealt with, they were sent home in the coach, leaving Olivia and Vivienne alone with Madame Annabelle. It was time to get down to the important business of the ball.

It soon became clear that Vivienne had been right when she guessed Madame Annabelle would be very much invested in Olivia's success. She was also kind, and for Olivia that would make all the difference. Once Vivienne could see the girl was comfortable with the modiste, even looking starry-eyed as they examined various dress patterns, Vivienne took a step back. As the other two sat with their heads close together, Vivienne wandered about the showroom. There were some pretty cloth samples, and trays of ribbons and beads. A finished gown had been set up on display, and Vivienne stood and admired it. It was the sort of gown a more mature lady would wear, rather than an innocent young girl. Olivia would need something in pastel or white, with flowers in her hair. Something that evoked unworldliness and innocence.

Olivia might not agree with the concept, and there had been times during the past fortnight when she had actively railed against it, but that was the way of their world. Her choices were narrow indeed—marriage or spinsterhood—and most chose marriage if they could.

Of course Vivienne knew of a few exceptions. Single ladies who refused utterly to be confined by the rules of society, and who set out to make their own way. Lady Hester Stanhope had traveled to exotic places, places that most women never had the chance to see. But these examples were few and far between, and the women usually had a fortune of their own and the backing of a powerful male relative. As much as Olivia may wish it were otherwise, she would have no option but to agree to her family's demands, although Vivienne hoped she might also come to enjoy her journey into the fashionable world.

With a sigh Vivienne ran a lime green satin ribbon through her gloved fingers. Did she envy Olivia her chance at a shining future in the ton? Vivienne had been her own mistress since she was a young girl, taking charge of Will and the house, playing lady bountiful to the tenants. That last was what had gotten her into trouble last year! And as for marriage…Who would have her? Penniless and ruined, with Sutherland as a stepfather?

Vivienne wondered if she would end up as one of those strange spinster ladies with decided opinions. The sort who appeared at major family events before they were hastily hidden away again, before they upset the others. Because if she could not have the man she really wanted, then she would rather not have anyone. And the man she really wanted was Gabriel. She suspected she was falling in love with him, and she didn't know how to stop.

The kiss they had shared was never far from her thoughts, but it wasn't just that. The sense of connection between them, the way they worked together, the ease and the understanding, and the feeling they were in accord. It all spoke of two people who were compatible. At least when it came to dealing with Gabriel's sisters.

And therein lay the problem. Gabriel's willingness to set aside his own happiness for his sisters' future.

Because even if he did feel for her the way she felt for him—and that seemed more and more unlikely the more he distanced himself—he would not act upon it. The dowager would already have a list of suitable wives drawn up, and Vivienne knew very well that her name would not be on it.

"Miss Tremeer, what do you think?" Olivia was calling her.

Vivienne approached and was pleased to notice that the girl's eyes were sparkling with excitement.

"My brother said I was to have several gowns to wear to various events, of course, but the coming-out gown is the most important. It will set the tone, you see."

"I do see." Vivienne looked down at the sketches the modiste had drawn, in particular the gown for the ball. She touched it gently with her finger. "Beautiful," she said. "Olivia, you will truly be the belle of the ball."

Olivia flushed with pleasure. "Do you think?"

"Oh, most definitely."

Olivia smiled but a moment later she was looking uncertain again. "They are all very…bland, are they not?"

Vivienne and Annabelle exchanged a glance. "Young girls have to abide by certain rules when it comes to the season," Vivienne reminded her. "I'm afraid if you were too bold in your color and style choices, you could be ostracized."

"I understand that. It's just…" Olivia shrugged awkwardly. "I wish I could enjoy this time without knowing what it is all meant for," she said abruptly, the words spilling out of her.

"What do you mean?" Vivienne asked, but she already knew. Olivia was no fool, and this could not sit easily with her.

"A good marriage!" She spoke resentfully. "Someone I will probably loathe."

Madame Annabelle's smile was sympathetic. "No, no. You must find yourself an indulgent husband, my dear. One who will do whatever you ask of him."

Olivia seemed to be considering this, and Vivienne

tried not to smile. Any gentleman who fell in love with Olivia could expect to find himself tied up in knots.

Next, undergarments and accessories were chosen, and by then the task was done. At first Olivia was quiet as they settled into the coach, and Vivienne was prepared to leave her to her own thoughts. But it turned out the girl was simply gathering her courage to say what she really felt.

"I never wanted to be like my mother," she said. "A child every year, always hoping it would be a boy. I would hate that for myself, so I'm not surprised she doesn't want anything to do with us now."

Vivienne wanted to reassure her, but she thought Olivia was probably right. And it made sense of the girl's repeatedly stated desire to be free of her birthright.

"I had hoped…By the time my father died, I thought perhaps I could make my own way in the world, but I see now that was foolish of me. Girls like me do not get that freedom. Then Gabriel came, and I thought he might champion me, but he is too busy trying to make the estate pay our bills, and apart from getting rid of Pascoe and letting you help us"—she gave Vivienne a smile—"he lets Grandmother make the decisions."

"I expect your brother must feel as out of his element as you, and he is relying upon the dowager to steer you all around the trickier bits. Have you told him how you feel?"

"About being auctioned at the marriage mart?" Olivia shrugged a shoulder in a very unladylike manner. "What's the point?"

"Perhaps you should," Vivienne said gently. "See what he says. He is not a tyrant, Olivia, very far from it."

"No, he is not a tyrant," she agreed. "I wish he were.

Then I could hate him. But he is trying to do what is best for us."

Vivienne reached for her hand and gave it a sympathetic squeeze. "Think how many girls would love a London season. Balls and parties and handsome gentlemen vying for your attention. I think you will enjoy yourself. You have worked hard to prepare for this. Why not put aside your frustrations and worries, and dive into your first season? You never know, you might find your future is brighter than you thought."

Olivia was silent as the coach drew up before Ashton House, before turning to Vivienne with the sort of intensity that reminded her of Gabriel. "Do you know, Miss Tremeer, I think I will. I'm so tired of being poor, and now I will have a wardrobe full of pretty dresses."

"And no doubt you will soon have queues of smitten gentlemen asking you to dance," Vivienne reminded her.

Olivia laughed. "That too. Thank you, Miss Tremeer." Her smile was beatific, and then she was gone.

The coach moved on to the Monteiths' house, where Vivienne found Annette waiting for her.

"Ivo's sister fell ill with a fever and the doctor was worried the rest of us could catch it. You know how Mama is about illness," her cousin explained. "She is already imagining a sniffle. But where have you been, Vivienne? Whose coach was that? Just as well Mama is resting. She has been asking, and I have told her so many fibs I can't remember half of them. If you are in trouble, I wish you would tell me. You know I would help."

Seeing her cousin's anxious expression, Vivienne could only imagine what she was thinking. She knew she shouldn't feel disappointed that Annette was back, but she was, because it meant that any chance of spending time with Gabriel and his sisters was over.

She had not planned to tell Annette the truth about her exploits, but now it seemed the time had come. She would swear her to secrecy.

And perhaps Vivienne had a flair for fiction after all, because she found herself effortlessly weaving fact and fiction. In Vivienne's version of the truth, the duke had asked her to help him with his sisters simply because he thought her the perfect role model and there was no mention of Will or a debt. Annette's eyes grew rounder and rounder as her tale went on. "Vivienne," she breathed. "Is all of this true?"

"I assure you it is true."

"That is why you didn't want to come with us to Ivo's house party. I see it now and I don't blame you. Why, didn't I tell you that you would be a perfect teacher for the duke's sisters. And the duke himself!"

"You must not tell Aunt Jane," she repeated. "You know what would happen if you did."

Annette nodded enthusiastically. "I will not tell even if she threatens to—to burn all of my books. My goodness. And what of you, Vivienne, spending your time with the handsome duke?" Her expression fell. "I do hope you have not compromised yourself, cousin?"

Vivienne sighed. This was just the sort of thing she had been afraid of. "We were never alone," she said patiently, refusing to feel guilty at the fib. "Wen was with me. Besides, it is over with now. I can't continue with my visits if Aunt Jane has her eye on me."

"That makes you sad, doesn't it?" Annette knew her too well. "You are fond of these girls? And the duke? Are you fond of him, Vivienne?"

More than Annette knew, but Vivienne wasn't going to admit it. She turned the questions aside, and moved the conversation on to Annette's time at Ivo's country house. That was when the joy seemed to leach out of her cousin, her smile taking on a forced manner.

"Nothing happened," Annette said glumly.

"You mean…?"

"He didn't propose to me. He had every opportunity, but he was more interested in galloping his horse around or racing his curricle. His mother arranged games inside when the weather turned foul, but he went off to the village instead. Harold and I sat in the conservatory and he told me about the latest books he'll be publishing." Annette's eyes sparkled and it was obvious whose company she preferred. They dulled again as she added, "Mama thinks it is my fault, I know she does."

It sounded to Vivienne as if Ivo had no intention of proposing and, if her cousin was ambivalent about marrying him, then wasn't that a good thing? It was a pity Aunt Jane did not think more of her daughter's future happiness than the title marrying Ivo would bring her.

But Annette had returned to their earlier subject. "I wish you didn't have to hide the truth about your friendship with the duke's sisters," she said.

Vivienne shook her head. "No, we cannot say anything about the past weeks. Aunt Jane would think the worst, you know that, Annette. As if I were wheedling my way into their family. I am not fit for polite company, according to her."

"And neither is the duke. Ergo you are perfectly suited."

Vivienne laughed, but quickly sobered. "Even if that were true, the dowager duchess will want him to make the sort of match she approves of. And that will never be me, Annette." Her voice wavered, but she firmed it. She was being ridiculous again, and she did not want Annette to feel sorry for her.

"I expect you're right," Annette said. "We are both sad cases, are we not?"

"Very sad." She returned her cousin's hug with affection.

Chapter Twenty-Three

May, the Coming-Out Ball, Ashton House

Margaret, the Dowager Duchess of Grantham, stood beside Gabriel as they prepared to greet their guests. She wore her usual black, with the Ashton emeralds about her throat and diamonds dangling from her earlobes. Despite her outward splendor, Gabriel thought she looked tired. Not that he would ever mention it aloud. His grandmother was far too proud to admit to weakness of any kind.

Since she had returned from Sussex, she had been busy preparing for the grand occasion of Olivia's ball. Gabriel could see her touch everywhere, from the decorations in the ballroom to the food that had been laid out in the room set aside for supper. She had harried the servants until everything shone and sparkled, and the scent of flowers filled Ashton House.

Gabriel had never seen anything like it, certainly nothing from his childhood compared. Olivia was similarly wide-eyed, but he also noticed her pallor and her lack of usual ripostes. The ball was weighing heavily on her, and for the hundredth time he wished Vivienne were here to lighten the mood. She had done so much to make this moment a success and deserved to see it play out. And any awkwardness between her and Gabriel was surely in the past. They could be friends if nothing more. Friends, he decided bleakly, was better than nothing.

With that resolution in mind, he had made certain she had been invited to the ball, as were her brother, aunt and uncle, and cousin. If his grandmother noticed, she did not say, despite her well-known enmity with the Viscountess Monteith. Gabriel got the impression that the dowager was willing to swallow old grudges for the sake of making her granddaughter's debut a success. She had called in a great many favors.

There were other names on the guest list that Gabriel wished were not there. Longley for one. When Gabriel grumbled about his inclusion, the dowager had reminded him that Longley had influential relatives despite his reputation. Remembering Vivienne, he decided not to press the matter. He would simply have to steer clear of him. And Charles and Freddie would be present, so he could find some comfort in them if things grew too nerve-racking.

His grandmother caught his attention now, her dark eyes skimming over him and then on to Olivia with a glow of satisfaction. He assumed that meant they both passed muster. Dressed in the traditional evening wear of cream satin knee breeches and stockings and buckled shoes, with his ruffled shirt beneath a black tailed jacket, he looked like a stranger. He *felt* like a stranger, but perhaps that was a good thing. He could put aside the past and pretend he was the duke he was supposed to be.

At his side, Olivia stood rigid. She was wearing the gown designed by Madame Annabelle and sewn by her seamstresses. Gabriel knew all about it because he had been privy to his sisters' detailed discussions for several days after the visit. Pale ivory in color, the gown was quite plain in comparison to some of the other ladies' outfits he had seen. No frills or flounces, but there was a smattering of embroidered roses on the bodice and the skirt. Her gloves reached above her elbows so that only a few inches of skin was on display before the fall of her sleeves. Olivia's dark hair had been swept up becomingly, and there was a mix of wax and fresh flowers pinned among the tresses. Grandmother had presented her with a plain string of pearls—suitable for a young debutante—and they were fastened about her neck.

Gabriel knew he was a novice when it came to fashion, but he thought his sister appeared both elegant and beautiful. Perfect, in fact.

"You look stunning," he said softly.

She glanced up, startled from her thoughts, and managed a weak smile. Her gaze slid over him. "So do you," she said, in an awkward attempt to poke fun. "All of the ladies will want to dance with you."

"Oh, will they? I'm dancing with you, remember."

"I hope you remember your steps," she whispered as the first guests began to arrive. Her eyes widened at the sight of them, and he squeezed her gloved hand. After that there wasn't a chance to speak privately for some time.

When a severe unsmiling man reached the head of the queue, the dowager stepped forward with a smile. "Gabriel, this is the Earl of March. And his daughter, Lady Edeline."

He made the correct bow, and greeted them as he'd

been taught. The earl might be austere, but his daughter appeared pretty and pleasant enough, although he felt no thrill as she responded to his pleasantries, and there was no mystery in her smile. *Because she isn't Vivienne.*

The earl moved on, and eventually they had come to the end of the guest line. Any who arrived late would have to be announced by Humber, who seemed to relish his task.

Now it was time for the dancing to begin, and Gabriel knew everyone present was waiting with bated breath to see the scandalous duke and his sister take to the floor before the rest of them could join in.

Olivia's eyes met his nervously. Was she thinking the same thing? That they would stumble and make fools of themselves? They had been practicing every day, and Mr. Marks had returned to the house to smooth out any hitches. Gabriel thought they were perfect, but there was always a chance things could go wrong at the crucial moment.

Just as they were about to make their way out onto the floor, their grandmother put a hand on Gabriel's arm and smiled at Olivia. It was unexpected, and there was an unfamiliar softness in her dark eyes.

She spoke quietly, for them alone. "When I was first married, I dreaded these grand occasions. I felt inadequate. I can see you are both skeptical, but it is true. I was seventeen, and had married into a family far more important than mine."

"You do not seem inadequate now," Gabriel retorted before he could stop himself. "You seem born to this life."

He could tell she was pleased to hear it. "Good. I have worked very hard to give that impression, Gabriel. It was a part I played, but over the years it has become the truth. I am Margaret, the Dowager Duchess of Grantham, and the seventeen-year-old girl is nothing more than an uncomfortable memory."

He could not imagine his grandmother as a nervous young girl, but then he glanced at Olivia and suddenly he could. They were similar in looks and stature, although Olivia was older than his grandmother had been when she married.

"You have done well, Gabriel." His grandmother's voice carried on beside him. "And you, Olivia. I am proud of you both."

There was a twinge in his chest, as if she had reached inside and squeezed his heart. This woman, who had abandoned him and persuaded him to step into a position he had no desire to be in, and yet who seemed to understand him in ways that still surprised him. Did he want her approval? It seemed that some part of him did, even if it was the young boy he had once been rather than the man he was now.

Olivia's hand was shaking as it rested on top of his. Her blue eyes were shiny in the light of the chandelier, and he knew their grandmother's words had affected her too.

"Ready?" he asked quietly.

"No."

"I'll take that as a yes," he said, and led her onto the floor.

The room seemed to hush as the orchestra prepared to begin and the guests watched on. Gabriel took a breath and the music started, and then he and Olivia began to dance.

As they turned, the faces became a blur, the clothing a kaleidoscope of colors…until he spotted Vivienne. As if somehow, for him, she stood out from the rest. His gaze clung to hers, and he saw her smile. A moment later she glanced sideways at the Viscountess Monteith, who had turned to glare at her, and dipped her head. Gabriel too was suddenly aware of all those eyes trained on him and the need for caution. Neither he nor Vivienne needed such attention.

"Mr. Marks said not to stare at my feet." Olivia's voice brought him back to the dance. She forced her chin up so that her eyes were in line with his cravat. "But it is very difficult when I'm not quite sure they know what they're doing."

He huffed a laugh. "Nearly finished. You'll be able to dance with some of the handsome gentlemen our grandmother has lined up for you. Try not to break their hearts."

She giggled involuntarily and then bit her lip. "She's planning a society wedding next, isn't she?"

Gabriel nodded. "She wants one for me too."

"Who?"

"The Earl of March's daughter, Lady Edeline."

"Oh, do you mean the insipid one? I thought..." She trailed off, as if rethinking her next words. "Never mind."

Gabriel had sometimes struggled with his relationship with Olivia, but lately they had been growing on each other, and right now his connection with her was as strong as it had ever been. Both had been pressed into a situation they neither wanted nor enjoyed. If he could ease her anxiety on the marriage front, perhaps she could take more pleasure in her first ball.

"You don't have to worry about marrying anyone yet, Olivia. There's plenty of time to decide what you want from the rest of your life. As head of the family, I give you permission not to do anything you don't feel comfortable doing."

She seemed startled, and then her expression softened.

"Thank you," she whispered. "I want to take my time and find someone I can like." She wrinkled her nose. "Well, I hope so anyway."

"I'm sure there will be dozens of gentlemen wanting to dance with you after me."

Her smile was back. "That is what Miss Tremeer said."

He almost stumbled as they negotiated a tricky step, and then they both sighed as the dance came to an end. Olivia curtsied and Gabriel bowed, smiling at each other as if they had performed some heroic feat, and then he led her back to their grandmother.

Justina congratulated them. She was not "out" yet, but as she was the next eldest and this was a private ball, the dowager had granted her permission to be present. Charles arrived, giving his friend a wide grin. "Well done," he said proudly. "You looked every inch a duke, Gabe."

The dowager's stare was repressive. "Perhaps you should dance, young man," she said. "There are plenty of ladies in want of partners tonight."

Charles looked unrepressed, but promptly turned to Justina. "Would you do me the honor?"

Charles smirked at Gabriel and Justina blushed as she accepted, and then they vanished into the crush of dancers. Gabriel felt a niggling sense of doubt. He loved Charles like a brother, but he also knew him very well. Knew his rakish ways. He had once boasted he could seduce a woman into his bed in ten minutes, just with his smile and his tongue. Gabriel didn't doubt it, and he wasn't sure he was happy with that thought when it came to his sister. Especially when Justina was gazing at Charles in such a rapt manner.

"Well done, Gabe."

Now Freddie was at his side, resplendent in his scarlet uniform.

"You're doing St. Ninian's proud tonight. If one of our boys can become a duke, then who knows what's next. King?"

"I'll leave that one to you and Charles."

Freddie just grinned.

It wasn't very long before the dowager declared, with a look of smug satisfaction, that the ball was a complete success. There were still guests trying to get in, and Gabriel was beginning to wonder if they would fit. He said as much to Lady Edeline when he partnered her in a dance, but she smiled in a puzzled fashion, as if he were speaking in a foreign language.

He told himself that Vivienne would have laughed and made some rejoinder that lifted his heart.

Thinking of her now sent his gaze searching the room. He found her a moment later, and what he saw didn't please him. It appeared that Longley was asking her to dance, and although it was obvious to Gabriel that she was refusing him, he had her hemmed in beside the windows and a marble goddess holding an urn.

Gabriel forgot about the watching eyes, or the necessity to be circumspect, or even the likelihood that Vivienne may not want his help. Fury surged through him, and as soon as his dance with Lady Edeline was finished, he hastened to return her to her father, and immediately turned on his heel.

The next dance was just about to start as he strode across the room, ignoring several tentative attempts to engage him in conversation, and came to a halt in front of Longley. The man's face was flushed, and his mouth dropped open at Gabriel's sudden appearance.

"What the devil!" he spluttered.

Gabriel ignored him.

"Miss Tremeer, dance with me," he said in a voice that brooked no argument.

She was flushed and obviously rattled, the expression in her eyes a little wild, but she didn't hesitate. "I would like that very much," she said.

Longley began to stutter a complaint, but it was too late; Gabriel had whirled her onto the floor as if he had been dancing all his life.

"That was rather rude," she said breathlessly.

"Did you want to dance with him?" Gabriel retorted, tightening his grip on her.

"No," she admitted. "He's a vile man. Why is he here?"

"He has important relatives," Gabriel spat. "My grandmother wants to find favor and overcome our scandal in any way she can."

There didn't seem to be much to say to that, and for a time they danced in silence. This polite and proper dance was very different from the time he had spun her around and around, both of them laughing until she was dizzy. Was it wrong of him to wish it back again?

"Your sister is enjoying herself. She looks beautiful," Vivienne said as Olivia floated by with yet another gentleman whose name escaped him. This one was red-faced and portly, but no doubt titled and rich. Olivia smiled at Vivienne, and then she was gone.

Gabriel cleared his throat, noticing Vivienne's gown for the first time. It was a color that eluded him—apricot perhaps, but softer, a match for the blush in her cheeks. Like Olivia, she was dressed simply and elegantly, and to Gabriel's mind she put everyone else in the room in the shade.

He was staring. He looked away and reminded himself that he needed to make conversation because that was what one did, but the feel of her in his arms, the familiar scent of her hair, was so intoxicating his mind was a blank.

"You were dancing with the Earl of March's daughter. According to my aunt she is quite a catch." She smiled as she said it, but there was a question in her voice.

"Is she?" he said with studied indifference. The last thing he wanted to do was talk about his grandmother's plans for him and the earl's daughter.

Vivienne's lashes swept down and she smiled again, but it seemed a pale shadow of the smiles he remembered from their moments together. She knew or she had guessed. Perhaps there had been gossip—he was beginning to learn that in the circles he now moved in, there was always gossip. He wanted to tell her that no, he had no intention of making an offer for Lady Edeline, but after his attempts to distance himself from her after their kiss, she probably wouldn't believe him. Vivienne was too steeped in the ways of society not to understand how it worked.

"She *is* a catch, you know," she went on blithely, as if they were discussing the weather. He remembered how very good she was at polite chitchat. "My aunt is right. She is the perfect choice, and she could open all sorts of doors for you. And your sisters."

But I want you.

The words shattered any illusions he might still have had about his true feelings. He almost spoke them aloud, but she had reminded him of his sisters and the Grantham heritage and the sacrifices that had already been made. Unlike Olivia, he did not have someone who could lift a little of that burden from his shoulders. It was all for him to bear.

"Gabriel?" She was watching him doubtfully, so perhaps she had seen something in his expression after all. "Grantham," she corrected herself. "Gabriel is too familiar, is it not? For us?"

"For us?" he repeated. He tightened his grip upon her, bringing her closer, too close probably, but he found he didn't care. What if this was the last time they ever danced together like this? "We are friends, are we not?" he asked, his voice gruff.

"Friends?" She looked sad, but a moment later she was smiling again. "Of course we are."

He could see that pulse beating beneath her skin, giving the lie to her flippant words. He bent his head so that his lips almost touched her cheek, and wished they were alone. He ached to kiss her, yearned to dance her out of this crowded room. But he could not. He had a job to do as duke. This was why he had distanced himself from her, and now that hard work was in danger of collapsing after a single dance.

Vivienne took a shaky breath and carried on. "Will is very happy. He tells me that Cadieux's is busy most nights. His friend Germaine tried to tempt him away, but he resisted. I don't think he was even that tempted really."

Gabriel pushed away his sense of desperation, the knowledge that the dance was coming to an end. Because who knew when he would get another chance?

He cast around for something to say, and noticed his rival glowering from the sidelines. "Does Longley bother you often these days?"

"Not often, no. Only when you are around I think. He is jealous of you."

"Jealous?"

She laughed uncomfortably. "Not because of me, or if he is, then it is just that he thinks…well." She changed her mind. "The club, I think. He wants it back."

"I'm not giving it to him. I'd rather hand it over to you."

Her eyes widened in startled amusement. "Please don't."

The dance was nearly over, and he wanted to stay with her here in his arms. He wanted to forget all the hard work he had put in to Olivia's success even as he knew he couldn't. Gabriel felt torn in two.

"It's quite a crush, isn't it?" she said, and her voice sounded small. Her gray eyes met his and held his gaze, as if she was determined to say the words. "The ball is a huge success. You should be proud of yourself, Gabriel. You deserve it."

"Vivienne…Miss Tremeer, this is all show." There was an urgency in his tone. "This isn't me, you know that? If it were up to me…" He stopped himself, because what could he say that she didn't know already?

"But it is up to you," she whispered, and when her lips threatened to wobble pressed them tightly together.

The music stopped. Olivia was a few couples away, in conversation with a fair-haired man, his face full of smiles.

"That's Ivo, the Duke of Northam," Vivienne murmured, seeing the direction of his stare.

Gabriel dismissed him. "One duke in the family is quite enough, thank you."

"Well, you would say that," she teased, but her expression grew serious when he turned to her with a frown. "You don't have to worry about him. If Aunt Jane and Ivo's mother have anything to do with it, he will soon be engaged to my cousin Annette."

"Good."

She searched around for something else to say, as if she wanted to keep him there a little longer. "The other girls must be wishing they could be here tonight. I imagine Edwina is very disappointed not to be able to dance with you."

He nodded upward. "They are here, in a manner of speaking. There's a spy hole behind the gallery wall and they're watching from there."

Vivienne followed his gaze. "Of course." She gave a surreptitious wave.

"Vivienne, we are going into supper." Annette had come up to them without either of them noticing. "Aunt Jane is asking for you."

And just like that, his time with her was over.

"Of course," Vivienne said briskly, and then offered Gabriel a curtsy. "Your Grace."

He bowed and she was gone.

Gabriel had no desire to go into supper. He needed time to gather his thoughts, to wrap himself once more in the role he was playing, because he felt as if his skin had been flayed from him. Leaving him raw and bleeding.

On impulse he made his way out of the ballroom toward the stairs to the gallery. There was a servant there, but as was proper protocol, they ignored each other. The rest of the guests were either enjoying supper or else in the cardroom that had been provided for those who could not go even a single evening without gambling.

He opened the door to the "spy room" as Edwina called it. The space was rather poky, only slightly larger than a cupboard, and he wondered how many Ashtons had peered down upon their guests, probably for centuries, plotting or laughing at their antics.

At the sight of him there were cries and excited smiles, while Edwina hopped up and down.

"We saw you dancing with Olivia," she babbled in her too-loud voice. "It was perfect."

"No, it wasn't," scoffed Roberta. "I saw them make two mistakes. At least."

He laughed. "Only two?"

"She seems to be enjoying herself. She's danced with an awful lot of gentlemen already." Antonia looked envious.

"Are you enjoying *your*selves? I asked for some food to be sent up."

"Oh, we've eaten that" was the response.

"We saw Vivienne…I mean Miss Tremeer, dancing with you too," Georgia said with a sly little glance.

"What color was her gown?" Edwina asked. "I think it is peach but Georgia says apricot."

"She's very pretty, isn't she?" Antonia added.

He wasn't sure what he was supposed to say to that, but it was true, she was pretty. In fact…"I think she's beautiful."

There was a gasp, and the girls exchanged smiling glances. "Do you think she can come and live with us one day?" Edwina whined. "I miss her."

Gabriel's chest felt heavy, as if there were a lead ball inside it. Their conversation at the end of their dance came back to him. After Vivienne had told him he should marry Lady Edeline, that she expected him to do what was best for his family. He had tried to explain to her that if it were up to him, he would choose her. And she had replied, *But it is up to you.*

He shifted uncomfortably. Only it wasn't, not really, and pretending things were different didn't help either of them. Vivienne knew as well as he that sometimes things weren't possible no matter how one longed for them to be.

He forced a smile and said, "Miss Tremeer has her own life, you know. We cannot be greedy with her company."

There was an uncomfortable pause, and then Roberta was talking about something else and he pretended to listen. But it felt as if all the joy had drained out of him, leaving nothing but a shell. A shell in the fine clothing of a duke. The tap on the door was a relief.

Will Tremeer peered in at them. "Lady Justina suggested I join you up here," he said awkwardly. "I apologize if I'm intruding, I'll…"

But the girls weren't having that. They insisted he come in, and with a shy glance at Gabriel, he did. It gave Gabriel the chance to make his own excuses. The dowager would be expecting him to beg another dance from Lady Edeline, and he went to do his duty.

Chapter Twenty-Four

Vivienne stretched under her covers and opened her bleary eyes. Her family hadn't returned home until after three o'clock in the morning, so she knew she would not be the only one in the Monteith household sleeping late.

The viscountess was not expecting any callers until this afternoon, some of her cronies, and it was unlikely Vivienne would be invited to take tea with them. And now that her time with the Ashton sisters was over, she had nothing to do but cool her heels.

She missed them. She missed their liveliness and their laughter and their confidences, and she even missed their bickering. But most of all she missed Gabriel. His wicked grin, so different from the stiffly polite man from last night, their shared confidences, and the sense that they were working together to achieve a goal. With a groan she covered her face with her hands.

I should have better guarded my heart.

Vivienne might have been in denial before, but the truth was perfectly clear to her now. Last night at the ball, the full measure of her folly had finally been brought home to roost.

She was in love with Gabriel.

That warm rush of pleasure as she had stood there in that elegant ballroom and admitted it to herself. She loved him. But the realization had barely had time to take root before her aunt had ruined it with one of her pithy observations.

Grantham would be a fool if he doesn't marry Lady Edeline. And while he might indeed be a fool, the dowager is not.

The happiness had seeped out of Vivienne. Because of course Gabriel would marry someone like that. It was inevitable.

The cold, hard reality of the situation had her seeking to escape, but Longley had followed and tried to browbeat her into dancing with him. Gabriel had promptly rescued her. As she had grown to know him better, she had discovered that although he might wear a stern veneer in public, he was actually a kind and generous man. Look how generous he had been when it came to the debt? His rescue of her was partly gratitude for the help she had given him with his sisters and partly because he considered her his friend. Had he not said so during their dance?

Only that wasn't true, was it? He felt more than friendly toward her. He had admitted it to her. *If it were up to me.* And even as she had answered, she'd known. His choices were driven by factors other than love and desire. As much as she would like a fairytale ending to her little romance, it would be very foolish of her to expect him to oblige. Gabriel was at heart a practical man. She had only to remember how he had stepped back from her after the kiss that still kept her awake at night, tossing and turning. He would quash any inconvenient feelings if they did not fit in with his future plans. And although he might tell her that he was not a duke, she could see that he was. He had grown into the role. Gabriel Cadieux had become Grantham.

But wasn't he the same man beneath that brittle shell? The man she had first met in his office above his hell, and never been able to forget? Fine clothing and proper manners did not mean he could not be reached. If she could burrow her way deeper into his heart, force him to change his mind…

Abruptly she sat up, unable to lie here in the company of her gloomy thoughts any longer.

It was ridiculous of her to imagine he would ever declare undying love for her. Beg her to run away with him so that they could be together forever. Laughable. Those were the dreams of a naïve young girl, a girl she had never been even before she was ruined. Surely by now she had learned her lesson. The world was not a kind place, and society was rigidly divided. Gabriel was so far out of her reach he may as well be residing on the moon.

She sighed. This really was all her fault, wasn't it? An inconvenience of her making. She had *allowed* herself to fall in love with Gabriel despite knowing how impossible it was. Now she would have to learn to untangle him from her heart. Although, at the moment, it felt as if he had wound himself around that organ tighter than ivy. Tough and difficult to detach, and even more difficult to eradicate.

She needed a distraction. Perhaps she could make some calls with Annette, ride in the park, visit the theater? After all there was always plenty to keep one occupied in London during the Season and Annette would enjoy her company.

The trouble was Vivienne didn't feel like doing any of that.

She was falling into a melancholy. All she wanted to do was wallow in her own misery. Ridiculous when you considered Will's debt, which had ruled her life these past months, had been wiped from the books and they were free of it. Will was happy and settled at Cadieux's and no longer needed her. She even had her nest egg safe again. She should be celebrating.

Vivienne needed to plan. She needed to consider her future and decide what she was going to do. Could she write another novel? *The Wicked Prince and His Stolen Bride* had been for Annette, to cheer her up, and Vivienne admitted that the idea of picking up her pen again did not fill her with the same passion. She had tried, after her time at Ashton House was over. She had begun a story about a governess who fell in love with a duke with many sisters. It had sounded so remarkably similar to her own experiences that she stopped.

Helping Gabriel sort out his problems, spending time in his company, looking up into his warm dark eyes, and knowing she was appreciated. That was what she craved, and anything else came a poor second.

Eventually she talked herself into rising and dressing. Jenny wasn't anywhere to be found, so she tied her hair back in a simple style and made her way down to the breakfast room. There was no one else there, which didn't surprise her, and in fact she was relieved she wouldn't be forced to make conversation. She wasn't sure she was up to it.

The silver tray that was used to convey the daily post to the family rested on a small table inside the door. Vivienne glanced through the pile of invitations and calling cards until a letter with her name on it caught her eye. Recognizing her mother's hand, she picked it up.

Vivienne poured herself a cup of coffee, adding cream and sugar, and made her way over to the bay window. Outside, the day was technically well underway, although for those members of the ton who did not believe in riding at dawn in Hyde Park, it was only just beginning. They would take breakfast in bed, and then prepare to make or receive afternoon calls, maybe indulge in some shopping, or if the weather was fine, perhaps set out with a group of friends and acquaintances to a local beauty spot. The evening could be filled with more formal engagements, before late to bed, and then next day it began all over again.

Vivienne had never really been part of that life. Most of hers had been spent in Cornwall, and although as the daughter of a baronet she had been privileged in many ways, it would be different for Olivia. For Lady Edeline. Who knew what Vivienne's future would look like? Whatever she decided, there would be plenty to do once she returned to Tremeer with Will, but the years in between…It suddenly felt like an eternity.

Her mother's letter lay waiting for her attention. At least it would serve as a distraction. Once the seal was broken, she found a single page, and as usual the writing was crossed, which saved on the cost of postage but made it more difficult to read. Impatiently Vivienne held the paper closer to her eyes, and had to retrace her steps several times when the sense of it evaded her.

Helena Sutherland wrote that she was full of despair over her situation. Could she come to London for a visit, did Vivienne think? Mr. Sutherland—whom she didn't seem to know had been in London alone—had been spending his nights out with friends, gambling and drinking, only coming home when his funds or his credit ran out. It wasn't exactly news. Vivienne had never liked or trusted the man, even in the early days when he had tried to make himself agreeable. Once her mother had declared herself in love with him, and despite the warnings of others, had married him, Sutherland had no longer pretended he was other than he was. A fortune hunter and a spendthrift. And yet Vivienne could still find it in her heart to sympathize. People made mistakes, and some of those mistakes were more life changing than others.

And now she felt the usual wave of guilt that reading about her mother's unhappiness always brought on. Before she came to London, Vivienne had been the one her family turned to in times of trouble. She couldn't do anything about her stepfather, but she could offer her mother some comfort and support. They may never have been close, but wasn't that what a dutiful daughter did? Support her mother in times of distress?

Her guilt gave way to resentment. The scandal with Benjamin was her own fault, she had never denied it. Sutherland may have been the one who tried to force her into marriage, but Helena had played her part. Once she had listened to Vivienne's story of the night in the inn and had commiserated, she had decided that marrying Benjamin was not such a bad idea. He was a local boy, the son of a tenant farmer, and certainly would never have been high enough on the social scale if Vivienne's father were alive. But her father was dead and her romantically inclined mother held sway.

No wonder Vivienne had taken flight to Aunt Jane.

Not that Benjamin was unkind or unpleasant. In fact he was handsome and cheerful and the sort of boy most girls would find perfectly adequate. But a marriage between them would never have worked. She would have been wretched, and she knew it now more than ever because she had a man to whom she could compare Ben. He was no Gabriel.

It hadn't even been a very exciting way to ruin oneself. A farm cart breaking down, and their making their way to the inn and then falling asleep. If she'd known they were going to stay the night, she would have insisted on separate rooms. Or more likely she would have trudged home in darkness through the rain rather than risk being compromised. When she had rushed out the next morning, the last thing she expected to see was the vicar staring down at her from atop his pony. He had just happened to be calling on a sick parishioner who lived near the inn.

He believed the worst. She had done her best to explain, but her flustered face and Benjamin standing behind her, looking guilty, and the smirking innkeeper… it all added up to one conclusion.

All hell had broken loose. The gossipmongers had spread the story far and wide, probably with Sutherland's support. Vivienne's reputation was in tatters, and when she learned of her stepfather's plan, she and Will left for London. Aunt Jane blamed Helena. "She could have nipped it in the bud if she'd had the least bit of sense!" she had declared. At first Aunt Jane had hoped the gossip of Vivienne's ruination would not reach London, but it had. At that point her aunt gave up on her. She was allowed to stay in Mayfair, Aunt Jane declaring that it was better she keep her distance from persons who did not have her best interests in mind—that was Mr. and Mrs. Sutherland—but she would never be completely welcome in society, and was unlikely to ever make an excellent marriage. Or even one that was middling.

Vivienne set her mother's letter down and sipped her coffee.

Vivienne tried not to think of Benjamin at all. If she did, then she suspected he would be wooing one of his commanding officers' daughters—he was handsome enough to catch a discerning eye. Affable and good-looking, with brown hair and eyes sparkling blue. Nothing had seemed able to depress his spirits, which in the confines of his mother's kitchen she had thought a cheerful way of looking at life, but later realized how utterly infuriating he would be if she had to live with him day after day. That merry smile and insufferably jaunty manner. She could not have borne it.

Vivienne set down her cup with a rattle and told herself to stop. Her thoughts were making her even more maudlin, and she needed to take herself in hand. What was done was done. Yes, it was true that perhaps if her reputation were spotless, she may have been able to set her cap at Gabriel, but she doubted it. A baronet's daughter, especially one who was related to Sutherland and his dissipations, was not high enough for a duke. The dowager duchess would warn Gabriel away. There would be no happy ending no matter how much she might want it.

She and Gabriel were fated to travel down different paths, and to believe otherwise was a waste of time. She had to stop. Life would go on; it always did. She knew that. Next time she saw him, she would make polite conversation, because as awful as it was to admit she was in love with him, it would be even more awful if he started to avoid her. Or pity her. Imagining his solicitous glances, she groaned again and rested her cheek against the cold glass of the window. At least she still had her pride to support her, and she needed to hang on to that, because if he ever started to feel sorry for her, she would shrivel up and die.

Chapter Twenty-Five

All morning there had been invitations and calling cards arriving at the door of the town house. When the family finally arose, the dowager had that same expression of smug satisfaction on her face Gabriel remembered from last night. Word was Olivia was a hit. Things were looking positive for their future.

"We have calls to make, girls!" His grandmother clapped her hands, startling the sleepy-looking faces around her. "There is much to be done. We cannot let the grass grow under our feet."

Olivia murmured a protest. "Must we? I thought I could walk in the park today."

"We can *ride* in the park," the dowager replied. "It is important you are seen. People will wish to speak to you because they hope some of your good fortune will rub off on them."

Olivia rolled her eyes at Gabriel but was soon trying to decide what to wear. She had taken to her new life in a way that pleased him greatly. If Olivia could be happy, then he told himself the sacrifices were worth it.

"Gabriel must come too," the dowager said with one of her commanding looks.

It didn't work on Gabriel. After last night, he needed some time in familiar surroundings. He needed some peace and quiet, if a gambling hell could be considered to offer such a thing.

"My apologies, but I am engaged to visit my club." Gabriel rose to his feet, tossing aside his napkin.

"White's?" she asked curiously. "You're not going dressed like that, surely?" Her gaze swept disparagingly over his brown breeches and fawn jacket.

"No, Cadieux's. I promised Charles." Yes, he was in his old clothing, but that was because right now he was not playing the part of the duke. He was Gabriel Cadieux, and it was just too bad if his grandmother did not like it.

She opened her mouth to protest and then changed her mind. "You are in one of your stubborn moods, Gabriel. Very well, go and play cards. We will talk when you return."

The club was quiet enough, but he had only just reached his office and begun to look at some of the decisions Charles had left for him to make, when there was a tap on the door. Thinking it was his friend, he asked them to enter, only to find it was a most unwelcome visitor—Sir Hubert Longley.

The man looked flushed and sweaty, as if he had been rushing, or perhaps it was the result of last night's drinking. Remembering what else occurred last night, Gabriel eyed him with suspicion.

"No need to fear," Longley smirked. "I am not here about your little turtledove."

"I beg your pardon?"

"Oh, don't get on your high horse, Cadieux. You

know who I mean. But that's beside the point. I am not here to discuss Vivienne Tremeer. I am here to make an offer on my club."

Gabriel ground his teeth. Not this again. He leaned back in his chair and tried not to show his feelings. Longley always seemed to rub him the wrong way, but he'd be damned if he'd allow him to know it.

"No," he said bluntly. "I haven't changed my mind since the last time."

He hadn't asked Longley to sit down, but the man did so anyway. "I want my club," he said, as if Gabriel must be hard of hearing. "You don't need it. Give it to me."

"No."

Longley carried on with a hint of baffled fury. As if he still couldn't believe that a man like Gabriel had won the club from a man like him, and was now refusing to give it back. There was no point in arguing and Gabriel remained silent, allowing the conversation to run its course. But when Longley seemed to show no sign of stopping, Gabriel rose to his feet and went to the door.

"Out," he said. "Or I'll have you thrown out."

Longley shot him a poisonous look as he left.

By now any possibility of Gabriel relaxing had gone. The man was insufferable. He had no intention of selling Longley the club, but because of him, the idea of selling it to someone had entered his head, and he found it would not go away. His responsibilities as Duke of Grantham were heavy and would probably increase as each of his sisters came of age. But the club was his. He had built it up from the dire straits Longley had left it in, and made a success of it. He felt as if the club were a part of him. He couldn't sell it.

Charles's arrival was a good distraction, and even better, he had brought Freddie. Their chef hadn't started work yet, so they sent out to the nearby tavern for hot pies and mugs of ale, just as they used to in the early days. But enjoyable as their time together was, Gabriel could not forget Longley's visit. When he told his friends about Longley's offer, they were angry on his behalf.

"That man is just waiting for a chance to bully you into selling," Charles declared. "Be careful, Gabriel. He's a liar and a cheat, and he'll use whatever he can to get the better of you."

"I am careful. Longley won't find anything compromising he can use to damage me."

"He's persistent, I'll give him that," Charles said. Then, with a knowing glance: "Or are you considering his offer?"

"No!"

"Good." Freddie drained his mug of ale. "If you have to sell to someone, make sure it isn't him."

Gabriel stared, not knowing what to say, while Charles leaned back, his belly full. "You *are* considering it, aren't you?" he said, eyebrow cocked. "I wouldn't blame you with all that you have on your plate these days."

"Dancing and paying calls to toffs, showing off in the park in your pretty clothes. Yes, you are very busy these days, Gabe." Freddie had a twinkle in his eyes.

Gabriel snorted. "I do a great deal more than that. The estate doesn't run itself."

"If you wait a little while, I can probably buy the club from you."

Gabriel looked at Charles in surprise. "You?"

"Why not?" Charles said defensively. "I have been running it more or less single-handedly for months now.

You'd have to give me time to find a backer who would lend me the blunt but—"

Gabriel held up his hand. "Charles, I'm not doubting you. It's just that I didn't think you would want to take the club on full-time. You always said you were going into importing spirits. French brandy and the like. No one is better at sourcing the top stuff than you."

Charles smirked. "I have my ways," he said, touching his finger to his nose. "All the same, I would rather take on Cadieux's myself than see it go to someone like Longley."

At that moment the door opened and Will Tremeer peered in. He looked guilty, his gaze sliding away from Gabriel's, leading him to wonder just how much of their private conversation the boy had overheard.

"Sorry," Will said. "I needed to speak to Mr. Wickley. There's a wager in dispute, and I can't find the betting book."

As Gabriel was aware, all wagers made on the premises were written down in their betting book. Charles and Will began discussing the matter, but every now and again the boy threw a worried glance in Gabriel's direction. When Charles went downstairs to look for the book, Freddie declared he needed to return to the barracks, and Gabriel was left with Will.

The boy hovered in the doorway as if not sure whether to leave or stay, and then he turned back to face Gabriel and burst out, "Are you really selling the club?"

Gabriel must have looked as surprised as he felt, because Will stammered an apology.

"I'm sorry. I just...I don't know what I will do if you sell Cadieux's. I feel as if I'm of use for the first time in ages, and if I have to go back to the way things were before...Vivienne has taken care of me for so long. That's what she does, you see. She takes care of people. I thought that, in time, I might be able to take care of her."

Gabriel stood up, suddenly needing to be on his feet. Although he was some distance away, Will took a step back, almost stumbling, and Gabriel felt it necessary to reassure him.

"Will, I'm not planning to sell the club. At least…if I do, then I will consider an offer from Charles. And I'm sure if that happens, he'll need your help more than ever."

Will's gray eyes widened, and then he let out a relieved breath. "Oh," he said. "That would be…thank you."

"I'm glad you want to take care of your sister," he added, suddenly as awkward as Will. At least her brother was there for Vivienne even if Gabriel couldn't be more than her friend.

"It hasn't been easy for her. I wish…" He chewed on his lip, looking young and earnest. "I wish there were someone who would love her for the person she is and forget about the past. But I suppose that will never happen. My stepfather and his debts will always be hanging over us, and that idiot she…" He stopped abruptly, as if aware he was about to discuss something that Vivienne may not want discussed. "Never mind," he muttered.

Gabriel wasn't sure what to say. His throat felt dry, and there was that ache in his chest again. He wanted to shout out that *he* was that man. The one to love her and spend his life looking after her. But he could hardly tell that to her brother when Gabriel could barely admit it to himself.

"I saw you dancing with her at the ball."

Will was looking at him now as if his words had some deeper meaning. Perhaps he had read Gabriel's thoughts even though he hadn't spoken them aloud. Before he could respond, they were interrupted by Charles returning, holding the betting book triumphantly aloft.

Gabriel left them to it.

Once he reached the town house, he had hoped to spend some time in the library, a place in which he could be sure he wouldn't be disturbed. Well, by anyone but Edwina. He needed to be alone with his thoughts, to remind himself of his priorities as Duke of Grantham. There was work to be done too. He had letters from Sussex, and one of his tenants was complaining about a leaking roof. Without a steward all these matters fell to him, but he didn't mind. It was something he was good at, and it took his mind off the rest.

But Humber waylaid him at the door.

"Her Grace, the dowager duchess, requested you attend on her as soon as you returned."

Gabriel's spirits sank, but before he could answer, Humber ran a critical eye over his attire and added, "It might be better if you changed first, Your Grace. Her Grace is very particular when it comes to dress."

Gabriel considered whether to simply ignore the man, but Humber knew his grandmother better than he. Besides, he would be more comfortable in his fashionable clothing, something he had never thought he'd feel at the beginning. By the time he came downstairs again, he was once more every inch the Duke of Grantham and ready to face anything his grandmother could throw at him.

He straightened his shoulders and took a deep breath before entering the blue sitting room. There was no putting it off. He had a fair idea what she was going to say, and he could only hope that he could withstand the barrage.

The dowager looked up with a smile of approval, so making an effort had probably been a good idea. Gabriel sat down, careful not to crush the tails of his jacket, and waited. She had requested this audience with him, and he had no doubt she would expect him to agree to whatever she said. In the early days, when he was first finding his feet, he might have deferred to her, but that was no longer the case.

"Olivia and Justina are visiting some acquaintances with their new companion," she said, pouring him a cup of tea from the pot before her. "I engaged her, as well as a governess for the younger ones, when I learned that Pascoe had inexplicably disappeared into the wilds of Scotland. Do you know anything about that?"

He considered pretending he didn't, but why should he play dumb when he knew he had done the right thing? "She was unsuitable," he said, taking the teacup. "I hope you have found someone better, or she might be joining Pascoe."

"Hmm." She narrowed her eyes at him but decided not to follow that train of thought. "I believe there was a young woman here while I was in Sussex. Was she someone you considered more suitable?"

"Was there?" He sipped his tea. "I was otherwise engaged with estate matters."

"Yes, you turned off the steward. I heard all about it."

"He was incompetent and a thief."

They stared at each other, as if preparing for battle, one Gabriel meant to win. In the end she must have decided not to follow that train of thought either, and he suspected she was keeping her powder dry.

"As for the ball, I am exceedingly pleased with how matters have turned out, Gabriel. Olivia has overcome any prejudice that may have prevented her from making the most of her first season. She is a hit. Of course I am not so foolish as to expect the unpleasantness surrounding her birth to disappear entirely, but I feel more confident. I know we can rise above the stain on the family name." Her smile was a little forced as she observed him.

Gabriel guessed "the stain" was his mother, but hearing her so described no longer caused him the same hurt. Harry had married her, had loved her, so surely that meant something? Gabriel had not known her well, vague recollections were all he had, but he hoped she would have been proud of the man he had become.

The dowager launched into speech again. "Family is everything. I think you know that now. And as the head of the family, you are expected to be an example to the others. You are required to marry well, for your sake and that of your sisters. Someone of impeccable breeding. In this we must choose wisely, Gabriel, or everything we have done thus far is for nothing."

"There is no 'we,'" he replied as calmly as he was able. "If I marry, I will choose my own bride." The handle on the teacup was tiny, barely big enough to fit his finger, and his shaking hand felt clumsy. He was angry, his emotions still stormy from last night, and he had a feeling he was about to get angrier.

"Unfortunately that is not something I can allow. Your own wishes in the matter are irrelevant. Your bride must be well bred and accomplished so that your children do not find themselves in the position you are now."

He tried not to grind his teeth.

"I do not talk often of my own marriage," she said, after a pause. Her voice was thready, as if the words were difficult, and Gabriel looked at her in surprise. "Your grandfather was not my choice, but I knew my duty. When I came to Grantham, I was young and unhappy. Humber was young too, a new footman in the household, and we formed a bond."

She looked uncomfortable for a moment, and he wondered whether that was because of her friendship with a servant—an enduring one, evidently, because Humber got away with a great deal these days. Or was it because any form of weakness on her part was to be denied?

She smiled. "He brought me flowers that first evening, while my new husband was visiting one of his mistresses. Oh yes"—with a glance at Gabriel—"he had several. Just like Harry. I accepted it. He had married me for the sake of the family, but he did not love me, just as I did not love him. Love was not part of the contract, and I had never expected it to be. He found his pleasures elsewhere, and I found mine in my son and running the household, and my social engagements. I was determined to play my part, and so I did."

"And was it worth it? Exchanging the possibility of a happy marriage for Grantham?" He was genuinely curious.

She met his eyes in surprise. "Of course! What else was there? I was born to this life, trained from childhood, made to understand it was my destiny. Marrying the Duke of Grantham was a great honor."

Gabriel set down his teacup with a clatter. "Why are you telling me all this, Grandmother?"

"Because when I spoke to Olivia about her possible suitors, she informed me that you had already told her you would not ask her to marry anyone until she was ready."

"I did. She was anxious you were about to force her into marriage when she was still finding her feet. This is all very new to her, remember."

She waved a heavily ringed hand dismissively.

"You are giving the girl unrealistic expectations. You are feeding her rebellious ways. She cannot return to the wild creature I first found when I arrived at Grantham."

"I don't believe she will. You saw her at the ball. She has taken to her season as a duck to water. But why can't she marry a man she has a chance of being happy with? Where is the harm in that?"

"Happiness is found in family and position. Romantic love is for servants."

"Or mistresses," Gabriel retorted, and earned a sharp look.

"Which brings me back to your own future, Gabriel."

He knew what was coming, he had no illusions as to his grandmother's agenda, and he tried to head her off. "I will not discuss my private life with you."

"Your life is no longer private, it belongs to us all. Let me finish, Gabriel. I was discussing the Earl of March's daughter. Last night when you danced with her, you were careless in your conduct. You returned her to her father somewhat precipitously to pursue a woman of dubious reputation. I have spoken to the earl and apologized on your behalf, and he has forgiven you. He was a young man himself, once. But he will not forgive you a second time, Gabriel."

Vivienne did not deserve to be slandered like this, and the words burst out of him. "That woman is worth ten of the Earl of March's daughter. No, one hundred. She does not need your seal of approval. And I was rescuing her from the unwelcome attentions of Longley, a creature *you* invited. Now there is someone with a 'dubious reputation.'"

"Oh." She nodded as if this made sense. "You are chivalrous. If you want this woman, then have her, but do it discreetly. Do you really want your sisters to suffer for your lack of self-control?"

She had said the very thing needed to make him doubt himself—his sisters' future. This woman saw everything. She knew everything. He felt as if she had reached into his chest and removed his heart, because that was what she wanted, wasn't it? For him not to feel. She wanted a frozen statue of a duke with no thought in his head but the advancement of the family.

"No." The word was louder than he expected, and his grandmother's eyes looked startled. Evidently people did not say no to her very often.

"No?" she echoed, the wrinkles in her face deepening in what might have been a scowl. "I have accepted an invitation on your behalf to accompany Olivia and the earl and Lady Edeline to a musical evening. You will attend, Gabriel."

"You should have asked me first."

"What else would you be doing? Playing cards?"

He'd had enough. "Trying to keep Grantham solvent," he said. "I am not going to marry Lady Edeline, so I will thank you to stop acting as if I am. This charade is over. I don't love her. I know that means nothing to you, but it means a great deal to me. Do you understand, Grandmother?"

She blinked at him, momentarily stunned, before her eyes blazed back to life. "You dare to speak like this to me? You are my flesh and blood and—"

Here was the formidable woman who once upon a time had visited her lonely grandson at St. Ninian's Foundling Home, and…left him there. But the dowager's fury only served to throw ice water on Gabriel's.

"It's a pity you didn't remember that when you left me

at St. Ninian's. I have wanted to ask you something ever since the day of my father's funeral. When you visited me at the foundling home…I was ten I think. You had never come to see me before, or after, and I wondered…Why did you come? You could not have known then that I was the legitimate heir."

She took a breath, struggling to calm herself. He wondered if she would answer, but a moment later she said, "I wasn't sure that you remembered the occasion. Just because I knew that placing you at St. Ninian's was the right thing to do does not mean I did not have regrets. You were a handsome boy, very like your father, and bright. A little wild, but it seems all of his children have that failing."

"You didn't tell me you were my grandmother."

"No. I didn't want to get your hopes up. And I knew I could not take you home with me. What would I say to Felicia? She was jealous enough of Harry's other women and half-mad with her desire for a son. No, you were better off there."

That last was an assumption he could not agree with. "Why though?" he persisted. "Why did you come?"

She sounded reluctant. "The thought of you had been playing on my mind, and I wanted to make certain you were being treated well. You were an engaging child. I…I came to set my conscience at ease."

Her conscience. She had felt guilty and she had come to check that he wasn't being too badly treated. He felt a wave of disappointment, but what had he expected her to say? That she was sorry, that she wished she had not done it, that if she had known him better…No, she was a woman who was ruled by a burning desire to do her duty. Not love, never that.

And she wanted him to do the same. Marry a woman he could not love for reasons that would have appalled him before he became a duke. And the worst thing was that her words had made terrible sense. He had been considering doing as she asked, he had understood her reasoning. The pragmatic and practical part of his brain had been in complete agreement.

But now his heart was staging a rebellion.

Chapter Twenty-Six

Helena Sutherland had arrived in London. It wasn't totally unexpected; she had been bemoaning the state of her miserable life in Cornwall, and threatening to come. The final straw was when she discovered her husband had visited the capital without her and without her knowledge. Aunt Jane was furious when her sister-in-law was set down at her door uninvited. Not that that would occur to Helena, and even if it did, she was very good at pretending ignorance of those matters that did not suit her.

With Helena here, Aunt Jane was forced to confront the sort of issues she usually preferred not to be reminded of. Such as her brother the baronet's unfortunate choice of wife. While the baronet had been alive, he had kept a watch on her more extreme flights of fancy, but once he was dead and she remarried the rackety Mr. Sutherland, all bets were off and Aunt Jane had washed her hands of her.

"I prefer to forget about that side of the family," Vivienne had once heard the viscountess declare to her cronies. "They are quite beyond redemption."

And now here was Helena, like a whiff of scandal, just as Ivo was expected to propose to Annette! Aunt Jane was obviously fuming, shooting glances like daggers at the oblivious Mrs. Sutherland.

And even worse, as far as Vivienne was concerned, her mother seemed to have made it her mission to interfere in her daughter's life.

"Benjamin is home from the army," she announced blithely as soon as the two of them were alone. "I always liked that boy."

"The boy who ruined my reputation?" Vivienne retorted.

Mrs. Sutherland gave Vivienne a little smile. "He asked after you."

"Did he?"

Vivienne gave the door of the parlor a desperate look, hoping someone would come in and interrupt them, but of course no one did.

"You should speak with him," her mother said with that mulish, determined look Vivienne knew well. Her heart sank. "It's over a year since that misunderstanding. You will find him quite grown up."

Misunderstanding? Vivienne stared at her angrily.

"And what are you doing with your life anyway," Mrs. Sutherland went on a little breathlessly, perhaps not quite able to ignore Vivienne's seething silence. "Wouldn't it be better to marry Benjamin and come home to Tremeer? What is there for you here in London?" She leaned in closer, as if she suspected Aunt Jane was listening outside the door. "You know your aunt will never forgive you for what happened. She was always one for holding a grudge. Your father said that from the cradle she had begun a list of people she believed had treated her badly, starting with the wet nurse. If you think she will help you to make a glittering marriage, then you are doomed to disappointment, my love. Come home with me and Benjamin. I promise you Richard will not get hold of your dowry."

Vivienne didn't even know where to begin. "I barely knew Benjamin, Mother," she said stiffly. "If he had woken me…you know this! I shouldn't have to go over it again. Benjamin was a mistake and one I'm not likely to repeat."

"Pffft," her mother responded. "Mrs. Jones was sure you would make a fine couple. She said you hung on Benjamin's every word that day in her kitchen." She fiddled with the lace on her neckline, avoiding her daughter's eyes. "He is in London, you know."

Vivienne's gaze sharpened. She really did not like this turn of events. "Benjamin is in London?" she said sharply. "I hope you didn't tell him I wanted to see him. If Aunt Jane—"

Her mother waved a dismissive hand. "Goodness me, what a fuss. We just won't tell her."

Vivienne stared. It amazed her how willfully blind her mother could be when it suited her. If Aunt Jane found out Benjamin planned to visit, she would wash her hands of Vivienne. But that was what Mrs. Sutherland wanted, wasn't it? For Vivienne to be sent home to marry Benjamin so that they could be wretched together.

"Vivienne?" Vivienne jumped, but it was only Will at the door. "Mother?" His gaze went from Vivienne to his mother and back again, and she wondered how much of their conversation he had overheard.

"My sweet boy," Helena cooed, holding out her hands.

Vivienne folded her arms and tried to stay calm as her mother gave her attention to Will. She would have liked to quiz her further, but what was the point? She had never listened to her daughter and probably never would.

That evening they dined at home, and Mrs. Sutherland waffled on about the beauties of Cornwall while the viscountess ignored her. Will was rather quiet during the meal, and Vivienne was glad to escape to her room before she could be called upon to share more of her mother's confidences.

The next morning, after a restless night, Vivienne agreed to walk with Annette in the park. During a moment alone at breakfast, Annette had confided in her that matters still weren't going as planned with Ivo.

"What do you mean?" Vivienne replied, concerned by her cousin's pale looks and shadowed eyes. Things must be bad indeed.

"He confided in me." Annette glanced over her shoulder, but they were quite alone. All the same, her voice was a harsh whisper as she went on, "As if I were his...his sister! As if everyone has not been waiting for him to propose all this time." Her chest was rising and falling with indignation.

"Annette, what did he say?"

She seemed to deflate. "He said he had met someone he liked. A woman. A girl. I don't know. Just 'someone.'"

Vivienne stared into Annette's bewildered gaze. "Someone he liked? *Who?*"

"He wouldn't say. He was almost coy." She pulled a face. "I was so amazed I didn't ask any more."

"But that doesn't mean he is planning to marry this someone. Does it?"

Annette's mouth trembled as if she was about to cry.

"It was the way he said it. He had a look on his face. I am not a violent woman, Vivienne, but I wanted to slap him."

Vivienne tried to think of something to say, but all she came up with was "Does Aunt Jane know?"

Annette shook her head wildly. "How can I tell her? Did you know she has an appointment with her modiste this morning? She's planning my wedding gown!"

The two girls stared at each other in horror, and a tear ran down Annette's cheek. Vivienne reached for her hand and gave it a squeeze. "I rather think I could slap him too."

"I never wanted to marry him anyway, so I should be relieved," her cousin admitted, "but I know Mama will blame me, and I hate it when she's angry."

"Once she gets over her disappointment, Aunt Jane will see you could be much happier with someone else," Vivienne said evenly. "Harold, for instance."

Annette gasped. "You know!"

"That you are partial to your publisher friend? Of course I do. I'd be a fool not to know." She was tempted to add that Aunt Jane was just such a fool. "Don't worry, I will stand by you when she finds out, and once it is over, things will be so much more comfortable for you."

Annette's mood had improved as they hurried upstairs to put on their outdoor clothes. Vivienne was ready first, and was waiting in the hall when her mother called to her from the front sitting room.

"Vivienne!"

She smoothed on her gloves as she went to the door. "Yes, Mother?"

Helena was seated on the green satin sofa, a tea tray on the table before her. She was smiling like a cat with a bowl of cream. There was a visitor on the chair opposite her, his back to Vivienne so that all she could see was his gold-streaked brown hair curling riotously over his collar. There was something almost familiar about that hair, but she dismissed her suspicions. Her mother could not be so brazen.

"Vivienne," Mrs. Sutherland said airily, "you remember Benjamin Jones? Well, how silly I am, of course you do!"

The man with the familiar hair stood up and turned, and there he was. Her heart sank like a stone. *Oh no!* Did she say it aloud? She put her hand to her mouth, but it was too late. His smile beneath a truly magnificent mustache wavered before he rallied.

"Miss Tremeer," he said with a bow. "It is so good to see you again. And I am Captain Jones now," he added proudly, as if his resplendent uniform were not clue enough.

She stared at him in fascination. She could not say she knew him well, but she thought the past year had changed him. His skin had darkened from the outdoor life of a soldier, but his eyes still sparkled in the way that she remembered, and he was just as handsome.

For a moment she felt dizzy as the past intersected with the present, and the dangerous possibilities of this visit swooped in on her. At any moment Aunt Jane would walk into the room and find him here, and she knew her aunt well enough to guess what conclusions she would draw.

"Benjamin," she whispered.

He came forward to take her hands, smiling down at her as if she was everything to him. "Vivienne...Miss Tremeer. It has been far too long."

Not long enough. She almost said that aloud too.

Behind him, her mother beamed as if she had single-handedly created a miracle. As Vivienne stood frozen before the man who had besmirched her reputation because he was too stupid to wake her when she fell asleep, Annette's voice sounded from behind her.

"Vivienne, are you ready?" she said, the words followed by a sharp indrawn breath. "Is this…?"

"Mother, what are you thinking!" Vivienne burst out.

And then her worst nightmare came true as her aunt's voice drifted down from the top of the stairs. "Who's there? Annette? Is there a visitor? It is rather early for callers."

The two cousins exchanged a terrified look.

"Don't let her in," Vivienne whispered desperately. "Please, Annette. I'll try to get him out of here before she sees him."

"Oh, I say…" Benjamin began, his expression one of mingled surprise and mild irritation, while Mrs. Sutherland squawked a protest.

When Annette didn't move, Vivienne pushed her outside into the hall and closed the door behind her. Then she stood, listening, holding her breath and praying Aunt Jane would not notice her daughter's white face and shocked eyes.

Annette's voice came through the door, sounding breathless. "Oh, Mama, I…I am just about to go for a walk. I wondered if you cared to join me? It is such a fine day."

"Join you?" her mother declared, as if she had never heard anything more absurd. "I am far too busy to go for a walk. I have an appointment with my modiste. Who is in the sitting room? I thought I heard voices."

"Oh, that was Mrs. Sutherland. She has a headache, so she is lying down on the sofa. I closed the door so she wouldn't be disturbed. Did you want me to ask her if she wishes to accompany you?" Annette added with casual brilliance.

Vivienne bit her lip on an hysterical laugh.

"No, I do not," her aunt replied sharply. The sound of their steps moved away, and Vivienne's shoulders slumped with relief.

Behind her she could feel two sets of eyes drilling into her back, and she took a deep breath before she turned. Her mother looked unrepentant, while Benjamin appeared confused.

"I had hoped…" he began, but she put her finger to her lips and he stopped with a disgruntled huff.

A moment later the front door closed and there was silence. Relief filled her, but it was not over yet. Vivienne set her shoulders and prepared to deal with the situation. It occurred to her that this was like being in Cornwall again, and another very good reason why she did not want to go home.

"Miss Tremeer…no, you are Vivienne to me," Benjamin said in a passionate voice. "I refuse to call you anything else. When I remember the night we spent together I—"

"I was asleep!" Vivienne whisper shrieked.

"I gazed at your lovely face in the firelight and I knew—"

"I'm sorry you have been invited here under false pretenses," she interrupted coldly.

Her mother gasped, but Benjamin hadn't finished.

"Vivienne, when you realize how much I still esteem you, I hope that you will allow me to—"

"Definitely not," she broke in again.

"Vivienne, you are being impolite," Mrs. Sutherland joined in.

"You do appreciate, Mother, that this will cause a great deal of trouble for us both."

Her mother waved a dismissive hand. "You exaggerate, my love."

Frustration threatened to overwhelm her but Vivienne pushed on, trying to make the two of them understand just how much trouble they were in. "I do not exaggerate. Remember when Aunt Jane heard about…" She glanced at Benjamin, deciding not to describe their liaison as "the disaster." "Remember how angry she was?"

Mrs. Sutherland did remember. She shuddered. To Vivienne's dismay, she also made her way toward the door and opened it, peeping outside to see if the coast was clear. "There is no need for me to play chaperone. I shall leave you two to discuss your future." She gave a vague smile, and slipped outside, closing the door again after her.

Vivienne stared. She shouldn't have been surprised by her mother's appalling behavior, her complete lack of a conscience, and yet she was. Well, it was done now, and however it had occurred, the situation needed to be resolved, and Vivienne was the only one who could fix it. She drew herself up and looked at Benjamin. He was smiling at her as if he truly believed they were about to be reunited. Two lost souls who had found their way back to each other, or some such nonsense. What on earth had Helena been telling him?

"You need to leave," she said bluntly.

His smile didn't waver. In fact he tilted his head to the side, as if humoring her. Vivienne closed her hands into fists and wondered if violence was the answer.

"Benjamin, you need to go. I did not ask you to come here. I do not want you here."

"I know that isn't true. Are you angry with me for not writing to you? You know how difficult I find putting pen to paper, and with the fighting…us army fellows do have a good time, even when we're not fighting!" His face changed, as if he registered he had said something he shouldn't have, but a moment later he was smiling again. "Since I've been back in England, I've thought about you. In fact I think about you all the time. I know we can be happy together. Your mother said…"

Vivienne had been listening to him in amazement. Once you got past his pretty face, there was nothing to admire, really, and she had always been profoundly grateful that she had not been forced to marry him. And that was what would have happened if Mrs. Sutherland had had her way. Aunt Jane may not like Vivienne very much, but at least she had her to thank for rescuing her from this idiot.

"No," she said, interrupting his flow. "We spent one day and one night together, and it has caused me a great deal of grief and suffering. There is nothing between us and never will be. I am asking you to leave."

"I can't go," he said reasonably. "My horse is in your stables. Your mother said it would be safe there and best if no one saw it, although I'm not sure why—"

Vivienne tried not to scream. "Of course she did." Ignoring him, she went to the door and opened it a crack. The house was empty, apart from a liveried footman. She knew she had to act quickly. Aunt Jane might return, and if she found her niece and Benjamin together. Alone…No, that couldn't happen. It mustn't.

She beckoned the footman over. "Please fetch Jem the groom," she said. "At once!" she added when the man looked about to question her order.

That tone did the trick. Vivienne closed the door again, counting the moments until finally Jem knocked upon it. As soon as he looked past her and saw who was in the room with her, his face reddened with anger.

"What the…?" he began in a low roar.

Vivienne hushed him. "Jem, we don't have time. I need to get him out of here without anyone seeing him."

"That's not going to be easy," he growled. "Your aunt has just returned home. The carriage is outside. Perhaps she forgot something?"

Vivienne wondered if she looked as shocked as she felt.

"Oh, is that the Viscountess Monteith?" Benjamin had joined them and was about to step past them into the hall. "I should pay her my compliments."

Jem grabbed his arm and held on to it. "I don't think so, you tuss. You are coming with me before you cause the maid any more trouble."

Benjamin's protests went unheard as Jem bundled him down the hall toward the back of the house. Vivienne followed, glancing over her shoulder as the door to the street opened and she heard her aunt's voice complaining about leaving behind some important fashion sketches. Then they were in the mews and a moment later inside the stables. Jem's face was so grim that even Benjamin seemed subdued by his escort. He had stopped arguing, probably remembering the day Jem sent him running when he found him lurking around the stables.

In a moment Benjamin was mounted on his horse and had trotted off, with a longing backward glance.

"What is he doing here?" Jem said.

"My mother thinks I should marry him and come home. Oh, and she probably needs my dowry."

Jem snorted in disgust. "You'd be better off with that gambling hell owner," he muttered.

Vivienne smiled as if he had made a joke. "Unfortunately I do not qualify. I am not wealthy nor well bred, and I do not have a spotless reputation."

Jem gave her a hard look, and she wondered how much he had seen during those times he had taken her to Gabriel's house or Cadieux's, or how much her voice had betrayed her. "You have something better than any of that," he growled. "He'd be lucky to have you at any price, maid, and if he doesn't know that, then he's as foolish as the soldier boy."

Vivienne didn't reply; what was the point? At least she had managed to avert disaster for the time being, but she had a hollow sense of foreboding, as if it was only a matter of time before her shaky house of cards finally fell down around her.

Chapter Twenty-Seven

The singer's voice rose to incredible heights, and Vivienne tried not to wince. She wasn't sure why she had agreed to come tonight to the soiree at Lady Elphinstone's, or rather she did know, she just wasn't sure it had been a good idea. She had come because Annette had begged her to. Ivo and his family were accompanying them, and it seemed that word had still not filtered through to Aunt Jane that the grand marriage she was expecting to arrange was not going to happen. At least Vivienne could be a distraction, according to Annette.

"If you and Aunt Helena are with us, she won't have time to ask me—or Ivo!—why we are dawdling."

"I hope you're right. Has Ivo told his mother about this other woman?"

"I don't know. She hurried from the room earlier, to avoid speaking to Mama about her visit to the modiste, so perhaps he has."

"It's nonsensical," Vivienne declared. "Is everyone afraid of Aunt Jane?"

Annette swallowed nervously. "You know what she's like. I…I think Ivo and I need to talk first. You were right. I was just so surprised when he told me there was someone else that I was mute. I should have asked him to explain. We need to think of a way to break the news without causing too much of a rumpus."

When Vivienne remembered the suffering this situation had caused Annette, she felt little sympathy for Aunt Jane. The Duke of Northam falling for another woman was the least he could have done and in Vivienne's opinion it was just a pity he had not done it earlier.

Dinner had been cold and half-cooked, but with the promise of the latest must-see operatic sensation to entertain them afterward, everyone was prepared to pretend the meal was delicious. But the singer was a disappointment too. Vivienne supposed she might be having an off night, or perhaps reports of her greatness had been very much exaggerated. Or, more likely, tonight Vivienne was difficult to please.

It didn't help that Gabriel and Olivia were also present, with the Earl of March and his daughter, Lady Edeline. They were seated toward the front of the room, and Vivienne was finding it difficult to keep her gaze from straying to them, counting the number of times Gabriel leaned in as Edeline whispered to him. Vivienne hadn't had a chance to exchange more than the usual polite formalities when they had greeted each other under Aunt Jane's watchful eye, and then at dinner they had been seated far from each other. It was hopeless, really. Even if Vivienne had wanted to make her way over to Gabriel—and that would be awkward enough—Mrs. Sutherland stuck to her side, insisting in a coquettish voice that she be introduced to simply everyone. Aunt Jane's mouth was growing tighter and tighter, so Vivienne suspected they would not be staying long once the performance was over.

She glanced along the line of chairs in her row. Her mother was smiling and tapping her toe while Annette sat stiffly between the viscountess and Ivo. On Northam's other side, his mother and one of his sisters whispered together like conspirators. The Viscount Monteith had had the foresight to escape the evening by pleading another engagement.

The singer hit another high note, followed by gasps from her appreciative audience, and Vivienne decided she had had enough. She would not be missed. Being on the end of the row, it was a simple matter to murmur an excuse, rise, and make her way unobtrusively to the back of the room.

Mr. Elphinstone had a fascination with Egypt and spent a great deal of his time digging up pharaohs' tombs, or paying others to do so. Annette had shuddered when she mentioned this to Vivienne, calling it "morbid." "He has an artifact room at his house, where he showcases his finds," she explained.

"Perhaps we can ask to see it?" Vivienne had suggested, but Annette only shuddered again. The footman standing outside the door gave her directions, and she made her way along a corridor and then up some stairs to the room in question. The sight made her stop and stare in amazed wonder.

The room was full of antiquities. Scrolls in glass cases and pieces of ancient stone covered in strange little drawings. There were books too, overflowing from the shelving that rose toward the ceiling. Several decorated mummy cases were on display, and painted ceramic heads were arranged in a central position, the long-dead faces strangely beautiful.

Mr. Elphinstone had had the ceiling painted too, and

as Vivienne gazed upward, she felt as if she had entered the world of these long-ago kings, with their chariots and falcons and scantily clothed bodies.

It occurred to her that most of the guests in the other room would probably be scandalized if they saw this, but Vivienne found it captivating. At least she had escaped the sight of Gabriel and the woman he was going to marry.

Slowly she turned around, taking in the exotic scene. It was pleasantly peaceful in here. Her mother hadn't given up on reuniting Vivienne with Benjamin, and used any moment she and her daughter were alone to put forward his case. It didn't seem to matter how often Vivienne told her she wasn't interested in him; her mother persisted. Vivienne was even beginning to suspect that Aunt Jane had guessed something was up and, guilty as Vivienne felt for thinking it, perhaps it would be a good distraction when her aunt's wedding plans for Annette fell apart.

Her thoughts were interrupted by the door opening behind her. Her solitude was short lived, and she was praying it was not her mother come to pester her as she turned with a polite smile. And stilled, her eyes widening. *Gabriel.* Her heart gave that swooping dive it seemed to perform whenever he was near, and she knew she was smiling. It was involuntary. His mere presence made her happy…and sad.

Hastily she rearranged her features. Their being more than casual acquaintances was as likely as Vivienne traveling into the deserts of Egypt with Mr. Elphinstone.

"Miss Tremeer." He bowed. He didn't seem surprised to see her, and knowing that he had followed her in here on purpose filled her with elation.

"Grantham," she responded calmly while her pulse was anything but calm.

He moved toward her in his dark tailcoat and cream silk breeches—formal wear for a formal evening. He was so immaculately turned out that she wondered if other gentlemen were thinking of poaching his valet. It had been known to happen. But there was more to Gabriel's appearance than his clothing, his good looks, or his charisma. It was the man himself.

"You are well?" he asked politely, but his eyes were saying other things. She couldn't be wrong about that, could she? Gabriel did harbor feelings for her.

"I…yes." She glanced about her, seeking some topic of conversation to return the moment to the ordinary and mundane. "What a wonderful room. Did you know about it? When Annette told me, I knew I had to see for myself."

She was babbling and stopped.

He glanced around as if he'd only just realized where he was. "No, I didn't, although our host was waffling on about his collection at dinner." If he knew nothing of the artifact room, then why was he here? As if he had heard her unspoken question, Gabriel answered it.

"At the ball you seemed…" He stepped closer. "You haven't heard from Longley?"

"No." She looked up at him in surprise. "You must have frightened him away."

"Unfortunately I don't think he frightens easily."

"Don't worry," she said in a confidential tone, "I can handle Sir Hubert."

His mouth twitched. "I've seen you handle my sisters, so I can well believe it."

She wanted to joke with him, but at his mention of his sisters, she felt a wave of loneliness. She missed them, and she missed him. She had felt as if she belonged in the midst of his cobbled-together family, and it hurt to have been cast out. Now she felt as if she were drifting in a vast ocean with nothing to keep her anchored.

"Your mother is visiting I see," Gabriel said after a moment.

She made a sound that could have been a laugh, and then covered her mouth with her fingers. She was a little overwrought. "My mother, yes."

Gabriel's gaze sharpened. He took a step closer. "What is it? What's wrong?"

She shook her head. "Nothing is wrong."

"I don't believe you. Something is the matter. Tell me at once."

Suddenly she wanted to tell him. He would understand; maybe he was the only one who would. Before she could stop herself, the words spilled out of her, how Benjamin—now a captain—had arrived, how her mother was trying to persuade her to marry him, that she didn't want to, that if Aunt Jane found out, she would be banished to Cornwall immediately.

Gabriel listened to it all, his frown deepening as the tale went on. There was comfort in sharing her troubles with him, and for an instant after she finished she felt so relieved. It didn't last. A moment later realization hit her, and she was appalled at herself; she wanted to take everything back again. "I'm sorry. Lady Edeline must be wondering where you are."

"I'm not worried about that," he said impatiently.

"But y-you don't want to hear my troubles. You have enough of your own, Gabriel. Truly I don't expect you to solve anything. It was just…I should go." But when she went to walk away, he caught hold of her arm.

"Vivienne." There was a note in his voice like a scold, or an endearment. "We're still friends, are we not? If you cannot tell me your troubles, then who can you tell?"

She gave a little laugh, which sounded more like a sob, and looked up. He was smiling, his handsome face so familiar and dear above his snowy cravat. He was still holding her arm, but now his grip slid down to her gloved hand, and his fingers intertwined with hers before he lifted their joined hands to his lips. Vivienne watched him, hardly believing this was happening.

"Gabriel," she breathed. She had so much more to say, but none of it seemed important now. Besides he knew as well as she how impractical, how impossible it was that they could be together. Perhaps she should just kiss him as she had been longing to ever since their moment in the library at Ashton House. It may be her last chance.

Vivienne stretched up and pressed her lips to his. He started, as if taken by surprise. She didn't want to see his expression, didn't want to know what he thought of her forwardness. Instead she transferred her kisses to his jaw, nuzzling against his smooth, recently shaven skin. His citrus pomade smelled wonderful, but then it always did. He still had not moved, and with a sigh she rested her cheek against his chest, ignoring the gold button on his coat pressing into her. He was unmoving for so long she thought he was going to abandon her here, walk away without a word, but then she felt his hand begin to caress her hair, so gently. If she could stay here forever she would, but he was already stepping back to put some space between them.

Swallowing her disappointment, she said, "I really should go," but once again he stopped her.

"Not yet." His voice had deepened to that gruff note that made heat pool in her belly. "My turn now." And his mouth closed on hers with rough urgency, as if he couldn't help himself either. With a soft cry of need and surrender, she leaned into their kiss.

Vivienne twined her arms around his neck, her fingers twisting in the crisp hair at his nape and probably disarranging his cravat. He groaned and cupped her face with his hand, angling her so that their kiss deepened. Became passionate and wild. He was as desperate for her as she was for him, and now they could hold back no more. His arm was an iron band around her waist as he pulled her closer and she was being crushed, her body helpless against his, while his mouth ravaged hers.

It was wonderful.

He broke away, taking a breath, nuzzling against her ear. Tingles of excitement gave her shivers, and her heart was pounding. She turned her head and found his mouth again, making a noise that was suspiciously like a whimper. His tongue explored hers, and this time when he groaned, Vivienne felt her knees give way, only his arms preventing her from falling. Nothing before had prepared her for this. The force of her desire was almost unstoppable, and she didn't care because she didn't want to stop.

Until a clinking sound pierced her foggy senses, and reality rushed in. Thinking someone had entered the library, she pulled violently away. All she needed now was for Aunt Jane to find her in Gabriel's arms. As she stood before him, panting, staring into his eyes, she knew with an awful clarity that she could not do that to him. Gabriel had too much to lose, and she wouldn't inflict her damaged reputation on a man who was working hard to overcome his own scandal. Because if he had too much to lose, she was already lost.

"I'm sorry, I shouldn't, we shouldn't—" She turned

and started toward the door in front of her. It was only when she pushed it open that she found this wasn't the door she had come through after all but another one, and it led into a different room. A billiard room. And it wasn't empty.

A cue clicked against a ball, and as it thumped into one of the pockets in the green baize table, Olivia Ashton gave a startled glance over her shoulder in their direction.

"Gabriel!" She gasped, blue eyes wide. "What are you doing here?"

Gabriel's brows had come down, and he let his gaze slide from his sister to the man on the other side of the billiard table. Vivienne recognized him. Ivo, the Duke of Northam.

She floundered to comprehend what the two of them were doing in here. The entertainment was still underway, she could hear the singer warbling. Why were they…?

"What are *you* doing here?" Gabriel said in a voice that should have sent a tremor of dread through his sister.

It didn't.

"I asked first," Olivia retorted, her eyes narrowed, her cheeks flushed. The two siblings glared at each other, and in that moment they looked very much alike.

Ivo had been observing them with surprise rather than alarm, and now he stepped forward with his friendly smile, as if it were perfectly normal to be playing billiards alone with a single young lady. "This is my fault," he said calmly. "I challenged Lady Olivia to a game when she told me she was a master player." He glanced at Olivia as he spoke, and there was something in his eyes…

Oh no, Vivienne thought as suddenly the pieces clicked together.

He said he had met someone he liked.

Ivo and Olivia dancing together at the ball. Olivia was that someone.

"And I have to concede she is a far better player than I," Ivo went on softly, fondly, and gave a little bow.

Gabriel must have sensed the situation too. Vivienne felt him stiffen at her side, like a guard dog. Olivia shot him a guilty look under her lashes and set down her cue. "No one noticed us leaving," she said, as if that were an excuse.

"Of course they did," Gabriel retorted, and there was no doubting his anger.

"Annette would have noticed," Vivienne said quietly, eyes on Ivo. "And my aunt."

Ivo's blue gaze narrowed, but he said nothing.

The silence became awkward while the siblings continued their standoff. Vivienne was aware that she was completely forgotten as this new drama unfolded. Or perhaps not, because Gabriel seemed to be doing his best not to catch her eye, not to even look in her direction.

Regret filled her. She never should have told him her troubles and reminded him of how unsuitable she was as his friend, let alone anything more. She never should have kissed him.

"Come with me," Gabriel said, holding out his arm, and Olivia didn't hesitate to slip her fingers into the crook of it. A moment later they were leaving, and Vivienne didn't know whose back was the stiffest.

Ivo's mouth twitched into a humorless smile. "After you," he murmured.

Vivienne felt flat, defeated. As if her encounter with Gabriel hadn't been turbulent enough, now this. She shot Ivo a censorious look. "What are you thinking?" she hissed. "Lady Olivia Ashton?"

Ivo seemed to consider her question seriously, and then he gave an awkward little shrug. "I don't think I am."

Chapter Twenty-Eight

Gabriel was furious.

"Don't you know Northam is near enough to engaged?" he growled at Olivia as they paused at the door to the drawing room. "What were you thinking?"

"No he's not!" she declared, and then…"Is he?"

Suddenly, she looked so young and vulnerable he found he couldn't berate her as he knew he should. Perhaps no one had noticed her absence, after all. But as soon as they walked through the door, his hopes were dashed.

The performance had come to a stop, the singer fussing with some sheets of music at her accompanist's side, and the guests were no longer focused on her. Heads turned toward Olivia, surprised expressions changed to shocked and knowing as Ivo and Vivienne followed behind her, and whispers filled the room like chilly breezes.

Vivienne's aunt half rose in her seat, her features tight with fury, no doubt on behalf of her daughter. Before she could let her feelings be known, someone at her side tugged her back down. Gabriel did his best to ignore the sensation they were creating, relieved when what seemed like a long walk was over, and they reached their seats.

He could feel the earl's chilly stare like icicles on the side of his face, but he did not meet the man's eyes. Good manners had ensured he keep tonight's commitment with March and Lady Edeline, but now he remembered his grandmother's warnings.

Olivia trembled beside him, finally aware of her faux pas, her face white and her eyes downcast. He reached for her hand, and her fingers squeezed his so tightly he could feel her nails digging into his skin. Gabriel felt his anger simmering and did his best to push it deeper, telling himself anything he had to say could wait until they were at home. Besides, it wasn't only Olivia he was furious with. He was glad when the singer resumed, hoping people would forget.

Instead the evening turned into a disaster.

The whispers continued as supper was served at the end of the performance. Guests congregated in groups, casting glances Olivia's and Ivo's way, despite the two of them being at opposite ends of the room. The Viscountess Monteith was busy, her hands waving about furiously, her vicious words not audible to Gabriel but obvious from the reaction of her companions. Someone tittered as Olivia walked by and she turned her head, startled, but the person showed her their back.

Gabriel moved quickly toward her, and noticed Vivienne doing the same. Of course she would help; he would expect nothing less. He hadn't anticipated seeing her here tonight, and when he'd turned his head from the front row and seen her slip away, he'd followed her without a second thought. He supposed that made him as reckless as Olivia. He'd only meant to ask her if Longley had bothered her again, but when she'd kissed him…he'd forgotten everything but the taste of her, the feel of her.

Now he asked himself, as he had been doing ever since she told him her troubles, how her mother could bring that boy back into her life. Hurt her like that. The anger he had tried to tamp down simmered to the surface again. Vivienne met his gaze, and he wondered what she saw because she quickly looked away. She had almost reached Olivia when the viscountess called out her name in a way that meant business. Vivienne hesitated but had no choice but to obey her aunt. The smile she sent to Olivia was brave and full of fellow feeling, but earned her a hissed reprimand from her relative.

Gabriel calmly took his sister's arm, aware how close she pressed to him, and turned toward their hosts. Only to find the Duke of Northam in his path.

The man was bowing, and when he straightened, his fair hair looked as if he'd been running his hands through it, and his face was pale and set. "My apologies," he said in a voice loud enough to be heard by those who were listening. "Completely my fault, Lady Olivia." Then, lowering his voice for them alone, "I promise I will fix this."

Gabriel was proud of his sister then, the curt nod she gave in response, and the way she lifted her chin proudly as they made their polite farewells to the Elphinstones. It wasn't until they were in the coach on the way home that her façade broke down.

"Gabriel?"

"What?" he snapped. She flinched and he was immediately contrite. "I apologize, I was miles away. You said something?"

"I didn't but I wanted to. Gabriel, I'm sorry. I shouldn't have been alone with Ivo."

"Ivo?" With raised eyebrows.

"His Grace the Duke of Northam," she corrected herself, "but he prefers Ivo."

"Olivia," he sighed. Were they having this conversation now? It appeared so. "You have worked so hard. You are beginning to find your place in society. It may not be what you wanted, God knows it isn't what I want, but I thought you were coming to terms with it. You seemed to be enjoying yourself, or was I wrong?"

"No, you weren't wrong," she admitted, her eyes shiny with tears as she looked up at him. "I *was* enjoying myself. It was so pleasant to be sought after and to dress in pretty things, and I was liking it very much. And now I've ruined it." Her mouth turned down in her misery, and a tear plopped onto her skirt.

He wanted to agree with her, but he wasn't their grandmother. Olivia knew how badly she'd faltered, and rubbing her nose in it was not the way to handle his headstrong sister. "We are still learning to live within the rules," he said. "Sometimes we can stretch them a little, or even bend them on occasion, but we must never break them."

"Do you think I have?" she said, sounding very young. "Broken them?"

"I don't know," he admitted. "You certainly caused a stir. Northam said he would fix things but how reliable is he, and how can he mend matters? Perhaps people will make allowances for your inexperience."

She sighed. "I am very sorry. I forgot for a moment where I was and what was at stake. I am trying very hard to be a duke's sister."

"Your life has been turned upside down," Gabriel agreed.

"So has yours. And don't tell me you don't resent it,

for I won't believe you," she said when he went to dismiss her words.

"Of course I resent it," he admitted, and heard the exasperation in his voice. "I wish it were different, but I understand why I have to change. It's for the sake of you and your sisters. If I had refused to take on the dukedom, then you would have been cast into penury, forced to live with relatives and strangers who had no care for you. How would you have felt about that? The estate was bankrupt, and although I have managed to claw it back to respectable limits, it will take time for us to be truly safe."

Her eyes had widened. "Do you mean we could still be cast into pen-penury?"

Not if I can help it.

"There is a possibility," he said evenly. "However, I will do my utmost not to let that happen. I may be a bad duke, but I am an excellent businessman."

She gave a shaky laugh. "You're not a bad duke. It was I who messed up. Grandmama will be livid, she is always going on about what is at stake, but I didn't realize how bad things could get until now. It's horrible to be treated like that. Especially when I was enjoying myself so much. I don't like it, Gabriel, I really don't."

They rode in silence for the rest of the journey, and Gabriel had a great deal to think about. He *was* resentful, Olivia was right, but not so much because his life had changed beyond all recognition. He had come to terms with that, and perhaps soon the losing of his club. He'd even begun to enjoy many of the aspects of his new life. No, he was resentful because his brain was still at war with his heart. Tonight, when Vivienne had kissed him, she had shown him what a love match would look like, and he began to hope again. Only for that hope to be immediately dashed when Olivia acted thoughtlessly. Now he was faced with that cold, hard truth. For the sake of his sisters and their futures, he must not marry the woman he loved. Vivienne was beautiful and vibrant, kind and generous, but he could not have her.

He had to keep his distance, which was especially difficult right now, when he was aware of how much she needed him. She had been distraught when the sordid story had spilled from her lips. He knew she regretted telling him immediately, but he didn't. If her family was conspiring against her, her mother and that soldier, then he needed to know. Even her brother, Will, who obviously valued her, still relied upon her to the extent that she had been willing to risk her aunt's ire and visit Gabriel at his club. Will was right when he said Vivienne was the one person everyone turned to for help. It was time someone stood beside her and fought the world on her behalf, time someone kept her safe, and Gabriel desperately wanted to be that person.

His anger over the situation was still there, simmering away, and as soon as Olivia was delivered safely home, he set off to find Freddie. He needed an address. He needed to look this soldier boy in the eye and warn him to leave Vivienne alone. After his talk with Olivia, it seemed hypocritical of him to even consider such a rash move—yes, Gabriel knew he was acting irrationally—but he couldn't help himself. Was he bending the rules or breaking them? He wasn't sure and he didn't care. All he knew was that it was more important to act to protect Vivienne than concern himself with the members of the ton. He may not be able to marry her, but he would save her from those who would do her harm.

Captain Benjamin Jones wasn't difficult to find. He wasn't staying at the barracks but in some lodging rooms nearby. Freddie had soon discovered the address—evidently Benjamin was happy to have visitors and exchange tales of derring-do with his fellows. He was well liked, Freddie had informed him, as long as his army tales were taken with a large grain of salt.

"A fool"—Freddie pronounced judgment on him—"but a harmless one."

The lodging house was rather like the one Gabriel had once roomed in, when he wasn't at his club, and before he moved into the Mayfair house. When he caught himself glancing askance at the grubby floors and wrinkling his nose at the smell of cabbage, he knew how much he had changed. He very much doubted he would be able to go back to the life he had once led, and in fact the thought of his new status suddenly being taken away from him was acutely painful.

Perhaps he would make a passable duke after all.

A knock on the door produced a muttered complaint about the hour, and stumbling steps, and a moment later it opened. The man had clearly gone to bed in his cups, his pantaloons with the braces dangling and his shirt untucked. Not that his rumpled and flushed appearance detracted from his handsome looks.

Gabriel felt a stab of jealousy at the thought of Vivienne in this man's arms, but his simmering anger overwhelmed it almost immediately.

"Who are you?" Benjamin said, blinking up at him with bloodshot blue eyes.

"I am a friend of Vivienne Tremeer."

It took a moment for the man to understand as he weaved back and forth in the doorway, and then he gave a beaming if somewhat drunken smile. "I'm going to marry her," he announced.

Gabriel lost any hold he might have had on his temper. The thought of someone else with the woman he had been denied was too much for him. He grabbed Benjamin by his shirt and pushed him back, hard, making him stumble into a stand upon which sat a washing jug and basin. There was a crash, and Benjamin flopped down among the debris.

He looked up at Gabriel, his mouth open in shock. It was his expression that brought Gabriel back to his senses. He had never been a violent man for the sake of it. The few times he had gotten into fights he had been defending himself or his friends, or breaking up an altercation at the club. If he had to put up his fists, then he could certainly hold his own, but this was different, out of character.

Gabriel took a heaving breath; his heart seemed to be pounding as if it were trying to escape his chest. "Give me your hand," he said gruffly, holding out his own. Understandably Benjamin hesitated before he obliged, and Gabriel hauled him to his feet.

"Vivienne sent you?" he asked in a doubtful voice. "I don't think she would do that."

"No, she didn't."

"Then…"

"Stay away from her. Whatever was once between you…can't you see you are causing her distress?"

"Distress?" He frowned as if trying to understand. "She knows I would never do that. She—"

"Cadieux?"

That voice. Gabriel closed his eyes briefly, but he

heard the steps come closer. He turned and, like a bad dream, there was Longley in the shadows, staring at him curiously. At that moment Gabriel remembered Charles's warning, and in this moment he knew it to be true. Longley had been keeping eyes on him, following him and searching for anything compromising he could use to punish him for refusing to hand over his club. Now his gaze went from Gabriel to Benjamin and back again, and he smiled.

It was the sort of smile that sent a chill of foreboding through Gabriel. Longley would destroy him if he could, and Gabriel had just handed him the weapon.

"Visiting a friend?" Longley asked in a sneering voice.

"Something like that."

Longley looked at Benjamin, who refused to meet his eyes, and then back at Gabriel. "You should have given me my club back," he said, and then he walked away. Gabriel waited until he was gone before he turned to Benjamin.

"Stay away from her," he hissed. "Do you understand?"

Benjamin gave a sulky shrug. "I didn't want to see her again anyway," he said. "It was her mother who insisted." And he slammed the door in Gabriel's face.

Before long the tittle-tattle was everywhere. Not only about Olivia—although Northam had made good on his promise, persuading the gossips it was his fault they had been briefly alone and he had been asking for her advice on a gift for his sister. But as soon as the heat died down around Olivia, it flared up again around Gabriel, who was the subject of this latest on-dit, and he had no one to blame but himself.

The dowager forgot herself so much as to come striding into the breakfast room with her dark eyes blazing and face ghostly white. She hadn't even stopped to put on her usual dazzle of jewelry.

Gabriel had been attempting to bring order to an argument between his sisters—their behavior had deteriorated recently. Olivia had backed him up, declaring the others ignorant and stupid, and said, "If any of you ruin my chance of an entry to Almack's, I will never forgive you."

How things had changed, Gabriel thought. Of course the others would not allow this about-face to go unnoticed, and there were shouts of derision. Their grandmother's sudden entrance brought that to a halt. Gabriel guessed what this was about. Olivia had already been the recipient of a tongue-lashing, and he didn't need the dowager's furious gaze fixed on him to know it was his turn.

"What were you thinking?" she said, her voice trembling with her anger. "Everyone is talking about you. I trusted you to behave like an Ashton, Gabriel. You have gravely disappointed me."

"Has Gabriel done something bad?" Edwina asked, and then shrank down in her chair as her grandmother turned that steely gaze on her. Only for Roberta to take up the baton. "What has he done? Are you going to send him home to Grantham? Can we go too?"

"Be silent!"

Gabriel snapped out of it. "This isn't their fault," he reminded her in a voice that strove to be calm.

"No, it's *your* fault."

He stood up. They glared at each other for a long

moment, and then the dowager seemed to become aware of the girls' gaping mouths and wide eyes. She took a deep breath, and suddenly she looked more like an elderly lady than a Valkyrie.

"Come to my sitting room. Now. We will talk there."

"Gabriel!" Edwina whispered as soon as she had gone, and her arms were wrapped around his legs. "Please don't leave us. Don't let her send you away."

And then the rest of the girls were there, surrounding him, anxious and tearful. He felt even worse now. He should have known better than to risk everything by such a rash action. He was not a rash man. And yet, in a moment of madness, he had rushed off and confronted Benjamin Jones. He'd put everything he and his sisters had worked for in jeopardy.

And it was worse even than that, because his actions were certain to affect Vivienne too.

He opened his arms, and the girls swarmed in, pressing against him, seeking comfort. For a long moment he simply held them because he needed comfort too. "It's all right," he kept saying. "I'm not going anywhere. I'm not. I will sort it out. I promise."

"We try to be good," Edwina said in a wobbly voice, "but it's so hard without Miss Tremeer to help. She made everything fun." A tear slipped down her cheek. "I wish…"

"Oh, do be quiet," Olivia snapped, but Gabriel noticed the shine of tears in her eyes too.

Eventually their trembling calmed enough for him to let them go, and after reassuring them again, he made his way to his grandmother's sitting room.

She was waiting in her usual seat, back rigid, but at least now she was composed. At her stiff nod to him, Gabriel sat down opposite her.

He had meant to let her speak first, but the words erupted from him. "It was Longley, I gather? That man hates me. You shouldn't believe anything he says."

"I wouldn't, he's a cad, but he has important relatives and *they* believe him." Her eyes narrowed. "Are you telling me that it isn't true that you accosted a soldier in his rooms and demanded he stay away from Miss Tremeer?"

Put like that, Gabriel could see just how irresponsible he had been. A rash fool, rushing off without thought to play the hero. Where was his usual pragmatic self? Too late now to think of other ways he could have helped her, less dangerous means he could have used. And yet he could not be ashamed of what he had done. It had seemed right at the time to stand up for Vivienne, and it still did.

"It is true," he admitted. "Someone had to confront the situation and put a stop to it, but I should have known Longley would take advantage. None of this is Miss Tremeer's fault."

"Once more you are playing the chivalrous knight for a woman who is nothing to you," the dowager retorted waspishly. "Or is she?"

Gabriel didn't reply, but it was no use. His grandmother saw everything just as she always did. He heard her weary sigh.

"She is not the wife for you, Gabriel. She has a past and everyone is well aware of it. The Viscountess Monteith offered her a roof over her head for the sake of her dead brother, but I doubt she will keep her now. Marriage with Miss Tremeer is out of the question. If you have other plans for her, then that is up to you, although I would advise against it. Emotional entanglements cause more problems than they are worth. You only have to look to your father for that lesson."

"I am not my father."

"No." She eyed him steadily. "You are stronger than him, but you have an odd kick. On occasion your emotions overwhelm you. Not always, but when it comes to your sisters, which is a good thing, and this woman, which is not. Emotion makes one weak."

Gabriel shook his head. "I disagree. Emotion makes one human."

"Well…we will not argue. Bad enough that Olivia has become a target for the gossips, and although Northam is helping to put out that fire, his reputation is not the best, so it still may flare up again. They are saying that all Ashtons are the same, did you know that? Lacking in morals, disreputable, and unworthy to be part of respectable society."

Gabriel knew this to be a lie. His reputation at the club was spotless, and to be slandered like this hurt.

"The only way to be certain we put a stop to the talk once and for all is for you to marry someone of impeccable character. Take on your role as head of the family with her at your side. Show everyone that you are serious about reforming yourself."

He said nothing. There was nothing he could say. She was right—his hard pragmatic head was telling him she was right—but his heart was another matter. And yet there was more at stake than his heart, wasn't there? Even Olivia had lost the will to rebel when she had been shown the consequences.

He took a shaky breath. He knew his face was pale and anguished when he turned to her, because her gaze softened. Perhaps she was not made of stone after all.

"What else can I do to repair this?" Gabriel asked, his voice husky. "What do I say to the gossips?"

"*We* say nothing. We neither deny nor agree with them. We ignore them. You will be seen with Lady Edeline as much as possible, and soon the rumors will fade. There is always some new on-dit to capture the ton's imagination."

He nodded his agreement. She was right, he knew she was right, but it didn't hurt any less.

Chapter Twenty-Nine

This time Vivienne went alone to Cadieux's. And instead of riding pillion with Jem, she took a hackney cab. Muffled in her cloak, her face hidden by the hood, she was as incognito as she had been the first time she came here. But things were very different now and, with a hollow feeling in the pit of her stomach, she knew this would be her last visit.

Will's amazed words from earlier rang in her head. *Grantham told Benjamin to stay away from you! He went to his lodgings and shook him like the rat he is.*

Will had burst in upon her as the maid, Jenny, was brushing out her hair in readiness for bed. Vivienne had stayed home, pleading a headache when the others went out to dine with friends. Jenny was sent off with an indignant squeak, while Vivienne listened to Will wide-eyed.

Will had been at the club but had hurried home to tell her the news. "Charles and Freddie…sorry, Mr. Wickley and Ensign Hart were teasing Grantham. They think he has finally run mad after all of his efforts to be prim and proper. And they think it is because of you, Viv."

"Because of me?" she had said in astonishment, while her thoughts returned to those moments in the Egyptian room at the Elphinstones' when she had been unable to stop herself from telling Gabriel about her mother's determination to bring Benjamin back into her life. Gabriel had said he was her friend, but then they had kissed in a manner very unlike friends. Seeing Ivo with Olivia had made her aware of how much the Ashtons had at stake, and she was even more aware of it when the guests turned on poor Olivia. Then Gabriel had looked at her in a way that made her think he was just as aware of the risks as she, that he was distancing himself again. Was that not the case?

"I don't understand," she had whispered.

"What is there to understand?" Will had given her a grin as if he'd won a fortune at cards. "He went and told that fool to stay away from you or else." His grin had subsided and his eyes clouded. "All the same, it hasn't done you any favors, Viv. The gossip is already running wild."

"Does Aunt Jane know?" She had voiced her first thought.

"No, probably no one dared until now. But they will. She's dining out tonight, isn't she? You can be sure someone will give her the news. Maybe you can plead innocent." He had given her a hopeful look.

"I am innocent! I didn't ask him to shake Benjamin like a rat." Her lips had twitched, as Will chuckled. "Stop it," she said, sobering. "It's not funny. I expect once Aunt Jane hears, it will give her a reason to finally send me home. Me and Mother, that will please her. Her house will be free of scandal."

Will had given her a hug. "At least Benjamin won't be

calling on you," he'd said, his voice muffled, attempting to cheer her up. "Come on," he went on, stepping back and squeezing her hands in his. "It mightn't be that bad. Perhaps she will think it a good thing that a duke is championing you."

"A duke she despises."

"All the same, a duke is a duke," Will said.

"Will, it isn't like that," Vivienne had protested wearily, because she could see her brother had some fairy tale in his head. She and Gabriel marrying and living happily ever after. Vivienne knew better than anyone that life wasn't a fictional fantasy, even if Will thought it was. She would be sent home to Cornwall, and that would be it. The remainder of her days didn't bear thinking of, but at least she'd probably be too miserable to care.

But Gabriel *had* rushed to her rescue. Perhaps that wasn't the most sensible thing he could have done, but his gesture, foolishly heroic, lifted her spirits. Would he have done it for anyone else? She wasn't sure, only that he cared enough for her to risk his own reputation. Yes, he had damaged hers, but it was already tainted. She wanted to thank him.

"Is Gabriel still at the club?"

"Are you going to see him? At this hour?"

"If Aunt Jane sends me home in the morning, I may not get another chance. I want…there are things to say."

He had looked hopeful again, and then downcast. "I should come with you. Home I mean, not the club. You shouldn't go alone, Vivienne. It isn't fair. After all you've done for me."

"Nonsense. I have my nest egg." She had reached for him again, holding him close. "Stay here in London. If Aunt Jane asks you to leave, then arrange to stay at Cadieux's.

Do you promise, Will? You're happy in London, and I don't want you to sacrifice yourself for me."

Grudgingly he agreed, and she was glad of that. Will was thriving here, and returning to the chaos that was Tremeer was the last thing he needed. She would do her best to keep him away until he came of age; perhaps she could serve some purpose after all.

Late supper was being served at Cadieux's as Vivienne made her familiar way through the kitchen, aware of the curious stares from the staff and the smirk from the cook. She had learned from Will that Charles Wickley had arranged for a first-rate chef to come and work at the club, and now the suppers were so good that many of the guests simply came to eat, and then stayed to play. Cadieux's was doing extremely well, and it was no wonder Sir Hubert Longley wanted it back. But there was more to it. Longley was jealous of Gabriel because of his success, and she rather thought that was what had driven his behavior in recent times too. Longley thought that Gabriel wanted her, and that had made her all the more attractive.

None of that mattered now. Gabriel would sell his club and continue down his ducal path. He would marry Lady Edeline, and soon no one would care about his past. Vivienne told herself she would be glad for him. He had been generous to her and Will, and he deserved to reap the benefits of his hard work and self-sacrifice. Yes, she loved him, but she had already decided he was better off without her.

The stairs that led up to the closed door of his office were in shadow. Vivienne reached for the balustrade, but before she could begin to ascend, she heard movement to her right. Someone was standing in the corridor to the gaming rooms. Startled, she took a step back, until she heard Charles Wickley's familiar voice.

"Can I help you, ma'am?"

Of course he did not recognize her with the hood over her face. She lifted her chin as he took a step closer, and from the frown line between his brows, she guessed he was not overly pleased now that he *did* recognize her.

She wondered why. He had never shown her enmity before, but then she remembered Will's words. Charles knew about Benjamin, and perhaps Gabriel's rush to her rescue wasn't something he approved of. Her voice was cool when she said, "I have come to see the duke. Is he here?"

"He's upstairs." Charles hesitated a moment and then came closer still. His blue eyes searched hers. "Gabriel is the sort of man who stands up for others. He tries to do the right thing. The right thing for everyone but himself. I hope you will not make matters harder for him than they already are."

"I have no intention of interfering in the duke's life. I wanted to speak to him. To say goodbye, that is all."

Charles sighed as if he didn't believe her, and then he shrugged and said, "Go up, and I will see you are not disturbed."

When he had turned and left her, Vivienne began to climb the stairs, her hand gripping the railing and her heart drumming in her breast.

The door opened to her knock, his silhouette against the glow of the lamp inside. He went still when he saw her, and she couldn't read his expression. Did he not want to see her? Perhaps Charles was right and she should not have come. Her being here would only cause him more trouble, and perhaps it was selfish of her, but she needed this moment. To thank him and say farewell. To draw a line beneath their ill-starred love affair.

"I wanted to—"

He interrupted. "Come in." His voice sounded gravelly, as if he was tired. He stepped back as she entered, taking care not to brush against him, and then he closed the door.

Now that she could see him better, Gabriel did look tired, as if he'd lain awake all night. There were frown lines in his brow, and shadows under his eyes. He hadn't shaved either, the dark scruff of a beard on his jaw and cheeks accentuating the pink of his lips. She could only think that he was suffering from the consequences of his actions, and that was her fault. Regret filled her—she shouldn't be here.

"I want…" she began at the same time as he said, "Please…"

He gestured for her to be seated, but Vivienne didn't want to sit down. Seeing him so worn down was worse than if she had not come at all, and she needed to say her piece and leave. But for some reason the words wouldn't come easily, and she stood in front of him, twisting her hands, trying to order her thoughts into something coherent.

"Before you say anything, I want to apologize," he said.

Nothing could have surprised her more. "Apologize? Why would you…Gabriel, I came to thank you. Will told me what you did with…with Benjamin."

Now *he* looked shocked. "I thought you'd come to give me a piece of your mind. I wouldn't blame you if you did. I'm aware I've made things worse. I was going to call upon you, but I wasn't sure you would agree to see me, and I know your aunt isn't happy with Olivia."

There were too many questions demanding answers, but the first one that popped out was "Why did you do it?"

"God knows," he huffed, reaching to tug at his neckcloth, but it was already hanging loose and crumpled about his throat. "No, I do know." His eyes flickered to hers. "When you told me what had happened, I was seething. I wanted to help you, but I wasn't thinking straight. There was that trouble with Olivia and Northam, and I just...Before I knew it, I was there at his door and...I suppose you know the rest."

He looked as if he hoped she didn't.

"Yes."

Gabriel groaned and shook his head. "I made it worse," he repeated.

Instinctively she put her hand on his forearm and felt bare skin. He had rolled up his sleeves, and her fingers lingered against warm flesh and coarse hairs. "Perhaps a little worse," she admitted, "but what you did was well meant and...and no one has ever done that for me before. Gabriel, no one has ever stood up for me like that. Well, maybe Will did once, at home in Cornwall when Sutherland was being horrible, but he was in his cups."

Gabriel gave a snort of laughter. "You probably thought I was drunk too."

"I think you are wonderful. I don't care what happens to me now. Well, I do, but I can bear it. Thank you. That's all I wanted to say, Gabriel. Thank you for defending my honor, and I am so sorry it has caused such an uproar."

This time he looked at her properly, his dark eyes searching hers, and what he saw must have convinced him she was sincere. The tired lines of his face smoothed out, and the hard line of his mouth softened into a smile.

"I should have known you would see it like that."

He reached out to take hold of her hood and lift it gently back over her head. When he brushed an unruly lock behind her ear, his fingers were incredibly tender. She stood and let him. She didn't move, she couldn't. She wanted to close her eyes and soak up this moment, put it with all the other special moments they had shared, so that she could remember it forever.

"That soldier," he said suddenly, interrupting her happy dream. "I don't blame him for wanting you. I want you too."

Her smile wavered a little. "Oh?"

"That evening outside the Farnsworths' when I was with Longley. The things he was saying…I told him to leave you alone and I said, 'She's mine.' I think you heard that, didn't you? I didn't mean I wanted to buy you or own you. I meant you were mine to protect from creatures like him. Like Benjamin. I felt like that even then, Vivienne."

"Benjamin and I…we didn't do anything," she said, wanting him to know the truth. "I fell asleep, and in the morning the vicar saw us. Everyone assumed the worst, and Sutherland let them assume for his own ends."

"You have been treated abominably." His fingers trailed down the side of her face, lingering over the sweep of her cheekbone, and her eyes began to close. But he cupped her chin, lifting it so that she had no option but to hold his gaze. Dark eyes, so meltingly warm, his desire for her plain to see. She remembered then the kisses they had shared, the desperate passion that had flared between them, and knew he wanted her as much as she wanted him.

This is a very bad idea.

"I should go," she said, sounding breathless. If he agreed, then she promised herself she would turn and walk away. She had said what she came to say and anything more would only compound his troubles.

"I have no right to ask this." He still held her, the pad of his thumb brushing back and forth across her lips, his gaze locked on hers. "But stay. Please."

Didn't he know that she was already lost? She couldn't have left if her life depended on it. The next moment they were in each other's arms.

He took her mouth with a groan. She thought she had remembered how good his kisses were, but they were so much more. His warm lips molding to hers, opening her mouth with a sweep of his tongue. The rasp of his jaw against her palm as she strove to get closer. It felt as if she had been waiting for him for so long. A lifetime.

"Vivienne," he murmured, his voice low and husky. His hand was beneath her cloak, pressed to the small of her back, and the other tangled in her hair. It was good, so good. Her body caught fire, a flame that spread from her breasts to her belly, and turned to molten heat between her thighs. She was trembling so much she had to lean against him to stay upright.

She reached for the ties of her cloak at the same moment as he, both of them fumbling until the garment slid from her shoulders to the floor. He lifted her out of it, up on her toes, and then they were kissing again. She ran her hands up his chest, hard muscled beneath his soft shirt, and traced the breadth of his shoulders, clinging a moment as he kissed her again, before sliding her fingers into that favorite place, the hair at his nape.

"Your hair was longer when I first saw you," she said, remembering the dark unruly curls. "I liked it."

"Too vulgar for a duke," he said, smiling against her lips. "I like yours better." He had removed her pins, and now the long strands came tumbling down and he lifted them to his face, rubbing against her like a cat, as if he wanted to cover himself in her scent.

"Gabriel…" Her voice was a moan. She licked over her swollen bottom lip, and the movement brought him to her again as if he couldn't resist, kissing her deeply. When they came up for air, she struggled to remember her own name.

His midnight eyes delved into hers. "Do you want me to stop?" he whispered. His body was melded against hers, a hand around her waist to hold her right where he wanted her, and she could feel his arousal. Vivienne was a country girl and she had heard others talk. She knew what making love entailed; she knew the particulars of the act. But no one had ever said how desperately she would want him, and how utterly impossible it would be to stop.

She shook her head and said, "Definitely not."

That made him laugh.

"Unless there is somewhere else you have to be?" she added, suddenly wondering if that was a possibility. An engagement with Lady Edeline perhaps…

"No. Nowhere as important as here." For a moment his expression changed and he looked lost, as if he could see into his future and it was a dark and empty place. Vivienne did not like that look on his face—she had seen a similar one on her own, when she knew they could never be together. Tonight was not the time for sorrow.

She tightened her arms about his neck. "We won't see each other again," she reminded him. "Who will care? Who will know? Our memories will be ours alone."

"One night," he agreed, and bent to nuzzle against her throat, finding the pulse that fluttered beneath her skin. She arched her neck to give him better access and then gasped as he sucked against her. "I've marked you," he growled. "You really are mine."

"For one night," she agreed.

"One night."

He reached for her hand then, his warm, strong fingers closing in a possessive grasp as he led her across the room.

There was another smaller room beyond the study. He released her, busying himself lighting a candle, which he set upon the windowsill. Outside, the darkness was broken by the flame's dancing reflection. This must be where Gabriel slept when he was working late, or before he had the Mayfair house to return to, she thought, watching him move about.

He was wearing his old clothes, faded brown breeches and a well-washed cream shirt, a far cry from his fashionable outfits. But it didn't matter if he was Gabriel Cadieux or Grantham, or both. She loved all of him.

He was watching her too, and now he drew his shirt over his head and tossed it aside. Her gaze snagged on the strong, flat planes of a chest with a thick swath of dark hair, and those broad shoulders. When she followed the line of hair that arrowed down to his breeches, she found herself dry mouthed, and when he rested his hands upon the waistband of his breeches, she had to swallow. Because he was even more glorious than she had imagined.

With trembling fingers she reached to fumble awkwardly at the hooks on the back of her gown, knowing she had to feel his skin against hers. In two steps he was there, spinning her about and swiftly completing the task for her. His mouth was warm, with a kiss for each inch of skin revealed. The gown slipped from her shoulders and pooled at her feet, and she stood in her chemise and stockings and shoes.

"Beautiful," he whispered, his breath tickling her. He brushed aside the tumbled locks of her dark hair and kissed her nape, sliding his hands around her to rest just beneath her breasts.

Vivienne tipped her head back against his shoulder, and their mouths met again, slowly this time, as if they were intoxicated. He cupped her soft weight with his palms, fingers brushing over the sensitive buds, which were stiffly upright now. She twisted in his arms, arching into his hands and wanting more. It was the work of a moment to unlace her corset before he dropped to her feet to remove her shoes. As he rose, he slid her chemise slowly up her body and over her head, and then he stood and looked his fill.

Her flesh prickled under his gaze, as if he were touching rather than just looking. Self-consciously she bent and began to untie the ribbons below her knees, which held up her stockings, but he stopped her. "Leave them on," he said hoarsely.

"But…oh."

He liked them on her otherwise naked body, she could tell by the gleam in his eyes and the clench of his jaw. Her momentary shyness vanished, and Vivienne reached for him, running her hands over taut skin that covered defined muscle and bone. There was delight in letting her tongue trace the flat nipples, especially when he showed his appreciation with a groan, and then to discover the pleasure of his coarse hair rasping against her naked breasts.

He found the tip of one and then bent his head to take the other in his mouth, rolling her nipple with his tongue.

She held his head, her words a garbled whimper, while the ache that had been building inside her turned into a desperate need. When he stopped she opened her eyes in dismay, only to see him push down his breeches, kicking them aside. Vivienne caught her breath. Now it was her turn to look her fill.

"May I touch?" she said, already reaching out.

He made a sound that could have been "Yes." He was velvet-covered steel in her grasp, and warm, very unlike the cold stone she had once compared him to. He moved his hips, thrusting into her hand, as if he couldn't help it. She would have liked to look for longer, but Gabriel drew her back into his arms, gazing down at her in amused wonder.

"I should have known you would not be shy," he said, with a slow smile that squeezed her heart. Then he kissed her, gently at first and then with passion, but it wasn't enough.

I love you.

When he lay her upon the narrow bed, covering her, she allowed her mouth and her hands to speak the words for her. Each one a declaration. Her soft cries of pleasure as he tasted her, worshipping her with tongue and lips. Taking his time so that she would feel pleasure too. "Beautiful Vivienne. Mine, mine…" And for tonight she was his, and she gave him everything.

Chapter Thirty

Gabriel opened his eyes. There was a moment of disorientation when he realized he wasn't in his large four-poster bed in his Mayfair house, before he felt a soft, warm shape curled against him, and the tickle of long hair across his shoulder. And then his mind filled with memories of Vivienne in his arms, their bodies straining and the pleasure slowly building. He had watched her eyelids flutter, the flush on her cheeks, and then the soft moan that turned louder as she reached that final starburst of climax. Followed by soft kisses and murmurs, and her gentle breaths as she slept.

He had watched her sleep in his arms. Her first time had been with him, and the thought had made him smile like a fool. *If only there were many more* had been his next thought, and then he too must have fallen asleep.

He lay in the silence thinking that it must be late, or early. The club was quiet, and no one had disturbed them. It was dark now, but he sensed that soon it would be dawn. He wanted to stay here and pretend she never had to leave, but he knew that was impossible. They had had their one night together and it was coming to an end.

He knew the moment when she woke, even before she stretched, and he admired her creamy bare skin and sweet curves in the faint light from the window. Suddenly she stiffened with awareness, and he propped himself on his elbow and looked down as she turned startled eyes to him.

Her loose hair was like a dark cloud, and he gathered it up, brushing it out of her face, breathing in the floral scent. When he leaned down to kiss her, something inside him shifted, a yearning he had never felt before. If only things were different and he was free to choose whom he pleased. But he was caught up in a tangle he could not see a way out of, a thorny mass of vines that would tear his flesh if he tried to escape them.

He wondered if this was how his father, Harry, had felt, when he had married Gabriel's mother. Because noblemen did not normally marry their soiled doves unless they were completely besotted, so besotted they had lost all sense and reason. For the first time since he'd learned the truth, Gabriel felt a kinship with his father. Because, despite the lies Harry had told afterward, he had been desperately in love, just for a moment.

Gabriel wondered if his own love would be as short lived. Would he forget Vivienne in the arms of his wife? Would he long to return to the night he had taken Vivienne Tremeer to his bed, or would he look back on this moment with regret?

"I won't regret this." He said the words aloud, more to himself than Vivienne, and then wished he hadn't. Her face fell, her gaze sliding away.

"Why should you indeed?" she asked coolly. "We both agreed to a night together, and now it is morning. Or soon will be." She glanced at the window as if expecting to see the sun high in the sky, and sat up.

"Vivienne." His hand on her arm stopped her from rising, but she kept her back to him, looping her hair over one shoulder. He leaned forward to bury his face in the curve of her neck, breathing in the scent of her clean skin and their night together. Just for a heartbeat she stiffened at his touch before relaxing again with a sigh.

"I wish…" he said, and couldn't finish it.

She leaned back against him, and he wrapped his arms around her tightly. "Gabriel, you know we can't meet again," she said, and he wished he could see her face. "You have your obligations, and I have sworn never to be a kept woman. I could not be happy with one small piece of you while your wife has the larger slice. My reputation may be tarnished, but I have my pride, and besides, I value my independence too much—the bit of it I have left."

Anger and hurt made him pull away. "I would never ask that of you. Not after what my father and his family did to my mother and me. I had hoped you'd think better of me."

She bowed her head and said regretfully, "I do. I'm sorry."

At the sight of her, at the edge of his bed and on the verge of leaving, his stormy emotions gave way to sorrow. He drew her onto his lap and held her there, resting his cheek against the top of her head.

Stay.

But he did not utter the word aloud, how could he? She was right; there was no future for them. They must go their separate ways.

"What if your aunt doesn't send you away?" he said, wondering if perhaps they could see each other occasionally, even knowing it was impossible. "Will you remain in London?"

"She will send me packing. Anyway, I'll be of more use in Cornwall. At least I can try to stop Sutherland from selling everything off before Will comes of age. It's better if I go."

"Is it?"

"Gabriel," she murmured, lifting her face to his, and he bent to kiss her once and then couldn't stop. She clung to him fiercely, belying her sensible words of a moment before.

His hand slid down between her thighs, brushing against the sensitive flesh, fingers busy until she moaned and writhed and arched against him. He watched as she reached her peak, petting her as she came down the other side, and he couldn't remember being with any other woman in this close, intimate way. Vivienne had swept them from his memory and replaced them with only her.

"Once more," he said, turning her so that she faced him, straddling his thighs. As Gabriel pushed inside her, he caught his breath, slowing and trying to make the moment last as long as possible. He thought he had managed it, but then she began to kiss him, arms around his neck, moving against him, and found he was too eager, too needy, too desperate. She cried out, stifling the sound in the curve of his shoulder, and then pleasure rolled over them again, in a great, warm wave, tumbling them along with it until they lay panting on the shore.

Gabriel had only barely caught his breath when a cock crowed in someone's yard, and Vivienne leaned back to look at the window, eyes wide. It was no longer dark outside, only the crowded buildings disguising the fact that morning was fast approaching.

"I must go," she said, and this time he did not stop her

as she rose, reaching for her chemise. "Soon the servants will be up and about, and I'd rather not be seen."

They dressed, and he helped her with her gown, frowning in concentration as he worked with the hooks. Once when he looked up, he caught her watching him, tenderness in her smile, before she sat to pull on her shoes. When she had tucked her hair inside the hood of her cloak, they made their way downstairs.

The club would not be stirring for hours. Gabriel went to fetch a hackney and its sleepy driver from the end of the street and then helped Vivienne inside. Their hands clung for a moment and then slipped away. In the morning light what he could see of her face beneath the hood appeared pale but resolute.

"Goodbye," she said. "I wish you a life full of contentment and joy, Gabriel. You deserve it."

"And you," he said, not sure what else to say. The things he really wanted to tell her could never be said as he watched the hackney trundle away.

Back inside the club, the silence seemed accusing and oppressive. He tried to busy himself with some of the bookkeeping, and even went so far as to go down to the cellar and count the bottles of liquor. As he trudged back up the stairs and closed the trapdoor, Charles appeared from the gaming rooms.

"Is she gone?" he said.

Gabriel thought about pretending he didn't know what his friend was talking about, but that seemed foolish. Of course Charles was aware of what was going on. He knew him too well. "Yes, she's gone."

"And will you see her again?" Charles was watching him carefully, as if the answer mattered to him.

"No. She's returning to her home in Cornwall."

"And you? What will you do?"

"I'll spend more time with Lady Edeline, show everyone that the gossips are wrong. No doubt some other scandal will capture their interest soon enough and my madness will be forgotten."

"This sounds like one of your bloody novels," Charles said irritably, hands on hips. "Love lost or some ridiculous thing."

"You don't understand."

Charles shook his head. He looked disappointed. "You're not happy," he said. "You had a chance—a very small one, it is true—but a chance to make a good life for yourself and you threw it away. You love that woman. Don't pretend you don't. I can see it. Freddie can see it. But you are going to deny yourself because you think that is what is expected of the Duke of Grantham."

"It's not that simple."

"Isn't it? Does it really matter what anyone else thinks or says, if you're happy?" Charles turned and walked away, muttering to himself. "If you're going to hang around here moping, then come and help me set up the tables!" he shouted over his shoulder.

Gabriel hesitated. Charles was his best friend, but he didn't understand, how could he? Gabriel had six lives depending on him, seven including his grandmother, hundreds more if one counted his servants and tenants. He'd already put a foot wrong for the right reasons; he couldn't chance making another mistake, or his carefully constructed world would come crashing down.

He clomped off toward the gaming rooms, as if he were heading for the guillotine.

Chapter Thirty-One

Vivienne had made it through the back door from the mews and slipped up the plain wooden servants' stairs to her room. She had to pause for a moment to press herself into an alcove while a maid bustled past with a pail and broom, having swept out someone's fireplace.

She felt light-headed from lack of sleep, or perhaps it was the cloud of enchantment she had been floating on. Loneliness and despair were yet to blow it away, like a snow-filled winter wind, and she tried to keep them at bay as long as she could. Gabriel's kisses, his tender attentions, and the soaring pleasure…Vivienne would never forget. She was a woman in love, and it was almost as if last night had drawn her even deeper into its sweet embrace.

What am I going to do?

She swallowed and blinked away sudden tears. Keep busy, that was what she was going to do. Occupy herself. Push her misery into a cupboard and lock the door and refuse to open it again. She was certainly not going to take to her bed like Olivia's mother, or marry someone like Sutherland. The man she loved and the family she had longed to be a part of might be denied her, but there was nothing she could do about that. She would become an eccentric perhaps, an oddity, and then people would leave her alone. Or maybe not. Maybe they would point her out and say, "There is that old woman who once loved a duke."

The maid had gone, and Vivienne set off again toward her bedchamber. She didn't meet anyone else and was congratulating herself just as she opened the door.

Aunt Jane and her mother sat in the chairs by the window. For a moment no one said anything, but her aunt's face was as red and furious as her mother's was pale and frightened. For Helena to look like that, there must have been a truly awful scene.

"You wicked, wicked girl!" The viscountess rose to her feet. She was smaller than Vivienne, but right now she seemed at least six feet tall. "I know all about you and that boy! Bringing him into my house, sneaking about. And as if that isn't bad enough, you have infected the Duke of Grantham with your disgusting ways. Not that I think it would take much to sway a man like him."

"I'm sorry," Vivienne managed. She felt sick. "It isn't what you think though. I mean, it isn't as bad as…" She looked at her mother, who refused to meet her eyes. No help to be had there then.

"Don't make excuses to me. I have done my best by you, ask anyone! I have ignored the advice of my friends and offered you my home, and this is how you repay me. I won't put up with it anymore, I won't. You will leave immediately, and I never want to see you again. Is that clear?"

Vivienne thought about arguing, trying again to explain, but it was clear Aunt Jane wasn't interested in listening. Vivienne didn't know how long she had been sitting here, waiting, but she had worked herself into a dreadful state. The only other time she had seen her aunt that angry was after the scandal with Benjamin.

Mrs. Sutherland cleared her throat nervously. "I'm sure you don't mean that, Jane," she said in a laughing voice, completely inappropriate to the occasion. "We are your family! Are you sending me away too? Your brother's wife? What do you think he would have said to such an insult?"

"Insult?" Aunt Jane roared. "I have put up with your idiocy and your spendthrift ways for far too long. I wash my hands of you. Of you all. I have no family. Leave!"

Vivienne heard a step behind her, and Will slipped his arm about her. "I say, Aunt Jane," he said, his voice rather unsteady. "Can't we have a think about this? No need to—"

She turned on him and screeched, "Out! You too. You will not take advantage of me any longer."

This time Vivienne tried to intervene. "No. Please, please let Will stay. He can't come home. His job at Cadieux's!"

"Viv"—Will gave her a wild look—"now you've torn it."

Aunt Jane stalked toward them. "Explain yourself, you wicked girl!"

"No, I…it was just…" Vivienne didn't usually stammer, but her aunt was incandescent with rage, and it was a frightening sight.

Will stepped in front of his sister. "I am working in the gaming room at Cadieux's," he said. "I write wagers in the betting book too. They pay me and I am learning the ropes. One day I hope to have a gaming hell of my own."

Aunt Jane was speechless, which was a good thing, but only briefly. Her voice rose as she listed their sins. "My nephew is working in a gambling club owned by the man who assaulted my niece's former lover. A lover who paid her a clandestine visit with the full approval of her mother! Do I have that right? Have I left anything out?"

No one spoke. No one dared.

There was nothing left to say.

"You will leave this house. You will not call upon me or write to me or in any way approach me ever again. I wash my hands of you all."

After the door had slammed behind the viscountess, Mrs. Sutherland slumped back into her chair. "What a to-do," she said shakily. "And she believes herself well bred! All that screaming…I have the headache."

Will and Vivienne ignored her. "What will we do?" he said in a dejected voice. He looked pale and sick, but Vivienne was sure she was the same.

"Go to the duke. To Mr. Wickley."

He shook his head. "And leave you to travel alone? No. I will write a note to Charles and then again from Tremeer. I am sure he will take me back when I explain."

Vivienne hesitated, but she was too grateful for his company to argue any further. "It won't be so bad." She tried to rally. "Go and pack."

Her mother and brother trooped off to do her bidding, and Vivienne sent a servant for her trunk. When it arrived, Annette followed, slipping nervously into the room with a glance over her shoulder.

"Should you be here?" Vivienne asked her, holding her briefly close. "Your mother…"

"I don't care," Annette said courageously. "I wanted to make sure that you knew it wasn't me who told her. The gossip is vile, Vivienne, and it was impossible for her not to hear. People are repeating it with such relish. I almost feel sorry for Grantham, but this is his fault. Why did he go to see Benjamin? What was he thinking?"

"I don't think he was," Vivienne admitted. "He was angry on my behalf, and it feels rather wonderful."

Annette stared at her with a curious look in her blue eyes. "You were with him last night, weren't you?"

There seemed no point in pretending otherwise. "Yes, I was. And now I am going home to Cornwall and I will never see him again."

Despite her efforts, tears stung her eyes. Annette didn't seem to notice, full of her own misery. "I will miss you so! What will I do when you're gone? Who will I talk to about Ivo?"

Vivienne thought that was the least of her problems, especially after the scene she had witnessed in the billiard room.

"How will I manage without you," Annette sobbed as she handed Vivienne a pile of clothing to place in her trunk.

"Perhaps you can visit me?" Vivienne suggested, although never in a hundred years did she expect such a thing to happen.

Annette gulped and thought a moment. Her smile was like the sunshine after rain. "I know! We will write another book together. Send me your letters, a chapter at a time. Won't that be fun? The time will fly."

"Let's not talk about it now." Vivienne closed the lid of the trunk and stood up. She had hastily changed into a traveling costume and was wearing the same cloak she had worn this morning. Had it only been this morning she had left Gabriel?

Will poked his head in the door. "The coach is ready," he said. "At least Jem will be driving us home."

Vivienne looked about her as Annette and Will embraced and said their goodbyes. She would have to leave some of her belongings behind to be sent on. The room had always been plain and small, and strangely it felt as if she had left very little impression on it. She had never been part of the Monteith household, not really. Her aunt had always resented her, and it was only Annette who had loved her and found solace in her company.

Outside, the servants were securing Vivienne's family's luggage onto the coach, and Vivienne was quite certain that several of the Monteiths' important neighbors were watching, enjoying the show. Aunt Jane would not like that. No doubt the gossip would soon spread, involving Gabriel in another round of whispers and speculation. Perhaps she would write a letter to him too, when the dust had settled.

She bit her lip on a hysterical laugh. Who was she fooling? Dust like this was unlikely to ever settle.

A footman handed them into the coach, his face impassive. They crowded together, making room for little Wen, who was returning with them. The girl's eyes were enormous in her pinched face, and she slunk into the corner as if worried she might catch whatever immoral infection Vivienne and her family were carrying.

Mrs. Sutherland fanned herself furiously with a pretty painted fan Vivienne recognized. It was one of Aunt Jane's, and she wondered what other items her mother might have secreted away in her luggage. For an instant she thought about making her hand it to one of the servants to return to the viscountess, but she didn't have the energy.

"Well," Helena said indignantly, "your father always said his sister had a coarseness in her nature. No true lady would behave as she did."

Will and Vivienne exchanged a look, and for a moment she thought her brother might burst into laughter. Or tears. Next thing the coach was rolling over the cobbles, leaving the Monteith house, and London, behind them.

Chapter Thirty-Two

By afternoon everyone knew that the Viscountess Monteith had sent her niece off to Cornwall in disgrace, with the command to never again darken her door. She had also sent away her nephew and their mother, who was her sister-in-law. It was as if she had called the ratcatcher in, and the house had been purged of vermin. If the pot of gossip had been simmering before, now it was boiling over.

"What am I supposed to do?" Charles said with a scowl on his handsome face. "Will Tremeer was the best apprentice I've ever had. Yes, yes, I know he was the only apprentice I've ever had, but that boy had a real feel for the work. I was going to take him on as my partner. Well, eventually."

Gabriel looked at him in astonishment. "Is that all you can say?"

"What else should I say? You knew what would happen. It was bound to."

"Not like this!" Gabriel shouted.

Charles folded his arms and stared him down. Gabriel slumped. Vivienne had warned him she would be sent packing, but he'd hoped it wouldn't be this brutal. Maybe he hadn't been thinking about much at all apart from holding her in his arms.

"She's gone," his friend said unsympathetically. "You said you couldn't marry Vivienne because you're a duke and you had to marry Lady Edeline. You'd better get on with it, hadn't you?"

Right now Gabriel's confidence about his future was wavering. He'd been so sure that he was on the right path, the only path. He'd swallowed the bitter pill of letting Vivienne go so that he could ensure his sisters lived the lives they were born to. And now, suddenly, he felt as if he had wandered into a thick fog and gotten lost. His footing was uncertain, slippery, and at any moment he might tumble down a mountainside.

He jumped as Charles clapped him hard on the back. "Buck up," he said with false cheer. "You'll think of something."

Think of what? His head was full of Vivienne and the expression on her face as the hackney drove her away. She had said they had only one night, as if she had never expected to be asked for anything more. She had foreseen the storm that would be unleashed, far more clearly than he, because it had happened to her before. And still she had come to him.

When he reached home, he walked in on another full-blown argument between his sisters. They were squabbling at the top of the stairs, and as he began to climb them, Georgia threw one of Edwina's dolls to its death. Edwina screamed, promptly launching herself at her sister, and it was only Gabriel's intervention that prevented a full-scale war.

Justina arrived to take over, ushering the two girls

back to the nursery and leaving Gabriel shaken. His sisters had been so well behaved for a time, but lately they had been reverting to the sort of conduct he had seen before Vivienne took them in hand. Vivienne had made these temper tantrums manageable, and his sisters had been good humored and willing to oblige. Oh, there had still been times when they misbehaved, but having Vivienne there had made it seem easier, as if they were a team.

Only now that she was gone did he fully grasp how much better his life had been, *their* lives had been.

He'd been hoping for some thinking time in his study, but of course as soon as she knew he was home, his grandmother was requesting his presence in the sitting room.

"Stupid, stupid woman!" The dowager tore the viscountess's character to shreds. "Such lack of decorum! Does she know nothing about the society she lives in? Well, we will not make her mistake. We hold firm. I have arranged for the Earl of March to bring his daughter to dinner tomorrow night. There will be a small, select gathering, close friends only, so you need not worry they will ask you awkward questions. We will tell them Longley mistook you for someone else. Everyone knows what a liar he is. They will take our part."

Gabriel had refused to sit down, instead pacing back and forth across the room. "I thought you said we should ignore the gossip."

"Yes, we should, but there is nothing wrong in spreading a little of our own."

He was so tired of this game. Give him a frank discussion anytime. The dowager closed her eyes briefly before pinning him with her dark gaze. "I want you to promise me that this will never happen again. Can you do that?"

He stopped his pacing to stare at her. Promise her that he would not fall in love? Promise her that he would never again come to the rescue of Vivienne, with her thoughtless mother and that idiotic soldier? Vivienne, who was always ready to help others, no matter the cost to herself? Who had made his life so much easier when she was in it, and who had come to him last night in what was undoubtably one of the most memorable moments of his life?

"I can't make that promise," he said, and it was a relief to say it.

Shock wiped emotion from his grandmother's face. She set her teacup down with a rattle, but it tipped to the side, and tea spilled into the saucer and over the lip, onto the table. She ignored the mess. "You will do as I say, Gabriel."

He almost laughed. He was a grown man, a man who had run his own life for years, and done so successfully. He wasn't going to make promises to her that he could not keep. Promises he did not want to keep.

"Gabriel!" Her voice cracked on the high note.

"I can't promise you that I will never make a mistake again," he said at last. "I probably will. We see matters differently, Grandmother."

She stared at him unblinkingly, and he could see her confusion. Then she nodded wearily. "Very well," she said. "I suppose that will have to do. Tomorrow night you will repair the damage done to our family name. You will be attentive to Lady Edeline and her father; it is your last chance."

Your last chance.

He felt disappointed. "You want me to win over Lady

Edeline by pretending to feel an affection for her I don't feel at all. Isn't that dishonest? Especially when I am in love with another woman. I'm sorry, I don't think I can do that."

His grandmother opened her mouth and shut it again.

Gabriel bowed to her before closing the door behind him. The sound of breaking china followed him up the stairs. He felt hollow, as if an important piece of him were missing, and he finally knew what it was.

Francis was waiting to help him off with his clothes, and although his valet was his usual kind and amusing self, Gabriel was silent apart from a grunt or two. Everything felt out of kilter. Wrong. He needed a good night's sleep, and maybe then the way forward would be clearer. Not easier, no, he didn't expect any of it to be easy. Gabriel was considering a course of action that would have dire repercussions for his entire family.

He must have slept, because when he woke, he found himself standing on the landing in his nightshirt. His brain felt fuzzy and confused until he realized he was sleepwalking again. The knowledge was like a dash of cold water and suddenly he was very much awake. Beside him a lamp flickered in a draft, and when he saw how close he was to the head of the stairs, like a cliff face disappearing into the shadows below, he gave a gasp and lurched to one side, clinging dizzily to the balustrade.

What if he had fallen? What if he had broken his neck? A sweat broke out on his skin. If he were dead, there would be no one to take care of the family. He had thought he was doing the right thing, putting aside his own happiness for the sake of his sisters, but he knew now he was wrong. Sleepwalking was another sign of his inner turmoil. He was miserable and he could no longer ignore it. He could no longer turn off his emotions and live a life that was not the one he wanted.

"Gabriel! There you are!" Edwina had pattered up behind him. "Georgia didn't know which way you'd gone!"

Gabriel turned, his head still reeling from his near miss. He saw that it wasn't just Edwina on the landing behind him. All of his sisters were gathered there in their nightdresses, hair down and faces pale and sleepy in the lamplight.

Georgia yawned and slumped against the others. "We've been taking it in turns to watch out for you," she said. "It was my turn tonight. I had to wake the others though, and by then you were gone."

"Watching out for me?" The thought of the girls caring so much for him that they would do that made his heart rattle in his chest.

"Gabriel, you cannot keep walking in your sleep," Olivia scolded him.

"I didn't know you knew," he said, looking in amazement from face to face. "Were you really taking turns to keep watch?"

"Of course! We've been worried about you. What if you fell down the stairs? What if you strolled out into the street and were run over by a carriage?"

He wanted to pooh-pooh the idea, but then he remembered that he had just come rather close to one of those things. "I'm sorry," he said in his calmest voice, but he wasn't calm at all.

"They used to tie him to the bed when he was little," Edwina disclosed with sad eyes. The others shook their heads in dismay.

"But why do you do it?" asked Roberta curiously. "Why do you walk in your sleep, Gabriel?"

He hesitated, but they had a right to know. Especially if they were worried about him, and it seemed that they were. "It happens when my mind is in a disturbed state."

"Disturbed about what?" Olivia said.

"I know!" Edwina shouted loud enough to wake the whole household. "It's Miss Tremeer, isn't it?" Justina tried to shush her but she wouldn't be quiet. "But it is!" she whispered furiously.

Gabriel met their stares and tried to think of a suitable answer, but he was tired and hurting and he blurted the words out.

"I love her and I let her go."

Edwina jumped up and down. "See, see!" she crowed.

Olivia put a hand over her youngest sister's mouth. "We know you do," she said impatiently.

After a brief struggle, Edwina pulled free. "Why did you let her go? You should ask her to marry you." She said it as if it were the simplest thing in the world.

Was he really having this conversation? Gabriel wondered. It seemed that he was. "Grandmother wants me to marry Lady Edeline."

There was a collective groan. Olivia pulled a face. "Please don't."

He was momentarily nonplussed. "But…isn't she the perfect wife for me? She will help us to secure our place in society. The scandals will be forgotten, and you can all make brilliant marriages, the sort of marriages the sisters of a duke should make." The words came easily, he'd repeated them to himself so often, but he no longer believed them. Brilliant marriages? Like his grandmother's? Like Harry's false marriage to Felicia? He must be a commoner at heart, because Gabriel believed contentment and happiness were more important than what passed for a brilliant marriage in the eyes of a cold and judgmental society.

"Well," Olivia said practically, "Lady Edeline may be perfect for Grandmama, but she isn't perfect for you. You would be miserable, Gabriel. You love Vivienne and she loves you, we can all see that. Ask her to marry you. She will be far more useful to us than Lady Edeline."

"Even if it means more scandal?" he asked gruffly. "There are rules, remember. I can't just break them when I feel like it."

But if he thought his selflessness would impress them, he was sadly mistaken.

Roberta snorted in disgust, and even Justina rolled her eyes. "Maybe some rules were meant to be broken," Olivia said. "When I became the subject of whispers and gossip, the only person in that room who cared about me, well, besides you and Ivo, was Vivienne. Why should we let such hateful people decide how we live our lives? You have worked so hard to make things better for us, Gabriel, and we want you to be happy. How can we be happy if we know you are not?"

He wondered if he should reason with them, talk about actions and consequences, but they weren't listening, and for once he was all talked out.

"I'd be happy to live in the country with a horse." Roberta pulled a thoughtful face. "Two horses and a dog."

"You said," Olivia began cautiously, meeting Gabriel's gaze, "that you are able to save the estate from bankruptcy. That we can be safe. You said that made you a good duke. Isn't ensuring we do not lose the estate and have a roof over our heads and don't go hungry what really matters? Balls and dinner parties are all very well, but we don't need them, not really. Of course, I will be sorry to lose them for now," she said with a sad smile, "but it will give me something to work toward, for my future."

He eyed her with pride.

"As for Grandmama...she will come around. She loves you, Gabriel, can't you see that? Oh, she will be angry for a time, but she will forgive you. She always does."

Her grandmother loved him? Gabriel couldn't believe that was true, but he set it aside to think about later. "And Vivienne...Miss Tremeer...will marry me? I wouldn't blame her if she said no. You think I should ask her?"

"Yes!" they all shouted, and if the whole house wasn't awake before, it was now.

He laughed and the misery in his chest was replaced with bubbles of happiness. Marry Vivienne, see her every morning and every night, hold her in his arms until cockcrow. For a man who had sworn never to love, he was head over heels. And for the first time in a long time, he was free.

The following morning, with his sisters' blessing, Gabriel set out for Cornwall.

Chapter Thirty-Three

When Vivienne and her family arrived at Tremeer several days later, they found it in disarray. Sutherland was stretched out in a drunken sleep on the dining room table, bottles spilling wine onto the carpet and half-eaten food scattered all around. Two of his cronies sprawled on the sofa, barely able to move as Mrs. Sutherland poked them viciously with her fan. Vivienne could only stand and stare in shocked dismay while her mother clucked about, exclaiming at the mess but seemingly unsurprised by it.

"Well, here nothing has changed," Will said angrily, his face looking older than his eighteen years. "I think I'm going to throw him out," he added with more purpose than she had ever heard from him.

She reached out for his arm to stay him. "Perhaps wait until we've unpacked?" she suggested. "I don't think my head can take any more noise."

The delayed journey home had been memorable for all the wrong reasons. It was slow, and service at the only inns they could afford to stay in was even slower. Their last night was particularly bad when one of the horses turned lame and they had to waste another day waiting for a replacement at a hostelry, where there was only one room left. Crowded in together—at least Will was able to sleep in the stables—her mother had insisted that none of this was her fault and how dare Vivienne set her thuggish duke onto poor Benjamin? The next morning Will had taken one look at their exhausted faces and demanded to know the reason. He promptly took Vivienne's side and told Helena that it *was* her fault. That had brought on tears, and Will was too softhearted not to comfort his mother. It had just needed Aunt Jane to come striding in and abuse them all over again.

And now at last they were home, and it was even more awful than Vivienne had been imagining. She wondered if she could feel any more melancholy. She had been trying so hard not to think of Gabriel, of their one night together, but whenever she closed her eyes, he was waiting to gather her into his arms. Not that she didn't want to remember, because she did, but right now it was too fresh. Too raw. And she thought that she might cry. In fact she wanted nothing more than to be alone so that she *could* cry.

"I knew the two of you would be back," Sutherland said in a sneering way. He had woken after his wife threw a goblet of wine in his face. After snorting and spluttering, he sat up. He looked dreadful, eyes bloodshot, clothes and body unwashed. A dashing, handsome man when their mother had married him; now he was falling into decrepitude.

"Where are the servants?" her mother demanded, barely holding herself together. "What have you done with them, Richard?"

"They went off and didn't come back," Sutherland replied, but he had a shifty look. Vivienne was sure he had turned them off to save some pennies, or maybe they had walked out after cleaning up after one too many drunken parties. Who did her stepfather think would do the work? Even if she and her mother and Wen could manage it between them, they would need help. And where was Wen anyway? she asked herself, looking about. Probably run off to hide. Aunt Jane's coach had already left to return to London, so Vivienne would have to walk into the village and beg the staff to come back, and probably offer them an increase in wages before they'd agree.

Her throat ached and her eyes stung, but she swallowed back her tears. Sutherland was watching her with a mocking expression, and she refused to cry in front of him. She hoped Will would throw him out, but she suspected he would inveigle his way around it somehow. Mrs. Sutherland had never yet followed through with any of her threats.

"No wealthy beau, Vivienne?" he said, sensing her weakness. "I thought you would be wed by now with a fine house and carriage, but here you are, back again like a bad penny. Well, don't expect me to pay for your upkeep."

"This is my house," Will reminded him coldly.

"Pooh! I am your father."

"Stepfather."

"Same difference."

"This is my house, and I say who lives here."

"Not until you turn twenty-one, and as far as I am aware, you aren't there yet, pup. I still intend to contest that will, don't think I won't."

Will's face reddened, and he was about to answer when they heard the arrival of a horse-drawn vehicle outside on the gravel driveway. Had the coach returned for some reason? Jem had promised that once he delivered it safely back to Aunt Jane, he would return to Tremeer. She had told him not to, but she was very glad when he'd retorted that he wasn't leaving her and Will alone in this calamity.

More likely the vehicle outside belonged to someone to whom Sutherland owed money, and they had come to remove more of the furniture. The paintings and anything of value were long gone, but there were still some sturdy old pieces and a portrait of her father Vivienne had hidden in the attic.

"Who is that?" Will demanded, striding to the door as if he really were the man of the house. On the journey home, Vivienne had seen the change in him. Their stay in London had done him good after all, or more likely his time at Cadieux's under the tutelage of Charles Wickley. Her brother had grown up, and she couldn't have been prouder of him.

She followed him, trailed after by her mother and Sutherland, the two of them still bickering. One of Sutherland's cronies had staggered out of the dining room and was now propped up against the wall, snoring his head off and completely unaware that one of the dogs was licking his face.

Will, who had reached the open front door, made a sound of amazement, and Vivienne hurried to join him. Plumb in front of their house was a light traveling coach with four fine horses to pull it. Who on earth would call upon them in such an equipage? None of their friends could afford such a turnout—even Sir Desmond, who was wealthy enough, made do with his ancient coach. There was an insignia on the door, but splashes of mud made it difficult to see—the driver had clearly been told to hurry. A footman rushed to open the door, and the next moment the occupant jumped down, shaking the dust of the journey from his many-caped coat. Vivienne blinked as he removed his hat from his dark hair and strode toward the front of the house in his fawn-colored breeches and shiny boots.

"Gabriel," she breathed, seeing it and not believing it.

Will was grinning from ear to ear. "Good God," he said, "it's Grantham!"

Mrs. Sutherland was conflicted by the arrival of the Duke of Grantham, but before she could open her mouth, Sutherland pushed rudely past her and placed himself in front of Vivienne. "What the devil?" he demanded. "Who are you and what do you want?"

Gabriel had reached the door now, and from his expression, Vivienne could see he wasn't at all sure he was in the right place. She shoved Sutherland aside, ignoring his complaints, and at the sight of her, Gabriel's expression cleared. "Miss Tremeer!" With a determined tread, he strode forth into the house, causing the others to give way before him.

"Miss Tremeer," he said again, and his gruff voice gentled. "Vivienne. I have come to…" He stopped, suddenly aware he was the center of attention.

"What *have* you come for?" Sutherland demanded. "Come on, out with it."

"Let him speak," Will said with a frown. "Don't you know who he is?"

"Maybe we could have some privacy," Vivienne began, but Gabriel seemed to have decided he would say what he came to say and be damned.

He reached for her hand and held it firmly between his two gloved ones. Awkwardly she became aware of how she must look—disheveled and tired, her hair a tumbled mess from the journey, and her gown wrinkled. What must he think of her? And why was he here? They had said their goodbyes, and to have to do so again… Vivienne wasn't sure she could pretend to be brave this time. And yet something about the way he was staring at her so fixedly gave her hope for the first time in weeks.

Gabriel did not seem to see any of her shortcomings; his dark eyes were full of relief. "Thank God I found you," he blurted out. "I thought I might catch you up on the road."

"It's a wonder you didn't," Will interrupted. "What are you doing here, Grantham? Not that we're not glad to see you."

Vivienne's hand trembled. "Very glad," she whispered.

"Vivienne." Gabriel's voice was deep and earnest. "I should never have let you go. I will never do so again. Will you marry me?"

Several thoughts went through her mind, like shooting stars across a dark sky. That she was definitely not the wife good sense decreed he should marry, that Aunt Jane would be furious if she found out her disgraced niece had been proposed to by a duke. That Sutherland would probably try to borrow money from him as soon as he got him alone, and that her mother would mourn the fact that he was not Benjamin.

But none of that mattered. It was inconsequential. Because she loved him, and he had come all this way at an obviously cracking pace to ask for her hand. He'd come after her because he loved her too.

"Yes," she said, her voice wobbly with emotion. "Oh yes, please!"

And she flung herself into his arms just as he reached for her. In a heartbeat she was pressed against his big strong body and his lips were clinging to hers. In the background she could hear Will cheering, while Sutherland kept asking in a petulant voice who "that man" was until Will told him, and then he was silent.

Vivienne looked up at Gabriel, and he gave her a smile that was absolutely devastating. They deserved their happiness, she told herself, as he gazed down at her as if she was the most wonderful sight he had ever seen.

"I love you," he said, serious again, giving her that intense look from his inky black eyes. "I've loved you for ages, Vivienne."

"Have you? I've loved you too. Even when I was telling myself I hated you for having a heart made of marble, I thought about you far too much for my own peace of mind." Was she crying? There was salty moisture on her cheeks as he leaned in to gently smooth the tears away with his fingers. "Are you sure I'm the wife you need?" There was a catch in her voice, because if he changed his mind…

"Vivienne"—and he frowned—"listen to me closely. You are everything I need. Without you life would be impossible. I've tried to be the perfect duke and I've failed because my plan didn't include the woman I love. I need you beside me, and bedamn anyone who doesn't like it."

She knew she had stars in her eyes, but there was one last question she needed answered. "Your sisters?" she whispered. "I know how much you were prepared to give up for them. What will happen if you don't marry a respectable woman?"

He laughed then, as if he was as wild with happiness as she. "My sisters informed me that they want you. I was glad to hear that, because I had already decided I couldn't live without you."

She hiccuped a laugh of her own. "I love your sisters," she told him, and then clung to him, kissing him again, beyond words now. But so happy, so very happy that the ending she had given up imagining could be hers had come to pass. To her! She had longed for someone to value her for herself, to want just her, and Gabriel did. He could have married an earl's daughter, but he preferred imperfect Vivienne Tremeer.

Her mother was weeping into her handkerchief, and perhaps she had finally set Benjamin aside. Will was grinning at both of them. "I am very glad," he said. "So very glad. Viv, you deserve this, the best of sisters. Anyone can see that the two of you are meant to be together."

Together, Vivienne thought, leaning against Gabriel, his arm around her waist as he smiled down at her. Yes, they were together. She would stand beside him no matter what confronted them, and he would support her through the difficult times and love her through the good. And she would love Gabriel right back, with all her heart.

Epilogue

One Year Later, the Farnsworths' Ball, London

It was one of those warm evenings, the scent of flowers drifting in from the terrace. The same terrace where the Duke of Grantham had first realized that with Vivienne Tremeer he had met his match.

She caught his gaze, her gray eyes sparkling, and smiled. She was happy. He made her happy, and if he did nothing else in this world, he could be content with that.

When they had been announced at the door, the noise inside the ballroom had fallen away into silence. Then the tittle-tattle had started. Everyone had their eyes on the Duke of Grantham and his new duchess, as enthralled as they had been from the first day Gabriel assumed his title. Scandal involving the Ashtons had rocked the ton, and although it was nearly a year ago now, they hadn't forgotten how he had run off and married this woman.

He should at least be repentant, or that was what the gossips said, according to Olivia. She would know. His sister had fearlessly taken her life into her own hands. He should show contrition. Instead he seemed to be blissfully unaware of his bad behavior. It was a love match, some of the more romantic members of the ton declared. As the former owner of a gambling hell, Gabriel already knew love was trumps.

Gabriel smiled down at his wife. They had been wed, quietly, in Cornwall before they returned to Grantham, and now here they were in London at the beginning of another season. Vivienne's gown was not as simple as those she used to wear, although it was the blush color she favored. The fabric was beaded, and there were delicate silk roses about the hem and neckline, and if that were not ornament enough, about her throat she wore the Ashton emeralds.

"Will you dance with me?" Gabriel said as the orchestra struck up. "I promise not to make you giddy."

Her smile put the diamonds in her ears to shame. His grandmother had gone above and beyond expectations when she stayed with them at Grantham. She had come to terms with Gabriel's odd kick, or at least was prepared to tolerate it. He had watched her carefully as she spoke with Vivienne, prepared to intervene, but he could see his grandmother being won over bit by bit. How could she not? There had been a small hitch when the dowager discovered Vivienne had written a novel called *The Wicked Prince and His Stolen Bride*, but his grandmother seemed to take it in her stride. Gabriel suspected she was getting used to her family's outrageous doings. The dowager had even agreed to leave her granddaughters in Gabriel's and Vivienne's hands, and return to her retirement.

"I love you," he whispered against Vivienne's cheek as they circled the room.

Her expression softened, her eyes warm with affection. "Gabriel, we are so lucky."

"Lucky? To have an estate drowning in debt and six irascible sisters?"

"Yes, lucky," she scolded him. "Because we have each other."

It was true. Last night, when he held Vivienne in his arms, their lovemaking leaving them both languorous, Gabriel had once again counted his blessings. He hadn't had anything to truly look forward to before, despite what he'd believed. For a boy from a foundling home, turning the club into a success had been vastly satisfying, and so had taking on the role of duke, as he worked to bring the estate back from the brink of disaster and learned to tolerate, and then love, his sisters. But he hadn't known what he was missing. There was a huge void inside him, waiting to be filled, and Vivienne had done that. Now he awoke each day with a smile on his face and a spring in his step and joy in his heart.

The door to the terrace was right in front of him, and it seemed the perfect moment to dance his wife out onto it. She looked about her, a little breathless—he was still a robust dancer—and then she laughed softly.

"Revisiting the past?" she asked him, her gaze darkening at what she saw in his. They were still insatiable lovers.

"Unfinished business," he said confidentially, leaning closer.

"Oh?" And then, her lips curling up in anticipation, "Oh!"

Gabriel grinned. "Besides, we don't want to become too respectable, do we? Whatever will the scandalmongers talk about then?"

She didn't answer him. She was already stretching up to press her lips to his, and he tightened his hold on her,

her soft curves fitting so perfectly against his harder body. "Love you," she whispered, "so much."

Gabriel let himself enjoy this moment. A year ago he never would have expected to be so happy. His future had been all about duty and others' expectations. It made him dizzy to imagine what might have happened if he hadn't come to his senses.

"What are you thinking about?"

He lifted her gloved fingers to his lips. "The future," he said. He rested their joined hands upon the barely visible swell of her belly. "Our child."

Her eyes shone. "Kiss me again," she said, "and then we can go home."

Don't miss the next breathtaking novel from Sara Bennett, coming Fall 2024

About the Author

Sara Bennett is an Australian bestselling author. She has written books set in various time periods—medieval, Regency, and Victorian—as well as women's fiction under the name Kaye Dobbie. Currently, she alternates between publishing independently and writing for traditional publishers. Sara was a finalist for the RITA award and the RUBY.

Sara lives in Victoria, Australia, in an old house in a gold rush town, with her husband and two important cats. She would love to spend more time in the garden, but there are just too many stories to be written.

You can learn more at:

Website: Sara-Bennett.com
Twitter @SaraBennett16
Facebook.com/SARA-BENNETT

Looking for more historical romances?
Fall in love with these handsome rogues and
daring ladies from Forever.

A LADY FOR A DUKE
by Alexis Hall

When Viola Carroll was presumed dead at Waterloo, she took the opportunity to live as herself. But Viola paid for her freedom with the loss of her wealth, title, and closest companion, Justin de Vere, the Duke of Gracewood. Only when their families reconnect years later does Viola learn how lost in grief Gracewood has become. But as Viola strives to bring Gracewood back to himself, fresh desires give new names to old feelings. They are feelings Viola cannot deny. Even if they cost her everything, again.

Connect with us at Facebook.com/ReadForeverPub

Discover bonus content and more on
read-forever.com

WHAT'S A DUKE GOT TO DO WITH IT
by Christina Britton

The last thing Miss Katrina Denby needs is another scandal. But when one lands in her garden and the rumors start affecting her friends, she will do anything to regain respectability and protect those for whom she cares. But her plans to marry one of the few men who will still have her are thrown into turmoil with the arrival of the Duke of Ramsleigh—the only man Katrina ever loved. And a man who is about to become engaged to another.

DREAMING OF A DUKE LIKE YOU
by Sara Bennett

When Gabriel Cadieux—orphan, gaming-hell owner, and polite-society outcast—discovers he's the legitimate heir to a dukedom, he must make a choice: accept the debt-ridden title and trappings of the ton who shunned him, or decline and leave his six newly discovered half sisters to fend for themselves. As much as he hates the idea, Gabriel can't abandon his sisters, even if it means making a deal with the most aggravating—and attractive—woman he's ever met…

Meet your next favorite book with @ReadForeverPub on TikTok

Find more great reads on Instagram with @ReadForeverPub

ALWAYS BE MY DUCHESS
by Amalie Howard

Because ballerina Geneviève Valery refused a patron's advances, she is hopelessly out of work. But then Lord Lysander Blackstone, the heartless Duke of Montcroix, makes Nève an offer she would be a fool to refuse. Montcroix's ruthlessness has jeopardized a new business deal, so if Nève acts as his fake fiancée and salvages his reputation, he'll give her fortune enough to start over. Only neither is prepared when very *real* feelings begin to grow between them…

MARRY ME BY MIDNIGHT
by Felicia Grossman

Isabelle Lira may be in distress, but she's no damsel. To save her late father's business from a hostile takeover, she must marry a powerful stranger—and *soon*. So she'll host a series of festivals, inviting every eligible Jewish man. Except that Aaron Ellenberg, the synagogue custodian, provides unexpected temptation when Isabelle hires him to spy on her favored suitors. But a future for them both is impossible…unless Isabelle can find the courage to trust her heart.

Follow @ReadForeverPub on Twitter and join the conversation using #ReadForeverPub

THE FORGOTTEN GIRLS
by Lizzie Page

London, 1943: German bombs rain down on London, but Elaine Parker knows her job transcribing letters from far-away prisoners of war is more important than her own safety. Then one soldier's letters have her questioning everything she thought she wanted.

Present day: When Jen finds an old photo of two little girls looking as if England hadn't just endured a terrible war, she wonders if the answers could finally be the key to mending the cracks in her past.